Heat Wave

JENNIFER ARCHER

"*Shocking Behavior* is well written and clever. It's an all around fun book to read."
—*The Romance Reader*

"*Once Upon a Dream* is an excellent magical story with a marvelous hero and an admirable heroine. . . . A fun, exciting, humorous, fast-moving story!"
—*Romantic Times*

KATIE MacALISTER

"Katie MacAlister has an easy voice that brims with wit and fun."
—Mrs. Giggles from *Everything Romantic*

Improper English is "charming and irresistible! A tale to make you smile and pursue your own dreams."
—Patricia Potter, *USA Today* Bestselling Author

SHERIDON SMYTHE

"A fast, fun and tender story sure to touch the reader's heart."
—*Romance Reviews Today* on *Those Baby Blues*

Those Baby Blues is "a compelling, sexy romp that leaves you smiling!"
—*New York Times* bestselling author Christine Feehan

JENNIFER ARCHER
KATIE MacALISTER
SHERIDON SMYTHE

LOVE SPELL NEW YORK CITY

LOVE SPELL®

June 2003

Published by

Dorchester Publishing Co., Inc.
276 Fifth Avenue
New York, NY 10001

ISBN 0-505-52539-9

Visit us on the web at www.dorchesterpub.com.

E D E N

Heat Wave

Bird of Paradise

KATIE MacALISTER

To Vance Briceland, the best critique partner a girl could have; to Kate Seaver, a fabulous editor who gets silly on Friday afternoons; and to Sherrie and Jenny, for being so much fun (as well as brilliant writers.)

HAWKEYE PRODUCTIONS MEMORANDUM

To: Michael Hawkins
From: Dara Thompson
Re: 30-second Eden promo spot text—please initial ASAP

The fabled Garden of Eden is brought to life this fall when two hundred single men and women descend upon a small Caribbean island in search of their own Adam or Eve. Will their dating experiences be made in heaven or hell? Will they find their perfect mate, or like the serpent of old be drummed out of paradise?

Watch the dramas unfold over six fun-filled weeks as one hundred couples live, love, and learn in their struggle to reign supreme in . . . *Eden*

Chapter One

"I'm with you on the need for the air horn in case you are forced to slaughter innocent animals in the name of sport, and I completely agree with the earplugs for the roller disco night, but why in the name of John, Paul, and Ringo are you packing this monstrosity?" Gemma held up a voluminous purple-and-black beruffled, skirted, blousoned swimsuit.

Hero made a moue at both her friend's words and the object held before her. "You left out George," she pointed out.

Gemma waggled the swimsuit at her.

Hero sighed and took the garment, folding it neatly and placing it back into the luggage. "You told me it was a crime against nature to go to the Caribbean without taking a swimsuit. That is a swimsuit."

"I said take *your* swimsuit, Hero, not your grandmother's," Gemma replied, much more acidly than Hero thought warranted, but then, who was she to say? She was only Gemma's best friend. Clearly her opinion counted for little in the Gemma scale of life. "That thing probably covers you from knees to elbows. You'll drown the first time it gets wet. It'll suck you right down to the briny depths. I know you think you're too Rubenesque for a bikini—"

Hero snorted at the word *Rubenesque*. She knew her friend was trying not to hurt her feelings by using such phrases as *prodigiously plump*, but really! Rubenesque?

"—but that's no reason to hide yourself. You're lovely. You should be proud of who you are, not hide yourself behind all those layers of clothing."

"I like my clothing," Hero said with great dignity that was lost upon the other woman.

"Well, no one else does! Hero, when are you going to realize that despite being a few stone heavier than you'd like to be, you're still attractive? *Very* attractive?"

"Gemma, give it up; we've been over it too many times before. I appreciate your vote of confidence, but I'm not at all comfortable wearing the type of clothes you do. I simply have too much flesh. An excess of flesh. Great, huge, vast stretches of it, in fact, which I prefer to keep covered decently so as not to frighten small children and the elderly. Now"—she held up two dresses—"which frock do you think for the fancy dinners—the navy or the ecru?"

Gemma plumped down on the bed next to the suitcase and frowned. "Neither, they both look like something my aunt Fran would wear to a convent in a blizzard during Lent. Hero, I don't like to duff you over this, but here you have the perfect opportunity to look over a large herd of eligible bachelors, and all you do is pack clothing guaranteed to keep you in purdah. You deserve better than that. You're going to a tropical island! Sun! Men! Beautiful white beaches! Men in thongs! Fruity drinks and pampering and fun! Men walking around with nothing more on than a really nice tan and a wicked glint in their eyes! I want you to promise me that you're seriously going to look at the men you'll meet on Mystique Island."

Hero silently shoved several pairs of lacy underwear into the corners of the bag. "I shan't be able to avoid looking at them, they are an integral part of my article."

"Hero," her friend said in a growl. "You know what I meant!"

Hero rummaged around in the bottom of her wardrobe looking for a pair of sandals. "I do, but as I'm participating in this ridiculous dating show solely to do a story, Gem, I don't feel your suggestion that I chat up the men in an attempt to find a potential husband deserves any comment. You know how important this article is to me. Besides, those men are Americans. We both know what that means—oversexed, egotistical, can't-keep-their-willies-in-their-trousers types. *Not* the sort of bloke I'm looking to tie myself to forever."

"You're half American," Gemma pointed out, removing the underwear and folding them tidily before replacing them.

"My point exactly. Mum got tangled up with a smooth-talking Yank engineer twenty-six years ago, and what was the outcome of that?" Hero tucked a pair of beige huaraches into the side of her bag and disappeared into the tiny bathroom to collect various sundries.

"You," Gemma called after her.

"Correct."

"Your parents were married."

"But Dad was never home! He wasn't happy at home; he wanted to wander the world. And now where is he? In Arizona with his new bit of crumpet, leaving Mum heartbroken."

"So heartbroken that when he left she said, and I quote, 'Good riddance to bad rubbish'?"

Hero emerged from the bathroom to wave that comment away. "That's merely a protective device so she doesn't have to admit how hurt she is by Dad's betrayal. Do you think I look too pale? Should I use tanning lotion?"

"Hero, your parents were married for almost twenty-five years. I think now is the time for you to get over their divorce and admit your problem isn't American men."

"No, my problem is to finish packing so I can make my flight

7

to Mystique, thus ensuring that I'll have a story on how desperate Americans will do anything to find someone to date, which will, in turn, keep Stephen from giving me the sack and me from going on the dole because no one wants to hire a blackballed tabloid writer. *That* is my problem." She held up a bronze bottle with a large yellow sun on it. "Yea or nay on the tanning lotion?"

"Yea, you look whiter than a fish's underbelly. And as for the other, you haven't been blackballed, goose. You can't really blame Stephen for putting you on probation after that last story; what you did was very much over the line."

"Perhaps," Hero mumbled as she flattened a roll of toilet tissue and added it to her suitcase. One never knew what one was going to find in the less civilized areas of the world. It was far better to be prepared than be obliged to use the local flora to tend one's personal needs.

"Perhaps? *Perhaps* your story claiming that one of the royal family had an alien love child was not so outrageous the outcry could be heard from here to John O'Groats? *Perhaps* you didn't almost lose your job, only hanging on because you begged the publisher to give you another chance. *Perhaps*, Hero? *Perhaps*?"

Friends. There were times when she really had to wonder why she was cursed with them. She zipped up the sides of the suitcase and turned to face her oldest and dearest friend. "What do you want me to say, Gemma? That I was wrong to try to increase circulation and save Stephen from losing his livelihood? That I was wrong to make up a story so patently false that only an idiot would believe it was true? That I was wrong to call those very same people mindless boobs on the telly? Well, all right, I admit the last was not in the best interests of either my career or the *Revue,* but the first two—no. Stephen knows full well it was my story that saved his paper, which makes it all that much more unreasonable that he should put me in the untenable position of having to turn in a fascinating story that will save my position without once using the words *alien* or *love child.* I ask you—can it be done? I have my doubts!"

Gemma laughed and held up a lacy bra. "I don't have any. You forgot this. Really, Hero, such scandalous smalls! For someone who looks so conservative on the outside, you do wear the naughtiest knickers and bras!"

Hero snatched the item and unzipped the luggage just enough to stuff it inside. "If you're quite finished ridiculing my choice of undergarments, perhaps you'll assist me in applying the faux suntan. I can't imagine it will fool anyone, but I'd much prefer to not have the streaks and blotches that I'm sure will happen if I try to do the backside of me by myself."

"No one will know your luscious golden tan came from a bottle," Gemma vowed as she followed Hero into the bathroom. "You'll dazzle every man there; just you wait and see. They'll all be eating out of your hand by the time the first few weeks are up."

Hero rolled her eyes. "For the last time, I'm not doing this to find a man! I'm simply trying to save my job."

"So you say."

"That's all. It's just an article. Nothing more."

"Uh-huh."

"Romance is definitely out of the question."

"Mmm."

"I certainly would *not* find myself attracted to an American."

Gemma started whistling as she applied the cream to Hero's now bare back. Hero tried to focus on how bronze and un-fish's-underbelly her skin would look, but other, less happy images invaded her thoughts. "And even if I were to find a man I fancied, I'm sure he'd be panting after one of those trim, tiny women who will no doubt be parading around with their fake breasts and toned thighs and pert bums with thongs stuck in between their cheeks and such."

"Hero?"

"What?" Hero's thoughts were dark with images of liposuctioned buttocks.

"Do you know what I think? You are setting yourself up for major trouble."

"Trouble? By not wishing to become involved with an American? How is that trouble?"

"Your prejudice against Americans has nothing to do with the matter—I'm speaking of women who deny themselves love, women who repress their honest, loving, and demonstrative natures, women who decry relationships on pretenses of standards. Such women inevitably end up falling for a man, and hard."

Hero rolled her eyes. "I'm nothing like that."

"They snap, that's what they do. They meet a man, they fall instantly and deeply in love, and voilà! Instant snappage."

"You're quite, quite mad, aren't you?"

"They call it the *Fatal Attraction* syndrome, you know. One moment you're a professional, intelligent woman in control of your life, the next you're completely obsessed with the man. It's quite tragic, really, and since I don't want to see you boiling up some poor innocent man's rabbit, I am warning you now."

"Obsessed," Hero scoffed. "I've never been obsessed with a man in my life. I'm hardly likely to start now."

"It's not as if you've had a great deal of experience, love."

"Just because you can count my relationships on one hand"—Gemma held up two fingers—"very well, just because I've only had two relationships of any duration—"

"A fortnight each, weren't they?"

"—doesn't mean I am naïve and inexperienced. I can assure you that if and when I meet a man I'm interested in, I will not snap, not that I'm likely to meet him where I'm going."

"Take heed, Hero! If you continue to deny yourself the natural expression of your affections, one day you're going to find yourself suddenly unable to think of anything but a man you've just met. You'll stalk him through crowds, you'll feel insane jealousy when you see him with other women, you'll concoct feeble excuses to seek him out because you must be near him; then, ultimately, you'll end up—"

"Stabbed to death in a bathtub?" Hero asked.

"Possibly. I prefer to think that it'll all end up happily, after your chosen man realizes that you're not truly insane."

"Thank you," Hero replied, mollified.

"I'm sure it won't take him any time to realize what the true problem is."

Hero cocked an eyebrow in question.

Gemma smiled. "You just need a right good shagging."

Adam Fuller was beginning to feel martyred. *Saint Adam*: it had a nice ring to it.

"Don't forget to take pictures of any man who looks like he's hitting on Sally. And names, I want names. Names are important. You got that?"

"Names. Pictures. I have it." He switched the black plastic cat carrier to his other hand and reached in his jacket pocket for the airplane ticket.

"I want to know what she does every minute of the day, and who she does it with. If she looks like she's having fun, I want to know that too. And don't forget the pictures of the men she's with. And their names."

Adam sighed.

"Who she has dinner with, who she dances with, who she does those stupid dating events with, who she smiles at—I particularly want to know that—who she talks to, who she—"

"I get the idea, Gar; you don't have to beat it into me. You want me to watch her. I understand the job; you'll just have to trust me to do it."

Edgar Holliday, famed throughout the NFL for his thirty-yard passes rather than his intellectual capabilities, glowered at the tall man walking next to him. "This is important, Adam. Sally isn't just any woman; she's *the* woman. I'm going to marry her one day. She's going to be the mother of my little quarterbacks.

11

I love her! That's why it's important you keep your eye on her while she's going through this difficult time."

"Difficult time? Gar, she kicked you out and told you she never wanted to see you again."

"She was mad at me because of that little thing with the cheerleader. It's nothing. Women like Sally get emotional that way. Probably was her time of the month."

"She got a restraining order against you. That doesn't sound like PMS to me."

"It'll blow over," Edgar said, supremely confident and utterly oblivious to the admiring looks sent his way as he and Adam strode through the busy airport. "It always does. She'll take me back; you'll see."

"She said the only way she'd ever want to see you again was if you were hanging by your balls."

"She's.just playing with me. That's why I need you to tell me every damned thing she does while she's on that TV show. It's important."

"I'll watch her," Adam agreed.

"Like a hawk?"

"Like a hawk. You're worrying about nothing—this may be my first job as a private investigator, but I think I'll be able to handle keeping an eye on one woman on a small tropical island."

"I'm paying a lot of money for this," Edgar reminded his friend. "It wasn't pocket change buying off the TV show producer, not to mention the guy whose place you're taking. And then there were the bribes to smuggle that monster of yours through customs. You think that comes cheap?"

The two men approached the waiting area for the charter flight to the island. Adam said, "I know it isn't, and I'm sorry about having to bring Jesus, but I couldn't leave him alone. Not after what he's been through. Dr. Miller says his last suicide attempt could well have been fatal."

"What sort of cat would try to kill himself by eating a box of crayons?"

"A depressed one with a very colorful litter box," he answered, slapping gently at the gray paw that emerged, claws extended, out of a breathing hole on the side of the carrier. Jesus had already snagged three people while Adam waited in line for his boarding pass; he had no desire to add Edgar's expensive silk suit to the list of damages owed. "Dr. Miller says he's lost his will to live, and if I don't do something drastic, one of these days his suicide attempts will succeed. And since his depression is all my fault . . ." Adam sighed again. "Well, that's why I'm here."

Edgar made no reply to that, just handed his friend a folder. "Here's the details on the guy you're replacing. There's a flight booked under his name for you from Miami to Mystique Island. Read the information and then destroy it."

Adam grinned. "You want me to eat it, just like the spies do?"

Edgar considered the suggestion.

"That might not be a bad idea. I wouldn't want Sally to find out what you're up to. She's mad enough at me for bugging her office—she'd be really pissed about me hiring you to follow her during this dating show." A sudden frown of suspicion blossomed between his thick brows. "Just because I want you to keep tabs on her doesn't mean you can date her yourself."

Adam thought of the aggressive tiny blond woman who had been Edgar's girlfriend and gave a mental shudder. "I wouldn't think of it."

"Is that right?" Edgar asked, still frowning. "You said that girl you lived with . . . Bethany . . . Betty—"

"Brittany."

"—left you, so why wouldn't you think of Sally? She's got everything, a hell of a lot more than that Brittany had. Sally is pretty and smart and goes at it like a mink in heat."

"She also has an ex-boyfriend who is now my employer,"

13

Adam drawled, nudging the cat carrier out of reach of a woman standing nearby.

Edgar's eyes narrowed as he studied Adam. Tall, blue-eyed, dark haired, Adam looked exactly what he was—a clean-cut man with few vices and a somewhat quirky take on life. "Yeah, but you're pretty good looking. For a guy," he added. "Women must like you."

Brittany's parting words as she had stormed out of his apartment still rang in Adam's ears. He tried hard to look suave and sophisticated and drop-dead sexy, and not at all like a man whose twelve-year relationship had ended because his significant other told him he was a lousy lover. "Regardless, the only interest I have in Sally is purely professional. So relax. I'll call you later tonight, after I've had a chance to look over the situation."

"Don't forget to destroy the evidence," Edgar warned. "Oh, hell, there she is. I have to leave so she doesn't see me with you, but don't you forget! Watch her but don't date her! And get me names! And pictures!"

Adam nodded, rescued a small tapestry-covered bag from the clutches of the gray arm extended from the carrier, and watched as his childhood friend, now employer, tried to make his huge self look invisible by skulking off through the crowd. Then he glanced casually over his shoulder to take note of where his quarry was, and was astounded to see her storming up to him with murderous look on her face. Even though she only reached his shoulder, he knew from the few times he'd met her that her petite size was misleading. Extremely misleading. He summoned a smile and tried to look as if he were not the possessor of a brand-new private detective's license.

"Hi, Sally. Long time no see."

"You!" she said in a snarl as she pushed past the people in line behind him to brandish a piece of paper clutched in her hand. "Is this true?"

Adam caught the name of a detective agency on the letterhead as she waved the paper under his nose. "Is what true?"

"This bull! Is it true that Edgar hired you to spy on me while I'm in the Caribbean? Is it? Did you agree to this?"

Adam blanched. She had a detective of her own? Watching him? Why? "Er . . ."

"Because if it is, you can just turn around right now and go home," Sally bellowed, crumpling up the paper in a manner that made Adam suspect she was envisioning his neck between her hands. Or worse. "It's outrageous! It's ridiculous! I won't have it, do you hear me?"

"I think just about everyone here heard you, Sally. Maybe we could talk about this—Jesus, no! Sorry, ma'am. It's my cat; he's a bit bored being in the carrier. Here's your magazine back. It looks like he only tore off a little bit."

"Look, Fuller, I don't give a damn what Edgar hired you to do; you're not doing it, OK? Now if you'll excuse me, I have a plane to catch. You can go home."

Adam grabbed the cat carrier and followed Sally to the back of the line, where she stood seething with fury and righteous indignation. "Sally, I don't know how you found out about Gar hiring me, but you have to give me a break. I've been on unemployment for more than a year; this is the first paying job I've had since the dot-com went under. I promise I won't get in the way. You won't even know I'm there!"

"I won't know you're there, all right." Sally stared straight ahead, growling in a tone reminiscent of Jesus when he was eating a particularly succulent piece of chicken. "Because you won't be there. Go home, Adam."

"I can't," Adam said quietly, trying to keep the pathetic pleading note out of his voice. "I have to go. I've already put a down payment on Jesus's surgery—there's no way I can afford the rest of it if I don't do this job. Besides, Gar promised to tell all his football buddies obsessed with their ex-girlfriends about me if he's happy with my work. So have a little pity on me, Sally. I'll take a few pictures, make a couple of notes—you won't even see me."

She turned to face him. The look in her eyes made him want to flinch, but he stood firm instead. He was a man, dammit, and he had a job to do, and it wasn't like it was illegal or anything. He did flinch at that. Not *very* illegal, he amended. "Stay away from me, Fuller. If I even so much as see you, I'll tell the show's producer who you are and have him kick your ass all the way back to California."

Her threats were very effective; Adam had to give her that. She was mean as a jackal and twice as vicious. Adam tried to look tough in response. He scowled. He added the tiniest sneer to the scowl, then threw in an Elvis lip twitch for good measure. "You do your job, and I'll do mine, babe."

The woman at the counter motioned for Sally to come forward. Sally ignored her for a moment, leveling her finger at Adam, then poking it in his chest. "Stay away from me, or else I'll have your balls. Understand?"

Adam straightened his shoulders and looked down his nose at the tiny blond jackal threatening him. "I appreciate the offer, Sally, but I'm really not interested in you that way."

She snarled something anatomically impossible before turning her back on him. Unseen by her, Adam let out a low sigh of relief as she moved to hand in her boarding pass. It was too bad that she'd found him out before he'd even set foot on the blasted island, but perhaps it was better this way. Now he knew where he stood (on the edge of a very shaky bridge), and could go from there. Handling Sally would require kid gloves, but that was no problem. He'd just explain it all to her once she had calmed down. No, it wouldn't be a hard job at all, he reflected a short time later as he tucked Jesus's carrier under the airplane seat with an admonition for the cat to keep his claws to himself. All he needed to do was keep a low profile and all would be well.

Five hours later, as the chartered plane took off from Miami headed for Mystique Island, Adam opened up the dossier on the man whose place he was taking and realized he was in deep trouble. Incredibly deep trouble.

"Hi, I'm Teri," a pert redhead sitting next to him had introduced herself a few minutes before. "You're going to be on the show too, huh? What's your name?"

"Uh . . ." Adam regretted the three screwdrivers he'd had on the flight from California that had led to his sleeping through most of the flight. He blinked at the bright-eyed redhead. "Uh . . . I have to . . . um . . . I'll be right back."

He grabbed the dossier as he ran for the nearest bathroom, locking himself in to read up quickly on who he was supposed to be. He stared in horror at the words until they swam before his eyes.

If the passengers nearest the bathroom were surprised by the sudden, profound burst of cursing emanating from the bathroom, they did not express it. They did, however, look with some worry upon Adam as he emerged. He bared his teeth in what he hoped was a smile and muttered something about needing to get more roughage in his diet as he stalked back to his seat. He was going to kill Gar; that's all there was to it. He'd *have* to kill him; there was just no other choice.

"Are you all right?" the redheaded woman asked with concern as he slumped into his seat muttering under his breath the variety of unpleasant things he wanted to do to his employer.

"Fine," he choked, then took a deep breath and held out his hand. "Monday. My name is Monday. Monday Marsh."

"Monday?" she asked as she gave his hand one of those little feminine squeezes that women thought passed as a handshake. Her blue eyes suddenly grew round with surprise. "Your name is Monday?"

Adam ground his teeth and nodded.

"Monday Marsh?"

The muscles in his jaw locked. He nodded again.

"*The* Monday Marsh?" The woman's voice was loud, strident,

filling the whole damn airplane. His stomach tightened and wadded up into a tiny lead ball. People around him started to murmur his supposed name, turning in their seats to look back at him. He tried to make himself relax. If the muscles in his jaw tightened any more, his teeth would crack. "The Monday Marsh who's on the radio? You're *that* Monday Marsh?"

"Yes," he said, his voice as cutting as razor-edged gravel on bare feet. "I'm that Monday Marsh."

"Wow!" the woman said under her breath, her eyes alight with wonder. "I can't believe you're sitting next to me. I listen to you all the time! I love your show! It's the best sex advice I've ever heard! That time you told the couple in L.A. to bring in her sister to explore the dynamics of a ménage à trois—that was such good advice! I loved your descriptions of the stuff they should do! I tried it with my boyfriend and his roommate, and it was the best sex I've ever had. You're going to Mystique for the show? Are you the sex consultant or something? Are you giving classes? Do you take private students?"

Adam ignored the hand caressing his thigh. "Yes, I'm going to Mystique, no, I'm not the consultant, and no, I'm not offering classes. I'm a"—he ground down another layer of enamel as he spat out the word—"contestant."

"He's a contestant!" the woman sitting in front of him told her seat partner. Both women eyed him avidly. Adam had sudden and complete empathy with every celebrity who had ever felt hounded by the public. "Would you say it for us? You know, the thing you always say on your show?" the woman asked.

"Yes, say it," Teri begged, her hand squeezing and caressing his leg through the thin linen of his pants. He shifted in his seat, uncomfortable at the looks he was getting, worried that Teri's hand would go roving. He'd never been the focus of so many women's attention—hell, he'd never been the focus of *any* woman's attention aside from Brittany. She was his first and only girlfriend. He'd never even thought about another woman until she'd left him a few months ago.

"Monday Marsh? The nipple guy? Hey, man, say that thing you say," a man two rows ahead stood up and called back to Adam.

"Say it, say it, say it!" The chant started up out of nowhere but quickly gained volume as word of who he was pretending to be passed among the passengers. Teri licked her lips as her hand slid toward his groin, her eyes sending him a blatant message of invitation.

"Say it, say it!"

Adam squirmed in his seat, unwilling to take the pretense any farther, unsure of how to stifle the attention he was receiving. He opened his mouth to yell out the truth, to end the farce before it went any farther, but the sharp pinprick of cat claws on his ankle reminded him why he was there.

"Say it! Say it! Say it!"

He disengaged Jesus's claws from his sock, standing with reluctance to face the planeload of chanting people. From where Sally sat in the far rear he could see her smiling a mocking smile at him.

"Say it!"

He straightened his shoulders.

"Say it!"

He lifted his chin.

"*Say it!*"

He sighed, and looked out into the faces of strangers, men and women he'd never met before, men and women who were gathering from around the country to participate in a six-week-long television show with the goal of finding someone special. Where had his life gone wrong? How had it all come down to this moment? He held up his hands for quiet. Instantly the voices were hushed, the silence expectant, a hundred or so people leaning forward to catch the words as they left his lips. Adam took a deep breath, swearing to himself that if he lived through this, he really would see to it that his name was put down for sainthood. "My friends, I am a contestant like the rest of you. I

19

am here purely as an amateur, not as an expert in the field of sexuality. I ask that you not treat me any differently than anyone else on the show. I appreciate the request, but I'm sure no one here really wants to hear that silly catchphrase. Thank you."

"*Say it!*" they roared back at him.

He sighed again, then gave in to the inevitable as gracefully as possible. "And then my nipples exploded in delight."

The entire body of passengers, himself and Sally excepted, burst into ear-shattering cheers. Adam forced a smile onto his lips, gave a slight bow to acknowledge the applause, and took his seat.

He really was going to have to kill Edgar.

Chapter Two

"Depraved, all of them. Nothing but a bunch of depraved, steroid-riddled sex fiends," Hero muttered to herself as she stood behind a large potted palm at the Mystique Island airport watching the men ogle the women. She was taking furtive photographs, unwilling to let anyone see her snapping their photos lest it lead to explanations she didn't want to make. She took a picture of a particularly lustful leer on a man's face, and corrected her statement. The men were ogling all the women but her, that is. Did she care? She did not! She had better things to do than allow a bunch of beefy, perfectly coiffed male American sex fiends to ogle her. She had some standards, after all. No matter what anyone else might think, she was not desperate; lots of women lived perfectly happy, successful lives without a man. She would simply be one of them. There was certainly nothing here to tempt her, no cause to be worried about Gemma's dire prediction.

"Jesus, no!"

The hoarse whisper caught her attention as much as the person tugging on the back fringe of her blue-and-purple batik cotton wrap. She hastily punched random buttons to turn the digital camera off and stashed it in her purse before she spun around in time to see the fringe disappearing into the hole on the side of a black plastic box with a handle on top. A man squatted next to the box, speaking to it quietly but firmly. "Let go of it, cat."

Hero's eyebrows rose. There was a cat in that box? Someone was bringing a cat to the island? She thought the television show had taken over the entire resort for the duration of the show— why on earth would a man bring his cat with him to film a dating show?

"How many times do I have to tell you not to grab at ladies' dresses?"

Her eyebrows arched higher as she looked down at the doubled-up figure of the man as he tugged her fringe out of the box. "Let go of it, damn you! I'll buy you your own fringe later. Jesus, drop it!"

A frown forced her eyebrows together. Honestly, American men! If they weren't sex fiend oglers, they swore at innocent cats. She wanted nothing to do with them, absolutely nothing. The next few weeks were going to be sheer and utter hell.

Still, she didn't like to see a cat in trouble.

"Perhaps I can help," she said as she knelt down carefully next to him, reaching for the material he was tugging out of the box. "I have a way with animals, and I'm very fond of cats."

The man looked up, blinking at her as she gasped in response, all the air in her lungs having suddenly disappeared. Dear Lord, he was gorgeous! Oh, not in the conventional manner, but in a much more devastating way, a way that suddenly made her feel extremely conscious of the fact that she had given up far too early on the latest diet guaranteed to whisk away unwanted pounds. He was perfection, he was manliness personified, he was everything she'd ever loved in a man—short black hair, two ebony swoops of eyebrows, lovely little laugh crinkles around dark blue eyes, a long nose that had a kink in the middle, and an indentation on either cheek that hinted at dimples. She swallowed hard, forcing herself to look away from him, suddenly aware that she was shaking.

Gemma was right! She had snapped!

"I'm sorry, Miss . . . er . . ."

"Hero," she answered, trying to get a grip on herself. It was worse than she'd imagined, this snapping. "Hero North."

"I'm sorry, Miss North, but when my cat gets bored, he has a habit of grabbing at passing items. He doesn't really mean any harm. I'll have your wrap free in just a minute."

Hero nodded, not trusting herself to look at him. She'd never had this sort of reaction to anyone before; why on earth did she have to have it now? And with an American man, of all things! One who, a few minutes before, was probably drooling over all of the tanned, fit women around him. She had to get hold of herself before the horrible snapping did any more damage. Taking a deep breath to calm her wildly beating heart, she tugged gently on the fringe until a gray paw came into view in one of the carrier holes.

"Excellent. If you hold him like that, I'll unsnag his claw from your dress."

Even his voice was sexy! It was low and sensual and rumbled around, striking a chord deep within her. She watched his long fingers carefully unhook the tangled fringe from the cat's claws. Maybe she hadn't really snapped after all. Maybe she was just so lonely that any man was starting to look good. Maybe there was nothing special about this one, other than his drop-dead-sexy voice and really nice fingers. Maybe thinking about all those sex fiends had triggered a hormonal moment. Surely she was better now. Surely this man was nothing special.

"There you go. I don't think any damage is done, but if there is, let me know and I'll pay for your dress."

She glanced at him as he released her fringe from the claw. Oh, Lord, she moaned to herself, it was worse than she first thought! His eyes were deep, deep blue, and the delightful laugh crinkles around them were evident as he smiled, and she was right: he did have the faintest dimples on either cheek. She just wanted to grab his head and kiss him. There was no hope for her now. All that was likely to be in her future were a few illicit weeks of pleasure before he moved on to another woman, leading to her eventual downfall to alcoholism, and quite probably insanity.

"Erm . . ." Oh, why had her brain chosen this moment to shut down? Why couldn't she remember how to speak? Why did those glittering blue eyes peering into hers make her forget those things said to people when you wanted to talk to them . . . *words*, that was it. Where had all her words gone?

He leaned his head in slightly toward her. "Is something the matter?"

"No. No, nothing. It's just that I . . . erm . . . nothing. Thank you."

He nodded and stood up, holding out his hand to help her to her feet. She stared at it stupidly for a moment, noticing his heart line curved up between his index and middle finger. "You're a romantic," her mouth said before her brain could veto the inane comment.

That startled his almost-dimples back into hiding. "I beg your pardon?"

"Sorry. I did an article on palmistry last year." She took his hand and got to her feet, mentally cursing at herself. *Stupid, stupid, stupid!* Here was a veritable oasis of a perfectly nice man in a desert of sex fiends, and she had to babble at him like an idiot. That was what snapping did to you: it turned you into a raving lunatic.

"Article? You're a writer?" His head tipped a little to the side in question, his smile doing all sorts of squishy things to her insides.

Oh, Lord, now what had she done? "Writer? Me? I . . . eh . . . just dabble in it."

"Ah." He looked at his hand. "How do you know I'm a romantic?"

Her heart did a little somersault as she traced his heart line, her finger tingling with the heat of his palm. "That's your heart line. The way it's curved indicates that you have a romantic nature."

"Ah," he said again, the baby dimples back. "What else does it say?"

She blinked at him, surprised he asked. Most men pooh-poohed having their palms read, but this one just stood there smiling at her with his nice eyes, and his almost dimples, and a cat whose arm was reaching out to snag other unwary travelers. A sudden spurt of hope came to life within her. Maybe she could turn her snappage into something good.

He obviously took her silence as reticence. "I'm sorry; you probably don't want to be bothered with my hand. Forget I asked."

"No, I love your hand," she said hurriedly, then blushed at her words. "That is, it's a very interesting hand. I'd like to read it for you."

"Perhaps later, then?" he asked with a look in his eye that turned the little trickle of hope into something stronger. Unbidden, her heart started beating faster. He wanted her to read his palm? Was he just being nice, making polite talk in the queue, or was he truly something special? Dared she hope that the wonderfully warm feeling his smile was spreading through her was reciprocated? Could it possibly be he was interested in her, as well? Had he snapped, too?

"That would be lovely," she managed to say without throwing herself on him. She allowed herself a moment of pride over her restraint, then immediately turned her thoughts toward more important matters. Should she take the chance? Should she be bold and courageous, as Gemma had advised, when meeting a man who turned her crank? Her lips curved in response to his warm smile. She would. She would take the chance. "Perhaps

25

if you have an hour free this evening after the orientation, I could read your palm. It really is a fascinating art, taking into account all sorts of things, like the size and shape of your fingers, fingernails, lines on your palm, mounts, and such. You would be surprised, for instance, what a person's thumb can reveal—"

"Excuse me," the dishy man muttered, picking up his cat carrier in one hand and a suitcase in the other. "I see someone I have to speak with."

Before she could blink he was off, hurrying down a dirty and dimly lit corridor leading out of the main customs area.

"Well, hell," she muttered to herself, staring at the luggage at her feet, trying hard not to cry. All of the wispy dreams and hopes beginning to solidify under the influence of his intriguing presence were dashed, her heart leaden and aching with the knowledge that no man, not even one with nice eyes and a warm smile, could find her worth his time.

She picked up her bag and rejoined the crowd queued up for customs, mulling over the tragedy of a freshly snapped mind as she waited. Moving forward when the customs official beckoned her, she answered his questions without thinking, aware only of the devastating truth made crystal clear by the nice man's sudden defection as soon as she stupidly opened herself up to him. When would she learn?

She blinked back a few tears of self-pity as the official stamped her passport, and started toward the outer reception area, where large groups of attractive men and women were chatting and flirting with one another. Avoiding the beautiful people, she retreated to the far corner, next to the corridor containing a line of offices. Her stomach roiled for a moment at the thought of what a personification of ugly duckling–ness she would make among the collective beauty of the other contestants; then her pride and determination and every ounce of fortitude within her surged to life. She turned her back to them and gazed down the corridor. So she had snapped and the snap-

26

pee wasn't interested in her, so what? She had a job to do, and by the saints, she'd do it, and do it so well that Stephen would have no choice but to offer her not only her job back, but also an immediate pay raise as well. Wasn't it an American who had said, "Damn the torpedoes, full speed ahead?" Well, she'd take a page from his book and show Mr. Nice Eyes. She didn't give a fig for what he thought of her. She couldn't have cared any less about his opinion. She had no interest in him, none whatsoever, not even the slightest bit of curiosity about what it was he was doing skulking down at the distant end of the corridor, speaking with a man in a customs uniform, handing over not only his cat carrier, but what looked to be a large handful of money as well.

Every journalistic instinct within her stood up and screamed at the nervous, guilty looks he was casting around himself. Hero glanced over her shoulder at the crowd behind her. Several members of the television show staff were trying to round up contestants and herd them toward the shuttles that would take them to the resort proper, but there were far more people than space on the shuttles. She probably had at least ten minutes before she'd need to be back in the main area. Still undecided, she picked up her bag and looked back down the hallway to where the man was disappearing through an unmarked door. She gnawed her lip for a second, then started down the corridor after him. She had no idea what was going on, but it looked to be the stuff that great stories were made of, so it could only be to her benefit to follow through on it.

She slipped through the door after the two men and found herself in large room reminiscent of a warehouse, stacked from floor to ceiling with large wooden crates. She ignored them and headed toward where she heard voices, pausing to peer around a towering stack of crates marked *Crescent Moon Resort*.

The customs official signed a paper, then handed it to the blue-eyed man. "Here is the quarantine certificate. I'll just add the stamps on the receipt, and you'll be able to pass through without comment."

Quarantine? Hero vaguely remembered a note about pet quarantine in the literature about Mystique Island that came with her acceptance on the show. The man was smuggling his cat through quarantine? What a personal interest story that would make! Not to mention it was highly, highly illegal. Hero grinned as she dug through her bag, her fingers closing tightly around the digital camera loaned to her by the newspaper. She hadn't had much of a chance to use it yet, but knew from those prior experiences that it could be tricky. If she could just get a photo or two of Mr. Blue Eyes and the customs official doctoring the quarantine information, she'd be a very happy woman. Ah, but revenge was sweet.

Both men spotted her with the very first picture.

"Bugger and blast," she said in a snarl at the camera as the flash went off, attracting their attention. The customs official disappeared instantly, leaving Hero to face the irritated-looking man who stalked toward her.

"Hello again," she said weakly, trying unsuccessfully to hide the camera behind her back. "Fancy meeting you here."

"You were taking my picture," the man accused her, and rightly so, she had to admit. His luscious black brows were drawn together in a frown that made him look even more adorable, if that were possible. Hero sighed to herself and promised a lecture to her libido at the earliest possible time.

"A picture? Why would I want to take a photo of you?" she asked, knowing innocence was not a brilliant subterfuge, but it was the best she could come up with under the constraints of a snapped mind.

"That's what I'd like to know. You don't work for Sally, do you?" He looked suspicious now, trying to see what she held behind her back.

"Sally? No, I don't even know a Sally. My, look at these fascinating crates. I wonder what could be in them. Isn't this a fascinating room? You know, I find the whole customs procedure simply fascinating. The rules, the regulations, the officials . . . oh! That must be what you saw! I was taking a picture of a customs man who was absolutely—"

"Fascinating?" he asked.

Hero nodded, slapping an insincere smile on her face. "Yes! That's it! He was fascinating. And now, if you'll excuse me, I believe the shuttles are leaving for the resort. I'll just dash out of your way and allow you to do whatever it was you were doing secreted away in this room with a customs official. Ta ta!"

"One moment, if you please, Miss North." The man's hand shackled her free wrist as she turned to leave. "I'd like to see your camera."

"See it?" Hero smiled wanly. "It's just a camera, I assure you. Nothing special about it. Has a lens and a flash and all that."

He pulled her toward him gently but firmly. "I'm afraid I can't allow you to keep the film in your camera."

"It's a digital camera; it doesn't have film," Hero retorted, beginning to be incensed at his high-handed manner. He set the cat carrier down and pulled her hand forward until the camera was between them. "You see? No film. Now please release me. I have things to do, and they don't include standing in a room with a professional cat smuggler!"

"So you did follow me!" the man said, taking the camera from her. She snatched at it but he stepped back, fiddling with the knobs and buttons.

"That's mine; you have no right to it! I must insist that you return it to me immediately!"

"You're English," he said, apropos of nothing.

"Yes, I am, as if that makes a difference to camera ownership. Give me back my property!"

"One moment." He frowned, not even looking at her as he pressed buttons until his image appeared on the small screen. "There. I'll just erase this picture—"

Hero ground an objection between her teeth, furious that he

was deleting her evidence, more determined than ever to have her revenge on him.

"It matters little whether I have a photo of you and that customs man falsifying quarantine documents," she said airily as he handed the camera back to her. "I imagine both the television show producer and the head of customs will be most interested in what I witnessed here. I'm sure a quick look at your passport and the false papers for your cat will reveal everything." She tucked the camera away in her bag and gave him a bright smile. "Good day!"

"Wait a minute; you can't tell anyone about Jesus!" The man looked horrified at the thought.

"Jesus?" Had the man snapped, too?

"My cat."

She blinked in surprise. "You named your cat Jesus? Isn't that rather blasphemous?"

"It's not intended to be blasphemous; it's just the only name he answers to," the man said, resignation written all over his face. He squatted down to release the door to the carrier.

"He *answers* to the name Jesus?"

"Yes," the man said, pulling out a huge gray-and-white cat, attaching a thin leather leash onto his collar. "I think it's because when most people see him, they say, 'Jesus, that's a cat?' Somehow the name just stuck."

Hero looked at the huge animal as it hobbled around. It was approximately the size and shape of a well-fed bulldog, was missing one eye, and had a pronounced limp. Altogether it was a very curious animal for a man to feel so strongly about that he dared risk imprisonment to smuggle it through customs for a six-week visit. "I begin to see your point," she murmured, watching the cat as it investigated the nearby crates.

"Do you know what they'll do to him if you turn us in?" the man asked. Hero squatted down when the animal limped over to her and smelled her shoes. She peered at his front.

"Is one of his legs shorter than the others?"

"Yes, he lost an inch and a half of bone on one leg when he was hit by a car. That's how I found him, as a matter of fact, a stray lying by the side of the road after some bastard had mowed him down. The vet was going to take the leg off, but offered to do reconstructive surgery instead. As you can see, it wasn't entirely successful."

"Poor puss," Hero cooed, stroking the cat as he rubbed against her, admiration for the sort of man who'd stop for a wounded cat—not to mention pay for its surgery—doing much to take the edge off her irritation with him. He might have named his cat inappropriately, but he evidently had a very soft heart. "I don't think very many people would take in such an odd animal."

A rueful smile curled the man's lips. "I seem to have a habit of acquiring them. Back home I have a maniac pheasant who likes to chase cars, a parrot that speaks only Mandarin Chinese, two dogs that have six legs between them, and a pygmy goat that's happiest when she's playing on a swing set. Him I found about a year ago."

Hero scratched behind the cat's ears. He leaned into her and almost pushed her over. "He must have suffered terribly."

"Yes, he has suffered, and he'll suffer even more if you tell the officials what you saw."

The man's eyes were dark with pleading. Despite her earlier vow of revenge, Hero couldn't help but be affected by his obvious love for the huge cat. "I'm sure they wouldn't harm him. They'd just put him in quarantine for a few months. The animals are very well taken care of, I'm sure."

"It would kill him," the man argued, his eyes soft as he scratched behind the cat's ear.

"Oh, you exaggerate. I'm sure it wouldn't be fun for Jesus, but I hardly believe quarantine would kill him. I'm quite sure the attendants are fond of animals."

"It's not that," he answered morosely, looking up and giving her the full benefit of his attention. Hero rocked back on her heels in response. Lord, but he was everything she could want in a man . . . except for his proclivity for smuggling, that is. "Jesus is depressed. Suicidal, in fact. That's why I'm here, in an attempt to cure his depression."

"Really?" Hero stood up slowly as the cat strolled over to her luggage and began investigating it. Her heart melted at the thought of a man who went to the trouble and expense he did just to find a partner who would love and care for his cat. He truly was one in a million. If only he could look beyond appearances to see that such a woman didn't have to come in a svelte, tanned package . . . "I suppose you're here to find him a mum?"

"What?" The man looked startled. "Oh . . . er . . . yes, that's it. I'm here to find him a . . . mum. Yes."

"That's terribly affecting, but you know, I have to say . . . What is your name?"

He stood up. "Adam . . . er . . . Monday."

"Adamermonday? That's an unusual name." Then again, his cat was named Jesus.

He looked intriguingly confused. "It's just Monday. Monday Marsh. Although my friends call me Adam."

Her eyebrows rose.

"It's . . . ah . . . middle name," he answered her silent question. "Prefer it. Over Monday."

"It's a pleasure to meet you, Mr. Marsh. As I was saying, your story is very affecting, but these countries have quarantine laws for a reason. I believe they are in place to prevent the spread of rabies from areas where that disease has been eradicated. You can see that it's not fair to the other animals on the island if your cat is allowed to bypass regulations."

He pulled out a small sheet of paper. "Here's his health certificate. The vet certifies that Jesus is free from any disease, rabies included."

Hero looked at the sheet. "Oh. Well, yes, I can see where you might feel it was acceptable for you to bring your cat if he poses no threat, but still—"

"You don't understand; I have no choice in this. He is deeply depressed and has had two suicide attempts already; I can't leave him alone. His therapist says now is a very critical time for him."

"Therapist? Your cat has a therapist?" Hero glanced over at the cat that sat cleaning his face by licking his front paw and wiping it over his long white whiskers. She'd never heard of a suicidal cat. "What on earth does a cat have to be depressed about?"

Adam glanced over to the cat, then leaned in toward her. "He's been neutered," he whispered.

"He has?" she whispered back.

He nodded.

She waited, but nothing more was forthcoming. "Are you trying to tell me that your cat is depressed because you had him neutered?"

"Shhh," he hushed her, sending worried looks toward the cat, still involved in grooming himself. "He'll hear you. It's bad enough without reminding him of the problem."

She eyed him from toes to nose. "I think you're a very nice man."

He turned his attention from the cat to her, his eyes crinkling again as he smiled. "Do you?"

"Yes. Very nice."

"Thank you. I like you as well."

She opened her mouth to continue on, to tell him that although he was nice, he was quite obviously a candle or two short of a candelabrum when it came to his cat, but the words never even formed. Warmth on her cheeks heralded another blush. "You do?"

His smile deepened. "Yes."

She couldn't help herself; she had to ask. "Why?"

"You have an affinity for animals, you are curious about things other than yourself, you're intelligent and honorable, but

33

most of all—" He stopped suddenly, looking a bit embarrassed.

Hero wasn't about to let him get away with that. He was bamming her, obviously, sweet-talking her so she wouldn't tell the officials about his cat, but even with that knowledge, she had to admit his words of praise were sweet upon her ears. She wanted more. "Most of all?" she prompted.

"You remind me of a statue. One of those Greek ones. A goddess."

She stared at him. He waved a hand toward her torso. "Your . . . er . . . shape."

Her shape? He thought her shape was reminiscent of a statue? Instantly the blush flooding her cheeks turned to a raging inferno. He was making fun of her, pointing out that she was the fleshy personification of fat ancient Greek women. A statue, indeed! And after she was thinking such nice thoughts about him!

"I see," she retorted, retrieving her purse from where Jesus the cat had dragged it over to a corner. "Regardless, I fail to understand exactly how a cat can become suicidal because of a simple operation, but I will accept your word that it is so. If you will excuse me, I believe I will return to the rest of the contestants."

"You'd be depressed too, if you had your balls lopped off," Adam pointed out, his brow furrowed as he watched her gather up the rest of her things.

"I highly doubt that."

"That's because you're a woman. You don't understand the male attachment to our reproductive organs. They're very important in our lives."

"No doubt," she ground out, refraining from adding that since most men thought with their penises, it only made sense that their testicles were ranked next in line in value. Unlike silly little things like manners and kindness and simple consideration for another human being.

"You seem to be mad at me all of a sudden," Adam commented as he watched her wrestle with her bags. "Did I say something wrong?"

"Ha, ha," she laughed gaily, or as gaily as she could with her heart shattering into little pieces at his cruelty. A snapped mind and a broken heart—oh, what a lovely way to start off her stay in paradise. "Ha, ha, ha, ha!"

She left the room, ignoring him as he called for her to wait and allow him to apologize for whatever it was he had said, hurrying past several curious guards to rejoin what remained of the contestants in the main lobby.

He followed her out a few minutes later, but she steadfastly refused to acknowledge him. The cat was back in his carrier, no doubt to facilitate his transfer to the resort. Even though more than half of the excited contestants had been spirited away to the main buildings, the crowd remaining was still sizeable.

Hero yanked her mind away from the contemplation of a pair of blue eyes and strolled through the outer doors to deposit her bag with the waiting luggage. Walking outside from the air-conditioned terminal was like entering into another world. The air slammed into her, a hot wall of humidity heavily scented with flowers. Greenery spilled onto the tarmac, the shrubs and bushes and trees alive with birdsong. Bright flashes of color flittered amid the branches, while high overhead sea birds—gulls and pelicans and terns—flew in lazy circles. Hero closed her eyes for a moment, soaking in the sensations of heat and noise and the smell of the tangy salt air and lush earth overlaying the more familiar scent of petrol fumes.

"It's beautiful, isn't it?" a small blond woman standing next to her said, looking out into the dense foliage. "Just like the TV promos said it would be—sun and sea and beautiful scenery . . . it truly is paradise."

Hero smiled her agreement.

"Or it would be if there weren't a serpent slithering around to ruin everything." The woman frowned over her shoulder at someone. Hero followed her gaze and was more than a little

35

surprised to find it focused on Adam. She looked back to the woman, her heart dropping as she took note of the heart-shaped face framed by thick, curly blond hair, a petite body obviously fit and well toned, and casual taupe linen trousers and a shirt that Hero suspected cost more than her entire wardrobe. If this woman was indicative of the competition, she was in very deep trouble indeed.

"A serpent?" she couldn't help but ask.

The woman glanced back at where Adam and a large cluster of women were approaching before opening her purse and looking inside for something. "Stalker is more like it. Everywhere I go, he's there. Well, he'll soon find out I mean what I say. Shoot, I don't have anything to write on. Do you have a piece of paper I could use? My lawyer told me to keep notes on exactly what he does in case I want to sue him."

Hero stared at her, shocked. Perhaps she was speaking about someone else. Adam might be a little off-kilter, but he didn't seem to her to be the stuff that stalkers were made of. Slowly she reached into her purse and pulled out a small tablet of notepaper she'd filched from work. "Erm . . . you're being stalked by someone on the show?"

. The blond woman fluttered her hands dismissively, taking the notepad and nodding her head toward Adam. "That man, the one surrounding himself with all the women. I've warned him and warned him, but I know how this is going to end— I'll have to have him removed from the island if he insists on pursuing me."

"He . . . he looks so nice," Hero said softly, wishing she could take notes herself, but at the same time having difficulty resolving the woman's claims with the warmhearted, animal-loving Adam. Perhaps the woman was referring to someone else. "You are talking about that man, the tall one with the dark hair and blue eyes? Monday Marsh?"

The blonde snorted and pulled out a pen. "Monday Marsh. Oh, yes, I'm speaking of the tall man. The one all the women are slobbering over, more fools they. The *Sentinel-Revue*," she read off the notepad.

The blood drained from Hero's face as she yanked her gaze back to the blonde beside her. Oh, Lord, what had she done?

The woman looked up, a frown on her lovely brow. "You're a journalist? An English journalist?"

Now what was she supposed to do? She could deny it, but any quick denial would sound suspicious. She could admit the truth, but she knew full well that the Eden rules prohibited journalists from being contestants. She decided to tell the truth—with just a bit of judicious fibbing—the same fibbing that had gotten her on the show in the first place. "I *was* a journalist. My editor fired me for writing a silly story about the royal family. Now, I'm just . . . here."

"Oh," the woman said, piercing her with a shrewd glance before turning back to make her notes. "A word to the wise— if you decide to write a story after the show is finished, you'll have to look no farther than our babe magnet over there for a very choice subject."

Hero turned to look, a frown on her brow. What *was* he doing with all those women? They were clinging onto his arms, laughing and giggling and smiling pouting little smiles at him. She sidled up a bit closer to do a little covert eavesdropping.

"Oh, Monday, your insight about multiple orgasms is *so* on the money!" a lovely brunette cooed at him, batting her lashes in a manner that screamed *wanton*. Multiple orgasms? He was giving women advice about orgasms? "I have been multiorgasmic ever since you suggested incorporating the use of a vibrator in love-play. I just can't believe I ever survived on only one orgasm during sex!"

"Oh, yes, me too," another woman interrupted as the pack moved by her. "One is just so passé now!"

Hero glared at Adam. How could she have been so misled by him? How could she have fallen for his Mr. Nice Guy story about his cat? How could she have snapped for a man who was clearly the United States Sex Fiend of the Year?

"I feel so much more in touch with my feminine side," yet another woman simpered, edging out a shorter woman to claim his arm as he stopped a few feet away from the shuttle sign, undoing the latch to the cat carrier. Adam, Hero noted sourly as he snapped the leash on Jesus to the stunned surprise of his audience, had adopted a little-boy-lost bashful look at the attention, no doubt carefully calculated to stimulate the women's maternal need to mother him. Lord knew, if the size of their bosoms were anything to go by, their maternal instincts might well kill him.

What a rotter.

"Just listen to them," the small blond woman said with a disgusted look at Adam and his groupies. "Fawning all over him and that monstrous cat. It's disgusting, isn't it?"

"I'm not quite sure why, but evidently they feel grateful to him for their newly found multiorgasmic abilities," Hero said dryly.

The woman next to her snorted. "If only they knew."

Hero turned to her. "Knew what? Just who *is* he?"

The blonde studied her for a moment, then held out a tanned hand. "My name is Sally Simmons."

Sally? Sally? It couldn't be a coincidence, not with her so obviously hostile to Adam. Hero wondered just why he had assumed she was working for Sally, and what the blonde's history was with him. Pushing her musing aside, she shook the offered hand. "Hero North."

"Well, Hero North, what would you say if I were to tell you that Monday Marsh is the U.S.'s premier radio sex therapist?"

Hero goggled at her. "Sex therapist? He offers sexual advice on the radio? Where anyone can hear it?"

Sally nodded. "He has an extremely large following, particularly among women, as you can see."

"And then my nipples exploded in delight!" Adam said suddenly. Hero turned to stare at him, her mouth hanging open in surprise. The women around him burst into laughter and applause, attracting the few remaining men from inside the terminal.

Dear Lord, what had she done? She'd snapped for an American sex maniac, one who discussed his nipples in public. With strangers. Along with orgasmic advice.

Three shuttles pulled up at that moment, fortuitously keeping Hero from contemplating the insanity that had gripped her. She followed Sally to the line of people queuing for the first bus, claiming a seat near the door. Sally sat at the front. Adam and Jesus, Hero could not help but note, remained with the swarm of women before the second shuttle. Just as the driver was about to close the doors, Adam leaped up the stairs and stood looking up and down the aisle, Jesus clasped to his chest. He glanced down at Hero. He noticed at the empty seat next to her. Her heart started racing at the warmth in his blue eyes. Had he sought her out? Had he left his adoring, orgasmic fans to sit with her? Could it be that he was looking for something not found in the shallow, vapid women who clung to him? Did he truly want . . . her?

"Hero," he said with a sigh of relief. Her heart did a few jumping jacks. "Do you mind?"

She scooted her purse out of the way and tried to look cool and unconcerned. "Not in the least."

"Thank you." He plopped the cat down on the seat next to her, and leaned forward over her. "He likes you; he won't be any trouble. Just don't let him try to kill himself."

She looked down at her hand in complete and utter surprise. There was a leash in it. She looked at the seat next to her. Jesus was considering her with his one good eye. She looked up. Adam had claimed the empty seat next to Sally, and was leaning close to her, arguing vehemently, if quietly. *Bloody hell!*

Pressure on her leg had her looking back at the cat. He curled up next to her, his huge head resting on her thigh. One side of his lip was curled under itself, exposing a fang.

He was drooling on her dress.

Chapter Three

"Orientation in the ballroom, ladies and gentlemen," the TV show producer was saying, waving his clipboard at everyone as they emerged from the shuttles. "Your bags will be taken to your rooms. Ballroom inside and to the left. Move along, please. We have a schedule to keep."

Adam retrieved Jesus from the Englishwoman, thanking her politely for watching the cat while he tried to plead his case with Sally. Hero seemed to be a bit peeved with him, although he couldn't understand why. She'd said she liked cats, and Jesus had obviously taken to her, something he didn't do with many women. He was about to ask Hero if it was her first time in the Caribbean when the women he'd tried so hard to escape earlier pounced on him, driveling on about his cat, and how thrilled they were to meet him in person. He shot Hero a look begging for her help, or at the very least sympathy, but she didn't take pity on him, strolling on ahead without so much as a glance back at him.

She really was something, he thought to himself as he followed the crowd into a brightly lit ballroom. Tall and statuesque with short, curly auburn hair, not to mention curves in places that would drive a monk mad, topped off with a charming English accent—why couldn't he have met her elsewhere? Why did it have to be here, where she would be sure to be swarmed with men wanting to get closer to all those delicious curves? His eyes followed her as she took a seat at one of the tables near the back of the ballroom.

"Excuse me, will you, ladies? I see someone I know. Yes, yes, later, I promise we'll talk. Thank you all for the kind words." He made his escape, hurrying toward the rear of the ballroom, his eyes on the tall Englishwoman. She was chatting happily with the woman next to her, a small woman with long blond . . . *Damn!*

"Ladies." He nodded as he pulled out the chair next to Hero. Both she and Sally turned gimlet eyes on him. He ignored the chilly reception and placed Jesus on the chair, taking the seat on the cat's far side. "I see we're just in time. Looks like they're about to start."

"Ladies and gentlemen, welcome to Crescent Moon Resort! Welcome to Eden!" A woman's voice blared out from speakers in the ceiling, and the ballroom suddenly burst into life. Huge arc lights lining the walls flashed on, making Adam and everyone at his table blink in response. Cameramen poured out of the doorways, spacing themselves around the room, their heavy shoulder-mounted cameras pointing at the people seated at the tables, shadowed by men and women with sound equipment, microphones that followed the sweep of cameras. A number of other people emerged as well, each clutching a clipboard with the Eden TV show emblem blazoned on the front. On a small raised dais at the front of the room, several men in suits joined a couple of women standing around a computer setup.

"Is everyone seated?" One of the women, a black woman with spiky hair and bloodred-framed glasses asked, looking around the room. "Handlers, do we have everyone? Yes? Excellent. Welcome, contestants, to Eden! My name is Dara Thompson, and I'm the executive producer of Eden. Standing to my left is the president of Hawkeye Productions, Mr. Michael Hawkins. Before Mike welcomes you and explains what will be happening in the next few weeks, I'd like to introduce someone whom I'm sure you'll all recognize—the host of our show, the fabulous Rupert Asterisk!"

The audience applauded while Adam wrestled his orientation packet from where Jesus had dragged it to his chair, returning the folder with one soggy, chewed-upon corner to the table. He dug through his pocket until he found a well-gnawed catnip mouse, giving it to the cat, who promptly growled and pounced on it, holding it with his front paws and rolling onto his back to kick at the mouse with his back legs. Adam glanced up to find Hero's serious gray eyes on him. He smiled at her. She started to smile in return, then suddenly shifted her gaze to the front of the room, where the show's host, the well-known diminutive actor/comedian, was entertaining the crowd with somewhat bawdy jokes about Adam and Eve. Adam smiled politely with the rest of the audience, but couldn't help but sneak a peek back to the woman sitting next to his cat.

She was studying Jesus's mouse with a perplexed expression. He grinned, and leaned across the cat to whisper, "It's a sock. Actually, it's three socks sewn together. Sturdier that way. I made it myself."

Her eyes met his, tiny lines of puzzlement between her arched brows smoothing out as she blinked at him. "You make him toys?"

"I have to. He eats regular cat toys. This one will probably last a week or less before he guts it."

She watched Jesus chomping on the sock mouse's head. "You put whiskers on it?"

"Well, it *is* a mouse. They have whiskers, you know. I wouldn't want to cheat him out of a proper mouse."

She looked at him as if he were the one with mouse whiskers;

then suddenly her eyes warmed up and her enticing lips curved into a smile. It lit up her whole face and, more amazingly, seemed to light him up inside, as well. "You really are a very nice man despite everything."

Despite everything? The warm glow her smile had started suddenly froze into a leaden lump of embarrassment. The women. She must have seen those blasted women hanging off him. *Hell.*

"I can't think of anyone else who would go to such trouble for a pet."

His heart started beating a bit faster at her praise. "He's not your average garden variety of pet, as you can see. He's had a hard life. A few toys are the least I can do to make up for what he's been through."

She looked like she was going to say something else, but the woman on the other side of him shushed them and pointed toward the stage. Asterisk had been replaced by a tall man with slicked-back blond hair who was explaining the basic rules of the contest.

"Now, as you all know, the show is divided into two-week sections. The first two weeks feature a variety of events and are intended to give you all a chance to find out how compatible you are with the contestants of the opposite sex. Each day of the first week you will have three dates: two during the day, and a third group date at night. At the end of every day you will be required to go into the special video booths set up in the lobby. We call them the confession boxes." The man waited for the polite laughter to die down. "The confession box is where points are awarded; if your date indicates he or she had a good time with you, and you say likewise, you both receive points for compatibility. If one of you states he or she did not enjoy the date . . . well, sorry, no points there. The second week you'll be paired off with those dates whom you've scored with— that's scored *points*, gentlemen. Anything else is up to you." The man held up his hands as if absolving himself of any wrongdoing as the audience hooted and whistled at his double entendre. Adam rolled his eyes. If the women who had hounded him at the airport were anything to go by, there wasn't anyone here he would have even the slightest romantic interest in . . . except perhaps the goddess sitting next to him. He slid his gaze toward Hero as the president continued.

"Couples rated compatible will be paired off, and judged on how well they work together as a team. They'll be faced with a variety of challenges, all geared to give them a better understanding of what the other is really like. Successful couples will be awarded points, while those of you not meant to be together will have the opportunity to pair up with someone else of your choice. At the end of the second week, the participants who have earned the most points will advance to the next round, leaving us to start the third week with only fifty bachelors and fifty bachlorettes. By the end of the sixth week, only one couple will be left to enjoy the grand prize of—say it with me—one million dollars and an around-the-world trip for two. As you can tell from the number of your fellow contestants, the competition will be tough, but remember! The goal of the show is to find that special someone, not to rack up points, so be honest in the confession booth. We've all had enough bad dates not to want to repeat them just to accrue a few points, right?"

The audience groaned their agreement. Jesus tugged on his leash, standing with his front legs on the back of the chair, giving the cameraman who was filming him one of his silent meows. The cameraman grinned in delight, tightening the focus of his shot as the cat squinted his eye at the light atop the camera, batting at it with one massive paw.

"Showoff," Adam grumbled, glancing up to see if Hero was watching. She was, but the smile that had started such a warm glow within him had faded. She looked worried now, pensive, tapping a finger against lush lips as if she was considering his fitness for some role. A surge of lust slashed through him, whispering to him exactly what role he'd like to perform with her.

"One final word and then I'll let you go all freshen up before dinner. You'll notice around you the cameramen and soundmen. They are here to capture your responses to your dates, as well as to film any interviews you might be requested to do with the illustrious Asterisk. Please do your best to pretend the camera crew is not present. We want your reactions to be as realistic and unstudied as possible. Be honest, be yourself, and above all, have fun here in our own little Eden!"

Dara, the executive producer, returned to the microphone with a few last minute announcements. "Dinner tonight is the first of this week's group dates. Each table will be playing a few icebreaker games to allow you to get to know each other. Points will be awarded to tables whose members complete the events. There will be a cocktail get-to-know-you hour before in the south patio. The orientation packets handed to you as you came in include your room key and a map to the resort, as well as a list of amenities, Eden rules, et cetera. If you have any questions, feel free to ask any of the show's handlers. They're the ones with the blue buttons and the wild looks in their eyes."

The crowd laughed and applauded the producer, chatting among themselves as they started filing out of the ballroom. Adam pulled Jesus back from where he was trying to climb onto Hero's lap.

"Sorry," he said. "He really likes you. You ought to take that as a compliment—he doesn't like too many women. My vet thinks it was a woman who abused him as a kitten."

"Abused him? How terrible. Poor puss," Hero said, stroking the cat's large head. Jesus made that peculiar rumbling deep in his chest that passed for purring, giving Adam a sly look out of his good eye. Adam looked over Hero's head.

"Er . . . Sally, if I could speak to you for just a moment . . ."

"You do, and I'll tell that producer the truth about you," Sally said in a snarl as she gathered up her things and stalked off.

Adam was torn between going after her to beg her to not turn him in, and staying to talk to Hero. He sighed. There were

Jesus's testicles to consider; duty had to win out. Feeling more a martyr than ever, he scooped up the cat from where he was making himself at home on Hero's lap. "I'm sorry about that; he really is a mooch when it comes to attention. I'll just take him off to my room and let him stretch his legs."

"I see." She didn't look like she saw anything that she understood; she looked confused. Delightfully confused, he amended, gnawing on a delectable lower lip as she eyed him speculatively.

He glanced out the glass doors to the long palm-lined walk that ran the length of the resort, knowing he should leave, but wanting to stay. Large clusters of people were still visible, including the retreating form of Sally. He really needed to talk to her, to make her understand that he didn't pose any threat to her whatsoever, and to get her to agree not to expose him. But Hero was an irresistible lure—especially since her hesitant expression told him she had something to say, but hadn't yet mustered up the nerve.

He sighed again and gave in. He could find Sally later. Just once he wanted to do something for himself.

"Erm . . . Mr. Marsh—"

"Call me Adam," he said, uncomfortably aware once again that she believed him to be someone he wasn't. He pushed that thought aside. There was nothing he could do about that now. Perhaps later . . . if he was allowed to have a later, that is.

"Adam, would it be possible to have a word in your ear? Privately?"

She wanted to talk to him privately. How fitting that he should be right there, willing to be talked to. *Privately.*

"Certainly. Er . . . let's see . . ." He juggled Jesus and his orientation packet for a moment, then set the cat down and rustled through the papers until he found a small brass key. "I'm in cabana seventeen. According to the map, that's just beyond the fitness center. Where are you?"

47

She held out a key. "Cabana one-twenty-two, next to the croquet court."

"You're closer. If you don't mind stopping to let Jesus do his business, I'll walk you there."

"I don't mind in the least," Hero said as they exited the ballroom. Long walkways lined with shrubs, small palms, and lots of flowers crisscrossed the main resort compound. Discreet signs pointed visitors to the various amenities. Adam and Hero turned right and headed toward the west side of the resort.

"To tell you the truth," she admitted with a shy smile that tugged on his heart, "I'm a bit overwhelmed by the resort. It's lovelier than anyplace I've seen. The flowers alone are breathtaking, and the scenery . . . it really is just as I imagine the Garden of Eden to have been."

Adam paused and discreetly turned his back when Jesus disappeared under a low-growing shrub.

"It's a big muggy, but I expect we'll get used to that in time." Dirt scattered on the paving stones before Adam's feet, kicked out from under the shrub. He shifted uncomfortably. Hero was dreamily looking off in the distance, past a line of coconut palms to where the roar and crash of the surf could be heard pounding onto a rocky outcropping. More dirt splatted on the pathway. He brushed it aside with his foot, wondering what Hero wanted to talk to him about. A small pink and white orchid, roots still attached, was flung out from under the shrub onto the tops of his shoes. He tugged on the leash, smiling wolfishly at Hero as she turned to him.

"He likes flowers."

Hero looked at the orchid Adam placed on the edge of the path.

"He does?" she asked with one eyebrow cocked in disbelief before turning back to gaze out toward the palms.

Adam fidgeted. He hated having to make chitchat. He never had been any good at it, and now here he was stuck with a woman who stirred his desire more than he'd felt in years, and his cat was evidently excavating to China. "Er . . . so, is this your first time in the Caribbean?"

"Yes."

"Ah."

He tugged a bit more persistently on the leash. The shrub trembled for a moment, a few twigs snapped sharply, and then a low, threatening growl heralded Jesus's arrival. Branches parted to reveal a feline rear end. The cat backed out of the leaves, rumbling softly to himself as he dragged a small piece of sky-blue cloth over to his owner, plopping his butt down on Adam's toes to present his find with a look of great satisfaction.

"What the hell . . . ?" Adam wrestled the cloth from the cat's mouth and claws. "Let go of it, dammit! Whatever it is, it's dirty. I don't want you to have it."

Hero watched in silence as he scooted the cat off his feet, squatting next to the animal, prying his mouth open to unhook the cloth from Jesus's sharp teeth.

Adam looked up. "I think there's a bit of retriever in him," he joked weakly, mentally moaning to himself. This was just what he needed, for Jesus to act up and make him look like an idiot in front of the one woman he wanted to make a good impression on. "Give it to me, cat! Damn it, I'm not playing with you, *give me the blasted thing!*"

Jesus spat out the cloth and turned to Hero, standing on his back legs and patting her knees with his front paws, giving her his piteous meow and a look that would do a starving orphan facing eviction into a blizzard proud.

"Oh, you poor thing!" she crooned, clearly falling for his pathetic act. She bent down to scoop him up, staggering a little when she tried to straighten up with the full weight of him in her arms. She recovered nicely, however, and glared at Adam over the cat's head. "You shouted at him!"

Adam held up his hand. A torn and dirt-encrusted pair of women's sky-blue underwear dangled from his fingers. "Yes, I

49

did. I have a rule that he's not allowed to bring home strange women's panties. I'm silly that way."

Her eyebrows went up. "You trained your cat to fetch knickers from women who are *not* strangers?"

"No, certainly not! He just likes them."

The look of disbelief on her face said it all.

"I mean, he just likes to find things and retrieve them. It doesn't matter what the object is."

She continued to stare at him, making him feel as though he were in fourth grade and caught kissing Betty Sue Seymore behind the jungle gym. "Look, he's a strange cat; I have little control over him. He likes to find things. I can count the number of times he's brought me panties on the fingers of one hand." He thought for a moment. "Well, all right, two hands, but that's only because my girlfriend was living with me at the time and there were panties everywhere. I couldn't expect him to just ignore them, now, could I?"

She pursed her lips, looking like she was going to argue the point, then shook her head and simply said, "I think perhaps we should let this particular subject drop."

"I think you're right," he agreed with no little sense of relief. What was it about this woman that made him feel as if he were a gauche young man on his first serious date?

Hero frowned at the underwear, then down on Jesus's head. The cat's look of smug satisfaction at being held melted into one of innocence and feline sainthood. Adam was not amused. He tossed the underwear into a nearby trash receptacle and retrieved his cat, setting him on the ground. "Behave yourself and I'll let you have a can of sardines later."

Jesus gave him a one-eyed, annoyed stare before leading the way down the path.

"He's limping quite heavily; don't you think you should carry him?" Hero asked as she strolled next to Adam, her eyes on the cat a few feet ahead of her. "His leg must be hurting."

"Just ignore it; it's an act. He's fine. When his leg hurts, he lets me know."

"How?" she asked, just as he knew she would.

"He bites me," Adam replied, enjoying the tantalizing scent of sun-warmed woman the soft ocean breeze carried his way. He breathed deeply, feeling the familiar prickles of arousal start to stir before he clamped down on the unwelcome sensation. What the hell was he doing? What sort of terrible things did it say about him that he was ready to take advantage of an innocent young woman while pretending to be someone else? What had happened to honor and pride? Had he really sunk so low that he would even contemplate lying—by word or by deed, they were both the same—to someone he wanted to have a relationship with? Had it really come to this?

Hero's hand brushed his as they walked down the palm tree–lined pathway toward a sweeping crescent of small cabanas lining a lush green lawn. Pure desire rippled through him at the contact.

"Yes, yes, it has come to this," he muttered as he stepped aside for her to open the door to the furthermost cabana.

"Did you say something?" she asked as she paused before the door.

"Nothing worth repeating."

The small puzzled frown was back between her eyes, but she said nothing as she unlocked the door and entered the cabana. Jesus marched in after her, his whiskers twitching as he surveyed the room, locating the whereabouts of anything that might be of possible interest to him.

"Don't get too comfortable; this isn't our room," Adam told him, unsnapping the leash before looking up at Hero. She was examining the room as well.

"This is quite nice, much nicer than I expected. Oh, I'm sorry, do please sit down. This won't take but a minute." She pulled a suitcase off a wicker chair and waved him toward it.

"I don't suppose you asked me here in order to cast yourself

51

into my manly arms and beg me to make you a woman tonight?" he asked with a smile that he sincerely hoped was not tinged with desperation.

Hero paused in the act of sitting down in the chair opposite his. "What?"

He tried to make his smile friendly and reassuring, and not in the least bit that of a sex-starved man who finds himself in a room with the living personification of Aphrodite and Venus all rolled into one tempting package. "That was a joke. A very poor one, I realize, but since you seemed to be a bit peeved with me earlier, and as my cat is probably even now sitting on your toilet playing in the water, I figured it might be called for."

"I see."

"Clearly it wasn't."

"Perhaps not," she agreed, her lovely gray eyes large with worry. She probably was concerned he'd pounce on her the second she looked away. He heaved a mental sigh. Wasn't this day turning out to be just jim-dandy fine? First she caught him in the blatantly illegal act of smuggling his cat through quarantine; then said cat retrieved a pair of underwear for him like he did that every day of his life, and now that she had invited him into her cozy little cabana for two, he was acting like a sex maniac. Oh, yes, his life was turning out very well, indeed.

"I have a proposition to make you," Hero interrupted his contemplation of recent events.

Adam sat up a bit straighter in his chair and casually crossed his legs so she wouldn't see just what sort of effect her nearness and the word *proposition* were having on him. He had to clear his throat before he could speak. "A proposition? What sort of proposition?"

Dared he hope it involved their bared flesh and a fresh mango or two?

"It's like this—I have a reason, which I don't care to reveal just now, to wish to be present at least through the third and fourth weeks of the show, and not eliminated at the end of the second week. It is vitally important to me, you understand. I assume if you've gone to the time and trouble, not to mention the risk of possible imprisonment, of smuggling your cat into the country, you must also wish to see the whole show through as well."

There was nothing he'd like more than to go home . . . assuming she'd like to come with him, but he supposed he shouldn't say that. He tried to look as though he were anticipating a grand and glorious time on the island of Mystique, and nodded his head.

"Excellent. Simply put, I propose—*Aaaiiiiiiiiieeeeeeee!* What the bloody hell is that?"

Hero leaped from a sitting position straight onto the seat of her chair and did a horrified little dance as she pointed a shaking finger toward the bathroom. Framed perfectly in the doorway, Jesus strolled nonchalantly into the room with a small creature perched on his head.

Adam sighed again, this time aloud. Jesus was going to be the death of him, he really was. Or if not him specifically, at least of his romantic life. "It would appear my cat has found a friend."

"But what is it? It's yellow! It looks poisonous!" Hero shrieked, still doing her fascinating little dance on the chair. Adam gave himself a moment to admire the flashes of leg that were visible as she bounced up and down, then turned his attention back to the cat, who had now wandered into the room and sat with his tail curled around his feet, looking for all the world like a feline version of Buddha.

One with a gecko on his head.

"Will it harm him? Where did he get it? Did he find it in my room? Oh, Lord, I'll have to have my room fumigated! I can't stay in a room with great herds of wildlife living in it!"

Adam rose and walked over to the cat to take a closer look. "It's nothing poisonous, and fumigating wouldn't do anything. It's just a house gecko, Hero, not a tarantula or anything that bites or is poisonous, although I did see a scorpion as we left the ballroom, so you might want to be wary about going around barefoot outside."

"Eeeeeeek!" Hero screamed louder, and scrabbled onto the tiny round table that sat between the two wicker chairs. "Geckos! Scorpions! Tarantulas! No one said anything about them in the promotional literature!"

He stroked a finger down the yellowish-brown back of the gecko. It was about three inches long, and looked back at him with shiny black unblinking eyes. "You just had to take on a hitchhiker, eh?" Adam asked his cat softly, giving him a quick scratch behind his ear where the gecko's tail curled. Jesus rumbled in reply. The gecko slowly blinked. Hero made distressed noises.

"Come here and meet the gecko," Adam said as he turned, holding out his hand for her. "It won't hurt you, I promise. It's just a harmless little lizard that eats bugs. You'll be thankful to have him once you see how many insects he takes care of for you."

Hero looked at him as if he'd ripped off all his clothing and painted his penis bright blue. "You expect me to touch it?"

The aforementioned penis twitched at the very thought of her words. He mentally pointed out to his genitals that she was referring to the gecko, not to them. "Yes, I expect you to touch it. Make friends with your house gecko, and he'll do right by you, that's what an old Bahamian once told me, and he was absolutely correct. Come on; I promise he won't do anything scary." He wiggled the fingers of his outstretched hand at her. She looked at his hand as if it were crawling with geckos and shook her head. He tsked, then grabbed her waist with both hands and swung her off the table. She slid down his chest in a manner that made his not-painted-blue penis cheer with happiness.

Her knees seemed to buckle once her feet hit the ground, so he held on to her waist until she was steady. That was the excuse he gave himself; the truth was he just liked holding her close to him. A breeze from the window ruffled her auburn curls, sending the flowery scent of her to dance a tantalizing dance around him, stirring his libido to new heights. He regretted the morning's choice of bikini underwear, and made a mental note to wear boxers from that moment on.

"You lifted me down," she said in breathy astonishment, her eyes wide with shock, her hands on his where they held her waist firmly.

"Yes," he agreed, unwilling to let her go. She was warm and soft beneath his fingers, and he had the most overwhelming urge to let his hands skim upward, to feel the heat of her breasts against his palms.

"You're holding me." Her eyes grew dark with emotion, but what emotion was it? Did he offend her, did she think he was a sex maniac, or was she feeling the same wild stir of attraction that was washing through him?

"I am."

"Close," she pointed out.

"Am I?"

"Yes."

"Oh."

A minute passed with the two of them just standing there, him holding on to her waist, both staring into the other's eyes. The muffled roar of the surf from the east side of the resort mingled with the jabber of birds and people as they strolled past the cabanas, laughing and talking excitedly. Inside, the room was quiet but for the loud beating of his heart.

"Do you want me to let you go?" Adam finally broke the silence to ask.

Her pupils flared. "It is probably for the best."

He said nothing, his palms warm with the heat of her through the thin cotton of her dress. For some reason, he seemed unable to move his hands from her waist.

"I . . . it's very difficult to speak with you when we're standing this close," she added.

"It is?"

"Yes."

"Why?"

The tip of her little pink tongue emerged to lick her bottom lip. Adam was possessed with the overwhelming desire to suck her lip into his mouth and taste it for himself.

"You . . . erm . . . standing this close . . ."

"Yes?" The blush that swept up from her chest intrigued him. Did women still blush over something like a little physical contact? He eyed her rosy cheeks and bright eyes that held a tinge of apology in them.

"It's a position people usually take when they are about to kiss each other."

He really had to let go of her; he knew that. Just standing so close to her, her thighs pressed against his, the tips of her breasts brushing against his chest with every breath, he was hard as a rock. She really would think he was a maniac if she knew he was reacting to her so strongly.

"Would that be such a terrible thing?" he asked.

"Mmm?" She looked confused by the question.

"Kissing."

Her eyes widened until she had a deer-in-the-headlights look of startlement. "You mean—"

He couldn't stop himself; there was nothing in the world short of spontaneous combustion or global nuclear war that would keep him from doing what he had wanted to the second he saw her. His lips brushed hers gently, tentatively, more a soft lip embrace than an actual kiss. The feeling of her mouth on his left him burning with the need to claim it properly, but he knew instinctively that she was poised on the edge of flight, so he pulled back and smiled at her instead.

She stared at him in bewilderment as he released her waist,

but captured her hand, tugging her over to where Jesus sat watching them interestedly.

"Look, it's just a gecko. It's not slimy or wet or anything; it's just a friendly little lizard that wants to eat the bugs in your room. He won't come near you; they're very shy of people. Most of them don't even come out until night."

She continued to stare at him as he stroked the tips of her fingers lightly down the back of the gecko.

"You kissed me," she finally said, then blushed even darker.

"Yes. Do I need to apologize?"

He was willing to bet he could fry an egg on the blush that was burning her cheeks.

"No," she whispered, then looked down at where her fingertips rested on the gecko. "I still don't want it in my room," she said in a stronger voice, slowly pulling her fingers from beneath his.

He grinned as he retook his seat. "I suspect that won't be an issue. Jesus seems to have found a friend, and until I can afford to pay for his new testicles, I'd just as soon he kept himself busy and his mind off his depression."

Hero closed her eyes for a moment, opening them again to shake her head. "His new testicles?"

"Yes, I told you that I was saving for his operation."

"But . . ." She looked at the cat as she sank into the chair opposite the tiny table. "Surely he's already *had* his operation?"

"Not that one, the next one. The one to implant his prosthetic testicles. It's a very expensive procedure."

She stared at him with a curious look that was part disbelief, part amusement. "Prosthetic . . . *testicles?*"

He frowned at her. "You're going to laugh, aren't you? Every woman I've told about the prosthetic testicles laughs—even my vet's partner laughed—but I assure you it's no laughing matter to Jesus. His self-esteem is involved. It's a very delicate situation."

She started to laugh. "I'm sorry, I have no intention of slighting your cat's testicles, or lack thereof. It's just that . . . prosthetic testicles! Only a man would think of such a useless thing."

"Useless! A man's balls aren't useless! They have a very specific purpose, and I don't mind telling you that we as a gender tend to be fond of them. We feel a definite lack if they are missing."

"We weren't talking about your . . . erm . . ." She glanced at his lap and then quickly away.

He ground his teeth together for a moment before speaking. "You said you had a proposition for me?"

"Yes," she said, her lips quivering slightly.

"What is it?" he asked crossly, trying to keep the scowl off his face.

Her lips twitched. "I will tell you, but I don't want you to be disappointed."

"Disappointed?"

"Yes." She lost the battle and began laughing. "It has nothing to do with tes . . . tes . . . testicles."

Chapter Four

It took Hero a good five minutes to stop laughing. It didn't help that Adam had shot her such an accusatory look, or that he turned to his monster of a cat and balefully told him it was all his fault. Wiping a few tears of hilarity back, she made an effort to get to the purpose of her proposal. "As I was saying, I intend on remaining through the duration of the show."

He stopped scowling long enough to look curious. "Would you answer a personal question for me?"

She gazed into his blue eyes and felt her determination not to allow him to affect her anymore begin to melt. Her fingers twitched, wanting to touch her lips, to see if they had been changed by the almost-not-there kiss that had rocked her world; then she remembered the women. His groupies. Indignation burned within her as she refortified her defenses against the sinfully handsome man opposite her. He probably kissed all of the groupies, too, no doubt as he was doing whatever he did to make them multiorgasmic. He probably did that on the plane to Mystique, she grumbled sourly to herself. He might appear to be a wonderful, warm, caring, handsome, ideal man who cared about animals and people, but the truth was, he was the biggest sex fiend of all. His nipples exploded in delight, *indeed!*

"A personal question? Possibly. What is it?"

"Why would an intelligent, pretty woman like yourself have to resort to a show like this to find a man?"

A warm kernel of pleasure formed and started to glow within her at his words. He thought she was intelligent and pretty? The growing warmth suddenly froze. Intelligent, yes, lots of men had called her that, but never pretty. He was just flattering her; he had to be. He was being nice to her because she knew his secret, and he didn't want her to tell anyone. She raised her chin and gave him what she hoped was a haughty glare. "My reasons for being here are my own, and have no importance to the proposition I wish to make to you. Simply put, I must be sure of making it at least to the second round, and since the first two weeks we are judged on compatibility with others, I find myself in the necessary position of offering you a deal."

"What sort of a deal?" he asked, leaning back in his chair, looking mildly curious.

"One that will be mutually beneficial: I will agree not to tell the Eden people and the Mystique officials that you smuggled your cat through quarantine, and you"—she took a deep breath—"agree to be my date once a day for the next two weeks."

The words didn't hurt nearly as much as she thought they would, at least not until Adam's eyes narrowed on her.

"You'd turn us in?"

"Not if you help me," she said miserably, feeling terribly guilty about blackmailing him, but seeing no other choice. It wasn't as if he really was a nice man. He wasn't. His nipples exploded on national radio every night. His appearance of niceness was all a sham, an act to make people believe he was the sort of man who'd care for a stray cat and adopt him when others would have ignored the animal, or had him put down.

Besides which, as the television show producer warned, the odds of making it past the first round of elimination were not good, especially for someone like her, who so obviously stood out from the rest of the tanned, fit women. "One date per day and positive comments each night in the confession booth should be adequate. That will leave you time to pursue Sally or any of the myriad other women who seem to wish to be with you, although I should warn you that Sally does not appear to be the least bit fond of you. You might wish to rethink your strategy with regard to your pursuit of her. She seems most adamant that you leave her alone."

"I wish I could," he ground out through his teeth, looking like he wanted to do someone bodily harm. Despite the gentleness of the kiss they had shared earlier, she had a horrible suspicion it was herself he was thinking of. No doubt he didn't appreciate her pointing out the fact that the woman he was smitten with wasn't interested in him. All of which would make his kissing her reprehensible, except it clearly wasn't intended as a sexual indicator. It was more of a sympathetic kiss, a kiss for a woman who posed no sexual threat, a kiss for a pathetic woman afraid of lizards, a . . . a pity kiss.

Oh, Lord, had it come to this? Pity kisses?

"I can't believe you'd turn us in. I thought you liked . . . er . . . Jesus," he said with a hint of steel in his voice.

She pulled her mind from the abject misery that was her life, and reminded herself that she was strong and completely capable of living her life without him. Happily. "I do, but this is business."

One glossy eyebrow cocked at that.

"What I mean, of course, is that I take the dating situation very seriously, very seriously indeed, almost as if it were my business. Which, in a way, it is."

"Let me see if I have this straight," Adam said, frowning at her. "You are blackmailing me into being one of your dates each day?"

She flinched at the baldness of the statement, then told herself that blackmailers had no right to be so squeamish. "Yes."

"Every day?"

"One per day will suffice, I believe."

"At the conclusion of which, I am to report to the confession booth that we had a wonderful time together and are completely compatible in all ways, and that I hope to date you again the following day."

"Well . . . whatever it will take to gain us the points. You might not have to lie quite so vehemently. Perhaps just a little exaggeration will be required."

He looked perplexed. "Why do you think I'd be lying by saying we had a wonderful date and I wanted to see you again?"

She stared at him in surprise. He really was a good actor. That or he believed she was so pathetic, he needed to bolster her ego a bit. Maybe he wasn't quite as hardened and jaded as she thought. That pity kiss had certainly done a lot for her, at least until she recognized it for what it was.

But there was the issue of his nipples exploding all over the place, not to mention his hobby of making women multiorgasmic.

She sighed, confused by the dichotomy of his character. There was a definite blaze of something in the depths of his blue eyes that didn't say he pitied her. It almost seemed as if desire lurked in the sapphire depths. She spent a moment in contemplation of what it would be like to stir such an emotion in him, then reminded herself that the proof was undeniable: he was a sex expert and no doubt knew how to simulate sexual interest. She couldn't allow herself to forget that she had him by the short and curlies, and in that situation he'd do anything, even pretending he desired her, in order to keep her mouth shut.

"It matters not," she said briskly, determined to get his agreement on the proposition. "You can see that my plan will benefit you, as well as me. You will also garner points with each successful date we complete; thus you, too, will make it to the

second round. I have no doubt Sally will, as will most of your
. . . erm . . . *admirers.*"

"My—Oh, them." He gave her a sheepish grin that turned
her insides all soft and squidgy. How could a sex fiend look so
adorable? "I don't encourage them, you know. It's a bit embarrassing, to tell you the truth. I never have been one for attention."

She was willing to wager he secretly loved it. All men loved
to have women fawn upon them. "Mmm. Perhaps then becoming a radio sex therapist wasn't the best career choice to have
made?"

He looked downright uncomfortable, leaving her to wonder
if what he said was true, that he honestly did not like the attention.

"About that . . . I . . . uh . . . hell. I can't tell you."

She eyed him for a minute, then stood up and held out her
hand. "Do we have an agreement?"

He looked at her hand, then stood to wrap his long, warm
fingers around hers. "I am completely at your mercy, as you
well know," he said stiffly, his eyes dark and unfathomable. "As
such, I have no choice but to agree."

The words cut through her like a hot knife. It was clear that
he was only agreeing in order to remain a part of the show, not
because he found any pleasure in the idea of dating her. Still,
it was better he be honest about it than try to make her believe
he really found her attractive.

She just wished that honesty didn't have to hurt so much.

"Thank you," she told him, pulling her hand from his, aware
of a profound sense of loss with the severing of physical contact.

He left shortly after that, taking his cat and the gecko (much
to her relief) with him. She took a tepid shower, had a rest on
a bed that was a bit too soft for her taste, and spent the remainder of the time alternately reliving the wonderful feeling of
being held by Adam as he kissed her, and remembering the
simpering looks on the women's faces as they clung to his arms.

Why had her mind chosen him to snap over, the one man who would have at least half the women on the island fighting for his attention? Well, at least she had his agreement for one date a day. He might not have chosen her of his own free will, but she suspected he was too much of a gentleman to ignore her during the dates themselves.

A few hours after the tête-à-tête, she headed off toward the ballroom and the evening group date. Cameramen dotted the walkways, filming contestants as they emerged from their cabanas, talking and laughing together in groups as they meandered toward the main complex. Hero paused at the door when her name was called. She smiled as Sally, dressed in a slinky gold-and-black dress that left more of her exposed than covered, hailed her from the arm of a large, beefcakey man with no visible neck and skintight pants that looked like they'd been painted on him.

"Isn't this a wonderful place? How was your room? Mine looks over the saltwater pool. This is Greg; he's from Chicago."

They exchanged pleasantries for a moment before Sally added, "Come sit with us at dinner, unless you have someone else you'd like to sit with."

Hero looked over Sally's shoulder and noticed Adam and his cat bearing down on them, a grim look on his face. She knew she shouldn't say yes; she knew that although she liked Sally, it wasn't for the sake of a friendly face that she wanted to agree. She couldn't even begin to pretend to herself that her true motivation was not in the fact that wherever Sally went, Adam was sure to follow.

Since there was no use denying it, she might as well give in.

"I'd love to join you, if you truly don't mind," she said with a grateful smile, and followed them past a barrage of cameramen into the brightly lit ballroom. It was a bit unnerving knowing that her every movement was likely to be caught on camera, a fact that had her checking obsessively in the small mirror in her bathroom to make sure that she didn't have a spot or something horrid hanging from her nose, or that the back of her tiered gauze skirt wasn't tucked up into her knickers. She tried not to look at the cameras, and took a chair next to Greg. He was grinning right at one, flexing his thigh-sized arms.

He probably ate steroids for lunch.

A minute later Jesus was deposited on the chair next to her, Adam taking the seat beyond that. "Evening everyone. Sally. Hero, you look lovely. Hi. Name's Marsh," he said to Greg, leaning across Jesus and Hero to hold out his hand. "And you are . . . ?"

She blinked at him as Greg introduced himself. Sally sent him a menacing glare, then ignored him, putting her hand on Greg's huge arm to draw his attention back to where she wanted it.

"Notice you have a cat," Greg said casually, but casually in an *I don't want you to see just how interested I am* sort of way. Hero wondered if Greg, noticing Adam's interest in Sally, was preparing to go territorial.

Adam's lips twisted wryly. "He's a bit hard to ignore, but yes, he's my cat."

"Brought him through quarantine, did you?"

Hero froze, not daring to look at Adam. How would he handle the question?

"Yes," Adam drawled, apparently unconcerned. Hero let out a breath she hadn't realized she'd been holding and glanced over at Adam. He was scratching the cat's chest, much to Jesus's satisfaction. "Spent six months in there, poor old fellow."

Greg tapped on the side of his plate with his fingernail. "Rather odd, isn't it, to put your cat through six months of quarantine for a six week vacation?"

Adam smiled, showing a great many white teeth. "Not odd at all. I'm hoping to settle in the area, and once your animal has cleared one quarantine in these islands, they can travel to the others with immunity."

"Huh. Is that so?" Greg replied, a shuttered look to his eyes.

Hero wondered if what Adam had said was true. It didn't sound right, but then, she knew he was lying. It might very well do as a cover story.

"So," Adam said, smiling at her and not too noticeably changing the subject, "what's the game plan for this evening? Dinner and then a group date, eh? What sort of a date will it be, do you think?"

Hero nudged the small card in front of his plate toward him. "The card says tonight will be an icebreaker date. I imagine that means silly party games."

Two more people wandered over, introducing themselves. Sally greeted them, her smile almost as bright as the arc lights shining down on them. Immediately two cameramen homed in on them, one camera on Sally, the other on Jesus, who was sitting at the table with a serious expression on his face, looking for all the world like a guest who had been invited to a dinner party. The gecko was still perched on his head. Hero stared at it for a moment, then glanced up at Adam.

"Thought he needed a bit of sprucing up," Adam whispered to her. "Jesus and I have our evening clothes on, so I thought it was only right the gecko should fancy himself up, too."

She looked back to the cat. She had to admit Adam was right. The gecko did look much more festive with a bright red bow around its neck. Jesus wore a different collar from the one she'd seen him in earlier. That was plain brown leather—this one was hot pink with little black charms dangling from it. She looked closer.

"They're mice. Friend of mine made it for him just for the dinners," Adam said. "Makes him feel like he's dressed up, too."

She wanted to tell him that he was the only man on God's green Earth who would think of his cat's feelings during a dinner date, but the camera was pointing at her now, so she just smiled and murmured something noncommittal.

Dinner was a bit of a trial. She realized midway through the escargot that the dinner in itself was an event—the food presented had to be the most challenging to eat politely in public. Each place setting had an appetizer fork, shellfish fork, salad fork, and main dinner fork, not to mention two spoons, two knives, and something that she thought was a tool to eat escargot, but might possibly be a gelding device. She giggled at that thought . . . until the snails were placed on her plate.

She slid a covert glance around the table. Everyone was laughing and eating and chatting quite amiably, and no one blinked an eye at the thought of eating escargot. Except Adam. He stared at his plate in horror, then looked up and caught her eye.

The urge to giggle was strong. "I'm from a working-class family," she leaned over Jesus to whisper. "Where I come from, snails are destroyed in the garden, not eaten."

A look of profound relief lit his eyes. "Thank God for you. I thought I might actually have to eat them."

"Do what I do when faced with something I don't wish to eat—say you're allergic to them."

"I have a better idea," he said with a wicked grin that lit all sorts of little fires inside of her. He picked up the gelding device and clamped it around a shell, then dug around inside until he pulled out the meat, and with a quick look to make sure no cameras were on him, placed the food on Jesus's plate. The cat sniffed at it, batted it around a bit with one heavy paw, then finally chewed on it with an indescribable expression on his face. Hero and Adam watched him carefully.

"He's going to spit it back up."

"No, he's not; he likes it. If he didn't like it, he'd knock it to the floor. There, you see? He ate it. Your turn."

They got rid of most of their snails in that manner. By the end of the meal Jesus was curled up on his chair, looking sated and sleepy. The gecko, evidently warmed by the cat below him, was quiet as well. Only occasionally did he rouse himself to flick his tongue, capturing an unwary moth or fly that flew too near the duo.

One cameraman or another was lurking around their table during the entire meal, making Hero feel even more nervous than she would in normal circumstances, but since most of the time the cameras were either on Sally, the three other women, or Jesus, she started to relax. Perhaps the party games wouldn't be so bad after all.

"Oh, how naïve I can be," she muttered a short time later as she and ninety-nine other women paraded around two lines of chairs that had been placed back-to-back. Loud Caribbean music blared throughout the ballroom. Lights from the ring of cameramen around them caused beads of perspiration to form on her brow. "Naïve and downright stupid. Of all the silly things I agreed to do—"

The music stopped suddenly. She lunged for the nearest man, plopping herself down on his lap even as she excused herself. "I do hope you don't mind if I—Oh, I am sorry. I didn't realize that was your . . . erm . . . yes. I'm sure it won't cause any permanent damage. You weren't planning on starting a family right away, were you?"

He didn't return her tentative smile.

Despite wishing she hadn't been so quick to find a free lap in the embarrassingly intimate game of musical chairs, she stayed perched on her unwilling host until the ten women unlucky enough to find themselves without men to sit on were excused, and another ten men and chairs were removed.

The music started again. She made it through three more excruciatingly embarrassing rounds, then finally was excused and returned to her table to watch the rest of the game with Adam's cat and the tablemates who were also unlucky enough to be caught without a man's lap to sit upon.

During the second round, in which the women sat on the chairs and the men raced around them, she was surprised to suddenly find Adam in front of her.

"Do you mind?" he asked with a wry smile.

Some of the smaller women, afraid of being squashed by

larger male companions, had taken to scooting over to inhabit a tiny fraction of the chair, thus leaving the men room to park themselves on a corner, but Hero was no tiny woman. She filled her chair. During the two rounds before, both men who had claimed her had sat on her without the slightest qualm. She couldn't help but be a little touched that Adam asked permission first.

Then again, he was a very large man.

"No, be my guest," she said, moving her hands from where her fingers were laced across her stomach. He sat down on her carefully.

"Am I too heavy?"

"No, although I will admit this is a novel experience for me."

"Never had a man sit on you before, eh? What a sheltered life you must lead." He grinned. She wanted to grin in response, but knew she shouldn't give in to his patently false charm.

But it was so very hard, especially when he was sitting sideways on her with a wicked glint in his eye, and an even more wicked grin curving those warm, soft lips. He looked like a rogue, a devil, a man who was the sort of trouble every woman loved. She doubted if very many people were allowed to see this Adam, the real Adam.

"I shouldn't humor you," she told him sternly, feeling her own lips twitch.

"Sure you should. I love to be humored."

"Heaven only knows if I do, it might make your nipples explode in delight."

The grin faded from his face. Hero wanted to kick herself the minute the words left her mouth. How stupid could she be? With a few ill-chosen words she had reminded him of the true nature of their relationship—blackmailer and blackmailee.

He opened his mouth to say something, but one of the show staff came up to tell her she had to relinquish her chair. She walked back to her table, reminding herself that this whole idea was hers, and she had no one to blame but herself.

It didn't help.

Adam lasted a few more rounds, giving her a curious look when he returned to the table, but other than asking her quietly if he had been too heavy for her, he said nothing.

Until the orange incident.

"I'm sure most of you are familiar with the orange game," the Eden host, Asterisk, said as a lead-in to the next event. Short, balding, famed for his comedic roles, he seemed to enjoy performing before the crowd of contestants, cracking all sorts of terrible puns and jokes riddled with double entendres that had the crowd howling and applauding wildly.

The cameras filmed every moment of it.

Asterisk held up an orange. "The object of this game is to pass the orange from one person to another—without using your arms or hands, and without letting the orange touch the floor. Each table will form a line, man, woman, man, woman, and pass the orange from one person to another. Points will be awarded to each contestant who does *not* drop the orange. So here's your chance, ladies and gents, to get a head start on the point count. Ready? Maestro, mambo music please!"

Loud, pulsing music poured out from the speakers overhead. Cameramen and sound people moved into place as each table obediently formed a line. Hero stood behind Adam (who, to her surprise, did not hurry to take a place next to Sally), and in front of a man with a skull-and-crossbones earring and tattoos of flames licking up his wrists.

It was going to be a long night.

Truth be told, she admitted to herself a few minutes later, it was an amusing game. The first person in the line held the orange under her chin, while the man next to her more or less embraced her in order to get close enough to try to take it from her. She giggled as he nuzzled her neck, trying to capture the orange under his own chin; he laughed when she writhed against him, trying to push the orange toward his neck; the cameraman tightened his shot on the two in a seemingly very intimate embrace; and Hero watched it all with her breath caught in her throat. Her eyes turned to where Adam stood in front of her, applauding when the man finally retrieved the orange. She was going to have to take the orange from him. She was going to have to stand very close to him, her arms on his, her jaw brushing his, to take the orange.

She had to be mad.

The next woman in line was Sally. She gave it a game shot, but dropped the orange. So did Greg, but Hero suspected that was because he had no neck to speak of, and thus no way to hold the orange. A short strawberry-blond woman took up the orange next, and giggled in Adam's ear as he doubled over to try to retrieve the orange from her. With some careful maneuvering, he managed to get it without too much trouble, and turned to face Hero with the orange clamped between his chin and collarbone.

"You can do it; it's easy," he encouraged her, his words somewhat slurred because he couldn't move his jaw. She stared into his glittering blue eyes for a moment, and wondered if the laughter she saw there was directed at her, or at the silly situation. It didn't matter, she told herself as she stepped up to him, placing her hands on his arms as she leaned into his chest. All that mattered was that she get the points. The points were everything. She couldn't afford to be left behind, not even with Adam as a ringer.

She had no idea what brand of aftershave he used, but she highly approved of it. The scent of him, part spicy aftershave, part something uniquely Adam, teased her senses as her jaw brushed his. She angled her head to capture the orange under her chin, ignoring the fact that her breasts, pressed up against him, were on fire with the contact. His breath was hot and rapid in her ear as his hands came around her waist to steady her. She could see the pulse beat rapidly in his neck. The scent of him, the heat from his chest touching hers, the slight abrasion of his whiskery chin against her neck, and the nearness of his

71

mouth to an ear suddenly turned into a highly erogenous spot almost undid her, but the flicker of light as the cameraman moved to a better angle reminded her that they were being filmed.

She bit back the desire to lick the pulse point on his neck and clamped her chin down on the orange. Adam groaned slightly and lifted his head to release the orange, but her grip wasn't as good as she thought it was. The orange slid from beneath her chin and started to drop. She shrieked and slammed herself against Adam, rocking him backward. He regained his balance, his hands tight on her arms.

"Of all the ignominious positions," she grumbled into his chest. She was half crouched, the orange caught slightly above her breasts, pressed into his stomach.

"Are you all right?" Adam asked, his hands warm on her shoulders.

"Yes, fine, the bloody thing is on my . . . it's between my chest and your stomach."

The others in their line called out encouragement and advice.

"If you slide down slowly you should be able to catch it under your chin again," Adam said, holding her firmly to him. She knew it was so the orange would not continue its downward path and *not* because he wanted her body pressed against his, but she couldn't help enjoy the contact.

"Is that the only way?"

"It'll be easy. Just move slowly," he told her.

She nodded into his chest, took a grip on his waist, and started to slide slowly down him. She almost had it under her chin when Adam jerked and yelled, "Jesus, no!"

The orange dropped six inches. She caught it by pressing it against Adam with her cheek. Breathing heavily with the effect of being so close to him, and the spurts of adrenaline that shot through her every time the orange dropped, she rolled her eyes to the side to assess where she was.

Her face and the orange were pressed against his crotch.

"Oh, Lord," she swore into his genitals, wondering if her life could get any worse.

"Jesus! Sit! No, damn it, that does not mean come here; it means sit! *Sit!*"

A loud crash indicated a chair had turned over, but it was the laughter and calls of the people at her table that told her what was going on behind her back. Adam had tied the cat's leash to the chair while he was participating in the games. Jesus didn't seem to mind, since he was curled up asleep after his meal of snails, but evidently he had woken up and suddenly felt the need to join in the fun.

He dragged the chair over to where Hero was face-to-genitals with Adam. She sighed.

"Any brilliant ideas how I'm to get it now?" she asked him, her words slurred because of the orange pressed against her cheek. She absolutely refused to look at his crotch. She refused to notice how strained his zipper looked, or acknowledge that his fingers were biting into her arms and his breathing was just as erratic as hers.

"You're going to have to turn your face a little so you can get it under your chin," he said, his voice hoarse. "Damn it, cat, I told you not to come over here."

She closed her eyes for a moment, ignoring the people laughing at her, at the cat, at everything, and tried very hard not to dwell on what turning her face toward Adam's groin was going to mean. The points, she needed the points. The points were everything. She had to do this.

A hard head butted her hip where she knelt before Adam.

"Leave her alone, cat," he said in a growl above her. Jesus paid no mind his owner and rubbed himself along Hero's thigh in an obvious attempt to get her attention.

She ignored the cat as she warned Adam, "I'm going to take the orange now."

A second cameraman joined the first. She ignored them as well.

"Carefully," Adam pleaded.

She smiled a grim little smile to herself and simultaneously rose a little and turned her face inward until her mouth was pressed against his belt, and the orange held firmly against her voice box. She lowered her chin carefully. Behind his zipper, Adam twitched. She stopped for a moment, feeling an answering twitch within herself, deep down where the heat pooled uncomfortably in her womanly parts. Deciding it was best to pretend the twitches never happened, with careful movements she clasped the orange between her chin and chest and pulled slowly away from him. The orange remained solidly under her chin. She gave a heartfelt sigh of relief, and with one hand on Adam's belt for balance, started to rise to her feet.

He jerked her head back, almost releasing the orange from her hold.

"What the . . . Damn. Hold on a minute; your hair is tangled on my belt buckle. No, Jesus, leave her alone—"

In the end it wasn't her hair caught on his belt, or Jesus crawling over her in an attempt to get her to pet him, thereby tangling her legs in the leash that led to the chair he dragged behind him; it wasn't even the cameraman who squatted down in front of her, laughing so hard he had difficulty filming her as she crouched red-faced next to Adam's groin while he worked her hair free. It was a small, insignificant thing that caused her to drop the orange and lose fifty points she well needed.

The gecko evidently decided that as her head was higher than the cat's, it would provide a better vantage point for insect sighting. The little creature leaped off of the cat and scurried up her arm and onto her head before she realized what it was doing.

An hour later she sat in a chair outside her cabana on a wooden lounge, rubbing the sore spot on her head. She hoped it wouldn't take long for her hair to grow back, but it wasn't really the lost of a shilling-sized clump of hair that pained her. No, it was the footage the cameramen had shot, no doubt gleefully, of her screaming and racing around the table batting ineffectually at her head while Adam chased after her, telling her to stand still so he could remove the gecko, finally achieving that goal when she tripped over Jesus and his chair, sprawling out on the ground in front of everyone with her dress hiked up almost to her bum. The TV audience would eat it up.

Her shoulders sagged until her head drooped down onto her hands. She didn't think life could get any worse, but she had no doubt it would. Fate was often like that.

Chapter Five

"Moonlight is the stuff that magic is made of," Hero said decisively to no one in particular, which, considering she was sitting alone on a bench, was good. "It's romance, it's fantasy, it's excitement and mystery. Moonlight in the Caribbean . . ." She gazed out across the velvety croquet playing field tinted black and silver by the waxing moon. She flexed her bare toes into the lawn, enjoying its coolness against the soles of her feet. It felt so good, she scooted off the bench and sat cross-legged on the ground, the grass tickling her bare legs. Absently plucking a piece of grass, she looked across the way to where a line of coconut palms rustled in the fragrant evening breeze, standing like guardians along a curved stretch of protected beach. The distant thunder of waves pounding onto the island was a muted undertone to air filled with soft noises of night birds and faint strains of Caribbean music from an open-air lounge on the far side of the resort, punctuated occasionally by a shriek and burst of laughter from the swimming pool next to the lounge.

She sighed and tossed the blade of grass away. "Moonlight in the Caribbean is the most romantic thing in the world, and should be outlawed when you're alone and have no one to enjoy it with and are feeling very sorry for yourself." She looked around. The line of cabanas was uniformly dark except hers. Evidently everyone had gone off to dance under the stars, or partake in the moonlight swim mentioned as part of the evening's after-hour activities.

Everyone but her. True, she had been asked. Adam, escorting her back to her cabana after the horrible orange incident, had said he'd heard several people were planning on enjoying a swim later, and would she be interested in joining them?

She had blanched at the thought then, and she blanched now. Appearing in front of everyone in her swimsuit was *not* her idea of fun. Although she told herself she cared little what Adam thought about her—nipple-exploding womanizer that he was— she knew she was lying to herself. She did care, rot his hide. And because she cared, she wasn't going to expose herself to the look of horror sure to be in his eyes when he caught sight of all her exposed flesh.

"Buck up, old girl," she told herself. "This too shall pass. Just a couple of weeks and you'll be home and he'll be forgotten and everything will be the way it was." With, she suspected, the exception of her heart. She greatly feared she was in danger of losing that particular organ to Adam. She wasn't happy about that idea, but as it was clearly the result of her snapped mind, there was little she could do.

Other than to repeatedly deny the attraction. And to reiterate his bad points to herself. And there was the matter of his fan club, as she'd taken to thinking of the women who seemed to chase after him everywhere.

"He's American," she told her bare toes as they bobbed in time to the distant music. "Which is always a black mark. He's a smutmonger, too, giving sexual advice to women on the radio. And he has an obsession with a woman who clearly wants nothing to do with him. Not to mention the fact that he enjoys discussing his nipples in public. No, he's quite obviously not at all the sort of man any decent woman would want to know. He's just too—Oof!"

A large gray animal landed in her lap, slamming into her chest and driving out all the air in her lungs.

"Jesus, down! Stop mauling Hero; you're getting dirt all over her."

Hero pushed the cat down until he was sitting on her legs, and glanced up at Adam, taking a deep breath to refill her lungs.

The breath strangled in her throat as he stopped before her. Her eyes bugged out a little at the sight of him. He was almost naked, wearing one of those skimpy little swimsuits that men in tropical climes seemed to favor. She'd never given them a thought before, but now she sent up fervent prayers of gratitude to whomever had the brilliant idea of allowing men to parade around in nothing but a bit of Lycra. Her eyes started at his bare feet and moved up over nice calves, cute little knees, and muscled thighs. Her gaze skittered over the Lycra-covered bits, and continued up to a lovely tanned stomach, a broad chest with just the right amount of chest hair swirling around two impudent nipples, and arms that were well muscled without being grotesque.

"I'm sorry about this; he got away." Adam slung the towel he held in one hand over a shoulder and held out a broken leash. "Are you all right? Did he hurt you?"

She tried not to stare, but she couldn't help it. His dark hair was wet, slicked back from his brow, emphasizing the slight widow's peak that made her heart beat faster. Oh, who was she trying to fool? It was all of him that made her heart race.

"Hero?"

"I'm fine, thank you," she finally said, tearing her gaze from him and looking down at the cat in her lap. The gecko, minus its partywear, was clinging to the cat's huge side. She stroked around it, shuddering with the memory of the beastly thing riding her head. "Jesus just knocked the breath from me. You've been swimming?"

"Yes, you should have come with us; it was great." He stared down at her for a moment, a smile flirting with the corners of his mouth. "Did we interrupt your meditation or something?"

Really, if her heart beat any faster, she was going to pass out. She had to get a grip on herself; such a reaction was foolish and completely ridiculous. She tried to force herself to calm down as she purposely avoided looking at the bulge in his Speedos; heaven knew *that* wouldn't do anything toward keeping her calm. And she was no where near calm with the hundreds of questions zipping through her mind: Was he going to sit with her? Had he left the swimming party because he missed her? Had he used his cat as a flimsy excuse to stop by and see her? Could it be that he left all those tanned, fit, attractive women just so he could be with her?

Had she completely lost her mind?

"No, it's nothing like that. I was just sitting here enjoying the evening. It's so lovely here, I almost can't believe it's real—the flowers and the ocean and everything. But the moon is so bright, and it's finally cooling down enough, so I thought I'd sit outside and soak in the local color. I can see why people come here for their honeymoons; it's very romantic. And peaceful."

He bent over to scoop up the cat from her lap, his fingers brushing her bare arm, sending little streaks of heat rippling up her flesh. "That it is. Well, I won't disturb your peace any longer. Good night."

With a flash of his teeth, he turned and strode off into the shadows of the croquet lawn. She stared after him with her mouth hanging open. He didn't want to stay and talk to her? He hadn't left the swimming party to be with her? He hadn't set up a broken leash as an excuse to stop by?

"Hell," she swore, still staring into the inky blackness that had swallowed him up. "I didn't even get to admire his bum when he left!"

Tears started in the corners of her eyes at the rejection, but she blinked them back before they had a chance to start. "Don't be stupid; of course you mean nothing to him, and you want it that way. He's a sex fiend, remember, and sex fiends are after only one thing. They are not interested in stable, long-term, meaningful relationships. They just want steamy, wild, hot jungle sex, and you don't do that, so stop imagining what steamy, wild, hot jungle sex would be like with him and thank your lucky stars that you don't have to worry about a sex fiend pestering you."

She sat lecturing herself for a good ten minutes, going over again her reasons for being there, his obvious many faults, and several excellent points regarding why a liaison with him—in the form of steamy, wild, hot jungle sex—would be a very bad thing.

It didn't do any good. She still felt like crying. What was wrong with her? Why couldn't she put him from her mind? Why was her silly heart so caught up with him when he was the epitome of everything she disliked in a man?

"And what's wrong with wanting steamy, wild, hot jungle sex?" she asked aloud, throwing a handful of grass into the wind.

"Is that a trick question?" a deep voice asked from behind her. Her heart did a few somersaults. Adam strolled over to her, now clad in a pair of black trousers and a thin linen shirt that caressed his torso like a lover's hands. "Are there multiple-choice answers? Because honestly, I don't think there's anything wrong with wanting steamy jungle sex. Do you?"

He sat down on the grass next to her, his long legs crossed at the ankles as he leaned back against the bench.

She stared at him. He came back?

"I left Jesus locked in the cabana as punishment for his bad manners. You're right; it is beautiful here. And peaceful, too. Very peaceful."

He came back? To sit with her?

"What I'm amazed at is how the scent of the flowers domi-
nates despite the sea air." He breathed in deeply, his eyes closing
to appreciate the perfumed air better.

He came back to sit with her? *Why* had he come back to sit
with her?

"Not that there's anything wrong with sea air. I like that too.
I'm from a small town in the mountains of California, and I
don't often get to the ocean."

He came back! Surely that meant something!

Adam glanced at her, suddenly looking a bit uncomfortable.
"I'm sorry; am I intruding on your quiet time? I'll leave if you
like."

Eeek! He was going to leave!

"No, please don't!" she said hurriedly, trying to gather her
scattered wits, scolding herself for being rendered so hen-witted
by a mere man. Except he wasn't a *mere* anything. "I'd like for
you to stay. That is to say, you're welcome to sit here. With me.
I was . . . erm . . . I was just sitting here. Not doing anything,
just sitting. So you're welcome to sit, too. Here. With me."

Lord, what an idiot she sounded. She wouldn't be surprised
if he left, but he didn't. He smiled. That smile ought to be
bottled and sold, she mused to herself when she couldn't help
but smile back at him. It was better than pheromones.

"Would you be averse to doing a favor for me?"

She looked startled at his request. Adam cleared his throat
nervously. "It has nothing to do with our *arrangement.*"

"Oh?" Now she looked relieved.

He swallowed back his nervousness. The worst she could do
was to say no. How bad could a little rejection be? His mind
went to the scene a few months before when Brittany had
stormed out of their apartment.

It could be very bad.

"What is the favor?"

The moonlight glinted on her auburn curls, making them a
glossy silver and black. His fingers itched to run through those

82

soft curls, to clutch them and hold her head in a position where he could plunder that sweet mouth until he could plunder no more. Reluctantly, he dragged his mind back from thoughts of plundering, damning his lack of self-control. He had seen the startled look in her eyes a few minutes back when she saw the reaction he had to her nearness. He had hoped getting into less obvious clothing would help the situation, but he was painfully aware that it hadn't. He was aroused and hard and hot, and he wanted her like he'd never wanted anyone.

"Adam? The favor?"

"Eh? Oh, the favor." He was mad, he was a lunatic, he was crazed and deranged for wanting to torment himself in this manner, but he had to ask her. She was smart; she was witty; she was everything every woman should be. Well, true, the blackmailing aspect to their relationship wasn't particularly desirable, but since he secretly approved of her plan to arrange for a date each day, that was a minor matter. Besides, there was no one else on the island whose opinion he was interested in, no one else he trusted to give him the truth.

Yeah, right, and pigs could fly. What was the use in lying to himself? He wanted her, pure and simple. "Would you be willing, purely for scientific reasons, to kiss me?"

Her mouth dropped open a bit before she snapped it shut. "You want me to kiss you? For *scientific* reasons?"

"I realize it's a strange request, but I do have a reason for it." Such as, she was an island of beauty and intelligence in a sea of bimbos. "My girlfriend left me a couple of months ago, and . . . well, we'd been together for a long time, so I haven't had an opportunity to kiss a lot of other women, and since she said I was a lousy lover, I thought maybe if you'd let me kiss you, you could evaluate me."

"Evaluate you?" She looked a bit stunned about the eyes, but he didn't think she was offended by the request. At least, he hoped she wasn't offended. She was obviously already of the opinion that he was a lust-crazed slobbering mound of testosterone, thanks to that stupid Monday Marsh catchphrase. Damn, he wished he could tell her the truth about himself. He hated lying to her, even if it was indirectly. "You want me to evaluate how you kiss?"

Maybe it wasn't such a good idea. Maybe he didn't want her to tell him he had terrible kissing skills. Maybe it would destroy him to know that he couldn't stir any passion in her. "Er . . . that's the idea," he said hesitantly. "I thought maybe you could tell me if Brittany was right, or if she was just getting in a parting shot before she left."

"But . . . you're a sex therapist. Why would anyone say an expert in sex was a poor lover?"

Well, she had him there. He looked at her sitting next to him, all innocent and beautiful and smart, and he knew he couldn't do it. He couldn't lie to her any longer. Hell, she already knew he was a cat smuggler; how much worse could it be to find out he was a private detective?

"That would be because I'm not really a sex therapist."

"You're not?"

He shook his head. "I'm not Monday Marsh. My name is Adam Fuller. I'm a private investigator. A detective," he said when he saw the question in her eyes. "I was hired to come to Mystique and pretend to be one of the contestants."

A puzzled frown settled between her brows "You were *hired* to be a contestant? But . . . everyone acts as if they know who you are. I mean, who you are pretending to be." She waved her hand about. "That whole nipple thing."

He sighed. "It's horrible, isn't it? My client, the man who hired me, paid off the real Monday Marsh so I could take his place. Turns out Marsh has agoraphobia or is terribly shy, or something along those lines. His producer was forcing him to do the show as a publicity stunt, so he leaped at the chance to get out of it when my client approached him. Gar bribed a couple of producers as well. I had no idea who I was supposed to impersonate until I was on the plane here, but I can tell you this—I will have my revenge on Gar one way or another."

"Gar?"

"My friend. The one who hired me."

"Oh." Her fingers pleated the soft cotton of her skirt where it lay on her thigh. "But won't people be able to tell that you aren't this Marsh person?"

Adam's brows drew together in a faint frown. "I worried about that too, but no one has said anything so far. I guess hearing someone speak in person is different enough from the radio that people are willing to accept any variations."

"What exactly were you hired to do here?"

He gave her a wry smile. "I can't tell you. Confidential."

"Would it have anything to do with Sally Simmons?"

He said nothing.

She nodded. "I see." She played with her dress for a moment longer. "Why are you telling me this? I'm already blackmailing you because of your cat. Why would you tell me something else to put yourself in my power?"

Why indeed? "I trust you." He shrugged. "You know the worst about me now anyway. It's certainly not illegal to be a private investigator."

"No, but I imagine the Eden people wouldn't be happy to know what you've done."

"Are you kidding? They'd love it. They'd save my denouement for the final episode. Anything to drive up ratings." He covered her hand with his. "The truth is, Hero, I'm a terrible liar. I couldn't think of kissing you knowing there were untruths between us."

Her eyes grew huge. "Untruths?"

He nodded. "I couldn't do that to you. I respect you too much." He gave a short laugh. "Ironic, isn't it, that we only met this morning? And here I am babbling on about respecting you and"—his gaze dropped to her lips—"kissing you. For purely scientific reasons, as I said before. My hope is, of course, that you won't reveal this secret any more than Jesus's, but I feel I can trust you. You have a quality of honesty about you that I greatly admire."

"Honesty?" she repeated, her eyes worried as she gnawed on her lower lip. "You think I'm honest?"

"I'm not often wrong about people," he said with a teasing smile. "So now that you know the worst of me, what about it? Will you rate me?"

She blinked her big gray eyes at him a couple of times while she thought over what he had said. "All right."

Hope—among other things—rose. "You're sure you wouldn't mind?" he asked, damning himself for giving her an out, but unwilling to force her into doing anything.

Her eyes were silver in the moonlight, warm silver with tiny black imperfections that caught him and held him fast.

"No, I don't mind." She smiled—a little worriedly, but still it was a smile. "I have always believed in furthering the knowledge of science."

Slowly, Adam, he told himself. *Don't pounce on her. Give her the respect she's due. Go slowly. Don't scare her. And for God's sake, don't let her see the desperation in your eyes!*

"Right, then."

"Right," she said, her eyes dropping modestly. God, but he wanted to touch her, to taste her, to taste all of her. He bit down the sharp edge of his desire and leaned toward her, his hands fisted into the grass to keep from grabbing her and pulling her under him.

Her breath was sweet on his lips, soft and warm and inviting. Her eyes were silver disks so beautiful it almost hurt to look into them. The soft floral scent of her skin merged with the heavier perfume of the night-blooming flowers, causing little pinpricks of heat to form on his skin, then sink inward and head straight for his groin. His lips touched hers, teased them, withdrew, then returned to tease them again. Her eyes closed as he tasted her lips, nibbling gently on her lower lip until, with a moan that went deep into his chest, she opened her mouth for him.

She was paradise; she was heat; she was desire. He kissed her deeply, stroking his tongue against hers, and almost lost control when she returned the caress. He pulled back enough so that he could see into her eyes. They were dreamy and filled with passion.

"Oh, Adam." She sighed, then grabbed his head and pulled him down over herself. Adam fought his desire for a nanosecond, then gave in, doing what he had wanted to do the first time he saw her; holding her head at the optimum angle and diving into her mouth as if he were searching for buried treasure. He growled into her mouth when she arched her body up against his, her breasts rubbing a heated friction against him, her skin warm and soft and infinitely inviting. He released the silken curls and slid his hands down over the loose cotton jacket she wore over her dress, sliding it off her bare shoulders, stroking his hands down the satin of her arms.

She kindled a fire deep within him, burning brighter and brighter with each moment that he drank in her scent, touched the lush curves of her breasts that surely had to be created just for his hands, and tasted the rapture found when their mouths met. The sound of approaching voices sent a signal through the haze of desire and need and something much warmer that he didn't want to examine too closely. They were in a public place. He could not continue out here, in the open.

His lips parted reluctantly from hers as he rose back on an elbow, her fingers still entwined in his hair. The soft cotton of her dress molded to the contours of her body, driving from his mind any consideration about privacy or the need to stop. He traced a finger up the curve of her shoulder, over to her breastbone, then down to the fragrant valley between her breasts. She stared back at him with heated eyes, her breath just as ragged and unsteady as his, her breasts heaving beneath the heat of his hand.

"Let me see you," he said, his voice thick with wanting. He pushed the light dress jacket from her completely, his hands moving quickly to the buttons on the sleeveless dress she wore underneath. "Dear God, you're beautiful. So beautiful. So sexy."

"No," she whispered, struggling to recapture the soft cotton jacket, tugging it back up her arms.

"What's wrong?" he asked, pausing with his hand on a button. A finger's breadth away, the heavy curve of her breast lay beckoning him.

"I don't . . . I don't want you to . . ."

Pain cut through him. He withdrew his hand. "You don't want me to touch you?"

"No." She moaned, her eyes brilliant with unshed tears. "It's not that. I don't want you to . . ."

"What?" he asked, almost desperate. "Kiss you? Touch your breasts? Make love to you?"

"See me!" she shouted, pushing hard on his chest, shoving him away so she could sit up and right her clothing.

What the hell?

"You don't want me to see what?" He looked around. "You don't want anyone to see us out here? I agree completely, and I apologize for starting it here, but I had no idea . . . well, I had no idea it would go this far. We can go inside to your cabana, if it will make you feel better."

"No," she said, buttoning up her dress and wiping at a tear that snaked down her cheek. "Not my cabana."

"Mine, then," he said, wincing at the note of desperation in his voice.

"No, you don't understand," she argued, not looking at him as she got to her feet, then bent to put on her sandals. "We can't do this."

He stood. "I had assumed because you were here that you had no impediments to a relationship. If that's so, it must be me that doesn't appeal to you. I guess I have my answer to the Brittany question."

"Oh, no," she said, turning to him, her face an agony of indecision and guilt and something that looked very much like desire. "It's not you. You are . . . your girlfriend was wrong, dead wrong. That kiss was . . . indescribable. Wonderful. Marvelous. Rhapsody."

Well, now he really was confused. He took her hand and rubbed his thumb over her knuckles. "I thought it was pretty damn good, myself. If it's not me, and you don't have someone else, then what exactly is the problem?"

Her silver-eyed gaze dropped as she pulled her hand from his. "I have to go now. Thank you for . . . thank you."

She turned and almost ran back to the door that let from the tiny patio to her cabana.

"Wait, Hero!" Adam started to follow her. Something was wrong, but he couldn't figure out what. If he could just get her to tell him, he could deal with whatever it was. "Why can't you—"

She whirled around at her door. "Oh, you stupid man, don't you understand? It's me, not you. Look at me!" She waved her hand in the direction of her torso. "I'm not pretty or tan or trim or any of the things those other women are."

He stopped, stunned at her words. She didn't think she was pretty? She was beautiful! She was a goddess personified! She was perfect!

"I'm not beautiful, and I'm not sexy, and I don't want you looking at me. There. Are you happy now? I hope so, because I don't think I can go over this explanation again. Thank you for the kiss; it was very nice. Good night." She opened her door and stepped through it.

"Hero, just wait a min—"

The door slammed behind her.

"—ute."

A lock clicked into place. He stood there for long minutes staring at her door, bewildered, confused, completely at a loss as to what to do to make her realize he didn't see her as anything but desirable and captivating.

He was in completely over his head, and hadn't the slightest idea what it was going to take to come to the surface.

"You're being unreasonable."

"Shhh!"

"I am not."

"*Shhh!*"

Hero's voice dropped to an almost inaudible whisper. "I simply do not wish to continue this discussion. Now may we watch the movie?"

Adam leaned close to her, his mouth next to her ear. Hero fought back a shudder of complete delight at his nearness. "Why won't you believe me when I tell you that I think you're beautiful?"

Hero smiled through gritted teeth as one of the cameramen turned to look at them. They were sitting in the back row of the theater, a room equipped with rows of comfortable seats and a large wall-sized plasma-screen television, and she would be damned if she lost points on her first official date simply because Adam insisted on driving her mad. As if the guilt riddling her because he thought her honest wasn't enough to do the job. That, or war between the need she felt to believe he truly admired her and the realization that he was just sweet-talking her to keep from revealing his secrets. Didn't he realize that she was nearly driven to insanity by the torture of having to sit next to him like this? The island paradise promised in the Eden promotional material felt more like purgatory to her.

"I'm not beautiful," she murmured under her breath, her eyes on the cameramen in the room rather than the movie. "You don't have to say I am; it's not part of our agreement. You don't have to worry; I've already said I won't give you away."

"That's *not* why I'm saying it," he said, a disgruntled look on his face. She smiled wildly as a cameraman headed their way.

"Smile," she said in a hiss. "We're supposed to be compatible, remember?"

He draped his arm over her shoulders. "We're going to have this out later, you and I," he promised softly in her ear. She shivered at the feeling of his breath brushing her flesh, but said nothing. What was there to say? She had made her bed; now she had to lie in it. Alone.

"That wasn't as bad as I thought it was going to be," Adam said later, as the movie ended. As it was a ladies'-choice day, the women selected the men they wished to participate with on that day's dates, both geared to please the female palate. Hero was obliged to pick Adam as her first date despite wishing she'd never thought up the grand idea of blackmailing him into helping her. "Then again, I never have minded chick flicks that much. Most of them are pretty good. Sorry Jesus ate your popcorn."

She strolled out of the theater with the other people, intending to duck behind a group to avoid speaking to him any more, but he had other ideas. He tugged her behind a cluster of palms and pinned her back with a steely blue-eyed look. Jesus and his attendant gecko took advantage of the break to investigate the shrubberies.

"Come on, out with it."

"Out with what?' "

"Whatever it is that you're holding in."

She frowned at him and crossed her arms over her chest. "What makes you think I'm holding something in?"

"You won't talk to me, you wouldn't let me neck with you during the movie, and for some reason you take offense when I tell you that you're beautiful."

She shivered when he ran his thumb along her lower lip, and jerked her head away. "I don't have time to discuss the cruelty of pretending you enjoy someone's company for your own gain. Nor do I have time to explain the arrogance inherent in men that drives them into thinking that all women are putty in their

91

hands with just a kiss or two. Be thankful I don't, because if I did have time, I would inform you in no uncertain terms that I found your ridiculous claims both hurtful and derogatory."

"What ridiculous claims?" he asked, a frown pulling those two lovely eyebrows together.

"You should know; you were the one making them last night."

He stared at her for a minute. "Are you talking about the fact that I wanted to make love to you, or that I find you a sexy, intelligent woman whom I'd like to know better? A lot better?"

She stiffened. "I have to go. My next date is in fifteen minutes."

He glanced at his watch. "Fine. You can spend five minutes talking to me."

"I don't wish to talk with you. Surely that is clear?"

"What's clear is that you have the erroneous idea that you're not attractive."

She waffled between the desire to grind her teeth in anger and the urge to cry. The anger won out. "Why are you doing this to me?"

"What?" He stepped back, surprised at her outburst.

"Why won't you be honest with me?"

"I have been honest with you."

"You have not. You say those . . . those . . . *nice* things, but you don't really mean them, not in the sense you want me to think you do."

He looked genuinely surprised. Obviously he did not realize she knew the truth behind his motivation. "Hero, what are you talking about?"

"I don't need your pity!" she yelled, shoving hard on his chest to push him back a couple of steps. "I'm not so bloody pathetic that I need your pity kisses and your pretended interest and nice words meant to make me feel like I'm something I'm not. You might think that you're the only man who's ever felt sorry for me, but you're not. I'm an expert concerning men who deign to notice me, and I can tell you right now that I'm not grateful for your attention *or* your kisses, so you can bloody well bugger off and go annoy some other woman!"

"Is that what you think I'm doing?" Adam asked, his voice a low growl, his eyes blazing with emotion. He took a step closer to her, no doubt to try to intimidate her. "You think I'm just hitting on you to make myself feel better, is that it? You think I'm so shallow that I'm incapable of looking beyond the surface for something more meaningful? Or do you think I'm just interested in meaningless sex with any woman who'll spread her legs for me?"

Hero raised her chin and glared at him, tears of fury pooling in her eyes.

"You paint a nice picture of me, Hero." His breath was warm on her face, his eyes hot enough to burn holes through her heart. "Is that what you really think?"

She thought her heart would crumble under the influence of the pain in his eyes, but she had no choice. It was him or her, and she didn't think she could survive seeing pity in his eyes when he looked at her.

"I don't want to see you again," she said, her throat aching with unshed tears. "Our agreement is canceled. Please do not accost me again."

"So I am to be tried and convicted without a hearing? Your faith in me is overwhelming, but then, I guess that's what I can expect from a woman who has to blackmail a man into dating her."

Hero turned away, her eyes closed against the pain of his words, pain she knew she deserved. She was the one who had lied to him; he had been honest, completely honest with her. Or had he? That was the worst part of having a mind that had snapped: she could no longer tell what was the truth and what was not. *Truth,* her inner voice whispered—like whether she was pushing Adam away because he pitied her, or if her guilt was the real culprit.

Without another word to her, Adam rounded up Jesus and walked away. She watched him leave, tears rolling down her cheeks, a sob caught in her throat. He was right. What sort of woman had she become that she would not even give him a chance to defend himself?

"I *am* pathetic," she whispered to herself as she dug through her purse for tissues to wipe the tears from her wet cheeks. "And I have just ruined my life, and my heart is destroyed, and I'll never be able to face Adam, and now I have to appear happy for millions of viewers when I go on dates with other men who don't even come close to being as wonderful as the man I just drove off, and damn it all, I'm out of tissues!"

Down the far length of the pathway the tall figure of Simon, her date for the trip out to the bird sanctuary, appeared and waved at her. A cameraman stood next to him.

"Bloody hell, what timing," she grumbled, sniffing heavily and waving back. She dashed behind a tree and used a leaf to mop both tears and nose, reappearing with what she hoped was a convincing smile.

It would never do to let the TV audience see that her heart was broken here in paradise.

Chapter Six

The following day was gentlemen's choice. Hero knew even before Adam and Jesus stalked across the crowded ballroom toward her that he was going to demand her as his date. What she didn't know was what she was going to do about it. Apologizing was out of the question; she had wounded his male ego the day before, which meant he was determined to prove her judgment of him was wrong. He would be all that much more prone to saying romantic things, to flattering her, praising her, and quite probably attempting to kiss her.

Lord, she hoped so.

She drove that rogue thought from her brain, telling herself firmly that she might love him more than life itself, she might have a shattered mound of dust where her heart had been, not to mention the snapped-mind incident, but she would not tolerate mutiny. That still left the issue of what she should do to stem the tide of affection he would no doubt be forced by his own sense of injustice to slather upon her.

"I know one thing . . ." she said to herself as Adam approached.

"Hero," he said as he stopped before her, a surprisingly grim look on his face. "Ten o'clock. The fishing dock. Boat fifteen. Got it?"

". . . I am not kissing you."

Immediately his brilliant blue eyes looked at her lips. "Hell."

That was her thought exactly.

"Boat fifteen. Half an hour," he said hoarsely, dragging his gaze from her lips to give her a heated look that left her knees melting into a puddle of water.

She summoned every last ounce of determination, and put it in one word: "No."

He frowned. "No what?"

"No, I won't go on a date with you." She made shooing motions with her hands.

He goggled at her. "Did you just shoo me away?"

"Yes."

"Why?"

"I told you—I'm not going on a date with you. I refuse your date."

"You can't. It's my choice. I choose you. So there."

"Ha!" she said as he started to walk away.

He froze and slowly turned around. "What did you say?"

"I said 'ha!' Disdainfully and with much scorn. And for your information, Mr. Adam Monday Marsh Fuller, I am not the sort of a woman who says 'ha!' disdainfully and with much scorn lightly. So there yourself!"

He glowered at her, positively glowered at her now. His jaw was tense and tight, his hands flexing as if they wanted to be around her neck; the words fired out through clenched teeth with all the warmth and friendliness of a bullet. "Boat fifteen. Fishing dock. One. Half. Hour."

"In your dreams," she called after his receding figure, using her favorite Americanism. She smiled smugly to herself for a moment, then turned to see the horrifying sight of a cameraman filming her. Despite swearing she was never going to notice them, she simpered repulsively and waggled her fingers at the camera. "I was just joking," she explained.

The cameraman leaned out from behind the camera lens and cocked an eyebrow at her.

She turned away and sighed. This was going to be *another* one of those days.

"Why are you doing this?" Hero demanded as she clambered aboard the boat assigned to take sixteen people on a morning date of fishing.

"We have an agreement," he said without looking at her, bent over a struggling Jesus. The cat twisted, forcing a buckle to slip between Adam's fingers. "Damn!"

"I canceled our agreement, if you recall," she said coldly. "I was quite clear about it."

"Insultingly so," he agreed, still bent over the cat, wrestling to organize a series of belts and buckles around the rotund furry body.

"I just want it understood that I am acceding to this date under protest."

"Consider it understood."

"I want it perfectly clear that the whole thing was your idea, and not mine."

"I will hold myself entirely to blame for any consequences of the date, if it will make you feel better."

"Good." She moved closer. "I apologize if I've insulted you. I simply wished to make myself clear."

"Oh, you've succeeded there; have no fear," he told the top of Jesus's head as he struggled to reach a recalcitrant buckle. "Stand still, cat!"

"Well . . . good. What is it you're doing to Jesus?"

Her lovely face came into view as she squatted next to him, stroking the cat on the top of his head.

"Putting his life jacket on. He's in a bit of a snit because I made him leave Gecko behind, and he's punishing me by refusing to wear his flotation device." He glanced up at her, caught the ghost of a smile on her lips, and smiled in return. "The things I do for this cat, huh?"

Her gaze dropped. "Something like that."

He got the last buckle snapped into place and stood up, straightening the lurid orange-and-blue feline life jacket and giving Jesus a pat on the shoulder. "Stiff upper lip, cat. Gecko will be waiting for you when you return."

Adam slipped on a pair of mirrored sunglasses, smiled cheerfully at the camera when it was pointed at him, and spent the twenty-minute boat ride out to a secluded lagoon watching Hero. She scratched Jesus's ears, ignored the cameramen, and sat by herself at the back of the boat, staring into the water. She did everything, in fact, but look at him. That gave him the time to watch her, and to try to figure out how the devil he was going to straighten out the mess he'd made of things.

The ship pulled alongside some trees hanging over the water before he'd come to any conclusion.

"You're free to fish anywhere in the lagoon," one of the show's assistants told them. "We have floats available if you want to do it from offshore."

"Shore or float?" Adam asked Hero, holding out a fishing pole for her.

She grimaced. "Shore."

"Shore it is." He gathered up Jesus and the fishing gear, and slipped over the side of the boat, wading to shore to deposit the cat and gear on a shady rock. "Stay put."

Jesus gave him a disdainful one-eyed glare and proceeded to lick his hind end.

"You're next," he said as he waded back to the boat where Hero was looking indecisively at the water. Several other people were wading ashore, claiming spots up and down the lagoon. The camera crew and sound people carefully held their equipment above their heads as they headed for the beach.

"What?" She looked up, startled at his words. "I'm next for what?"

He stood next to the boat in waist-high water and held out his arms. "I'm the ferry to the shore. Put your arms around my neck."

She stared at him, horror mingling with disbelief in her beautiful gray eyes. "You can't be serious!"

"Never more so. Come on; if we don't get to it, all the fish will be caught."

She wrung her hands. "You can't carry me."

"Why not?"

She looked around quickly, then leaned forward over the edge of the boat, allowing him a delicious view down her loose tunic. "I'm too heavy."

He rolled his eyes. "You're not too heavy."

"Shush!"

He lowered his voice. "Hero, you have three choices: you can stay on the boat and not get any points, or you can wade ashore yourself, or you can let me carry you the ten feet it'll take to put you on solid ground."

She wrung her hands even harder, then raised her chin and reached for him, stepping over the rail of the boat to the outer ledge. "If you drop me I'll never forgive you," she whispered as he slipped an arm behind her legs, swinging her away from the boat.

"You mean like this?" he asked as he released her for a moment.

"*Adam!*" she shrieked, clutching him, then scowling something fierce when he started laughing. He carried her to shore with her scolding him every step, and knew as he set her on the rock that whatever it took, whatever he had to say to convince her, whatever acts of bravery and heroism and valor she demanded he perform, he'd perform, all because he had to have her. She was the woman meant for him.

The problem was to get her to recognize that fact.

"So," he asked a short while later, leaning back against the rock and watching the float on his line bob merrily in the waves. "This isn't such a bad date, is it? Better than that horrible one yesterday."

Hero looked like she didn't want to ask him, but she did. "The movie?"

"No, the other one. The shopping-for-shoes one. I don't know what you did, but the woman who was with me insisted on modeling every single pair of shoes the shop had and asking for my opinion on each. It was a horrible experience. I've never thought up so many adjectives in my life. How you women can take a simple act like buying a pair of shoes and turn it into a two hour torture session is beyond me."

His comments riled her up, just as he knew they would. "I quite enjoyed my afternoon date. The gentleman I was with had particularly good taste in espadrilles."

"Honey, a man who spends two hours giving you advice on shoes has only one thing on his mind."

She rustled around in the large purse she carried everywhere with her before looking up. "A shoe fetish?"

Adam shook his head, fighting a smile. "Let's just say I bet he's trying to get you somewhere—and it isn't into a good pair of shoes. Hey, I think I have a nibble."

"Oh, really?" Hero pulled a small can out of her purse and turned to face the water. Adam leaped to his feet when a loud blast startled everything within, he was guessing, a five mile radius.

"What the hell is that?" He swore, dropping his fishing line and lunging for her.

She danced out of his reach, holding a small can with a white plastic horn behind her. "It's my air horn."

He was too quick for her, snagging her arm and grabbing the air horn before she knew what he was doing.

"Your what?" He stared at it as people up and down the lagoon shouted and called to each other. Adam yelled to a fast-approaching Eden assistant that it was all right, just a mistake and nothing more. A cameraman and sound woman trailed after the assistant.

"Why on earth do you have an air horn?" Adam asked her before they were set upon with questions.

"You obviously haven't noticed, but I'm a vegetarian."

He stared at her. "I had noticed, and so . . . ?"

"I do not eat fish. I do not condone the slaughter of fish for sporting purposes. Hence, the air horn to scare them away so you won't catch them. I couldn't possibly have the death of a fish on my conscience as a result of our date."

He stuffed the air horn in the roomy pocket of his knee-length shorts, shaking his head and muttering to himself before turning a bright smile on the cameraman as he puffed his way up to them. He explained the mistake to the assistant, apologized, and tried to look as if he were having a great time.

"You really are a terrible actor," Hero told him once the crew had scurried off to film one of the couples who had fallen off their float and were floundering around in the water trying to retrieve the woman's missing bikini top. "No one will believe you're having a good time. You look like you want to strangle someone."

"I wonder who that could be," he said with a tight smile as he leaned back against the rock, forgetting the air horn he'd securely pocketed. The sudden sensation of an icy blast hitting his genitals coincided with another ear-shattering blast, causing him to jump at least three feet straight off the ground, and whirl around clutching at himself.

"Air horns gain their power from compressed carbon dioxide," Hero said helpfully as she watched him fall to his knees, both hands cupped protectively over his groin. "I assume that sounded in the close proximity of flesh, you might feel a certain sensation of . . . shall we say, discomfort?"

"You might say that," Adam said, his voice sounding rather

as if he were chewing on gravel. "The words 'henceforth not able to father any children' also come to mind."

Hero giggled.

Adam relaxed despite his frozen testicles attempting to suck up inside his body. If she could giggle, he had a hope that all could be made right. All he had to do was make her see herself through his eyes, to show her that she was beautiful and warm and smart, and that he had only the most honorable of intentions toward her.

In other words, he had to pull off a miracle.

He watched her wade knee-high in the sun-warmed water, laughing at his cat when Jesus followed her from the safety of dry land. Adam could only think of one way he was going to have his miracle.

"Sorry, old boy," he said softly, smiling as Hero tossed a piece of seaweed to Jesus. "I think those prosthetic balls of yours are going to have to wait a bit longer. This is even more important than restoring your manhood."

Hero was ecstatic as she skipped down the stone path toward the ballroom. The last three days had been blissfully wonderful, all because of Adam. He had been attentive to her at every opportunity, sitting with her at dinner, laughing with her when they met during the day, teasing her, talking to her, and best of all, kissing her every night outside her cabana. He hadn't made love to her yet, but she knew it was inevitable. His constant, unfailing interest in her, his gentle patience and unstinting devotion, had turned her anger and uncertainty toward him into something that made her heart soar.

Once or twice it occurred to her to wonder why he was spending every available moment with her and none following Sally—not to mention the question of just *why* he had been hired to follow Sally in the first place—but she pushed those questions to the back of her mind. Sally had probably told him off again, and he was wisely keeping his distance. It certainly didn't seem to bother him, and Lord knew she was enjoying every second they spent together.

The truth was, she was most definitely in love.

Hero giggled like a schoolgirl; she was so eager to see Adam again, to have another date. Everything was looking wonderful—her dates with other men were pleasant, but not thrilling, and both Adam and she had full points for every event, ensuring they'd make it to the next round. Every evening she sat up in her cabana and worked late into the night on her story, much happier with it after she changed the focus from poking fun at Yanks desperate for love to one that reflected the reality of dating in today's world, and the intrepid few who went beyond the norm, who went the extra distance—like becoming a contestant on a reality dating show—to find that special person, that someone marvelous enough to spend the rest of their lives with.

Someone like Adam.

Hero sighed happily, then giggled at her sigh, then giggled at her giggle as she raced into the ballroom. The announcement was being made about the day's events. She couldn't remember what was on the day's schedule for dates, but she was confident that as it was the gentlemen's choice, Adam would pick whichever date would allow them the most time together.

The show's host, Asterisk, was doing his usual routine, relating some of the more memorable comments on the confession-booth tapes, making the audience laugh over amusing incidents during the previous day's dates—Hero's airhorn adventure had even made it into his morning routine—and generally setting the crowd up for their day in paradise.

She stood to one side and searched the crowd for Adam, finally spotting him and Jesus at a table across the room. He was evidently watching for her, because he lifted his hand in greeting. She smiled in return, and leaned against the cool wall, watching without listening as the Eden producer expounded about some point or other. Whatever it was, it didn't matter. Nothing could possibly matter when she was so very happy.

"Hero?"

Sally's voice pulled her out of the daydream involving Adam and that big bed in her cabana. "Good morning, Sally. How are you?"

Sally looked nervous, chewing on her lower lip and casting a quick glance over her shoulder. Evidently Hero had missed the whole of the morning announcements, because the men and women were separating to either side of the ballroom in preparation for pairing off for the day's dates.

"Hero, there's something I want to talk to you about. Something . . . well, something that I shouldn't have done."

Hero's attention switched from admiring Adam as he approached to the smaller woman in front of her. "You didn't say anything to the television show people about Adam, did you?"

Sally's frown deepened. "No. He's left me alone these last few days; I told him if he left me alone I wouldn't expose him. This doesn't have to do with me, not really, you see . . . Oh, it's confusing. . . ."

Hero, relieved as soon as she knew Adam was in no danger, gazed over Sally's shoulder and smiled as Adam and Jesus strolled up. "I'd be happy to talk to you at lunch, Sally."

"Morning, Sally," Adam said politely, his eyes only for Hero, even when Sally muttered something inaudible and moved off. A warm kernel of pleasure formed within Hero. How could she have ever doubted his sincerity? Oh, to be sure, he still had silly notions about her admitting she was attractive, but she hadn't once seen a look of distaste or pity on his face when he kissed her. "Hero, as always, you look lovely."

She blushed gently and beamed at him as he chatted politely when they were joined by Phillip, a man she had dated the day before. Phillip was interested in another woman, and posed no threat to her peace of mind. He certainly wasn't anywhere near as fascinating as Adam.

"I thought you'd prefer the first one over the second, since we can take a lunch along," Adam was saying to her. She dragged her mind back to the present and smiled. He was no doubt talking about the day's dates. Anything that would extend her time with him was all right by her!

"Absolutely," she said under her breath, uncaring what she agreed to. Perhaps, she mused as she admired him as he talked to Phillip and another woman, sheepishly declining the opportunity to offer the woman advice on the best way to find her G-spot, perhaps Adam was one of those men who liked fleshy women. There were some men like that, or so she had heard. She'd never met one, but Adam was unique. If anyone would be able to overlook her obvious flaws in the body department, she was sure he would.

Adam grinned at the G-spot woman and leaned his head toward her when she whispered something in his ear, causing him to laugh out loud.

A small doubt burst out from nowhere, dampening the pleasure that glowed within her. What if he *wasn't* the sort of man who liked women of abundant form? What if he just didn't realize exactly what she looked like beneath the loose gauze of her jackets and cotton dresses and voluminous skirts? What if the sight of her body without clothes repulsed him? How would she survive such a devastating occurrence? A cold chill gripped her, making her almost sick to her stomach as she watched him from beneath her lashes. He was laughing with another woman now, one who was squatting next to Jesus and his gecko. A very fit woman.

"How about it, Hero? Care to bowl with me this afternoon?" Phillip was asking her.

She smiled wanly, fighting down the uncertainty that roiled within her. There was only one thing she could do—she'd just have to make sure that Adam never saw her naked. If they made love—and she fervently hoped they would very soon—it would simply have to take place in the dark. "I'd love to, Phillip."

"Great. Well, guess I'd better go get suited up. Nancy, I'll see you down at boat fourteen."

The Jesus-stroking woman agreed, and said something about going to fetch her swim fins; then she, too, strolled out of the ballroom.

Adam took her arm and steered her out the double doors into the heat of the morning. "I thought rather than joining everyone else, we'd take advantage of Dead Man's Cove. I've already rented a sailboat, so if you go change now, I'll meet you down at the docks. We have the *Calypso Sunset* for the morning."

She blinked at him. Sailboat? Change? Maybe she should have been paying attention earlier rather than daydreaming about him.

"Don't forget your snorkel equipment," he called as he turned down the path toward his row of cabanas.

Snorkel equipment? A wave of horror crashed over Hero, causing her to stagger for a moment. Snorkel equipment? A sailboat? Change? As in . . . donning a swimsuit?

"Oh, dear God, no!" She moaned, blindly heading for her cabana. "He's going to see me in my swimsuit! What a ghastly turn of events!"

Chapter Seven

Hero was not one to face life's little trials with fluttering hands and cries of "Woe am I!" She had come prepared with supplies for horrific eventualities leading up to, and including, death and dismemberment, but in truth, she knew she'd rather face both than the epitome of horrors, the pinnacle of dread, the zenith of everything loathsome—appearing in public in her swimsuit.

With that repulsive thought in mind, she had purchased not one, not two, but *three* beach cover-ups, all of which modestly covered her swimsuit-clad body from breast to midcalf. True, she reflected as she padded down the wooden dock, looking for the sailboat named *Calypso Sunset*, the cover-up was ventilated with hundreds of holes intended to keep its wearer cool, but she had critically examined herself in the mirror and couldn't see that any untoward expanses of her flesh were exposed.

Adam was already on board the sailboat, stowing a picnic basket. She greeted a petulant-looking Jesus, the cat once again peeved because he had been wrestled into a life jacket, as well as parted from his boon companion, and settled herself down to enjoying the unexpected pleasure of time spent with Adam at one of the resort's three secluded beaches that were reachable only by boat.

"Do you know how to sail?" Adam asked as he handed her a life vest.

"No, but it isn't that difficult, is it? Don't you just point the boat in the direction you want to go?"

Adam coughed what sounded suspiciously like the beginnings of a laugh, but he quickly regained control of his esophagus and explained the principles behind sailing, ordering Hero to sit with her hand on the tiller. Before she knew it, they were heading out of calm waters protected by a reef to the north side of the island.

Dolphins rode their bow, splashing and leaping ahead and alongside them with wild abandon. Hero leaned back, the wind ruffling her short hair, feeling an odd combination of peace and excitement at the day's outing. A short time later Adam pointed out their destination: a small, white-sand beach edging a corner of the wildlife sanctuary. It was lined with palms and dense vegetation that left a ten-yard-wide swath of sand that stretched out into a small spit. Adam dropped anchor, carried the picnic basket, blankets, and Jesus to a shady spot at the base of the spit, then turned to wave at Hero.

"Come on, the water's only waist-high. We can have a swim before lunch."

"Hell," she muttered quietly to herself, smiling and waving back at him. "I just knew this was going to happen. Well, make the best of it, Hero. You don't want to ruin this lovely time simply because you're too embarrassed to get in the water."

"Is something wrong?" Adam called out to her, peeling off the T-shirt and cotton shorts he wore over his teensy-tiny blue swimsuit.

She closed her eyes at the sight of all of his marvelous tanned flesh, flesh that called to her, flesh that she craved to touch and taste and stroke. Oh, no, nothing was wrong. Nothing other than that there was much too much Hero for her liking, and most of that dyed a bronze that she suddenly realized made her look as if she had a severe attack of jaundice.

"Just coming," she said, opening her eyes to see him swimming toward her. "Eek! No, stop, go back!"

He paused midway to the boat and stood up. As he predicted, the water was only waist-high. "What's wrong?"

"Nothing, I'm coming; you just have to . . . erm . . . turn around for a moment."

"Turn around?" He frowned and started half swimming, half walking toward her. "Why? You've got your suit on under that, don't you?"

"Yes, but I have to take the cover-up off to get in the water. Please don't come any closer."

He ignored her and kept coming. "So?"

She would *not* die of embarrassment, she would *not* die of embarrassment. . . . "If you don't mind, I do not want you watching when I get in the water."

"I do mind," he said, reaching the side of the boat, which swayed slightly with the gentle roll of the waves. "And it's about time we had this out. I don't know why you want to hide yourself from me, but you don't have to. There are no cameras here now; it's just you and me."

"Yes, but—"

"I've told you I think you're beautiful, and you know what sort of an effect you have on me. It's about time you realized how stunning you are."

Hero recalled rubbing up against him the prior evening when he kissed her good-night. Oh, she knew she had an effect on him, but . . . "Yes, but you haven't seen *all* of me. And I don't want you to, so please do the gentlemanly thing and turn around so I might get into the water."

Once she was in the water, she'd be safe. She'd be half-covered. She just wouldn't go into the very shallow water, or she would paddle around until he had to go pee before streaking for the safety of the blanket he'd spread out and its accompanying stack of beach towels.

He squinted up at her, his hand shading his eyes against the bright sunlight. "You won't get in the water unless I turn around?"

She nodded. He sighed pointedly, but turned around. Hero approached the ladder leading down the side of the sailboat into the water, peering at him suspiciously, but he remained looking in the opposite direction. Halfway down the ladder she peeled the cover-up off, and jumped the rest of the way into the warm ocean.

"Now," he said, turning around and wading toward her with a dangerous glint in his lovely blue eyes. "You and I are going to have a little talk."

"Talk?" she asked weakly, her knees melting under his gaze. "You want to talk?"

"In a manner of speaking," he said in a growl, wrapping his arms around her and pulling her up to his chest seconds before his mouth descended upon hers.

Hero's senses swam. His tongue was so hot, so demanding, she could do nothing but moan softly against his lips and open her mouth to him, allowing him to sink into her and fill her mind with the addictive taste of him. She wanted him; she wanted him not just then, but for the rest of her life.

The water was warm around them, but his hands were warmer, stroking the bare flesh of her shoulders and arms, smoothing a path down her back and around her sides, then up to where her breasts ached for his touch.

And still he kissed her.

Pressed against each other, they moved together in the waves, their bodies gently swaying with the rhythm of the water around them, but everywhere his body touched hers, she felt as if she were on fire. Unable to stop herself, she let her fingers sculpt down the long planes of his back, reveling in the sensation of his sun warmed, sea-dampened skin that lay like velvet over thick ropes of muscles.

He was so beautiful, and she was so—"Stop!" she cried, suddenly pulling back from him, tearing herself from the hot lure of his mouth.

"No," he said, his voice a low rumble that echoed deep within her, touching all of those magical little places that only a man could touch. He tangled the fingers of one hand into her wet hair, and tipped her head back until her lips were offered up as a sacrifice to their passion.

"You can't . . . I don't want . . . ." The words came out jumbled in between gasps of air, but he had no mercy.

"Yes, you do, just as much as I want to. Have you ever made love in the water, Hero?" Her eyes widened as he leaned down to nip her lips. "I promise you it'll be something you won't soon forget."

He took possession of her mouth once again, and this time it was too much. She couldn't keep fighting him, fighting the need that she had for him, fighting her love. With a groan that came from her soul, she dug her fingers into his shoulders and pushed his tongue from her mouth, only to invade his. He moaned as she writhed against him, tasting him, teasing him, nipping at his lips and sucking his tongue, aware that his hands were busy stripping the swimsuit from her upper body, but for once uncaring because she knew that as long as they stayed in the water, she would not be entirely exposed to his view.

"Oh, Hero, my beautiful Hero, how can you think you are anything but desirable?" Adam kissed a hot path down Hero's breastbone, setting her skin afire. "You are a goddess, meant to be worshiped and venerated."

His hands tugged on her swimsuit until suddenly she stood free of it, her bare skin surrounded by warm water on the backside, and Adam on her front. He tossed the wet garment into the boat, and stifled her protest with his mouth.

Flames licked from his fingertips as they danced down her

111

spine, the fire heightened, not extinguished by the soft caress of the sea on her sensitive flesh. His hands were everywhere, stroking her behind, swooping along the curves of her hips, teasing her breasts until her nipples were hard and aching in the heat of his palms.

"Talk to me," he murmured in her ear as he kissed and suckled the spot behind her ear. Hero moaned in response. "Tell me what you're feeling."

"Can't. No air."

He chuckled as he pulled away from her long enough to kiss her waiting lips once more. "I know the feeling. There doesn't seem to be enough air on this beach, does there?"

She frowned at him. "Why is it *you* can still talk while I'm completely witless? I must not be doing something right."

"Oh, baby, you're doing everything right," he crooned, his fingers hard on her hips as he pulled her to him, plundering her mouth for another one of those brain-numbing kisses. She arched her back against him, her breasts rubbing sinuously against his wet chest, and realized what it was she was doing wrong. "Honey, you couldn't possibly be any beh . . . beh . . . behhuuuUUUUUUUUHHH!"

She smiled at the look of astonishment and absolute bliss on Adam's face as she stroked his Speedos, curling her fingers into the waistband and tugging them off. She could almost hear the *boing* as his penis—more erect than she thought humanly possible, visions of the redwood forest coming immediately to mind—sprang free of the skimpy material.

"So it wouldn't please you at all if I did this?" she asked, grasping his heated length with both hands and mapping out every bump and contour.

"Haaaarng," he groaned, swallowing hard.

He was so hard and soft at the same time, velvety smooth skin riding over steel. Hot steel. Hot steel that spasmed quite a bit.

"I suppose, then, you wouldn't like it if I were to do this, either?" She reached lower, dipping at the knees to take his balls in her hand, gently scratching her nails along the tender flesh at the same time she took one insouciant brown nipple in her mouth.

"Gwaaahhnan," he burbled, his eyes rolling up in his head as his hands spasmed helplessly. She bit gently, so very gently on his tiny little nipple nub, and was rewarded with his body going stiff.

"Condom!" he shouted, his eyes snapping open.

She blinked at him, then began patting herself down, just in case a condom magically appeared on her person. Alas, the condom fairies were busy elsewhere that day. "I don't have one!" she wailed.

"Boat!" Adam said, maintaining his hold on Hero as he lunged awkwardly toward the side of the boat. His arm flailed around in the net bag sitting on the seat, then emerged with a shiny silver packet in his hand.

"Hurrah!" applauded Hero, and leaned forward to grab the condom from him at the same time he leaned forward to apply the slippery bit of latex.

There was an audible "thunk" as their heads cracked together.

"Oh, Adam, I'm so sorry," Hero apologized, rubbing her forehead. "Never mind that," he snarled. "The condom's escaping! Quick, grab it!"

Hero snagged the white object, then turned to apply it, but as his penis was wet, and the condom was slick with lubricant, the beastly thing kept popping off him. All the while she was trying to get it on, Adam twitched, groaned, and sobbed pleas for her to finish before he died.

"Done!" she said at last, giving him a beatific smile.

"Are you sure?" he asked, his jaw tense and tight with strain.

"Pretty certain. Mostly certain. Maybe I should just check it."

"Now!" he bellowed, startling her.

"Now?"

"*Now!*" He grabbed her by the hips and pulled her close to him and up in one smooth move. Her breasts rubbed on his wet chest, the heat of him suddenly sending the slow burn inside her into a raging inferno. She wrapped her legs around his waist, digging her heels into the hard muscle of his behind. She felt the hard, pointy bit of him probing her, bumping against her, nudging her everywhere but the spot she wanted him, craved him, *needed* him. He poked again, a whimper escaping from her mouth as the touch of him drove the inferno inside her into a veritable firestorm that threatened to burn her up on the spot.

"Lower," she cried, almost sobbing with frustration. Why couldn't the man aim properly? "No, up a little. To the left. No, too far, back to the right. Now you're too high again—"

"For the love of God, woman, help me," he pleaded, desperation mingling with desire and need and something that looked so much like love that it made her want to burst into "God Save the Queen." Help him? Help him? Of course! Why didn't she think of that? She reached between them and placed him where he was guaranteed a heartfelt welcome, then slid her fingers into his wet hair and groaned her pleasure into his mouth as he sank into her.

They stood like that for a moment, savoring the sensation of being joined, but soon Adam was pounding into her hard and fast, all gentleness gone, but that was just fine with her. She dug her heels into his behind, urging him on, clenching all those inner muscles she rarely ever had a use for around him until she squeezed a moan of absolute ecstasy out of his adorably manly lips. She rocked against him, sobbing now with pleasure as the fire inside her burned scarlet, then white-hot, knowing that she was going to explode into a thousand little fragments—sated and happy fragments to be sure, but still she was certain she was going to die from the rapture of their joining.

She didn't die. She roared out his name so loud Adam was deaf in the ear nearest her mouth for a week, but he never once complained. The joy he found in her arms, in her eyes, just plain *in* her was more than enough compensation for something as meaningless as a functioning eardrum. Her body tightened and shuddered around him, driving him on to find his own moment of absolute pleasure, a moment that went beyond anything he'd known and entered the realm of mythic eroticism. He came hard, arching his back and pumping into her every drop of life he had to give, filling her with his heart and soul and love and anything else he thought she might want. He gave so much of himself, he wasn't sure there would be anything left of him, but when the world stopped spinning around him, when he regained enough of his wits to realize that he was standing waist-deep in the Caribbean Sea, the woman he loved draped limp and wet over him, he knew that somehow everything would be all right. He had Hero; nothing else mattered.

True, he staggered as he waded back to the beach, her arms and legs still wrapped around him, but he figured she wouldn't hold that against him. Not even Superman would have been able to walk straight after such an experience.

Hero stirred in his arms as he walked toward shore. "Did I die? Is this heaven?"

He mustered together enough strength to move his grin muscles into place. "Not heaven, just paradise."

She kissed a lazy line along his jaw. "Mmm. Paradise. With Adam. That must make me Eve?"

"Well . . ." He stopped long enough to kiss her silly. He loved her when she was silly. "I think there are some apples in the basket."

"Good. You're going to need a lot of sustenance. Adam?"

"Hmm?"

She bit his chin gently. "That girlfriend of yours was dead wrong."

He looked down at the woman in his arms. "She was?"

"About you being a poor lover. You're not; you're very, very . . . *mmmrowr!*"

He grinned. He'd never been called *mmmrowr* before, with or without the implied italics. It felt good. It felt damn good.

Hero suddenly pushed back from his chest, looking around them wildly. "What are you doing?"

He grinned again. He loved her when she was bemused. "I'm carrying you to the blanket in the very best romantic-hero tradition."

She struggled against him, unwrapping her legs and trying to drop down his body. "No! The water's only up to your knees! Stop!" Suddenly she went rigid, then slapped a hand over his eyes, her legs wrapping themselves around his hips again. "No, don't stop! Take me to the towels!"

He laughed out loud. He even loved her when she made no sense. "Baby, I can't see where I'm going."

"That's not all you can't see."

He turned his head until her hand slid from his eyes, saying nothing until he stood holding her over the blanket.

"Hero—"

"I don't suppose you'd care to bend down and let me grab a couple of those towels before you let go of me?"

She was clinging to him like a limpet. He felt a rumble of laughter start in his chest, but knew she would be offended if he laughed at something that she did not find funny. "No, I'm not going to let you cover yourself up. Hero, I love you. I have since that first day when you ambushed me in the customs room. I love you and I want to spend the rest of my life with you. I don't care what you look like. You're beautiful to me, all of you, every last square inch of you, and if you'd just loosen the stranglehold you have on me, I'd be more than happy to show you just how much I worship you."

She mumbled something into his neck.

"What?"

"There's too many square inches of me."

"No, baby, there's not; there's just the right amount," he said, but knew when he felt the hot tears on his neck that it was going to take more than words to convince her. He sank to his knees on the blanket with her still clinging to him, draping a beach towel around the back of her until she grabbed the ends and pulled it around her front. She slid off his legs, looking anywhere but at him, trying to pull the towel down over her as she moved to the far edge of the blanket.

He wouldn't let her.

"Here," he said, pulling her back to him as he stretched out on the blanket. She frowned at him and clutched the towel closer.

"You're not wearing anything."

"I know." He ran a fingertip along the curve of her breast before it disappeared into the towel.

Her breath hitched. "Don't you think that's a little risqué? What if someone should see you?"

"No one can see us." He rubbed his leg against hers, leaning over her and throwing his heavy thigh over her legs.

She glanced over his shoulder. "Jesus is over there."

"Jesus has seen me naked before." He started nibbling on her neck, pushing aside her wet hair to taste the sensitive flesh beneath it.

"But . . . but . . ."

"Hero, you are the most beautiful woman in the world."

She snorted.

"To me you are," he said with a smile, then sat up and ran a palm down her smooth calf. "Look at your legs; look how shapely they are."

"They're stumpy," she said with a mutinous glare. He bent down to kiss a path down one calf, pausing to nibble on her ankle, then kissing down the top of her foot until he reached her toes.

"I could never love a woman with stumpy legs," he murmured, sucking a toe into his mouth for a moment. She moaned. "Your legs are long and muscled, and you have stunningly gorgeous heels. I bet men fawn upon your heels all the time."

She giggled as he turned back toward her.

"And your arms," he said, holding out one arm and kissing a wet trail up to her shoulder, "are pieces of art. They are the arms of the *Venus de Milo*."

"The *Venus de Milo* doesn't have arms," she said—somewhat breathlessly, he noted, smiling to himself.

"That's because no one else can have arms as lovely as you," he murmured against her collarbone. "But they have rivals to the title of loveliest limb, because those must go to your legs, particularly your thighs—"

She squealed and tried to push down the towel as he peeled it off her upper legs. "No, please, Adam, don't!"

He bent over her legs, sliding a hand between her thighs, nibbling her soft flesh gently until she shuddered and allowed him to spread her legs. "Your thighs are almost perfect enough to be part of a sculpture, but not quite, because yours are warm and soft and inviting."

"They are?"

He heard the wistful tone in her voice and prayed she would learn to see herself as he saw her. "Almost perfect," he repeated, kneeling between her thighs as he tried to pull the towel from where she clutched it between her breasts. "Let me, baby."

"No."

"Please."

"No." Her eyes were filling with tears.

He kissed her long and deep. "Let me see you."

Slowly he pried the towel from her fingers and laid it back, exposing her breasts, those glorious breasts, breasts that would make any man's mouth water. "Oh, Hero, they're exquisite," he murmured, his fingers stroking and caressing; then he paid homage to each pert, rose-tipped nipple with his mouth.

"Exquisite." She moaned, writhing against him, thrusting her breast into his mouth, screaming when he suckled hard. He paid due attention to the other breast, making her gasp with the pleasure, then kissed the warm valley between them as he slid down.

118

"But the best part of you . . ." He nudged the towel down.

"No!" She tried to grab it and cover herself up. He wouldn't let her.

"The best part . . ." He pushed the towel down until her belly button was exposed, pausing to lave it with his tongue. She jerked beneath him.

"No," she whimpered, her hands fluttering in his hair.

"The very best part of you"—he brushed the remainder of the towel aside and gently bit her belly, sliding his hand up her inner thigh until he reached his own personal paradise—"weeps tears of joy for me."

He leaned down until his mouth was against her heated core, his nose inhaling the scent of her, the scent of him, their passion mingled into something earthy and salty and so essential he had to taste her.

She bucked beneath him so hard that he held her hips still, licking and nibbling her until her back bowed and she screamed his name.

He lay next to her, twining a finger in her damp hair until she was able to open her eyes.

"Now tell me I don't find you beautiful."

She slapped a hand on his chest and pushed him onto his back, looming over him with a scowl that would do a misanthrope proud.

"Just what do you mean by saying that my crotch is the best part of me? Whatever happened to loving my mind, hmmm? Whatever happened to my charming wit and my delightful sense of humor and all the other things you have been praising these last few days? There's more to me than just my genitals, you know!"

He laughed and pulled her down over him, and kissed the disgruntled look right off her face. "I was wondering if you were going to say anything about that."

"Oh, I'm going to do more than just say something about such a gross understatement of my many charms," she said, a wicked look in her eye that warmed him to his toes. She leaned over to kiss him, and squeezed a groan out of him as she wrapped her fingers around his penis. "I'm going to do much, much more than say something. I'm going to demand penance."

He tried to capture one of her ripe nipples in his mouth, but she squirmed out of his reach. "What sort of penance? Will it involve whipped cream? Handcuffs? You parading around me in naughty lingerie?"

She sat back on her heels, then suddenly bent over him and flicked her tongue along the sensitive underside of his penis.

He stopped breathing.

"No," she whispered, curling her fingers around him. "Your penance is that you're going to have to make love to me again. Right now."

"Such a taskmaster." He sighed, then tried to grab her and pull her over him.

"No, no, not like that, anyone can make love like that," she teased, getting to her feet and running toward the water. "We're going to do it the hard way."

"Oh, baby, you have no idea how hard it is." He grinned as he jumped up and chased after her.

Jesus lay in a cool spot directly beneath a broad-leafed shrub and watched with interest as Adam hauled Hero to a spot next to the blanket.

"What do you mean, it's poisonous? I thought you ate sea urchins? How can you eat something that's poisonous?"

"It's just a mild poison, Hero, on the spine. It's nothing serious. Here, stand on one leg and let me look at your foot."

Hero stood naked, tears pooling around her eyes, her wet hair streaming water down her back as he held her foot up and bent over it. The bottom of her foot stung, but that ominous word *poison* kept ringing through her head.

"It's not bad at all—the spines barely punctured the skin—

120

but even if we left right away it might start to swell up before we made it back to the resort."

"I've been poisoned by a bloody sea urchin?" She couldn't believe it. She had medications for every other eventuality, but who knew that treacherous little spiny things lurked under innocent patches of seaweed? She just thanked her lucky stars that she stepped on the little bugger after they had made love, not during. "What are we going to do? I don't want to be poisoned; I just let you see me. All of me! It's not fair that I should go through that and then die because of sadistic sea life lying in wait for me!"

"Hero——" Adam looked at her with an odd expression.

"What?"

"There is one thing I can do."

"Well, then, do it," she said, trying to peer over her shoulder to look behind her at her foot.

"Sea-urchin spines can be dissolved with ammonia."

"And you have some?"

"Well——"

"For the Lord's sake, put it on! I don't want to be puffy-footed; tonight is mambo night! I want to mambo with you! We could get at least two hundred points if we beat everyone else!" Keeping her injured foot off the ground, she hopped toward the picnic basket and gestured toward it. "Go ahead; get the ammonia and put it on my foot. I'm getting tired of standing like a flamingo."

Wry amusement and embarrassment mingled in his handsome eyes. "The ammonia isn't in the picnic basket; it's in, uh . . ."

"Well?"

"My urine."

She stared at him, her mouth hanging open slightly. "Your *what*?"

"Urine. Urine contains ammonia."

She continued to stare, sure she must have misheard him. "You want to pee on my foot?"

His lips twisted into a half smile. "They do it all the time down here. It's very common."

"You want to *pee* on my foot?"

"It'll help dissolve any bit of spine that's in the wound, and should keep it from swelling. We'll get you back to the resort and let the medical people have a look at it then."

"You want to pee on my *foot?*"

He sighed. "It's the only thing I can do until we get back to the resort."

She glared at him for a moment, then turned her back and raised her foot until the sole was facing him. "I am going to pretend this is not happening. I am going to pretend that I am soaking my foot in warm water and Epsom salts. I am going to pretend—Good Lord, man, what are you, a camel? How much do you have in you?"

He carried her out to the boat a short time later, instructing her to keep her foot out of the water despite her inclination to wash it off in the warm salt water. With his help she shimmied one-footed into her swimsuit, then pulled the cover-up on and resumed her seat by the tiller while he fetched Jesus and the picnic things.

She thought that nothing could ruin such a fabulous, breath-takingly glorious, stupendously wonderful, marvelous, perfectly lovely day—lovely with the minor exception of having had the love of her life pee all over her foot—but as she found out, even such a day of almost bliss as they had shared could be crushed until it resembled nothing so much as a stomped-upon sea urchin.

Chapter Eight

"I wonder what's going on over there?"

Adam looked where Hero pointed down the dock. He had just tied up the sailboat and was unloading Jesus and the picnic things, preparing to help Hero hobble to the resort infirmary, but stopped when he saw the group of television people coming toward him. They had the ubiquitous cameraman and sound person in tow, he noted.

Hero gnawed on her lip and hopped to the edge of the boat, allowing Adam to swing her over the side. She no longer had any doubts that he truly did find her attractive, and with that knowledge came the freedom to love him with every atom in her body. She leaned against him, wanting the warm contact touching him gave her. "Have we kept the boat out too long?"

"No." He shook his head, snapping a leash on Jesus and handing it to her as he scooped up the blankets and towels, adding them to the picnic basket.

"They don't look very happy." A twinge of guilt streaked through her at the sight of the Eden producer, her assistant, someone sweating profusely in a suit, and a cameraman headed straight for them. She had meant to tell Adam the truth about her participation on the show during the sail home, but somehow they ended up kissing more than talking, and she just hadn't mustered up the nerve to tell him. She would tonight, though. The first moment they were together alone, she'd explain about more or less losing her job, and having one last chance, and the need for her to keep her intentions quiet. Surely he would understand.

He had told her the truth about himself even before he kissed her.

She pushed that niggling thought aside and smiled at the approaching people, Adam's arm strong around her waist.

"Adam Fuller."

She felt Adam stiffen beside her and wondered why, then realized the show's producer used his real name, not the name he had assumed for the show.

"Hero North," Dara Thompson said with a smile that most definitely did not reach her eyes. "How very fitting we should find you both together."

"Is it?" Adam asked smoothly, his arm tightening around Hero. She had a horrible presentiment of what was coming. "Well, I'm afraid that whatever you have to say to us is going to have to wait. Hero stepped on a sea urchin and she needs medical attention."

"I'm sorry to hear that," Thompson said, her eyes expressing anything but concern. "This won't take a minute. Mr. Jenkins?"

The sweaty man in the suit oiled his way forward. "I'm Robert Jenkins, of Dowitcher, Prog, and Epile. I represent Hawkeye Productions, and the TV show *Eden* in particular. Mr. Fuller, we have here an affidavit from one Samuel Fife, producer, stating that he received payment of five thousand dollars in order to doctor a legitimate contestant's file in such a way as to admit you to the show in place of the contestant."

Oh, Lord, they'd found Adam out. Hero slid a glance at him.

He stood beside her, not gnashing his teeth or frothing at the mouth, or doing any of the things she would be doing in his place. Instead he looked mildly bored, as if nothing the horrible lawyer was saying was of any importance.

"Further investigation has revealed that you were party to the illegal act of smuggling a live animal onto the island despite the quarantine restrictions."

Hero wanted to put her arms around Adam. They'd found out about Jesus, too?

"As you are aware, such an act carries with it not only a substantial fine, but a jail term, in addition to the destruction of the animal in question."

"No," Hero shouted, surprising everyone, including herself. "That's ridiculous, utterly ridiculous—"

The evil man held up his hand. "I will attend to you in a moment, Miss North." He turned back to Adam, pulling out a handkerchief to mop his sweaty brow as he spoke. "Because of your actions, you have been disqualified from the competition. You have an hour to remove your things from the hospitality of the resort. Transportation will be provided to the Mystique Island Airport, whereupon officers of the commonwealth will be waiting to discuss your violations of quarantine policy."

Hero stared in horror at the man.

"I understand," Adam said, his voice rumbling around her, drawing her eyes to him. He looked nothing more than mildly annoyed. He understood? She didn't understand! And she certainly wasn't going to let some nasty little solicitor push Adam around.

"I believe that even on Mystique the accused is allowed to face his accuser," Hero snapped at the man. "Just who exactly tattled on Adam?"

Jenkins turned to her. "Ah, Miss North. Who exposed Mr. Fuller is not at issue here."

"Isn't it? I think it is, although it really is a moot point. There's only one other person here who knows who Adam is—Sally Simmons."

"Miss Simmons reluctantly verified information, yes, but she did not bring the initial complaint to our attention. That was done by a Mr. Gregory Barstow."

Greg! Greg of the thigh-sized arms. Hero's eyes narrowed as she recalled him questioning Adam the night of the first dinner. And Sally knew she was a journalist—had she told that to Greg as well? Hero couldn't help but being hurt, even though the man had said Sally was reluctant to verify the truth. She had *liked* Sally; how could she be so cruel to Adam?

"Miss North, I have here a copy of your application to participate on *Eden*, and a notarized statement concerning your background. Nowhere in it does it state that you are currently employed as an investigative journalist for a British newspaper."

She felt Adam twitch next to her, and crossed her fingers behind her back, praying that she had the time to talk to him before he thought the worst of her. If it wasn't too late, that is . . .

"Would you like to explain this oversight?"

She raised her chin. "Explain it? No, I would not *like* to explain it, but I will nonetheless. I was employed by a newspaper, but as of three months ago I was forced to take a leave of absence. I am no longer on the payroll of the *Revue*."

"Do you deny that you applied for a spot on the show with the intention of using your experiences here in an article to be published by the *Sentinel-Revue* at a later date?"

"That was my intention, yes."

"And you willingly provided false information to the show's producers that would mislead them into believing your sole interest was in participating in the show in good faith?"

What must Adam be thinking of her? She shuddered to think. "No. I did not provide false information."

"You did not reveal your recent employment by a British tabloid known throughout England for its outrageous and often fantastical and inaccurate stories. You do not consider that providing false information?"

"I assume there is a point to this?" Hero asked, wanting to lean into Adam, but unsure of his reception to such a move. "My foot hurts. If you are going to throw me off the island, too, please say so now so that I might see the doctor before I have to leave."

The man nodded, mopping at his face again. "You are also disqualified from the show. You have one hour to remove yourself from the Crescent Moon Resort. Further, you will be hearing from the Hawkeye Productions legal department regarding the falsifying of statements on your applications."

Hero wanted to tell the man where he could stick his falsified statements, but the camera was on her and Adam, so she just smiled instead.

"Do you need me to carry you?" Adam asked as the group turned around and left without further word. Hero wanted to look at him, wanted to assess the damage the fact that she'd lied to him had done, but hadn't the nerve.

"No, I can walk," she said, her head down.

"Hero."

His hand on her arm stopped her.

"What?" she asked into his chest, ashamed and embarrassed and close to tears with the knowledge that her stupid plan had hurt the one man she loved more than anything else.

He raised her chin and looked down at her with eyes so blue they looked like the brightest sapphires. "You could have told me."

"I know. I'm sorry, so very sorry, Adam. I didn't mean to not tell you, but there never seemed to be a good time, and I didn't want you to think badly of me, and I didn't know how you feel . . . *felt* . . . and I was going to tell you tonight, but now you probably don't even want to hear me out—"

He leaned forward until his breath was warm on her lips.

"Honey, it would take more than a little thing like this to change how I feel about you."

She blinked back her tears, shivering despite the warmth of the day. His eyes were so warm, so full of love, she wanted to do a few back flips down the dock despite the fact that their world was falling apart. "It would? What would it take?"

His lips brushed hers in the sweetest kiss imaginable. "Oh, I don't know . . . global destruction? No, not even that could change my mind. You're the best thing that's ever happened to me, Hero. I love you now, I'll love you tomorrow, I'll love you always. You're my bright, beautiful goddess in my very own Eden."

"Maybe I'll change my name to Eve," she murmured, sucking on his lower lip, releasing it to add, "But what about you? What will you do if you can't follow Sally? And what about Jesus?"

They both looked down to where Jesus had plopped himself in the shade Hero provided, sitting with his one good front leg tucked under him, the other stretched out straight.

"We can't let those quarantine people take him and put him down. We can't!"

Adam's eyes, heated with passion the moment before, turned to ice. "We won't. The only thing Jesus will have to sacrifice is his balls, and I already told him those were on hold when I decided to give up the job on Sally so I could court you. He'll be OK; his balls'll just have to wait until later, once I can scrape together enough to pay for the surgery."

She touched his cheek. "Once *we* can scrape together enough for his surgery. It seems a shame he should lose his testicles a second time."

He grinned at her, the grin fading a moment later. "Hero, I hate to do this to you, hate to start out our life together with something illegal hanging over our heads, but—"

"I have three hundred pounds in traveler's checks, and a Visa card. Will that be enough to bribe someone into taking us off the island?"

He laughed, pulling her against him, kissing her soundly. "With what I have, yes, it will be enough. You know that Dominica is just a short hop away?"

"Dominica?"

Adam smiled and brushed a curl out of her eye. "It's a small island, one that doesn't have animal-quarantine laws. I'll call Gar from there—if his past is anything to go by, he's probably already engaged to someone else—and apologize and send him back his money."

Her smile answered his, love alight in her eyes. "Sounds marvelous," she said under her breath, giving him one more kiss. "This has the makings of a great story! My editor will love it!"

Adam laughed as he scooped her up in his arms. "Come along, my little fugitive from justice. Jesus, heel. We have a daring escape to plan."

"Escape to paradise." Hero sighed, snuggling against Adam, filled with love and hope and happiness, but most of all, filled with the knowledge that all her feelings were returned. "What a lovely headline that will make."

Breaking the Rules

JENNIFER ARCHER

For Molli, Don, and Jeff, my fellow island blackout survivors.
Thanks for the memory!

HAWKEYE PRODUCTIONS MEMORANDUM

To: Michael Hawkins
From: Dara Thompson
Re: Rules of the Game—Week Three

1) All remaining 100 contestants will meet poolside after dinner on Saturday night to compete in the first challenge of the second round. Winners will choose their dates for the next three days and nights, after which the second challenge will be announced.

2) Contestants will report to the confession booth once per day to report on their interactions with other contestants.

3) Contestants are reminded to stay out of restricted areas of the resort and/or island as indicated on the maps provided at the game's inception. Those in violation of this rule are subject to removal from the game.

4) Contestants and *Eden* employees (i.e., hotel staff, production crew, etc.) are not allowed to fraternize outside of normal and necessary exchanges required by the competition. Employees in violation of this rule risk immediate termination. Contestants in violation are subject to removal from the game.

Chapter One

Claire Mulligan drew a breath of salty air. She'd never ventured this far down the beach. The quiet cove was dark and deserted. Just the sort of place she craved following the hectic frustration of the last few hours.

After a long deluge of wind and rain earlier in the day, the storm had finally eased. Brief lightning to the south assured the reprieve wouldn't last long. A heavy blanket of clouds obscured the moon and stars.

Claire scanned the area, her gaze settling in the distance on Crescent Moon, home these past two weeks for her and the other *Eden* competitors. Bright lights surrounded the resort, reflecting off the water like a treasure of jewels beneath the surface. Shimmering golden lanterns hung low in the trees along the walkways and around the pool. Guitar strains drifted on the fragrant night breeze . . . a sultry love song intended to send Cupid's weapon of choice straight through the hearts of would-be lovers or to sharpen the arrows in couples already shot.

Claire sighed. Leave it to James to ruin an evening picture-perfect for romance. She thought of how he'd ignored her at every turn and sighed again. Tonight was a mixer; no teams, no pair-offs. Rupert Asterisk, the show's host, had instructed the players to mingle and get to know one another better. Claire nibbled her lower lip. Apparently James felt he knew her as well as he cared to.

When tears threatened, she blinked them back. James's behavior tonight was no different than on any other night since a week or so after the game started. Since he quit trying to hide his fascination with her female competitors.

Claire sniffed. It had been a mistake to let him talk her into this. She wasn't the sort who relished airing private matters on national TV. But James had insisted it would not only be fun, but a great chance to possibly win an awesome honeymoon and a whole lot of money. Money they could use to bail their floundering business out of debt. He'd said a lot of other things, too. Comments that had made her feel dull and uptight. So, rather than disappoint her fiancé, she'd agreed to audition for the show.

They had pitched themselves in a different light from the other competitors—as a committed couple out to test their relationship. Would their bond unravel or tighten? She'd been so naïve that she hadn't taken that question seriously. In her mind, it was only a sales ploy to win over *Eden*'s producers. And it had worked. But now here she was . . . alone on a deserted beach while James alternately flirted with the cameras and every female in a bikini. Had she been so dull she'd driven him away? If so, she could change; she *would* change.

After another quick glance in every direction, Claire drew a deep breath, then reached for the bathing suit string at the back of her neck. She couldn't let James fall in love with another woman. She couldn't lose him over a silly game show. The money and trip weren't what enticed him; she'd known that from the start. His desire to appear on *Eden* was a direct result of that stupid B movie filmed on location in Prairie last year. If not for James's bit part in it and the ridiculous line he'd ad-libbed that had caught everyone's attention, he wouldn't have the slightest interest in *Eden*. His brief brush with celebrity had muddled his common sense. He'd snap out of it and become his old self again just as soon as they got off this island . . . she had to believe that.

Claire closed her eyes and pulled the string. Then she said a quick prayer that James would take the bait and follow her here. She'd made certain he'd watched her leave. And he'd have to be blind not to see that she was upset. If she ever meant any-thing at all to him, surely he wouldn't let her venture off alone in the dark in this state of mind.

Though she wasn't the least bit cold, Claire's teeth chattered. "You can do this," she whispered as she let her bikini top fall forward.

Yes, that ridiculous low-budget film had changed everything. *Rodeo Romeos*. What a laugh. James might sell feed and tackle, but he did so wearing leather loafers, not leather boots. The movie was the first time she'd ever seen him in a pair of Wran-glers. James had become addicted to the adrenaline that accom-panied his fifteen minutes of fame. When the high had worn off, he went looking for another fix. He'd found it in *Eden*.

With fumbling fingers, Claire reached back and unhooked the clasp between her shoulder blades. After dropping the strip of fabric in the sand beside a palm tree, she pushed the lower half of her suit to her ankles and stepped out of it. With a kick, she sent the bottoms toward the tree, too.

The ocean offered thunderous applause, appreciation for her impromptu striptease. The breeze blew warm against her naked body.

Exhilarated by her daring, Claire glanced over her shoulder. A line of cabanas was snuggled cozily in the palm trees several yards back, their shades lowered against the night like sleepy eyelids. Only the slivers of light around a few of the windows hinted at life inside. The crew's living quarters. She'd seen them on the Crescent Moon Resort map. Which meant she'd wandered into a restricted area, off-limits to players. If caught here, outside the boundaries, she could be kicked off the game—a disaster she should avoid at all costs. Just the thought of leaving James alone on the island with all those half-dressed bimbos made her blood boil.

With a nervous laugh, Claire looked back at the water. On the other hand, maybe getting in trouble with the show's producers would work to her advantage. Maybe she'd snag her fiancé's attention and he'd see her in a whole new light. Considering the women he'd flirted with these past couple of weeks, James was in the market for someone with a wild streak.

Lightning flickered again in the distance. A low rumble of thunder followed. Claire drew a shaky breath. She cast one last glance at the lights of Crescent Moon. "Here's to breaking the rules," she yelled. Turning, she ran toward the water, then plunged into the waves.

"Here's to breaking the rules," Mitch Talbott mumbled. Smiling, he watched through the lens of his camera and continued to film as the naked woman dove into the water.

He'd been headed back to his cabana when he spotted her standing at the edge of the surf. The combination of overcast sky, the late hour, and the fact that she'd kept her back to him while she stripped prevented him from identifying the woman. He assumed her to be one of the *Eden* competitors. No female crewmember owned a body like that.

Mitch leaned against the palm tree he stood beneath, aiming the camera at the spot where she'd disappeared. Just his luck: the producers had rules against the crew getting friendly with contestants. He guessed it didn't really matter, though. Great body or not, the simple fact that she'd signed on to humiliate herself on national television soured any interest he might have had in her otherwise.

When the woman's head emerged from the water, Mitch

steadied the camera. As far as he was concerned, anyone who'd go on a game show to compete for a potential spouse was a few feet short in the depth department. The *Eden* contestants had pretty much confirmed that suspicion for him. They were a bunch of shallow-minded, self-absorbed, silly imbeciles.

The camera seemed to dig a little deeper into Mitch's shoulder. Hell, maybe he wasn't any different from the rest of them, even if he did only work behind the scenes. Like the players he scorned, he'd chosen to sacrifice his pride for something he desperately wanted: a chance to prove himself to the president of Hawkeye Productions, Michael Hawkins, and maybe land a job on one of Hawkeye's more serious projects. Specifically, the documentary on the lost tribes of Africa Hawkins planned to film next year.

Mitch zoomed in on the woman's bobbing head, hoping for a clearer look at her. But she turned away at the crucial second, and all he saw was the back of her head.

Pride. That was what separated him from the contestants. As far as he could tell, none of the *Eden* competitors possessed any pride to sacrifice.

The woman laughed and shrieked as she rode a wave to shore, then turned and dove in again.

Mitch stopped filming and lowered the camera to his side. His job was to invade her privacy; she'd agreed to have it invaded when she signed on for the show. But if anyone found out she'd ventured this far outside the restricted boundaries, she'd get the boot. He didn't want that to happen. Not now that she'd sparked his interest by taking the plunge in her birthday suit.

Mitch walked the few steps to his cabana and set the camera inside the door. He thought of the hazy glimpse he'd caught of her nude body a few moments ago. If not for those damn rules, he supposed he wouldn't mind passing a few idle hours with a woman who liked to skinny-dip. He could sure think of worse ways to spend his off time. Maybe he could forgive her for destroying her own dignity. Who was he to judge, anyway? Maybe, like him, she had reasons for joining up with the show that went beyond the obvious.

Here's to breaking the rules, she'd said.

Mitch tugged his shirt from his waistband, then unbuttoned it and kicked off his shoes. Maybe she'd be worth the risk. He was bored . . . tired of hanging out with a bunch of burned out crewmen.

Ambling closer to the ocean's edge, he picked his way around shells, pebbles, and matted strands of seaweed. What was the worst that could happen if he was lucky enough to score a night or two with the woman? He could get caught and fired, lose his chance to ever work on another Hawkeye project. Two weeks ago, to risk that possibility would've been out of the question. But he hadn't so much as uttered "Hello" to Michael Hawkins. In fact, he'd seen the production company's president only once. From a distance.

Mitch rolled up the sleeves of his shirt. He'd thought tonight might be his chance when a rumor circulated that Hawkins would be visiting Crescent Moon Resort for dinner. He'd even used nearly an entire can of spray starch ironing his best shirt for the occasion. But Hawkins didn't show.

Waves lapped at Mitch's feet, swallowed them, then curled away, only to return moments later. He searched the dark ocean, worried he could no longer hear or see the woman in the water. No sane person would be out there anyway. Not at night, and especially not with a storm brewing.

When he heard her shriek of laughter a few feet away, he smiled and relaxed. But he tensed up again as a burst of lightning illuminated the water. *Crazy woman*. She'd fry herself if she didn't watch out. Thinking he'd warn her about the dangerous combination of lightning and water, he started toward the sound of her splashes and squeals.

Before he'd gone more than a couple of steps, the woman

cried out. Then everything went black. Crescent Moon Resort no longer glittered in the distance.

He turned.

The pencil-thin beams of light from the cabana windows had vanished.

The electricity, Mitch thought. *An island blackout. Dandy.*

"Help me!" the woman cried out behind him. "I'm hurt! "Someone help me . . . please!"

Chapter Two

Claire held a hand inches from her face. Panic rolled in like the wave that carried her to shore. She couldn't see anything. Not her fingers. Not a glimmer of light. Nothing.

A whimper worked its way up to her throat. She touched the spot where she'd bumped her head on her tumble toward shore. She didn't feel a scratch, not even a goose egg.

Another incoming wave sent Claire to her knees. Her fingers grasped sand as she crawled forward to a place where the water lapped gently, then receded. She sat, shivering and licking salt from her lips, shaking her head to sling strands of hair from her face. Tentatively, she reached out. "Help!" she yelled again. "Someone . . . help me!"

Sounds she'd taken for granted before, night sounds, ocean sounds, amplified. The hiss of the wind . . . the growling surf . . . a trickle of water alongside the place where she sat. She sensed a presence even before she heard a shuffling of feet. "Hello? Is someone there?"

"I'm here," a man answered. "Are you OK?"

His voice sounded quiet as the distant thunder. Claire realized he stood beside her, so close she might touch his leg if she reached out. She pressed her knees to her chest, wrapped her arms around them. "I need help."

"Are you hurt?"

The words came to her from eye level, indicating he knelt beside her. Claire drew back, cringing, embarrassed by her nakedness. "Please . . . don't look at me."

His laugh was short, baffled. "How could I?"

She swallowed a sob, her dignity as bruised as her skull by his comment. "I bumped my head. I . . . I think I've gone blind."

"You've what?"

"I think I'm blind." A wave lapped around her. Her teeth chattered harder. "I . . . I was swimming. When I came up for air, I couldn't see anything. I still can't."

The man's sudden laughter had a new fear clawing its way into her mind. Of all the people who could've found her, she had to get the island maniac. He might be a sadist . . . a rapist . . . worse. "I'm okay. You can go now."

"But you're hurt."

Claire let go of her legs, dug her fingernails into her palms, scooted backward. "Please . . . I'd like to be alone."

"You're not blind," the man said. "We've had a blackout. Probably because of the storm. The entire island must've lost power. There's no light anywhere."

"But I can't even see my hand in front of my face! It can't get that dark, can it? We'd have to be in a cave."

"This island's miles from civilization. And the clouds camouflage any natural light."

Relief swept over Claire. The lunatic made sense. She rubbed her palms up and down her thighs. "You didn't have to laugh at me. I made an honest mistake."

"Sorry. You must've been scared to death." He cleared his throat. "I'm Mitch Talbott."

"I'm—" Claire stopped short of speaking her name. She had

stepped beyond the contestants' boundaries, breaking a show rule. The fact that he was here, too, told her he was probably affiliated with *Eden*'s production in one way or another. That is, unless he, too, was a contestant and had wandered too far. But she couldn't take that chance, wouldn't risk being kicked out of the game, leaving James here alone with a harem of willing women. "Just call me Amphitrite," she blurted. "You know, Poseidon's wife? Goddess of the sea?"

"I think you mean Aphrodite."

"No," Claire said, "Aphrodite is the goddess of love and beauty."

"Maybe so, but I seem to recall that she was born from the sea foam of Uranus's genitals. And since you just sort of washed up here on shore—"

"I think I'd rather be Poseidon's wife than some goddess born from the sea foam of . . ." Claire paused. Talking about genitals, even mythological ones, with a strange man she couldn't see didn't seem the wisest course of action. "Just take my word for it; the name's Amphitrite."

"Okay. Aphrodite who?"

Claire was too tired to argue mythology any longer. If he preferred Aphrodite, why should she care? Her mother's maiden name popped to mind. "O'Malley," she said

He cleared his throat again. "Well, Aphrodite O'Malley, I'd shake your hand if I knew where it was."

"Don't touch me!"

"Whoa! I'm not going to hurt you."

"I know that."

He was quiet for a few seconds, then said, "It is sort of strange, isn't it? Meeting and carrying on a conversation with someone you can't see?"

"It's more than strange." Claire squinted, turning her head one direction, then another. "Have you ever seen anything so black?"

"Only Sadie."

145

"Sadie?"

"My sister's Labrador retriever. She's as black as she is good-natured."

Claire relaxed some. The madman liked animals. That was a good sign. And he smelled of shaving cream. Clean. Fresh. No cologne. Considering the circumstances, she guessed she couldn't blame him for laughing. Besides, his tone, his manner, everything about Mitch Talbott suggested he was harmless and friendly. And sane. Now if she could only find her way to the palm tree where she'd dropped her suit before the electricity revived.

"So," she said, "do you have any idea how we might get back to the resort?"

"I'm staying in one of the cabanas just down the way."

"So you're part of the crew?"

"Yeah . . . a cameraman."

A cameraman. Claire folded her arms over her breasts. Was he on duty or off tonight? Could he have followed her here? "Oh, really," she said slowly. "I'm starting not to notice the cameras anymore. They blend in with the scenery."

"Guess we're doing something right, then. We're supposed to try our best to stay inconspicuous."

Claire pressed her knees together. Had he been so *inconspicuous* that she hadn't noticed him tailing her from the resort? Had he watched her as she . . . "Which cameraman are you? Maybe I'd recognize you."

"I'm the good-looking one."

"Ah . . ." She laughed. *A maniac with an ego.*

"If we can make it to my quarters, I might be able to rummage up a flashlight or some candles. Then you can see for yourself what I look like." He paused for several beats before adding, "And I can get a look at you, too."

Claire's breath caught. Something about the change in his voice on those last words bothered her. "It's not far, is it?" she asked cautiously. "To your cabana, I mean. When I went into

146

the water, the crew's quarters were right behind me." *Could he have been right behind me, too? Him and his trusty camera?* Her heartbeat kicked up. "Where were you before the lights went out? At your cabana?"

"I was finishing up my shift."

"So you weren't at your cabana?"

"No, not yet. I was headed that way."

"But you weren't there yet?"

He laughed. "What's with the interrogation? Do you have something to hide?"

"No, I don't," she fibbed. "It's just that I left my bag under a palm tree. I need to find it."

"You drifted. We're a ways away now. But no one's going to find your stuff in the dark. Us included. Let's try to make it to my place. I'll be happy to look at your things when the lights come on."

She blinked. "What did you just say?"

"When the electricity comes on, I'll be happy to look for your bag. Until then, I'm sure it'll be safe."

Maybe so, Claire thought, *but I won't.* "I don't care." She squared her shoulders. "I'm going to try to find it."

"Fine," he said, still sounding too amused for her comfort. "I'll help you, but I think you'll change your mind after we get started and you understand what we're up against. If I could find a flashlight or candle, we could try to make it back to the main area of the resort. But otherwise it's too far and risky. It'll be tricky enough finding my place." He paused. "Here. Take my hand."

Sensing he reached for her, Claire leaned back. She cringed at the thought of which bare body part he might encounter if he touched her. "Wait! I mean . . . let me."

"I promise I don't bite."

"I know that. It's just, well, I'm claustrophobic." *And naked.* "This darkness makes me nervous." She lifted an arm toward the sound of his voice and came in contact with what felt like a shoulder beneath a starched shirt. *Strange beach attire.* She'd felt softer sandpaper.

"There you are," Mitch said, taking her hand in his.

She was pulled to her feet as he stood. "Well, Mr. Talbott, will you lead the way, or should I?"

"Call me Mitch. Mr. Talbott makes me feel ancient."

Claire felt too close to him, too aware of his deep, almost intimate tone of voice. Now it wasn't the breeze or nerves that caused her to shiver. "You don't sound old."

"I'm thirty-four."

"Ahh," Claire said, her throat going dry. "Then I was wrong. You're a decrepit old geezer after all."

"So what I have here is a rebel," he said, laughing. "You've sneaked off to see if you can get away with something that's strictly forbidden by your *Eden* contract."

"I didn't intend to cross the line. I just needed some space. The game . . . it's starting to wear on my nerves. All those strangers . . . the egos. I needed to get away for a while." *And I was hoping that, instead of you, James would follow and find me in the nude.*

A moment of silence stretched between them. Claire waited, feeling his presence as though it were a touch.

"I feel the same way," he said quietly. "And I'm not one of the competitors. But risking your place in the game is one thing; risking your safety is another. You really shouldn't swim in the ocean at night. Especially not alone."

"Believe me, I'm old enough for a midnight swim without a chaperon."

"No one's that old, Ms. O'Malley."

"I'm a very good swimmer." The nerve-tinged sound of her own laughter surprised her.

"Good swimmer or not, swimming alone in the ocean at night, especially when a storm's threatening, is dangerous."

"I felt like being a little dangerous tonight."

"Okay, then. Since you're a daredevil . . ." Mitch gave her arm a tug. "Come on. Let's give this a shot. I'll go first, since I've walked the route recently. Ready?"

"Lead the way."

Claire shuffled along behind him, worrying over what would happen if he made a sudden stop and they collided, worrying even more that the lights would come back on before she found her suit. She'd never felt so vulnerable in her life, so completely exposed. The rain-tainted breeze swept over her wet skin, teasing her nerve endings. She tried her best not to shiver, but couldn't restrain the reaction. Even her goose bumps had goose bumps.

"Cold?" Mitch asked.

She flinched. "Why would I be?"

"You're shaking. I could put my arm around you."

"No!" Her heart jumped to her throat. "You're imagining things. I'm warm as can be."

She told herself she should swallow her pride, tell him she was naked, ask for his shirt. She started to do just that, but the words stuck in her throat. What did she really know about Mitch Talbott? True, she liked the reassuring sound of his voice and the solid, secure feel of his hand around hers. But for all she knew, he might very well be the lunatic she'd first thought him to be.

"So," Mitch said, "do you like to hang out on the beach when you're at home, too?"

"Hang out?" She swallowed, her gaze instinctively lowering to her chest. She'd hung out on a beach or two in her life, but never quite like this. "Prairie—the town in Texas where I live— is landlocked. A lake's about the best we can do when it comes to a body of water."

"I see."

They traveled another few feet. "This isn't working," Mitch said. "I feel like I'm about to run head-on into something. I'd do better if I had both hands out in front of me. Here." He placed her palm at his waist. "Hold on to me."

Claire didn't argue, though she felt ridiculous walking choo-choo style behind him down the beach. Then there was the matter of his waist. Not a pinch of fat beneath that cardboard-textured shirt. Though she told herself to get a grip, steamy pictures of Mitch's possible appearance strolled a lazy pathway through her imagination.

A quick flash of lightning split the sky over the ocean, providing a brief glimpse of Mitch's back. She was right—the shoulders were broad, but the body beneath was lean, almost lanky. He stood at least four inches taller than her five-foot-nine-inch frame.

Darkness again. His hair. What color was it? Dark brown, or maybe black. She didn't catch a long enough look. She told herself she shouldn't care, anyway.

Mitch reached for her wrist, came to a halt, and turned. "That was too close for comfort," he said, his voice strained. "We shouldn't mess around with that lightning striking so close. At least it did the trick, though. I know where we are. It's a straight shot to my cabana."

Claire dug her heels into the sand. "My bag. I need to find that tree." She had the distinct feeling Mitch Talbott was counting to ten, the way her father used to do when she'd pushed him to the limit.

"Several trees line this beach. Groping around in the dark trying to find the right one isn't my idea of a fun-filled way to spend the night. Or a safe way, for that matter. You hear those waves?"

As if on cue, one crashed nearby. Water swallowed her feet and rose all the way to her knees before receding. The tug of the undertow had her stumbling.

Mitch grasped her wrist tighter, steadying her. "The tide's getting stronger," he continued, before she could answer him. Slowly he led her farther out of reach of the waves. "Our best bet is to make it to my place."

"And if you don't have any candles or a flashlight?"

"Then we'll stay put until the electricity comes on or the sun comes up."

"But the current might wash my bag away." She stepped back, though he kept a grip on her arm. "I get your point, Mitch. But if you won't help me, I'll go alone. It's been nice knowing you. Somewhat bizarre, but nice nonetheless. Thanks for getting me this far."

Mitch's sigh seemed a mixture of exasperation and reluctant amusement. "Okay, Aphrodite, you win. You're probably the most stubborn woman I've ever met. Whatever's under that palm tree must be pretty damn important."

Despite her predicament, Claire grinned. "You have no idea."

Chapter Three

Mitch turned toward the water as the woman's hands settled at either side of his waist. When he'd found her cowering in the sand she'd seemed sweet . . . fragile. *So much for first impressions.*

The blackness felt like a blanket over his head. Extending both arms, he took a few hesitant steps. When his toe hit something solid, he stopped short. "Dammit!"

"What's wrong?"

"I kicked a rock."

"Are you okay?"

Balancing on one leg, he lifted the opposite foot and touched his toe. Nothing oozed. He lowered his foot to the sand, wishing he'd been smart and kept his shoes on. "I'm fine," he said. "Just dandy. Next time I might not be so lucky, though. This is crazy, and I'm crazy for letting you talk me into it. We could get toasted by lightning or sucked out to sea by a wave."

What had started off as a fun and sexy game had begun to lose any appeal for him. Her stubborn streak didn't seem quite as cute now, either. He really didn't give a rat's ass if she was naked or not. They needed to get off of this beach and into his cabana. Pronto. He only had nine toes left, and at this rate they wouldn't last long.

"I'm not forcing you to help me, Mr. Talbott," she said, as if reading his mind. "You can retreat to your cozy little cabana and curl up safe and sound until the blackout is over. That's okay with me; I'm not afraid of the dark."

Yeah, right. Her words might be brave, but her voice wasn't. "Neither am I. And I wish you'd call me Mitch. I told you I'd help, and I will." Never mind that the good sense he'd ignored before, with toe-throbbing results, told him to run far and fast from Aphrodite O'Malley. Never mind that the woman was willful and certifiably nuts.

"Let's get this over with," Mitch huffed. He waved his arms out in front of him, found no resistance, then crept toward the roar of the ocean. "So what made you decide to try out for a spot on *Eden?*"

She was quiet for several seconds, then finally said, "A . . . um . . . *friend* talked me into it."

"What kind of friend would want you to go on a nationally televised game show to try to hook a husband? Sorry, but I can't imagine anyone being that desperate."

"I don't need to *hook* a husband. I wanted to have some fun, that's all. If, in the process, I win a lot of money or a vacation, or even fall in love, well, so much the better."

"Why is it that every woman I meet is in such a rush to get married? Happily ever after is highly overrated."

"I see," she said, her tone curious and defensive. "If you're so down on marriage, then why are you working on a program that promotes it?"

"Don't tell me you really believe that? *Eden* isn't about love or marriage. It's about titillation for the nation's viewing pleasure."

She didn't respond, which was fine with Mitch. He was alone in the dark with a woman wearing nothing but skin. The last thing he wanted to talk about was marriage. Titillation, on the other hand, had definite possibilities.

When his left palm hit a rough, solid surface, he stopped. "Here's a tree. Let's hope it's the one where you left your . . . *bag*." He stooped to feel in the sand for her suit.

The woman grabbed hold of his arm. "Wait! I'll do it."

He heard the urgency in her voice, the ring of panic, and grinned. "Of course." She didn't want *him* to find her suit and ruin her little charade. "Go for it, goddess."

Her hand slid down his arm until their fingers connected. Mitch hadn't considered holding hands to be a big deal since junior high school. But now, with a naked woman he couldn't see, a warm night breeze, and ocean waves crashing around them, he found it oddly seductive.

Their fingers remained linked as she stooped to pat the ground. "Well?" he asked.

"Nothing here." She stood. "Wrong tree."

"Ready to give up?"

"No."

"Why doesn't that surprise me?" Mitch guided her hand to his waist and smirked. She was in a no-win situation. If the blackout continued, they'd have a hell of a time finding her suit. But if the electricity suddenly came on again, she'd be exposed . . . literally. "Let's see what we can stumble onto in this direction." He inched forward.

"Owww . . . !"

Mitch stopped. "What?"

"It's nothing," she said, her voice pinched.

"You sure?"

"I said it's nothing."

"Fine." He took another two steps. Though he couldn't be sure, it felt as if she hopped behind him. She moved so slowly, she practically dragged him backward.

Mitch paused again. The situation had gone from funny to ridiculous. If she didn't confess in a second, he'd just have to admit he knew about her dilemma. Sure, she'd be embarrassed. But if the power came back now, she'd not only be embarrassed, he'd get to see her blush. All over. "Hey . . . if I'm going to help you, you're going to have to be straight with me. What's the problem?"

"I stepped on something. I think my heel's bleeding."

"Great."

"If you want to say 'I told you so,' go right ahead," she snapped. "Say it. I can tell you're just dying to."

He was. "Can you walk on it?" he asked instead.

"I don't think so. It really hurts."

"Probably not good to get sand in the wound anyway. We should give up the search and go to my place. Agreed?"

"Agreed," she answered, sounding resigned.

Unable to resist a little good-natured torture, Mitch bit back a chuckle and said, "I'll carry you."

"No! I can hop along behind you. I'll make it okay."

"At least put an arm around my neck. It'll be easier."

"I prefer to hop."

He imagined the persistent lift of her chin, the set of her jaw. His amusement shifted to exasperation again. "Have it your way. If you develop gangrene and lose your leg it won't be my fault."

"It's just a cut."

Mitch started walking again. *Time to tell her the truth.* Then they could both quit playing games. What did she think he'd do, anyway? Lose control of himself? Turn into a sex-crazed beast? Or was she just too proud to admit the predicament she'd placed herself in? He'd bet on the latter. She was stubborn, that was for sure. The type of woman bound and determined not to listen to a man come hell or high water. Or, in this case, blackouts. Never mind that he made clear common sense and she didn't. Not only was she stubborn; she was reckless. And careless, too. Aphrodite O'Malley, goddess of the sea, obviously thrived on chaos.

Mitch opened his mouth to confess, then reconsidered. If she wanted to flirt with disaster, why should he care? He'd let her keep her dignity intact for a little while longer by playing along with her silly game of pretense.

After a few seconds of her struggling to keep pace, Mitch heard what he interpreted as an acquiescent sigh.

"Mr. Talbott—"

"Mitch."

"Mitch . . . stop."

"I wouldn't dream of it. You're an independent woman. You don't need advice from anyone. I respect that." Another step. Her fingers dug into his waist.

"Stop!"

"Why would I want to do that?" He took another step.

"I won't let you carry me because I'm—"

Mitch's shin hit something hard. He twisted and tumbled over it. *A lounge chair.* There was a clatter, a whoosh of air from his lungs, a startled exclamation, a thud.

Mitch fell onto his back in the sand, his legs sprawled over the chair. Aphrodite landed facedown on top of him, her breasts pressed against his bare chest where his unbuttoned shirt fell open. On reflex, his arms went around her, both palms settling on her rump.

"I'm naked!" She gasped.

"I noticed."

"Let go of me!" Claire's heart pounded as she scrambled up, favoring her injured left foot.

"Let me remind you, lady, it wasn't my idea to stumble around in the dark. I warned you this might happen." He paused a moment, and when he spoke again, she detected a hint of humor in his tone. "Though at the time I warned you I had no idea how much fun it would be."

"You *knew*, didn't you? You knew I was naked."

"What if I did?"

She hugged herself to cover her breasts. "Why didn't you say something?"

"I didn't want to embarrass you."

"And you think this didn't?"

"Hey, it also wasn't my idea to stroll around stark naked on the beach."

"Very funny. For your information, I wasn't strolling; I was swimming. And if you think for one minute I believe you were trying not to embarrass me by keeping your mouth shut, then you can think again. You enjoyed making me look like a fool."

"If you would've just admitted you were naked, I would've offered my shirt. End of problem."

"How was I supposed to know you're not some weirdo who'd take advantage of the situation?"

"After that fall, the thought crossed my mind. But no need to worry. I'm a gentleman. Not that it's ever gotten me anywhere."

An awkward silence ensued. Finally Claire huffed a sigh. "You filmed me, didn't you?"

"It's my job."

"How much did you see?"

"Not as much as I would've liked."

Claire closed her eyes. "Oh, God. You know what I look like. If I left you right now, tomorrow you'd see me and know who I am."

"Not unless you're walking around in the buff."

"But you saw me."

"I wasn't looking at your face."

She hugged herself tighter. "Very funny. So you don't know what my face looks like?"

"You can rest easy. I didn't follow you. I just happened to stumble upon you right at the start of your very intriguing strip-tease. I tried to see your face, but it was too dark and I was too far away." He whistled a tune beneath his breath. "By the way, you have talent. If you're ever in need of a job, there's a little club back in L.A.—"

158

"You are *so* amusing." Claire tapped her uninjured toe in the sand. She was cold . . . and still in a precarious situation should the lights come on. "Does the offer of your shirt still stand?"

"I'm taking it off now. Here."

She groped the air until she came in contact with the garment in Mitch's outstretched hand. "Thanks."

Instinctively she turned her back to him, slipped it on, and began to button up. The crisp cotton felt stiff, almost scratchy, against her bare skin. "When did it die?"

"When did what die?"

"Your shirt. Must've been a while back. Rigor mortis has already set in."

"I don't think you're in a position to complain."

She couldn't argue with that.

A single raindrop drenched the end of Claire's nose. Another plopped onto the nape of her neck. Lightning bursts provided a moment of vision. Claire looked over her shoulder, but before she caught a glimpse of Mitch, the world went black again. Exasperated, she listened to the grumbling thunder and finished buttoning his shirt.

"My place is behind us," Mitch said. "I saw it again in that flash of lightning. Are you decent?"

"Depends on who you ask."

Mitch laughed. "What I meant was, are you dressed yet?"

"Yes." This time she didn't flinch when his arm found her waist and encircled it. Leaning into him, Claire placed an arm around his waist, too. Careful to walk on only the ball of her wounded foot, she moved guardedly alongside him.

"How's that heel?" he asked.

"It hurts like crazy."

"Sure you don't want me to try carrying you now that you're dressed? I don't mind."

"I'm not *that* dressed."

"Have it your way. We'll take it one step at a time."

It seemed his previous irritation with her had eased a bit.

Realizing how other men might've treated a woman in this situation, she found herself believing Mitch Talbott might actually be a gentleman, after all, not the madman she'd first thought him to be.

A steady, gentle rain began to fall as they inched toward his cabana. Overhead, palm trees swished with a sudden rise of the wind. Mitch stopped. "Here's the porch. Two short steps up. Careful."

They took the steps slowly. Upon reaching the top, they were shielded from the weather. Raindrops hammered overhead on what Claire guessed must be an extended tin roof. She heard a rattle, then a squeak as Mitch opened the door.

The sound muffled only slightly once they stepped inside. "I'll try to find a flashlight or some candles," he said. "But no matter what, nobody's going anywhere until this storm passes."

Shivering, Claire released Mitch's hand and hugged herself. His shirt, now damp and limp, clung to her like a second skin. Her teeth clicked together.

"We'd better get dry or we'll catch pneumonia," he told her. "My clothes are in the bedroom. Have a seat while I look for a light and get some things together. The couch is about five steps ahead of you."

"Thanks." Arms outstretched, Claire limped forward, counting each step. Mitch was nothing if not precise. When she reached five her toe bumped something. She leaned forward and patted nubby-textured cushions with her palms. She collapsed onto the sofa, realizing for the first time how grubby and miserable she felt. Sand coated her feet. Her lips were parched from salt water, as was her skin, with the exception of the clammy area covered by Mitch's wet shirt.

"I couldn't find a flashlight or any candles," Mitch said when he returned. "But here's my robe, a dry shirt, and a pair of shorts. Where are you?"

"Here." The clothes hit her face then fell around her.

"Take whatever you want."

"Would you mind if I borrow your shower? I itch."

"Help yourself. I'll lead you to it."

Scooping up the clothing in one arm, Claire probed for Mitch's hand with the other. Her fingers landed upon his stomach instead, her thumb settling atop his naval. The skin there was warm—smooth, firm, and dusted with coarse hair. She snatched back her hand. "Oops. Excuse me."

"No problem," Mitch muttered, his voice hoarse again. His hand covered hers. "Ready?"

Ready, willing, and able. Stunned by the direction of her thoughts, Claire reined in her galloping libido and silently scolded herself for her brief escape into fantasy. Not only was Mitch a stranger, but she'd made a decision, a promise to herself: she would do whatever it took to bring James back to his senses . . . back to her. And though becoming more bold and daring and exciting might help her to recapture her fiancé's interest, she didn't think James would like her taking an eyes-closed, headfirst plunge into temptation with Mitch Talbott.

True, James might very well deserve a taste of his own medicine, but she liked to think she was above using a man like Mitch for petty revenge.

Chapter Four

When Aphrodite finished in the bathroom, Mitch took a shower. A cold one, though the tank held plenty of hot water. Making his way around in the dark searching for soap and shampoo was a trick. Dressing was no easier feat. Somehow he managed to locate his first-aid kit in the medicine cabinet. He took it with him to join his guest on the couch. "Let's look at that cut. Put your leg in my lap."

After she removed the towel she'd wrapped around her heel, he felt her shift sideways to comply. Mitch skimmed his fingers down her calf. "Guide my hand to the spot."

She grasped his fingers and slid them to the sole of her foot. "Right here. Careful. Ouch! That's the spot."

"I'm going to use some disinfectant. It might sting." Mitch kept one hand on her foot while he fumbled inside the kit for alcohol and cotton. He spilled half the bottle on his pants while attempting to soak the cotton ball. Finally he applied the cotton to the wound. He heard her quick intake of breath, but contin-

163

ued. When he lifted her foot and blew on the abrasion to dry the alcohol, she shivered.

The darkness made the procedure seem all the more intimate, and he tried to concentrate on anything but her. The wind raging outside. The muted stutter of rain on the roof. The antiseptic odor in the air. Still, he noticed her foot was long and slender, her ankle small and smooth.

It took another ten minutes to rummage up a bandage and place it over the cut. That done, Mitch lowered the kit to the floor. "That ought to do until tomorrow. You might have the doctor check to see if you need a stitch or two."

"Thanks, I'll do that."

They sat in awkward silence. Mitch smelled the fragrance of shampoo in her hair, the clean scent of her skin. "So . . . how are you faring in the game?" he finally asked.

"Okay. But I'll have to do better if I'm going to win."

"You don't sound like you're enjoying it."

"It's not something I'd sign up for again."

"What? No prospects?" When she didn't respond, he added, "Potential husbands, I mean."

"You live to tease, don't you? I admit it's not working out like I expected. But, since I'm here, I might as well go after the money and the trip."

"And if, in the process, you just happen to fall in love . . . You said that, too," he reminded her.

"And you're not going to let me forget it, are you?" She shifted. "What about you? You never told me why you took this job when you have such contempt for reality TV."

"I'm trying to get in on a future Hawkeye project. A documentary Michael Hawkins is planning on filming in a remote area of Africa next year." He braced himself for her laughter, waited for her to tell him he was wasting his time. He'd heard it all before. From his father and more than one girlfriend just before the door slammed behind them. Everyone knew Michael Hawkins hired only top talent when it came to his serious projects. The man had won Oscars for his documentaries. Who did Mitch think he was, anyway?

"How exciting!" she said, catching him off guard, bringing his chin up. "Any luck?"

"Not yet." The weight of frustration he felt over that fact was becoming as familiar as his camera on his shoulder. "The guy's hardly ever around, as you probably well know."

"Not really. I haven't paid much attention."

"I think programs like *Eden* are only a means to an end for Hawkins. A way of financing the projects he's really interested in pursuing."

"Sounds as if the two of you have something in common then. You're using *Eden* as a means to an end, as well."

"So are you. The money, the trip, that heartthrob you just might fall for."

"Here we go again," she said with exasperation.

"You ever been married, Aphrodite?"

"No."

"Smart girl."

"I take it you have?"

"I came close once." *Damn.* How had they maneuvered themselves to this subject? He'd rather pluck a nose hair than discuss his breakup with Sarah.

"Well, just because your relationship didn't work out doesn't mean everyone is destined for failure. I assume staying unattached is top priority for you?"

"Exactly. No marriages, no divorces. It seems pretty simple to me. Which is why I just don't understand all these people clamoring to get hitched."

Mitch told himself it was stupid to be telling her all this when he could be instigating some fun and a little relaxation instead. Circumstances had provided him with the perfect opportunity. Pitch darkness, seclusion. An almost naked woman. And here he sat, philosophizing about marriage.

"Let's change the subject," he said. "I'm boring you."

"No, go on. You're not boring me at all. I'd like to hear a man's perspective on the subject of marriage."

"Okay. Let's just say that Sarah, my ex, wasn't honest with me. I was up-front with her from the start about what I wanted to do with my life. She pretended to be okay with it. Until she had my ring on her finger, that is. Then she set out to change my way of thinking."

"So you believe that's the problem with relationships these days? A lack of truthfulness?"

He nodded. "Not just these days. Since the beginning of time. A man and woman meet. They play up the good points about themselves and gloss over the bad. Or leave them out altogether. If there's chemistry, they each say what they think the other wants to hear." Mitch shrugged. "That's the way it is. People should learn to accept it and not get caught up in all the romantic garbage."

"I think you're talking about your own experience, not people in general."

Maybe so, Mitch thought. He'd been given the shaft by more women than Sarah. Maybe he'd become cynical when it came to the man-woman thing.

"A lot of couples have honest relationships," she insisted. "My parents, for instance. They've been together thirty years."

"How do you know they're honest with each other?"

"I can tell. It's obvious."

"Things aren't always what they seem."

A rhythmic beat competed with the patter of rain on the roof. Mitch realized her uninjured foot tapped the floor. "Okay," she said, "let's examine your theory. Suppose you and I just met."

"We did."

"But suppose there wasn't a blackout. What if we could see each other and we were both attracted?"

Intrigued by the direction in which she guided the discussion, Mitch flexed his fingers. He waited a heartbeat, clenched his teeth, then placed a hand on her thigh. "Who says you have to be able to see someone to be drawn to them?"

Lightning flashed at the window. She jumped at the following crack of thunder, then quickly removed her foot from his lap. "Don't be cute," she said. "If we'd just met, liked what we saw, and were both open to starting something, according to your theory you'd tell me a favorable thing about yourself. Enhancing the facts a bit, of course. Then you'd avoid exposing anything unfavorable. Correct?"

Mitch grinned. "That about sums it up."

"What's one true thing you'd tell me about yourself?"

"Who's your ideal man?"

"You didn't answer my question."

"Answer mine first," Mitch insisted.

"Let's see. Tom Hanks's sensitivity, an Abercrombie and Fitch model's body, and Brad Pitt's looks, I guess."

"Okay. I'd hold the door open for you, pull out your chair, then tell you I'm a muscle-bound, bronzed blond with a scruffy five-o'clock shadow."

"No fair," she said. "I could see that for myself."

"But you can't now, can you?"

"This is supposed to be hypothetical, and that was supposed to be the honest thing you'd tell me. I can't wait to hear what you'd avoid."

Mitch scratched his chin. "Well, *if* I were attracted to you, and *if* I reacted like most men, I'd probably be smart not to tell you what we've already touched on."

"Refresh my memory."

"I don't think I'm long-term material when it comes to becoming involved with the opposite sex." Which was why he'd been dumped so many times, he guessed. "Women want forever. Stability. A home. I want to traipse around the world with my camera. And basically all I own right now, all I care to own, fits in a suitcase. Women don't usually like to hear that sort of thing."

"Oh, I don't know. Some women are turned on by a challenge."

He leaned closer to her. "Speaking for yourself?"

"Don't jump to conclusions."

Enjoying himself, Mitch grinned. "The fact that women like a challenge is exactly what I'm talking about. Sarah didn't care what I wanted; she only cared about changing me into what suited her."

"Sarah's not every woman."

"And you're not making sense. First you plug honesty. Then you say women like a challenge. For instance, a man who needs to be changed. In their opinion, I might add."

"I didn't—"

"Just a minute. It's your turn," he said. "In this hypothetical situation, what truthful bit of information would you reveal? Your name might be a good start."

"I'd rather tell you about my business," she said smugly, smoothly bypassing the bait he'd dangled. "My grandparents and their best friends started a feed and tackle store in Prairie two generations ago. Their children, one of whom was my father, inherited it. And now it's mine. At least half of it is. I . . ." She coughed. "I have a partner."

Mitch tried to imagine the soft, sweet-smelling woman beside him selling feed and tackle . . . and couldn't. "Do you like the business?"

He thought he felt her shrug. "It's what I do."

"That's no answer."

She seemed to hesitate. "I've never really thought about it. I grew up knowing I'd inherit it. There was never any question in my mind that I'd make it my business."

If anything, she sounded indifferent about her occupation. Mitch didn't blame her. Feed and tackle wouldn't thrill him, either. "So what would you lie to me about?"

"Lie to you?"

"Your hypothetical situation, remember? Where the two of

168

us meet, et cetera, et cetera. You've told me one truthful thing about yourself. What would you lie about?"

"Nothing."

"Not even your *name*?" he asked, smiling.

She sniffed. "I don't agree with your theory."

"Come on. Surely there's *something* you wouldn't eagerly confess to a potential love interest." When she didn't respond, he asked what he'd been itching to know since he'd watched her strip on the beach. "How about an explanation as to why you were naked when I found you tonight?"

"I already told you I was swimming."

"Most people wear a suit."

"I like to swim naked. I do it all the time."

Now, there was a lie if he'd ever heard one. She sounded about as convincing as a kid assuring a teacher the dog ate his homework. "At night? In the ocean? With a storm on the way? You don't seem stupid. You must know that's dangerous."

"I've always done crazy, spontaneous things." She gave a jittery laugh. "Wild and unpredictable, that's me. It drives my family and friends nuts."

Mitch wondered if she heard what he did in her voice. Uncertainty. Fear. A woman trying to convince herself of something. "Well, control yourself when you're alone on the island. I'd hate to find out something bad happened to you."

An image flashed to mind of her standing naked at the ocean's edge, a silhouette, waves lapping at her feet.

On impulse, Mitch leaned forward, then just as quickly pulled back. He thought of the contract with the show that forbade him from cozying up to competitors.

Thunder rumbled.

He thought of the lights from the resort casting a hazy glow on her slick, wet body.

His heart bounced haphazardly against his chest.

"To hell with the rules." Mitch leaned toward her again.

"What?"

"Nothing." Misjudging the location of her mouth, his lips brushed the tip of her nose instead. It reminded him of eighth grade, when the girl he'd loved to distraction turned her head at the crucial moment, landing his tongue in her ear. "Sorry," Mitch muttered.

"That's okay," she answered softly.

He gave it another shot, and this time hit his target.

Chapter Five

Claire couldn't remember when anything had felt as good as Mitch's mouth on hers. At first it was little more than a silky whisk of lips. Then warm, thick tension twisted inside her, and she allowed him to deepen the kiss. He cupped her face in his palms, and Claire shifted to wrap her arms around his neck.

When he finally broke away from her, she had to remind herself to breathe. *I'll tell him about James and end this here and now.* "Name your ideal woman," she murmured instead, sliding her hands through his hair.

"Tall and slender." He kissed her again. "Impulsive."

She laughed, flattered by his observations. "You're playing it safe. Tell me what she looks like."

"She looks like you."

"No fair."

"It doesn't matter what she looks like," Mitch said.

"You're not getting out of this."

He touched her damp head. "Her hair is short and wavy."

"Go on."

He released an exasperated breath. "Okay. Brunette. Eyes dark, skin brown."

Claire thought of the coloring she'd inherited from both of her Irish parents: red hair, green eyes, skin easily burned by the sun. The exact opposite of what he'd described. She'd already lent credence to his theory about men and women and dishonesty by not telling him she was engaged. What was one more little indiscretion? "I thought you said you didn't see me?"

"You're joking."

"Nope. People tell me I'm very exotic-looking. Guess it's my Latin heritage."

"But your name's O'Malley."

"Oh, that. My father is Irish. The Latin blood comes from my mother," Claire lied. She tried out her sexiest Mae West impression. "I inherited her dark looks along with her hourglass hips and buxom chest."

"You forget. I've seen you . . . and *felt* you naked. Not that I'm complaining. Buxom isn't my thing."

His hands moved down her back. Claire was acutely conscious of the fact that she wore nothing beneath Mitch's T-shirt and shorts, and suddenly afraid of what the two of them had started. She'd never intended her first taste of recklessness to turn into a feast.

"Mitch," she said, easing away from him. "We really shouldn't be doing this. We both have a lot to lose."

"Didn't you say you were famous for being wild?"

Thunder rattled the windows. Wind creaked in the rafters. "Yes . . . I said that."

"Don't change now. Be wild with me."

She caught her lower lip between her teeth, afraid of what he implied, afraid of the emotions churning inside her. Desire. Temptation. Fear. A dash of irritation.

"I like you, Aphrodite, and I think you like me."

"I like my hairdresser, Raoul, too, but you won't catch me crawling into bed with him."

Claire had been dubbed "Most Serious Senior" in her high school yearbook. But Mitch's laughter made her feel like Lucille Ball reincarnated.

"Maybe not," he said between hoots, "but have you ever tumbled naked on a beach with Raoul?"

It had been a long time since anyone had brought a smile to Mitch's face, much less made him laugh as easily as this woman had tonight. But when the muscles in Claire's back tensed beneath his fingers, Mitch suddenly sensed the tug-of-war going on in her head. He chided himself for causing it. She was right to resist. They were strangers . . . and he was out of line.

Mitch listened to the staccato beat of rain against the roof, remembering the kiss they'd just shared, the way his heart had slammed against his chest at that first tentative touch of their lips, the desire that had risen like an almighty wave to consume him. He removed his arm from her shoulder. "I wasn't implying we should go to bed together."

"You weren't? I mean, I just thought . . ." She groaned. "Boy, oh, boy, I really put my foot in it this time."

"Not that the idea of sleeping with a sea goddess doesn't appeal to me, but what I really had in mind was raiding the refrigerator and pantry."

"Sounds good to me," she said. "I'm starved. Let's make a game of it. I can guess what I'm eating."

Mitch found his way slowly into the tiny adjoining kitchen. He rummaged around in the dark, then returned minutes later with paper goods, a bottle of wine, and a sack full of assorted stuff from the pantry. After some awkward maneuvering in the dark, they sat opposite each other in the middle of the floor, the groceries between them.

"Ready for a taste test?" Mitch asked, straining to see, hoping for more than the occasional hint of her vague silhouette.

"Bring it on."

"Hold your nose."

173

"Why?"

"The smell might give it away."

There was a pop, then a crackling of paper. Mitch grinned. "Here you go."

"You sure I won't regret this?"

"Trust me." Her breath fanned warm against his hand as she took a bite.

"Ughh! It tastes like a cracker topped with slimy dead fish smothered in mustard."

"It is a cracker topped with dead fish smothered in mustard. Sardines." He heard a sputtering sound and guessed she had spit the sardines into the napkin he'd shoved into her hand. "I take it you don't like them?"

"You take it right. By the way, next time you say to trust you, I'll think twice."

They continued their picnic, concluding with wine from paper cups. And sometime during it all, every ounce of tension Mitch had carried around since arriving on the island slipped free and disappeared. The tile floor was cool beneath his skin. He leaned back on his forearms, full and content. "How about some music?"

"Don't tell me. In addition to being a cameraman and a junk-food connoisseur, you're also a musician."

"Afraid not. But I do have a radio. Battery operated." Mitch gathered up their trash and set it aside. He scooted backward toward the couch, then felt around atop an end table until he located the small radio. After switching it on, he turned the dial. "Let's see, our musical options are Reggae, reggae, or reggae. And all with a good deal of static. What's your pleasure?"

"Reggae would be nice."

"Good choice. I was afraid you might say Tejano, considering all that Latin blood running through your veins."

The sound of her laughter aroused him. That wouldn't have worried him much if it were only lust stirring. While his ra-

174

tionality battled his instincts, he sat back and listened to the music.

After a minute, Mitch felt her fingers brush his arm. "Let's dance," she said.

The shorts Claire had borrowed from Mitch after her shower hung loose on her hips. Through the fabric of her T-shirt, she felt his hands, large and warm against her back. Because of her bandaged foot, she couldn't dance to the wild beat of the music playing on the radio, so, laughing at themselves, they swayed to an awkward rhythm of their own.

She wondered how she could feel so secure in his arms—the arms of a man she'd just met, a man whom, as far as she knew, she'd never seen. But she did feel secure, and she felt other things, too. Emotions that had nothing remotely to do with safety.

Her heart beat much too fast and, as if to compensate for her lack of vision, her other senses became fine-tuned. The pace of Mitch's breath was slow and even, the length of his body lean and solid. He smelled like Dove soap and warm male skin. And when he lifted her chin to kiss her, his lips tasted faintly of wine . . . and sardines, but she found the secondhand flavor more to her liking.

The song's tempo increased and they spun once, then crumpled to the floor, out of breath and laughing. Mitch tugged the cushions off the couch and they stretched out side by side on top of them, talking and teasing.

Claire pushed aside thoughts of James and the game. She tried not to analyze the reasons why, since the moment she'd met Mitch, she'd avoided telling him she had a fiancé. After the past few days of heartache and humiliation and fruitless competition, it felt good to just relax and be herself. Yes, she wanted to marry James; that hadn't changed. But she refused to turn away from this moment; she wouldn't question the right or wrong of it. Not once in the past had she fantasized about a secret lover, a one-night rendezvous. But now the prospect tantalized her. One night of carefree pleasure. No strings . . . no commitments.

"You're a great dancer," Mitch said.

"And you're a terrible liar. I'm clumsy and gangly even when both feet are working. Always have been. You, on the other hand, have been concealing your true identity. You're really John Travolta. That's some rhythm you've got. What else have you been keeping from me?"

"Let's see. I've been called obsessive and self-centered by a woman or two."

"Self-centered, huh?"

"Yeah. And one of them even followed up that accusation by saying something derogatory about my mother."

"Your mother?" Claire mulled that over for a second.

"She said something to the effect of 'you obsessive, self-centered son of a bitch.' "

Claire choked out a laugh. "That was rude."

"That's what I thought, too. She'd never even met Mom."

He fingers gently tapped on Claire's forearm, keeping time with the music. "What else do your old girlfriends say about you?" she asked.

"I seem to recall the words 'control freak.' And then there was 'problem avoider.' " He paused. "No, it was 'conflict avoider,' I believe."

"Are you?"

"I don't know." She felt his shoulders lift, then lower. "Maybe. I don't like being pushed into a corner, if that's what it means. I don't like being caught off guard, either. As far as I'm concerned, the fewer surprises, the better."

"You kind of bombed out this trip, didn't you? First the storm, the blackout, then me? I'd say that's quite a few surprises in one day."

"The weather can't always be predicted. Neither can power outages. But you can bet I'll never travel again without a flashlight and fresh batteries in my suitcase. Now, as for you, stumbling across a goddess every now and then is a nice surprise. I don't mind that kind."

Claire trailed a finger across his collarbone. "I'm not usually a surprise, nice or otherwise. I lied to you earlier about being impulsive. I'm normally dull and predictable. This is the first time I've ever been spontaneous."

"Being on *Eden*, or skinny-dipping?"

"Both. And this. You and me. Here. Now. I normally avoid setting myself up for future regrets."

"Why do you think you'll regret this?"

Anxiety forged a jittery path toward the pit of Claire's stomach. Beneath the banter, the conversation had somehow turned serious. "You don't believe in romance or commitment. I do. Still, here we are together, and I'm liking it very much. There you have it—the perfect recipe for future regrets on my part."

"What's wrong with just enjoying the time we have together?"

"You mean tonight?"

"I mean however long we're both on the island."

Claire took her hand from Mitch's shoulder. "Even if our being together weren't against the rules, we're too different." She forced lightness to her tone. "We'd only leave each other with bad memories."

"We have things in common," Mitch insisted. "You're a woman who likes to swim naked; I like women who like to swim naked. See there?"

"Ha, ha. You're such a comedian."

Mitch took her hand in his and pressed a gentle kiss into the palm. "You're beautiful."

She smiled. He made it too easy to forget about James and the game, her inhibitions, and everything else. "How do you know I'm beautiful? You've never even seen me."

"I don't have to see you."

Starting at her forehead, his fingers moved down her face, touching her eyes, her cheekbones, her nose and mouth. "Your skin is smooth," he said quietly. As if on cue, the music changed to a soft, romantic tune. "Your eyes . . . they slant some. Your nose turns up. Your lips are full."

Pleasure shimmied through her before the worries and guilt she'd just pushed aside returned full force. Why had she allowed this to happen? She wanted Mitch Talbott, and he was giving every signal that if she just said the word, she could have him. At least for a while. But that was impossible. She belonged with James. They owned a business together. They shared a history. A future. Just last month they'd started the wheels in motion to buy a house.

Claire leaned away from Mitch and forced herself to think about James. She couldn't risk doing anything that might ruin her plan of getting her life back on track.

"Mitch, there's something I should tell you."

"It doesn't matter." He slid his hands beneath her shirt to leisurely rub her back. "So your hair's really purple and you have a tattoo on your forehead. I can live with that."

"Mitch, seriously—"

"You talk too much."

She didn't protest when his mouth covered hers, ending any further discussion.

He didn't press for more, only talked and touched and held her close through the night.

Later, with his hands still warm beneath her shirt, Claire nestled against him, listening to the steady beat of his heart. Mitch had fallen asleep.

She wished she could be as lucky.

Chapter Six

Mitch tossed a handful of peanuts into his mouth. He still had a few minutes left on his dinner break. Then he would return to the confession booth to film more of the same dim-witted babble he'd listened to all day. Until then, though, he didn't want to think about the game.

A few feet away, in a shimmering turquoise pool, couples splashed and dunked and shrieked. Others reclined a safe splashing distance from the water, eyes hidden behind dark glasses, oil-slicked bodies bared to the receding sun.

Mitch scowled. How was he supposed to forget about the game of *Eden* when the playing pieces lay scattered everywhere? He shifted toward the resort's large outside deck. Overlooking the ocean, it offered a view of the crimson sun as it slowly melted into the water. Couples were arriving for dinner. Mitch studied faces, looking for a woman who fit the description of the goddess he'd met last night. Aphrodite O'Malley. He hadn't run across her today. At least if he had, he didn't know it.

Reaching inside the canvas drawstring bag at his side, he retrieved her emerald-green bikini and studied it. *Swimsuit*, he amended. Modest by *Eden*'s standards. He shifted his attention from the sculpted bra top to the high-waisted, shortlike bottoms. Modest by *anyone*'s standards. Anyone born in the last three decades, at least. On his way to work, he'd found it beneath a tree across from his cabana. The suit smelled faintly of jasmine.

A dark-skinned man with cottony-white hair, his teeth squared-off pearls, approached from the other side of the bar. He lifted Mitch's half-empty bottle of beer, then set it down again. "You no done yet, mon?"

Frowning, Mitch peered up at the bartender's fine, weather-worn features. "What do you make of this, Winston?" He extended the swimsuit for the older man's inspection.

Winston took the bra top and bottoms, dangling each separately between the thumb and index fingers of both hands. "Forgive me, mon, but if I must explain de clothing of a woman to you, I know why you live alone."

"I know what it is." Mitch raised his eyes to the thatched roof overhead. "I'm asking about the fragrance. Do you recognize it?"

"You ask de right man when it come to da ladies." With a deep, rich chuckle, he pressed the fabric to his nose and breathed deeply. "Yea, mon. I think it is Poison."

"I should've guessed," Mitch grumbled. She'd poisoned his mind, all right. Taking the garments from Winston, he placed them on top of the counter and stared at them while twisting a green strap around one finger. So she wore Poison. That was a start. But what else did he know about Aphrodite O'Malley other than the scent of her perfume and the fact that she'd lied about her name? He knew she stood five feet, nine or ten inches in height, possessed long, slender, silky legs, a contagious laugh, a powerful stubborn streak. And she had a penchant for swimming in the nude.

He gave the strap another twist. What else? Her hair was short and dark, or so she'd said. And her husky Texas drawl was his new definition of sexy.

Mitch heaved a sigh that sounded more like a groan. He knew the shape of the woman's features, the taste of her lips, the feel of her. And, despite his resolve to follow the rules for the sake of his job, he knew he ached to find her, to meet her a second time, to see her.

Mitch glanced up at the bartender. "What do you think, buddy? Would the sort of woman who wore that suit and that perfume be worth sidetracking your plans over?"

Winston picked up Mitch's bottle again then wiped a damp cloth across the counter. "Big plans?"

"They're important."

"And de lady?"

"She's . . ." Mitch recalled the sound of her laughter.

The bartender's teeth flashed against his dark skin, his smile all-knowing. "Don't worry. You are not de first brother to fall. She is an *Eden* player?"

Mitch quickly met the other man's eyes.

Winston lifted a hand. "Your secret is mine, mon."

Relieved, Mitch nodded his thanks. "I stumbled across her during the blackout. She stayed at my place all night, then ducked out this morning before I woke up."

The bartender's eyelids lowered to half-mast. Chuckling, he pressed a hand to his heart. "You in big trouble. Next time we link up, I will tell yuh a story or two. Mebbe Winston can show yuh how to romance de lady."

Mitch pointed out a moisture droplet on the counter. "You missed a spot," he said, and then reached for more peanuts. The last thing he needed was to romance an *Eden* contestant and jeopardize his plans for the career he'd been pursuing for as long as he could remember. He needed to find this particular goddess and confirm that she was nothing more than a seductive, though unconsummated, one-night stand.

"She disappeared," he muttered, wishing he could get her off his mind and proceed with his previous plans. But he couldn't stop thinking of her. Nothing he'd seen or done today had nudged her from his thoughts.

Mitch looked over his shoulder. He was pitiful. A poolside of bathing beauties just footsteps away and, for the life of him, he couldn't kindle one spark of enthusiasm. "I don't even know which one she is," he mumbled to no one in particular as he pushed to his feet.

"Go along 'bout yuh business. You don't need help wit dat problem. Your lady wants to be found." The bartender tugged at the bra top Mitch held. "Why else she leave this behind for you, brother?"

Ignoring her friend's pacing, Claire gave her toenails one last inspection before putting aside the pink polish, then sliding off the bed. She'd had time to paint only the first three toes of each foot. No matter. The others wouldn't show in her sandals.

"Good Lord, Claire," Ally Kendall said, nibbling at a cuticle. "We were supposed to meet Rico, James, Marcus, and that horrible Darla bimbo five minutes ago. Would you please hurry?"

"Brimbeau."

Ally stopped short and frowned at Claire. "What?"

"Darla's last name. It's Brimbeau, not Bimbo."

"Whatever." The pacing resumed. "You've already missed breakfast and lunch. You don't want to miss dinner, too, do you? The first challenge of the second round is tonight."

Ally was a fellow Texan and one of the few contestants Claire had met so far whose company she truly enjoyed. During the first two weeks of the game, they'd been in the same group at dinner on more than one occasion. "Don't be so nervous," Claire said. "James will understand if we're a little late. I'm sure the others will, too."

Pulling her finger from her mouth, Ally stopped in front of Claire. "Aren't *you* nervous? Or even the least little bit antsy?" She waved her hands as if trying to catch Claire's attention.

"Hello? This is James we're talking about here. You and James are meant to be. That's all I've heard from you since we met. But where were you last night when lover lips was playing blind-man's buff in the dark with Darla and the rest of the bimbo brigade? And where were you all day today when you could've been keeping an eye on him? If you've lost interest in your fiancé, the least you can do is help me watch out for Damien."

Claire continued to blow on her wet toenails.

Ally tapped her foot. "Are you going to tell me where you were during the blackout last night?" Her foot tapped faster. "Do you think James'll be happy when he finds out you stayed out all night?"

Claire limped to the closet for her sandals, trying to concentrate on the routine of getting ready. Trying to dodge the memories that hurtled toward her like baseballs in a batting cage. The tousled head of black hair she'd seen when she first opened her eyes this morning. The weight of Mitch's arm draped across her waist. The heat of his palm on her breast. She glanced over her shoulder at Ally. "You're the only one who knows about it. James won't find out unless you tell him."

Ally wiggled her eyebrows and grinned. "Maybe I should. You seem . . . I don't know . . . different. In a good way. It's not like you to straggle in at dawn after a night of doing Lord knows what." She winked. "Come on, 'fess up now. Which one of the guys were you with? He must've been something if he's swaying you away from James."

"Nobody's swaying me away from James. I wasn't doing anything wrong." *Not that it didn't cross my mind.*

"Of course you weren't. There's not a thing in the world wrong with playing the field. In case you weren't aware, that's what this game's all about, Claire. If you score a point or two along the way, all the better."

Afraid the heat suffusing her cheeks told more than she cared to admit, Claire averted her eyes from Ally's scrutiny. But the memories came at her again, catching her off guard when they hit, shattering her composure. She thought of Mitch's olive-hued skin. His long, lean body. The sprinkle of silver dusting the hair above his ears. *Think about something else. Anything.* She threw three pairs of shoes behind her into the center of the room before finding her sandals.

"Don't think you can pull one over on me, Claire Louise Mulligan," Ally said, wagging her finger, her smile still in place. "I've gotten to know you like the back of my own hand. And I'm not blind. You turned up this morning wearing a man's shirt and pants and little else. You looked like you'd slept in the eye of a hurricane. I want the juicy details. All of them."

"I wandered too far down the beach last night, is that juicy enough for you? I was out of the boundaries when the lights went out. Thankfully, a guy stumbled upon me." *He has laugh lines around his eyes and a crease on his left cheek that probably turns into a dimple when he smiles.* Claire swallowed, hoping her voice wouldn't betray the scattered rhythm of her pulse. "We managed to make our way to his cabana before the storm hit."

"So he's one of the contestants?"

Claire bit her lower lip. "Can you keep a secret?"

Ally leaned forward and nodded.

"He's a cameraman."

"Now we're getting somewhere." Ally moved to the bed and sat. "Go on."

"There's nothing more to tell. We fell asleep and, when I woke up this morning, I left. End of story."

"You can at least tell me what he looked like."

He'd been sleeping like a baby when she'd slipped out of his cabana at dawn. But Mitch was no baby; that was for sure. He'd looked very much like a full-grown man . . . a wonderfully rumpled one. "He looked like an average guy."

As Claire backed away from the closet and started toward the bed, Ally grabbed something off the nightstand and held it out, her expression amused.

"I don't like to wear my engagement ring in the water," Claire

NAME: _____

ADDRESS: _____

_____

_____

TELEPHONE: _____

E-MAIL: _____

_____ I want to pay by credit card.

__ Visa   __ MasterCard   __ Discover

Account Number: _____

Expiration date: _____

SIGNATURE: _____

*Send this form, along with $2.00 shipping
and handling for your FREE books, to:*

Love Spell Romance Book Club
20 Academy Street
Norwalk, CT 06850-4032

*Or fax (must include credit card
information!) to:* **610.995.9274.**
*You can also sign up on the Web
at* <u>www.dorchesterpub.com</u>.

Offer open to residents of the U.S. and
Canada only. Canadian residents, please
call 1.800.481.9191 for pricing information.

said, taking it and slipping it on. She'd never noticed before how tight it felt around her finger.

"Don't explain to me. It's James you should worry about."

Hobbling the remaining steps to the bed, Claire sat, then shoved her sandals on, ruining her six-toe pedicure. She winced as the leather strap rubbed against her bandaged heel. "Who knows? James might be thrilled to hear I spent time with another man. I'm starting to think this thing he's going through isn't temporary at all. Maybe he really wants to get rid of me. Maybe that's what coming on *Eden* was really all about. Maybe he doesn't want to marry me."

"Or he could just be playing hard to get. You know, to spice things up." Ally tapped her chin. "It might just work to your advantage to drop a few hints about last night. Make him jealous." Ally glanced down at Claire's ankle. "You never said what happened to your foot."

"I cut it on a rock or something during the blackout."

"So what are you going to tell James?"

"That I cut it on a rock or something during the blackout."

"Good Lord." Ally sighed and shook her head. "I meant about last night."

"I won't tell him anything."

"What if someone else besides me saw you coming in this morning and they say something to him? Everyone knows you and James are engaged. The show's producers are just slobbering for someone to come between the two of you. They're *encouraging* it." Ally giggled. "I wasn't supposed to tell you that. I'm also not supposed to tell you that they think you're pathetically boring. They're afraid you'll have viewers yawning, Claire."

Claire felt a surge of defensiveness. "Why's that?"

Ally raised a finger. "Number one, your unwavering devotion to James. It may be sweet, but it's not good for ratings." She lifted a second finger. "Then there's that gawd-awful two-piece swimsuit you wear. Has your belly button ever seen the light of day?"

Claire scowled. *Pathetically boring.* She hated being *pathetically* anything. "I don't really care what the producers think of me. As for James, if he asks about last night, I'll tell him just what I told you. The truth."

"Sure you will." Ally's grin looked wicked. "I think the producers are wrong about you, Claire Louise. You're pulling a fast one on everybody, acting like you're so prim and proper and all. I know better, though."

Claire gathered her guilt-strewn wits and stood. "Let's go. I need to make a quick stop by the confession booth before we go to dinner."

Ally scooted off the bed. "Thanks for reminding me. I have a confession or two of my own to make."

Mitch peered into the camera that sat behind the confession-booth curtain. *Eden's* creative team had decided contestants might speak more freely if they couldn't see the person filming them. It worked. Over the past couple of weeks, he'd heard intimate details explicit enough to make Hugh Hefner blush.

The contestant who'd just entered the booth sat in the chair facing the camera, then cleared his throat. "Damien Dimeola from Jersey," he said for the record, as all the contestants had been instructed to do.

Damien leaned back. Balancing on only two chair legs, he crossed his arms over his sculpted pecs, which were apparent despite the silky black dress shirt he wore. "Ally," he said, as if tasting the name. "Ally, Ally, Ally." His mouth curled up at one corner. "She wants me. *She*"—his brows bobbed—"*wants*"— they lifted and fell again—"*me.*" On the final bob, the chair legs hit the floor with a *thunk*.

Mitch lifted a brow of his own. *It's really a shame you don't have more confidence, buddy.*

Damien uncrossed his arms. "The woman hung on every

word I said. She was eating me up, you know what I'm sayin'?" He leaned in toward the camera. "Eating me up, I'm telling you. She couldn't even speak. The lady was speechless, she was so into me."

Ally wasn't the only one speechless. Mitch zoomed in for a close-up of Damien's smug face. *And what do you think of her?* he wanted to ask.

Damien saved him the trouble. "I think she thinks I'm the one for her. *The. One.* We're not in the same group for dinner tonight, so I'm gonna make her suffer some. Catch her eye while I'm giving the other chicks their chance. Make her work for it, you know what I'm sayin'?"

Yeah, yeah, yeah. I know what you're saying. Over the past two weeks, he'd waded through different versions of the same bullshit more times than he could count.

Tuning Damien out, Mitch let his thoughts meander to the modest green suit in the canvas bag at his feet. Maybe it was just his imagination, but he thought he could smell her perfume. Poison, the bartender had said. A more fitting brand name would've been Aphrodisiac.

He became so caught up in his thoughts of Aphrodite O'Malley that he didn't realize Damien had left until the door to the confession booth opened and a woman with shoulder-length curly brown hair stepped inside.

"Ally Kendall. Dallas, Texas," she said, taking her place in the chair.

Mitch snapped to attention. Ally Kendall. The woman who was "so into" Damien. He grinned. *This ought to be good.*

The woman nibbled on a cuticle a second, then examined her nails before lowering her hand to her lap. "How can I possibly express to you my deep feelings for Damien Dimeola?" she asked, staring directly into the camera. After a dreamy sigh, she opened her mouth wide and stuck a finger inside of it, gagging herself. "The only thing I found even remotely interesting about Damien was the crustacean hanging from his left nostril. Tenacious little ol' thing. I kept waiting for it to drop off, but it held tight all the way through dessert. I couldn't take my eyes off of it. Good Lord, the thing struck me mute."

Mitch didn't even try to muffle his laugh.

Ally scowled. "Why is it all my dates have been duds? Are there any men playing this game who won't bore me to tears? I'm starting to have my doubts." She tilted her head to one side. "Hmmm. Maybe I should just follow the lead of one so-called *committed* female contestant and look to the crew for a little fun on the side."

Startled by that last comment, Mitch waited to hear more, but Ally Kendall stood.

"Anyway, that's all I have to say about my last date. When it's time to boot someone off the island, Damien gets my vote." She turned, then glanced over her shoulder at the camera. "And when he leaves, he can take his crusty little friend with him." Opening the door, Ally stepped out.

Mitch leaned back away from the camera. That last little tidbit of information had been no slip-up. Ally had an agenda, no doubt about it. Before he had a minute to determine if her sly revelation had anything to do with him and the goddess, he heard someone else enter the booth.

Mitch peered into the lens of the camera and saw a woman. A redhead. Pretty. Hell, they were all pretty. Even Damien. Weary of it all, he slumped on his stool and yawned.

The woman sat in the chair facing the curtain, her back erect, her feet crossed at the ankles. Her toenail polish was a mess. She had something on her heel, too, though he couldn't tell what. He lifted his attention to her face. A sprinkle of freckles crossed her nose and fanned onto her cheeks. *Cute.* Mitch yawned again.

Lifting her chin, she stared at the camera . . . and blushed. "I . . ." Her left eye twitched. "This ritual is humiliating."

Mitch slammed his mouth shut and sat up straighter. *That sultry Texas drawl.* He'd recognize it anywhere. His foot hit the tripod the camera sat on and he had to grab quickly to keep it from toppling over.

"Everything okay back there?"

"Fine," he rasped.

"Okay, then. I'm Claire Mulligan from Prairie, Texas."

So she wasn't a complete liar. At least the Prairie, Texas, part had been true.

"I think I know what you're hoping I'll say. You'd just love to hear that James and I are on the outs, that he's playing hoochie-coochie behind my back or that I'm doing so behind his."

Mitch frowned. *James? James who?*

"Conflict is intriguing," Claire went on. "So is deceit. And that's what this show's all about, right?"

Mitch opened his mouth to answer her, then remembered she spoke to the camera, not him.

"Well, I'm afraid I'm going to disappoint you by being *pathetically boring—*"

Pathetically boring? Aphrodite, goddess of the sea? Born of Uranus's genital sea foam? Mitch thought of her striptease on the beach last night. Even from a distance, even considering the fact that, at the time, he couldn't see every gorgeous detail he was looking at now, she'd knocked his socks off. Or she would've if he'd been wearing any. Claire Mulligan . . . alias Aphrodite O'Malley . . . was definitely the least pathetically boring woman he'd met so far on this island. As a matter of fact, she was the least boring woman he'd ever met, period.

"But the simple truth is," Claire continued, "James and I will leave this island every bit as committed as we were the day we arrived, if not more so."

Committed. That was the word Ally had used in reference to the player who'd "looked to the crew for a little fun on the side." The puzzle pieces began to snap into place in Mitch's mind. He recalled talk of one committed couple competing among the other contestants. An engaged couple the producers had tossed into the mix of singles to see if they stuck together or were ripped apart. Of course, being producers, they hoped for the latter. This was prime time television, after all. He had never met up with the couple because, during the first round of the show, they had not been in the group of contestants he'd been assigned to follow and film.

Claire lowered her gaze to her pink polish–smeared toenails and kept it there. "Nothing's changed. Nothing except . . ." She glanced up at the camera and burst into tears. "Nothing except the fact that I've become a total and complete liar."

Not a very good one, either, Mitch thought. Damn, he hated it when women cried. It was all he could do not to part the curtain and go out to comfort her.

"James is treating me like yesterday's newspaper. He's flirting with anything in a bikini, and that's not me."

Thinking of the prim green suit, Mitch smiled.

Claire swiped at her wet cheeks with the back of one hand. "Last night, I couldn't stand it another second. I went off alone, hoping he'd follow me so we could hash this out without everyone else around. But he didn't. And then the island blacked out. And then . . . and then . . ." Her voice rose an octave. "I ended up sleeping with a *stranger*." She shook her head and sobbed. "Not *sleeping* sleeping. Sleeping literally. We didn't do anything." With a sniff, she glanced at the camera, then quickly averted her eyes. "Well, not much anyway. Just enough to . . . to . . ." Bursting into tears again, she lifted a hand to cover her face. "Just enough to make me feel guilty, which makes me mad at myself, because James obviously doesn't feel guilty about being touchy-feely with other people, so why should I?"

She took a moment to pull herself together before risking another glance at the camera. "The man . . . the one I was with last night. I . . . he . . . I can't quit thinking about him," she said in little more than a whisper. "We *connected*. This morning when I woke up, he was still sleeping and he looked so . . ."

Claire's eyes widened suddenly, as if it had just occurred to her that everything she'd revealed could be broadcast to the entire nation unless the show's producers chose to cut it out. And Mitch could guarantee that the footage would not end up on the cutting-room floor. It was exactly the sort of material the producers wanted.

"Oh, God." Claire closed her eyes. "Forget what I said. Please, forget all of it. I'm not going to see the man again, I can promise you that."

There you go, lying again. She would see him. He'd make sure of it.

"Nothing happened between us and nothing's going to happen." Pushing back her chair, Claire stood, then ran from the booth without looking back.

Switching off the camera, Mitch balanced it on his shoulder while grabbing the drawstring bag at his feet. Carrying both, he went out the rear entrance and found Coot, his replacement, whose break wasn't up yet. "I'm having trouble with this camera," Mitch fudged. "Fill in for me while I go check it out, okay?"

"Yeah," Coot said, stuffing the last bite of a hot dog into his mouth. "Sure thing."

Mitch started off toward the editing bungalow. When he was sure Coot no longer watched him, he veered left toward his cabana. It wouldn't take more than a couple of minutes to erase the segment of footage he'd just filmed of Claire and to make a few choice cuts in Ally's, too. Then he had some business to take care of.

Some red-haired, freckle-faced business.

Chapter Seven

Claire heard James's toast and the musical clink of crystal tapping crystal. But as the others in her group lowered their glasses to drink, hers remained in midair.

Mitch headed toward her table, a determined expression on his face, a drawstring bag slung over his shoulder, his camera at his side. The khaki shorts and white short-sleeved shirt he wore brought out his tan. Starched, pressed, and combed, he seemed a far different version of the rumpled man she'd left behind that morning. Either way, Mitch Talbott was too great-looking for his own good. Or hers.

She searched for cameras. To her relief, the only ones she spotted were busy filming other disasters-in-progress.

"Claire? Are you okay?"

Ally's voice tugged her gaze from Mitch. Claire managed a tight smile for the benefit of her table companions. "Why wouldn't I be?" She lowered her drink and sipped. What was Mitch thinking? He would get them both into trouble if he let on that they'd spent time together.

"Claire?"

It was Mitch's voice now. For one woozy, light-headed moment, fainting seemed her best option. The perfect escape. A nice little nosedive into the shrimp dip. Effective, but messy. She looked up and smiled. "Hello. Do I know you?"

The corner of his mouth quivered as he set the camera down beside him. Claire noticed that his eyes were the softest shade of brown and brimming with curiosity. They held her gaze like gravity, tugging her heart every direction but the one she wanted to go.

"Oh, I recognize you now! You're one of the camera crew, aren't you?" Every stare at the table seared into her like laser beams.

"Yeah, I am, and—"

"Oh! Your voice!" She laughed. "You're not . . . ?"

Mitch rubbed a hand across his mouth, but not before Claire noticed the dimple in his left cheek—the one she'd known would be there. "Everyone, this is the man I told you about. The one who found me on the beach last night during the blackout." She returned her attention to Mitch. "Mitch isn't it? Mitch Talbott?"

"That's right."

When she set down her glass to shake his hand, the goblet toppled forward, spilling wine down her dress.

James's eyes narrowed a fraction, his gaze alternating between her and Mitch.

Ally calmly slipped Claire a napkin, squeezing her fingers on the handoff.

"I guess I owe you one for taking care of my fiancée last night, Mr. Talbott," James said. He shook Mitch's hand. "I'm James Watson."

Fiancée. Claire winced. She didn't miss the shift in Mitch's expression over the F-word. Why, oh, why hadn't she told him she was engaged? Mitch's theory about couples and honesty came to mind and she winced again.

194

"I owe you, too," Ally said. "Claire's become a friend over the last couple of weeks. If you hadn't come along when you did last night, she might be dodging barracuda out in the middle of nowhere as we speak." She giggled. "Of course, that would mean one less competitor, so maybe I shouldn't be thanking you." She turned. "No offense, Claire."

Claire's cheeks sizzled as she dabbed the front of her dress with a napkin. She sent a pleading look Mitch's way, a look that clearly said, *Leave.* "It's good to see you again. I'm glad you stopped by. We won't keep you." She nodded toward his camera. "I'm sure you have work to do."

"I'm not in any hurry. I'm on a break."

Okay, Claire thought. *So that's the way it is.* Rules be damned; he would see to it she was punished for withholding information.

Claire cleared her throat. "Well . . . thank you again for helping me last night."

Marcus Wilkins, the man sitting next to Ally, crossed his arms and leaned back in his chair. "Just how much *help* did he give you, Claire?"

Her throat constricted. Her right eye twitched. Once. Twice. Again. The return of an old nervous tic she thought she'd seen the last of long ago. She attempted a laugh but managed only a squeak. "Now, Marcus. Quit playing detective." Smiling, she glanced up at Mitch. "He's a police officer. Suspicion goes with the job, I suppose."

"You didn't answer the question, Claire," James said, eyeing her with more interest than he had since they'd been on the show.

"I believe I said that he led me back to the hotel."

"Yeah, but isn't it a game rule that contestants and crew don't fraternity?" asked Darla, drawing every male eye at the table her way. Sending James an undisguised wink, she continued to smear her puffy lips with cherry gloss.

"I think you mean 'fraternize,' Darla," Ally said. "A 'fraternity' is where you spent all your time and energy back in college, remember?"

Mitch's gaze met Claire's and stuck, nailing her to the chair. "I wasn't fraternizing; I was making sure she didn't drown," he said.

It took a moment for Claire to find her voice, a moment more for her to pry her gaze from Mitch's. "Really, James. Don't you think the blackout qualifies as an extenuating circumstance? No one's going to get all bent out of shape over a crewmember showing me the way back to the hotel."

"That depends." Darla pulled out a compact and checked out her glossy mouth. "Just what else did he show you?"

"As I was saying, Mitch," Claire said, ignoring Darla's question, "I appreciate everything you did for me."

The corner of his mouth quivered again. "My pleasure." He slipped the canvas bag from his shoulder. "I almost forgot. I found something on the beach this morning. I thought you might've left it last night."

Envisioning the swimsuit she'd never located, Claire held her breath. She could've sworn his dimple deepened as he offered the bag to her.

"Is this yours?" Mitch asked.

Tension seeped from her body like air from a balloon. "The bag? No, someone else must've left it." She sent him a silent thank-you with her smile.

Lifting his camera, Mitch bade them good-bye, then made his way across the deck.

Claire rolled her wine-dampened napkin into a cylinder as James's assessing gaze narrowed on her. He knew her well. Maybe too well. Sensing someone else watched her, too, she turned to see that a cameraman had arrived and was filming her. Pinching the tip of the napkin cylinder, she curled it up like a snail's shell. "Why is everyone staring at me?"

"You seem edgy," Rico said.

"That's ridiculous. I'm fine."

Her face must've indicated otherwise, because the camera moved in for a close-up.

Releasing the napkin, Claire watched her nervous handiwork unravel. A sideward peek revealed the suspicious look on James's face. Claire's stomach flip-flopped. "Would y'all excuse me? I think I'll check out the ladies' room."

Mitch returned to the poolside bar and propped his chin in his palm. He sneaked a peek at Claire's table. *Fiancé. Great. Just dandy.* An island full of beach bunnies who would've been eager to break the rules with him, and he had to hook up with someone's wife-to-be. If she'd told him about what's-his-name last night, he would've backed off.

He recognized James Watson. Yesterday, before Mitch found Claire on the beach, he'd noticed the sunburned clown gushing and strutting every time a camera moved toward him.

As Mitch watched Claire on the sly, she pushed back her chair and stood. He wondered if the camera-ham knew his future wife was a shameless skinny-dipper. He wondered, too, with a worrisome tug that felt a little like jealousy, if Watson ever bared his pale behind and joined her. Somehow Mitch couldn't imagine it. Maybe he just didn't want to.

Claire started away from the table. For a woman of Latin heritage, she had the reddest hair, fairest skin, and greenest cat eyes Mitch had ever seen. He found himself wishing she really did have purple hair and a tattoo on her forehead, as they'd talked about last night.

As she made her way toward the door leading from the outside deck to the inside restaurant, Mitch stood. "Winston, old buddy," he said to the bartender, "would you mind keeping my camera behind the bar for a few minutes?"

"Sure, mon. No problem."

He'd find those desperate beach bunnies. Damn right he would. Right after he had a word with Claire.

Mitch started for the restaurant entrance. Inside, he caught a glimpse of Claire's white dress just before it disappeared around a corner. On guard for cameras, he pursued. Upon reaching the corridor he saw her facing the ladies' room at the narrow hallway's far end. "Claire!"

She whirled around and paused, her hand on the door. "What are you doing? Someone might've seen you follow me."

"They didn't. I checked." Stopping in front of her, Mitch stared into her eyes. He listened to the tapping of her foot, watched her skin tone change from pale to pink to crimson.

Claire crossed her arms and quit tapping. "Look . . . I want you to forget about last night."

"Have you?"

She stared at her feet. "I'm trying."

"Maybe we should talk."

"I can't. Last night was a mistake. Anyway, nothing happened between us, so what's the big deal?" She gave the ladies' room door a push. "Good-bye, Mitch."

"Just a minute." He pulled her swimsuit from his bag.

"Put that away!" Wide-eyed, she glanced down the hall.

"What do you want me to do with it?"

"I don't care; just get it out of sight," she said in a hiss. "Aren't you afraid of losing your job?"

He thought about that for a second, maybe two. So far this job wasn't accomplishing what he'd hoped it might. He hadn't seen hide nor hair of Michael Hawkins. Mitch shrugged. "I'm not worried about it."

"What about me? They could ask that I leave the show."

"Do you care? I thought you hated it." He shrugged again. "If you're concerned, go ahead. Hide. But I'll stand right here holding this suit until you agree to talk to me."

"Don't do this!"

"It's your choice."

Her foot started tapping again. "Okay, I'll talk."

"When?" He dangled the suit higher in the air.

"When's good for you?" Claire snapped sarcastically.

"Now's perfect."

Voices drifted from around the corner at the end of the hallway. The color drained from Claire's complexion. "That sounds like Ally. . . ." Frowning, she leaned forward, as if straining to hear. "And James!" She grabbed at the swimsuit.

Mitch lifted his arm, holding the garment just out of her reach. "When are we going to talk?"

"Damn you, I can't think." Claire nodded toward the restroom door. "Get in here. Hurry!"

"Whatever you say."

"Wait!" The voices drew nearer. She scanned the space around them, her attention settling on a closet across the hall. The door stood ajar. Claire grabbed his arm and headed for it. Swinging the door wide, she shoved him inside, then followed. She pulled the door to, leaving it slightly open.

Except for a sliver of light at the door's edge, darkness surrounded them. The closet barely had room for two people, barely room to breathe. Claire stood against one wall with a broom handle jabbed into her side. She tried to ignore the feel of Mitch's breath on her forehead and the familiar, clean scent of his skin.

"What is it with you and me and the dark?" he asked with a soft laugh.

"Shhh!" She heard people outside the door.

"Go on back to the table, you two," Ally said. "I'll check on Claire."

"I'll just wait here," James answered, sounding suspicious. "She was acting strange."

"She was acting *guilty*," Darla added, huffing a laugh.

"I don't think she's feeling well," Ally said.

Claire held her breath as she stared at James's back through the tiny space at the edge of the door.

"She's not in the rest room," Ally said a moment later.

"That's interesting." James leaned against the door, clicking the latch shut, leaving the closet in total darkness. "Where could she be?"

"Now don't you worry," Ally told him.

"I'm not worried," James assured, making Claire frown.

"I'm sure she just went back to her room on the spur of the moment," Ally said. "If there's one surprise I've recently learned about Claire Louise, it's that she's more impulsive than she appears on the surface."

"Yeah, must be a new trait," James said. "The old Claire wouldn't open the mail without asking permission. . . ."

The voices faded. Claire released her breath in a noisy rush. "I have to get out of here."

Mitch's hand grasped her forearm. "When can we talk?"

"Talking will only make things worse. We'll screw up both our plans."

"Forget the plans for a minute. If not for that, why would it bother you to see me again?"

The suggestion in his tone made her tremble. "I only meant . . ." She sighed. "I'm going to marry James. That's that."

"Why?" His hand slid up to her shoulder. "Why do you want to marry him?"

Her mouth went dry. "Because I love him, of course."

"Do you?"

His arm went around her waist, pulling her to him, closing the small space between them. His other hand found her chin. And then he kissed her, slowly, possessively. A toe-curling, head-spinning, knockout kiss.

"Do you?" Mitch asked again when she pulled away.

His whisper sounded almost as shaky as her knees. Fumbling for the doorknob, Claire found it. She eased from his embrace. "Forget last night."

"I've tried," he said, his voice low and insistent in the darkness. "Believe me, I wish I could."

Claire turned the knob. Nothing happened. "Oh, no!" Pressing one hip against the door, she turned the knob again and shoved. "The door won't open."

"What do you mean?"

"I mean it *won't open*. I think we're locked in here."

Chapter Eight

Mitch squeezed in next to her and tried the door himself. It wouldn't budge. "If we cause a commotion, someone's bound to walk by and let us out."

"No! We can't let anyone find us alone together."

"Then what do you suggest?"

"Let's keep trying."

Mitch closed his mouth. After last night on the beach, he knew reasoning with her was useless. "Move away from the door. I'll try to pick the lock with my room key."

Claire stepped back.

"Watch out!" Mitch snapped. "You're on my toe."

"Sorry. These aren't the most spacious accommodations."

"Just move to the side a little more."

"Something's in the way. I think it's a vacuum cleaner. If I can just . . ." Grasping a handle, she shoved. The bulky appliance rammed into the opposite wall. "There."

"Oww! You waylaid me with that thing."

"Sorry. It was an accident."

"I didn't need that shin anyway."

"I said I was sorry."

The keys jingled as he pulled them from his pocket and reached for the doorknob. After locating it, Mitch stooped and rubbed one finger over the face of the metal knob. "There doesn't seem to be a keyhole on this side."

"Try running the key between the door and the facing. Maybe it'll pop the lock."

"Good idea." The door rattled as he slid the key down to the latch. "It won't move," he said after several unsuccessful attempts.

"Let me try."

"Have at it." Mitch extended the keys in the direction of her voice. "But I'm telling you it won't move. I still say we should yell for help. We'll think of some excuse to tell whoever finds us."

"What about—"

"Lover boy? You'll come up with something to tell him, too. You might try the truth for a change. Funny thing, the truth. Helps a person avoid all kinds of turmoil."

Claire considered stepping on his other foot. Instead she reached for the keys and her hands landed squarely on his chest. His shirt felt crisp beneath her fingers and she wondered if he had some sort of wrinkle phobia. Or a starch fetish. Maybe that was it. "Oops," she said. "Bad aim. You'd think I'd be getting better at this by now." When she started to pull her palms away, his hand covered hers.

"You'd think so." Mitch laughed softly. "We've had our share of experience groping in the dark." He moved the key to her hand and closed her fingers around it. "Here."

To end the intimate silence settling around them, Claire knelt before the door to try her luck. After a minute she stood, bumping against him. "I can't do it."

"Well, then," Mitch said. "We either start yelling or start talking. Which is it?"

"I don't like either option."

"If you're committed to what's-his-name, what was last night about? Was I just a fling before you tie the knot?"

"No! I don't have flings. The way I behaved last night was because of the situation. The blackout. I got a little swept away, that's all. It didn't mean anything. As I said, nothing really happened between us."

"We didn't have sex. Is that what you're getting at?"

"Exactly."

"That may be true, but we made love all night long."

Claire finally understood why women in the old days swooned. How did he know exactly the right words to charm her speechless? Despite every intention to keep a level head, to hide what she was feeling, she sighed his name.

Mitch slid an arm around her and pulled her close. He moved his hand up her back, then combed his fingers through the hair at the nape of her neck.

"You don't want to get involved, remember?" Claire asked. "Relationships are based on deceit."

"I remember," he said, soothing her tensed shoulders with his other hand until the muscles eased.

"Well, I lied to you about my appearance. And I didn't tell you I'm engaged. I've proven your point."

"And I told you I was a muscle-bound blond. We were playing a game. As for you keeping quiet about Jimmy, I'm still trying to decide what I think about that."

"If you don't want to get involved, then why do you even care about James and me?"

"Because he's a jerk. Didn't you hear the way he talked about you just now? Haven't you seen him with the other women on this island? If you haven't, you're either blind or suffering from a serious case of denial. Marrying him would be a mistake. The guy doesn't love you, and you don't love him."

"How can you say that? You don't even know me."

"I know enough." He tucked a lock of hair behind her ear.

"By the way, I've changed my mind about the ideal woman. She's a redhead instead of a brunette."

His lips touched the hollow beneath her throat, his kisses warm, teasing. The last remnants of Claire's resolve melted with the rising heat. "Oh, really? Why?"

"I saw this woman in the restaurant. She has hair like fire and the sexiest freckles I've ever seen."

To her own annoyance, Claire giggled like an adolescent in the throes of puppy love. Mitch's lazy strokes across her collarbone scattered goose bumps over her skin. She needed to stop this now. To tell him she wasn't interested, that she wasn't going to jeopardize her place on the show and James along with it. Case closed. But she found it increasingly difficult to concentrate on the messages being delivered from her conscience. She placed her palms against his chest. "How were you so sure it was me at the restaurant? You didn't get a good look at me last night."

He traced each feature of her face with his fingertips until he found her mouth. "It was the shape of your mouth, I think. Or your legs; they caught my attention right off."

When he replaced his fingertips with his lips, she didn't resist. Mitch pressed his back against the wall, bent his knees, and slid to the floor, easing Claire with him. After a moment, he shifted their positions so that she sat between his legs, her back against his chest, his arms around her. The vacuum cleaner still jabbed into one hip, but he couldn't have cared less. "You're all wet," he said, skimming the fabric at her waist with his fingertips, trailing kisses down the back of her neck.

"I spilled my wine. You made me nervous."

"I noticed. Are you still determined to marry Jimbo?"

"His name is James," she answered unsteadily. "I know it's difficult for you to understand, considering . . . well, *this*, but yes, I'm going to do everything in my power to see that we leave this island the same way we arrived: together."

"Tell me about him."

Claire sighed. "I've known Jimbo . . . I mean *James*, all my life." She tried to keep her mind on the subject and off the sensations Mitch stirred in her. "We each inherited fifty percent of the same business from our parents."

"So he's your partner in the feed and tackle store?"

"Yes . . ." She felt him lift her hair and run his fingers through it, sweeping every coherent thought from her mind. Then he massaged her neck and she went limp against him.

"Go on. Tell me more."

"Umm . . . James is two years older than me. When we were kids he used to tease me, just like a brother. Then in middle school, he offered me pointers on surviving puberty."

"Like a brother?" Mitch gently nipped her earlobe.

"Hmmm?" Goose bumps scattered up her arms. "Oh . . . exactly. When I turned fifteen, he was a senior. I think that's when I fell in love with him. But the next year he left for college and our paths didn't cross as often for a while. I missed him, but I resented him some, too."

"Why would you resent him?"

"Whenever I messed things up, which was often, Mother and Daddy would mention James. What would he have done if he'd been in my shoes? Why couldn't I be more like James?"

"So that's why you want to marry him? Because you think you'll mess up without him?"

"I told you, I'm marrying him because I love him."

"Like a brother?"

"Yes . . . no!" Claire slapped his hand and sat up. The abrupt movement upset a broom propped in the corner. Stiff bristles scratched her face. She shoved them away. "James is not at all like a brother to me. Not anymore."

"He's not?"

"No. He's my partner in every way. He's patient with me. And reliable. He's never missed a day of work. And he's never late. He believes in establishing a routine and sticking with it."

"How exciting," Mitch muttered.

"At least, he was all those things and believed all of that until last year when that stupid movie came along."

"Movie?"

"A horrible low-budget film called *Rodeo Romeos*. They filmed it in Prairie. James snagged a bit part in it as one of the cowboys." She drew a shaky breath when she felt the warmth of Mitch's breath against her neck. "His one line was to take place at the rodeo concession stand. He was supposed to say, 'I'll have a chili dog,' and the girl taking the order was supposed to eye him with interest."

"So what happened? She wasn't that good of an actress?"

"He spoke his line," Claire said, ignoring Mitch's sarcasm, "and when the girl looked down at his tight jeans, he ad-libbed, 'and you can hold the wiener.' "

Mitch made a choked sound.

"The director loved the line. From that point on, James had the acting bug. Which is what I think *Eden's* all about. It was his idea for us to try out for the show. I was against it, but I let him convince me. He implied I was boring, and then he dangled the money over my head like a carrot. Our business is struggling. We could use it."

"You want to marry a guy who said, 'You can hold the wiener'?" Mitch asked, as if, after that particular revelation, he hadn't heard another word she'd said.

"He's just having some sort of an early midlife crisis. He'll come to his senses and get back on track. The old James is who I need . . . who I *want* to share my life with."

Mitch splayed the fingers of his right hand wide against her stomach, then slid his palm slowly from her waist to her neck, molding her breasts along the way. "When James touches you," he said, tilting her chin to one side and muttering the words against the corner of her parted lips, "does your pulse jump like it is now?"

Longing bloomed anew, then fluttered through her like wind-tossed petals. Claire tried to fight off her traitorous emotions, but he cupped her chin, holding it gently yet firmly in place. "Mitch . . ." she whispered.

"Answer me, Claire. Is it hard for you to breathe when you're with him?"

"I can't . . ."

His fingers left her face to fumble for the button at the top of her sundress. Then his other hand was on her inner thigh, stroking gently just above the knee, slowly moving higher. Claire's head fell back to his shoulder. She couldn't tell him to stop. She didn't want to.

He undid the first button and moved toward the second. "Does he make you forget everything else but him?"

The straps of her dress slipped from her shoulders. Mitch's finger trailed between her breasts toward the third button. Heat singed Claire's skin, her breath escaped in erratic gasps, her heart pounded. She lifted a hand to help him with his task.

"Does he, Claire?"

"No," she said under her breath, bumping knuckles with him while struggling to free her remaining buttons.

The closet door flew open. Blinding light spilled over them. Claire jumped. Gasped. Squinted past the broom braced haphazardly across the doorway.

"Oh, my . . ." an unfamiliar woman's voice muttered.

"*Claire* . . . What in the . . . ?"

Her heart dropped. She knew the second voice all too well. Her chin fell to her chest. The straps to her sundress dangled at her elbows, the buttons opened to just above the waist exposing all but the tips of her bare breasts. In her and Mitch's journey to the floor, her short hemline had hiked to the tops of her thighs, which were wedged between his veed legs.

Lifting her head, she blinked the faces above into view. She skipped past the amused eyes of a cleaning lady to focus on James's shocked ones. "James . . . please . . ." she said, pulling her dress together. "I can explain."

He turned and walked away.

Claire shifted to her knees, crawled out of the closet and stood next to the lady from Housekeeping. Buttoning her dress, she started down the hallway after James but made it only a few steps before Mitch grabbed hold of her arm from behind and stopped her. "Let me go!"

"Hey, slow down." He turned her to face him. "I don't understand why you want him, but you obviously do." His eyes softened. "Don't worry. He'll come around now that he thinks you're interested in someone else."

"How do you know that?" Claire blinked back tears.

He swept his thumb underneath her eye, wiping away the moisture. "James wants what he doesn't have. He thought you were a sure thing, so he went after all the other women just to see who he might catch. It's not that he really wants them, Claire. It's an ego thing. And now that he thinks you're fooling around, he'll be chasing after you."

"James isn't that shallow."

Mitch didn't need to respond; the lift of his brows conveyed his opinion.

Claire eased from his grasp and stepped back. "I'm sorry I got you into the middle of all this." Confusion sifted through her as she looked into his eyes. She rubbed the warmth of his touch from her arm. They'd met only last night. The thought of leaving him shouldn't make her feel so hollow at the center. "If James turns you in to the producers, I'll vouch for you."

He shrugged. "It wouldn't be such a big loss. I'm just spinning my wheels here, anyway."

"You'll make it, Mitch. With or without Michael Hawkins."

"That's nice of you to say, considering you've never seen my work."

"It doesn't matter. I know you." She smiled a watery smile. "Good-bye, Mitch."

Claire hurried down the hallway, trying to focus her thoughts on finding James. She knew her fiancé, too. He'd be angry. So angry that she didn't doubt for an instant that he wouldn't stop at turning Mitch in; he'd turn her in, too.

Eden's remaining one hundred contestants crowded the deck surrounding the swimming pool. Rupert Asterisk, the show's host, stood at the end of the diving board, making bad jokes as he bounced up and down.

Ripples of laughter wove through the crowd as Mitch made his way over to the bar. Winston looked up at him as he neared. Then the bartender knelt, rising a moment later with Mitch's camera in hand.

"Thanks," Mitch said, trading it for the canvas drawstring bag, which still held Claire's suit. "Hang on to that for me, would you?" Balancing the camera on his shoulder, he went to work, filming the tanned faces around him until he found her.

She stood next to Watson, across the pool from Mitch. Mitch zoomed in for a close-up. Claire seemed unaware of anything going on around her; her worried eyes studied her fiancé, though he pretended not to notice her beside him. Mitch shifted completely to the scrawny jerk and found him flirting with the nearest camera. A scab lined the sunburned bridge of his long, narrow nose. *Yes, sirree.* The guy had true Hollywood leading man potential. No doubt about it.

"Okay, folks," Asterisk finally said, ending his bouncing. "Onto the first challenge of the second round. You're about to take part in a good old-fashioned swimming-pool chicken fight. Ladies, you'll sit on your male partner's shoulders and try to knock off your opponent. Gentlemen, I'll start at the end of the alphabet. When I call your name, choose a partner. I'll assign each couple an opposing pair. The team whose woman falls off first loses."

He motioned to the bar side of the pool. "Winning couples immediately leave the pool and stand on this side. Losing couples stand on the opposite side. The winning couples have the privilege of choosing their dates for the next three days and nights. Any questions?" When no one responded, he reached into his pocket, pulled out a sheet of paper, opened it, and called the first name. "James Watson."

Mitch cut to Claire. She looked unemotional. Impassive. As if her face would crumble if she so much as blinked.

Jimbo smiled at her. "I choose Claire," he said.

Her face did crumble then, and for a moment Mitch thought she might cry. But then she grinned and threw her arms around her fiancé's neck.

Mitch cursed under his breath. Why did she have to look so damn happy? And worse than that, why did it bother him? He should be glad Claire and her sweetheart were back in each other's good graces. Now he could concentrate on the reason he'd taken this stupid job in the first place: Hawkeye Productions' elusive Michael Hawkins.

When the remaining forty-nine male contestants had chosen their partners, Asterisk pitted each couple against another pair; then everyone jumped into the gigantic pool, clothes and all. The women climbed on the men's shoulders, Asterisk blew a whistle, and the fighting began.

Mitch tried to keep his camera aimed at anyone other than Claire. Why should he be bothered by the fact that her dress was white and wet and molded to her body? He wasn't interested. He was just doing a job and doing it for one reason only: to further his career.

He panned the camera around the screeching, splashing crowd in the pool, passing by Claire with ease, then slicing back to her as her opponent, Darla Brimbeau, reached for Claire's hair. Mitch winced. Of all the women Asterisk could've chosen to fight Claire, Darla was the worst. The woman wasn't only an Amazon; she was a ruthless Amazon. She'd introduced herself to every member of the cast and crew on *Eden* the moment she arrived on the island. And she'd made it clear she'd do whatever it took to win, moral or not.

Claire shrieked and swayed and wobbled atop James's shoulders as Darla tugged her hair.

When it appeared certain Claire would fall, Darla flashed her too-white teeth at the nearest camera. But her smile turned into a sneer when Claire caught her balance and righted herself. Darla glanced down at James, who stared up at her. In one swift move, Darla pulled her halter top over her head and dropped it in the water.

Wide-eyed, James staggered backward at the same instant Claire lunged forward, using her entire body to tackle Darla. Both women went into the water, but Darla hit first.

Mitch chuckled. He didn't know why Claire's aggression surprised him. She'd proved last night that when she wanted something she went after it with gusto.

He watched James Watson choke and sputter on the chlorinated water he'd apparently swallowed while ogling Darla's enormous set of buoys. *Fine.* If Claire wanted a life with the guy, he wouldn't interfere. Mitch liked her too much to do anything that might rob her of her wish.

He winced and groaned as Watson puked into the pool, scattering contestants in every direction and bringing the entire camera crew running to film him. "That-a-boy, Bozo," Mitch mumbled. It looked as if the camera-ham had finally figured out how to get the attention he craved.

Chapter Nine

Mitch took his place behind the curtain in the confession booth and prepared for the first contestant to step inside. A part of him hoped it might be Claire. He wished he didn't want to see her, but he did. For the past three days and nights he'd avoided bumping into her. But that didn't mean he hadn't thought about her. Constantly. Luckily, he hadn't been assigned to film any of her dates with the pukemeister since the evening the two of them stood among the winners of the chicken-fight contest and chose each other for all six dates.

Claire seemed stunned James chose her, while Mitch wasn't in the least surprised. The guy was as predictable as rush hour traffic in L.A. on a Friday afternoon. Maybe Watson had been faithful to Claire prior to *Eden*, but now he'd sampled a taste of the chase, and he liked it. Mitch had known that once Watson thought Claire was seeing someone on the side, his interest in her would return.

He adjusted the camera on the tripod. This morning was his first time in the confession booth since he'd filmed Claire a few days back. He hated listening to the baring of shallow souls, and wasn't looking forward to the next couple of hours.

The outside door squeaked open. Mitch switched the camera on and looked through the viewfinder. He jerked back involuntarily at the sight of the man facing the curtain.

"James Watson, Prairie, Texas."

Speaking of shallow souls . . .

Watson settled in. He puffed out his cheeks, which were blotchy and peeling from too much sun. The scab on his nose still hung tight. "I have something to get off my chest."

Mitch knew it wasn't hair. The guy didn't have so much as one short and curly between his bony shoulder blades.

James's Adam's apple bobbed. "Claire thinks I've only been dating her these past three days, but the truth is . . ." He averted his eyes. "The truth is, I've managed to sneak in some time with Darla on the side."

Mitch stifled a yawn. *You and every other male contestant on the island.* Hell, for all he knew, maybe some of the women, too. Darla and her wardrobe of thong bikinis in every color of the rainbow were a big hit on *Eden.* The woman not only loved to show them off; she loved to *take* them off. Especially on-camera.

"Anyway," James continued, "I guess I'm feeling sort of guilty. We *are* engaged. And I did talk her into coming on *Eden* even though she had reservations. But the thing is, she's acting prudish with me lately. Not that she's ever been all that spontaneous or anything, but up until now she's never acted like a nun, either. What am I supposed to do? Be content to sit around with her and stare at the freakin' scenery? I'm a man, damn it. It's time she treated me like one."

That-a-boy, asshole. Turn this around. Make it Claire's fault. I know you can do it.

James squared his shoulders and jutted out his chin. "If this is how she's going to treat me for the rest of our lives, then who'd blame me for making the most of this experience? How could *she* even blame me? She knew when she agreed to come on here that there'd be dozens of beautiful women intent on seducing me."

In your wet dreams.

"She knew that was part of the bargain. I wouldn't be human if I didn't give in to temptation from time to time. It's only natural in a situation like this. And, you know? Maybe now's the time to get all that out of my system. In the end, Claire will probably be glad I did. Getting through this will make us a stronger couple. If she can't admit that, she's only being child-ish."

Mitch wondered what method of torture would cause Lover Boy the greatest discomfort. The guy craved attention; maybe solitary confinement would make him squirm the most. Odds were good that the door could be barred before Watson knew what was happening. The confession booth could easily be transformed into an isolation booth. It would be the first time Mitch had ever enjoyed this shift.

As Watson continued to talk himself out of his guilt, Mitch reminded himself that Claire had chosen to marry Bozo of her own free will. She'd known him all her life. Surely she had an inkling of what she was getting. *This game can't change a person that quickly or easily.*

"So." James pushed back the chair and stood. "It's Claire for dinner tonight." He wiggled his brows and leered at the camera. "And Darla for dessert."

Mitch narrowed his eyes. *Or can it?*

That evening Claire drained her glass of merlot and gazed at the sunset over the waves just outside James's patio where the two of them ate dinner. She wondered what Mitch was doing. Was he off for the night? Breaking the rules with some other *Eden* contestant?

She scanned the lush foliage surrounding the large patio deck. Across from her, a glowing red eye hovered amid the greenery. She spied another to the side of the walkway leading to the beach. The cameramen attached to both had successfully hidden themselves behind coral blossoms and glossy dark leaves.

Claire stared at the closest light. The light stared back. Her heart hiccupped. Maybe Mitch was working tonight. Doing his job. Spying on people who had come here knowing their privacy would be invaded and broadcast to the world.

Across the table, James drained his own glass, poured himself another, then asked a question. Though his words didn't register in her Mitch-preoccupied mind, she nodded.

"Is that a yes, you want to take a dip in the hot tub, or a yes, it's too humid to take a dip?"

Drawing a breath of salty air, Claire glanced from James to the red light and back again. "The second one."

The hopeful glow in his eyes extinguished, leaving behind an alcohol-induced dullness. "That's what I thought." He picked at the remains on his plate.

Claire reached for her fork, but immediately laid it back down. What was the matter with her? She had wanted James to pay attention to her, to spend time with her, and now he was following through. "What the heck," she said. "Heat is a *good* thing for two engaged people, right?"

James's fork paused. "What are you saying?"

"I'm saying I'm glad I wore this outfit, since I'm going to get wet."

"I like it, by the way." He downed half his wine in one gulp as he glanced at her breasts. "The outfit, I mean."

He'd had too much to drink; she could tell by the slur of his words. Still, drunk or not, the desire in his eyes should've pleased her. Instead she felt herself shrinking away from it and what it promised. "Thank you."

While coercing her to make the purchase this afternoon at an island boutique, Ally had promised Claire the ensemble would please James. And though her friend was obviously right, Claire felt as if she dined in the nude. The string-bikini top wasn't made to lift and support, only to cover the essentials. And the short sarong tied around her hips was so transparent that the barely-there bottoms were visible beneath it.

"Well . . ." James glanced at his watch, then pushed away from the table. He held out a hand. "I'm ready if you are."

Claire cast a quick look of longing at her untouched key-lime pie and two looks of dread at the piercing red eyes hiding in the foliage. "Are you in a hurry?"

"As a matter of fact, I am." James's grin was slow and sluggish. "I'm anxious to see what your new outfit looks like when it's wet."

Mitch was anxious to see Claire's outfit wet, too. But he wasn't in a hurry for the rest of the world to enjoy the same privilege. And, fiancé or not, he didn't want James Watson ogling her, either. He had no right, but every time the guy looked her up and down, Mitch wanted to pound him.

He considered turning off the camera, but it wouldn't serve his purpose. Ray still filmed across the way, just at a different angle. Besides that, Mitch had already pushed his luck by getting involved with Claire and then erasing both her and Ally's confession-booth footage.

Because the hot tub sat a few feet from the patio table, Mitch had to shift position in order to bring it into view. The leaves rustled, and Claire shot a nervous glance in his direction. He was glad for the abundance of plants and bushes and trees surrounding the deck. In the dark clothing he'd worn, if he were careful, Claire would not be able to identify him. He felt bad enough filming her. If she knew he held the camera, he didn't think he could continue.

Watson pulled off his shirt, slipped out of his slacks, and stepped into the water wearing only boxers. He turned a knob and the water began to bubble and gurgle and steam. He looked up at Claire. She stood at the edge of the tub, frowning. "Get in. It feels great," James slurred.

Alternately eyeing the place where Mitch hid and Ray's spot in the opposite bushes, she fussed with the knot at her left hip that held that sexy little bikini cover-up in place. Finally she sat at the tub's edge, dangling her feet in the water. "That does feel nice." Quickly she pulled the cover-up free and tossed it aside as she slid in next to James.

Determined to capture only above-the-shoulder images of Claire, Mitch zoomed in for a close-up. She looked like a wary, caged animal; Jimbo, on the other hand, appeared eager to put on a show.

James drew Claire closer to him, positioning her so that they sat face-to-face. "See," he said quietly, "now, wasn't this a good idea?"

"It's nice," she answered, her laugh nerve-tinged.

"Just nice?" He nuzzled the side of her neck.

"Don't," Claire said, turning her head and pulling back. "Please."

"What's wrong?"

She looked toward the camera. Mitch flinched, unnerved by the illusion that she stared directly into his eyes.

"It's . . ." Blinking, she returned her attention to James.

"Relax." He slid his hand down her back, toyed with the tie between her shoulder blades. "It's just you and me."

Claire let James kiss her, but when the kiss became more heated, she backed off again.

Good girl. Mitch smiled. *He isn't worth the lipstick.*

James's brows drew together. "What's the matter now?"

"It's not just you and me. It's you and me and"—she motioned toward the bushes—"and *them.*"

"Come on, Claire. I've missed you." He pulled her to him again. "Things haven't seemed right between us lately."

Mitch squinted. *Whose fault would that be, buddy?*

"I'm not comfortable with this, James." Claire started squirming, but he wrapped his arms around her waist. "You're not the same man I said I'd marry. You've changed. Being in the spot-light brings out a side of you I don't like."

James laughed as Claire's increasing struggles only rubbed her up against him. "Aren't you being a little melodramatic? I'm the same as always. But the stranger fantasy could be fun, too. Is that what this game's about?"

"It's not a game. I don't know you anymore."

"Let me refresh your memory." Ignoring her attempts to break away, he leaned down and kissed her shoulder.

"Did you hear me?" Claire asked more firmly, still wiggling. "I don't want to be with you. We can go inside away from the cameras to talk things out, or I'm leaving."

"So that's it, huh?" James laughed. "You're playing hard-to-get. I like the new you, Claire. The teasing"—he glanced down at her chest—"the way you dress. We can go inside if you want, but I don't want to talk."

When he removed one arm from around her and slid his hand up to cup her breast, Claire slapped him.

His head snapped back. When he looked at her again, his eyes glittered like gemstones. "You know what, Claire?" he said. "I'm sick of you being so uptight." He jerked her bikini top string until it untied completely.

"That does it." Mitch lowered the camera to the ground. "I've had enough." He heard Claire cry out his name as he burst from the bushes and strode toward them.

The next seconds passed in slow motion.

Lover Boy dropped his hands from Claire and looked up.

Claire backed to the far side of the tub.

Jimbo's mouth opened but no sound emerged.

Mitch dove. The water was hot. He hit Watson hard, landing on top of him and shoving his head under the water.

Time sped up again.

"Mitch!" Claire screamed. "What are you doing?" She scrambled from the tub.

"I'm"—he dodged a flailing fist—"teaching this son of a . . ."

221

James grabbed Mitch's ear and twisted. Mitch lost his hold, and James came up for air. "Some manners," Mitch gasped, then threw a punch that hit James square in the nose, knocking him back against the hot tub's steps.

James tried to stand up but fell forward instead, landing face-down on top of an air jet. A stream of pink bubbles swirled out from beneath his head.

Mitch quickly considered the pros and cons of letting him drown. Above him, he heard Ray's voice. He looked up and found the crewman calling for help on his walkie-talkie. Ray continued to film, though, capturing the scene in the tub.

Cursing under his breath, Mitch reached over, grabbed a handful of James's hair, and jerked his face out of the water.

James sputtered and coughed as Mitch dragged him over to sit on the steps.

Claire tossed James her cover-up. "Press that on your nose," she snapped, keeping her eyes on Mitch. "You're messing up the water." When a commotion sounded inside, she looked past the sliding glass doors into the cabana.

Mitch followed her gaze. Michael Hawkins and two other Hawkeye Productions executives walked through the door.

"So this is what it takes to finally get to meet the elusive Hawkeye president face-to-face," Mitch muttered.

Claire turned, her face pale as the moon rising behind her. "Oh, Mitch," she whispered. "What have you done?"

Chapter Ten

Crazy. She must be insane. Sneaking out at three in the morning. Darting from shadow to shadow. Risking Mitch's job, if he hadn't lost it already.

Claire knew she should turn around, wait until tomorrow to look for him. But if the Hawkeye executives had fired him, he might leave first thing in the morning. She couldn't let him go without telling him she was sorry, couldn't risk not having a chance to say good-bye.

Earlier at James's cabana, Michael Hawkins and his sidekicks had questioned them all separately—her, James, the other cameraman, and finally Mitch. Afterward they apologized to her and James for Mitch's behavior, then took Mitch away, leaving her worried about his fate.

Claire left James soon after without saying a word to him. Just the sight of him disgusted her. What disgusted her more was the fact that she'd let him manipulate her for years. That she'd let him pull her strings like a spineless puppet, a hunk of wood with no brain, no courage, no life at all. Before meeting

Mitch, she'd thought she couldn't survive without James's guidance. How could she have been so blind to his weaknesses or to her own strengths?

When she finally reached Mitch's cabana, she stood beneath a palm tree and breathed in the tangy, sharp scent of the sea to calm her nerves. His lights were on. She closed her eyes, felt the wind on her face, in her hair. What would she say to him? Why was she really here?

Before she could answer those questions or talk herself out of knocking, she walked up the steps and did just that. *Is this about caring, or lust?* she asked herself. *Some of both. A lot of both.* Not a bad combination, she guessed.

The door creaked open. Mitch's brows drew together when he saw her. "You're up late," he said.

She ignored the fluttering in her stomach. "You too."

Stepping aside, Mitch opened the door wider. "Come in."

Her conscience tried to step on the brakes. If something happened between them tonight, it would only be temporary. Mitch had a bad case of wanderlust; she had a business in Prairie to run. But was temporary so bad? And if not, could she handle it? "You sure it's okay for me to come in? I don't want more trouble for you with Hawkins."

"He can't do a thing to me now. We're no longer associated." He motioned her inside. "Have a seat."

The tiny spark of hope she'd nurtured snuffed out. He'd been fired. Because of her. She walked past him into the cabana, noting his packed bags on the floor beside the sofa. "I'm sorry, Mitch. I can't help but feel like this is my fault. If I'd told you about James that first night—"

"Hey, I knew the rules. I chose to break them."

Glancing down at his bags, she sank onto the sofa. A video-cassette lay on top of a suitcase. Claire picked it up and saw Mitch's name printed down the spine. "What's this?"

"Nothing." He started into the adjoining kitchen. "Can I get you something to drink?"

"It's some of your work, isn't it? You brought it hoping Michael Hawkins might take a look."

He took two glasses out of the cupboard, then faced her and shrugged. "It was a stupid idea. Hawkins hires only the best for his serious projects."

"And what makes you think you're not?"

Mitch set the glasses on the counter, then opened the refrigerator, his back to her. "I only have a little lemonade left. You want it?"

Claire put down the cassette. She stood. "What makes you think you're not one of the best?"

He turned, surprise flashing across his face when he found she'd walked up behind him and now stood close. "Maybe I've been accused of chasing rainbows for so long that I've finally decided to believe that's what I'm doing."

"Accused? You mean by your father and your old girlfriends?"

He let the refrigerator door close. Their gazes met slowly and held. "Yeah."

Claire touched his cheek. "I've always wished I had the nerve to chase a rainbow," she whispered. "To be brave enough to go after something that seems off-limits or out of reach." She wrapped her arms around him. "You'll catch yours, Mitch. I know you will."

She still wore her new skimpy outfit, so she felt his body acutely as he pressed close to her. And then she melted, bone and muscle dissolving against him.

In his eyes, worry clashed with desire like water on rocks. "Claire—"

"You don't have to promise me anything," she said softly, sliding her fingers across the laugh lines around his eyes, down to his lips to stop further protests. "I understand how you live. I'm a big girl, Mitch. I'm going after what I want." Claire brushed her mouth against his. "You're my rainbow tonight. Let me catch you."

* * *

Lust and tenderness flared inside him, twin flames, equally hot. Mitch pulled Claire closer, his hands moving down her body, skimming over her shoulders, down her breasts to her stomach, sliding around to cup her bottom. With his mouth still on hers, he mentally measured the distance to the bedroom. Making his way blindly across the room, he took Claire with him, clinging and kissing, staggering and turning, again and again. At the bedroom door he pulled back for air.

The prospect of making love with her had been simpler before he'd started to care too much. Now he was terrified of what he saw in her expression, of what it made him feel. They were about to become lovers. He'd always sensed they would . . . from that very first night, long before he'd had a clue what she looked like. But now that the moment had arrived, he didn't want regrets later on when he left her, when they said good-bye and resumed their separate lives. He cared about her too much to hurt her. They should set things straight. Decide what this meant—and what it didn't.

"Let's slow down, Claire. Talk about it."

She made quick work of undoing the buttons down the front of his shirt. "I'm not in the mood to talk."

He laughed, then drew a breath. "I can see that. But I'm trying to be sensible here." His thoughts weren't sensible at all, though, when she kissed his bare chest, trailing her tongue along his collarbone to his throat. "How am I supposed to think straight when you're doing that?"

"You're not."

"Claire . . . as much as I want you . . ."

Her mouth—those gorgeous full lips that had played a starring role in his recent dreams—touched his neck now, soft and warm and arousing. He closed his eyes. "God knows I want you a lot," he said, swallowing hard. "I need you."

She nibbled his earlobe. "How much?" she asked, her voice teasing, seductive. "More than food? More than water?"

"More than air. More than . . ." Forcing his eyes open, he

looked down. He threaded his fingers through her hair, then tilted Claire's head back. "I don't want to rush into this and have you end up sorry about it. I want you to be sure."

"Do you see any uncertainty here?"

Something clutched in his chest at the sight of the pink-tinted, freckled face staring up at him. Her clear, true eyes, the flaming hair. The last of Mitch's resistance slipped away.

Claire clung to him as he turned down the sheets on the bed, then lowered her onto it. She nodded toward the doors that led to a back patio. "Open them," she said. "I want to hear the ocean."

The breathy hiss of the wind mingled with the sea's distant whisper as Mitch threw the doors wide, then returned to the bed. With restless hands she tugged at his shirt. Just as impatiently he shrugged out of it and tossed it behind him. Reaching for the nightstand, he slid open the top drawer and found a condom packet. He placed it within close reach before untying her cover-up and tossing it, too. He pulled the bikini top string at the back of her neck, freeing the tie between her shoulder blades at the same time. Her top fell to the bed, baring her breasts. They were smooth and firm and high, pink and pearly white as the center of a shell. "You really are a goddess." He touched her. "Aphrodite . . . goddess of love and beauty."

Her smile made the blood drum in his head in a primitive, steady beat. He lifted his gaze to hers and saw a hint of something that stunned and frightened him before she quickly glanced away. Behind the provocative teasing, behind the laughter, lived something vulnerable. Something hopeful but afraid.

Needs he'd never known existed sprang up in him. Needs deeper than lust or longing. Needs that brought with them a desperation all his own, an intensity and fear that equaled what he saw in her eyes.

So, though he'd intended to be tender, had ached, at the sight of her naked body, for slow, drawn-out pleasure, he didn't stop her when she took the lead at a wild, frantic pace. Instead he responded in kind, tugging her bikini bottoms down her legs as she did his shorts. Learning the contours of her body as she did his—not with gentle sharing, an intimate give and take, but with a raw lustiness as emotionally painful as it was exciting. Every nerve ending he possessed felt exposed. Bare. Excruciatingly sensitive.

As if Claire sensed this first time might be their last, she held nothing back physically, gave everything she had to give without inhibition. But emotionally Mitch sensed she held back . . . and so did he. She'd uncovered needs and wants he'd just as soon stay hidden. And he was afraid.

For the first time Mitch acknowledged and examined those unearthed emotions, admitted they were more powerful than his fear of what they meant. His instincts urged him to drive himself into her until they both found the release they yearned for. But with Claire, he realized he wanted more than sex. He wanted it all. Emotion. Vulnerability. Everything.

"Look at me, Claire," he said, rolling on top of her, propping his elbows on either side of her head. "I need you to look at me."

Her eyes opened slowly, and he stared into them for the longest time, his heart exploding in his chest. "I think . . ." He took a shaky breath as the truth spread through him with a force so sweet he thought his heart would break. "I—"

"Don't," she whispered, cupping his face in her palms, searching his face for a hint that the words she knew he'd planned to speak were born of a passion that would pass with the night. But nothing less than sincerity stared back at her, and she realized she was more stunned by his attempted admission than by the truth of it. Maybe she'd known the truth all along, from that very first night, but feared it would slip away like the wispy remnants of a dream if she tried to hold on to it. So she'd run back to safety, to what was familiar, rather than reaching for something that seemed too good to be real. She was still afraid it would slip away, but she wouldn't run this time.

"Don't say anything," she whispered. "Just be with me." Tears dampened the hair at her temples as their lips brushed together, then parted and met again. Her hands drifted over his torso, discovering every rise of muscle, each dip and hollow. The jut of his hipbones, the flat plane of his stomach. The skin covering his rib cage was smooth. A small, thick scar stood out on one shoulder blade. Coarse hair filled the hollow beneath his throat.

Earlier, she'd told herself she could bear it if he left her and never looked back, that the little bit of himself he shared would be better than nothing at all. But when he'd turned away from the patio doors to join her on the bed, her flimsily built confidence crumbled and washed away like a sand castle on a wave. What if he saw how much he meant to her? If he realized the pain he could cause? Taking this beyond the physical would expose her heart, and he'd be scared away before the night ended.

He would still leave her, she thought as his mouth found the pulse at her throat, then moved lower. But it wouldn't be so easy for him now. And she'd always know he had cared about her, what it had cost him to turn away.

So she joined him in the slow ebb and flow, the gradual climbing of sensation and emotion. Throwing caution aside, she gave her heart and soul along with her body, knowing there'd be no regrets when she looked back on this memory. For them, it had happened fast . . . too fast. But she'd never felt more beautiful, more wanted or loved. No matter what happened tomorrow, she'd remember this night, this moment, as perfect.

Claire closed her eyes, anticipating, as he reached for the packet on the nightstand. A moment later, she murmured her pleasure as he ran his fingers upward along her inner thigh to her most sensitive spot. Her breath caught when he touched her and her stomach muscles tightened. She thought nothing could possibly feel any more wonderful, but then he entered her and her breath caught again. She closed her arms and legs around him, arched against him, the pressure inside of her growing stronger with each stroke and caress, with every whispered word.

The muscles in Mitch's back trembled beneath her fingertips as they moved together on the rumpled bed, slowly at first, then gradually faster and faster. And then Claire cried out, her body quivering uncontrollably as they both let go.

Much later, when their heartbeats had returned to a more normal pace and their breathing slowed, they continued to hold one another, each only vaguely aware of the gentle rain starting outside the window or the lazy passing of time.

Chapter Eleven

A pounding noise roused Mitch from a dreamless sleep. Blinking awake, he sat up. Claire lay beside him, the sheet pulled to her chin, her green eyes sleepy and confused.

"We're coming in," a man called out.

Mitch leaned forward and peered into the den. He thought he recognized the voice. "Is that . . . ?"

"Rupert Asterisk," Claire finished for him as the door burst open and Coot, the cameraman, rushed into the cabana, followed by Asterisk, Darla Brimbeau and . . . "Ally," Claire whispered.

Mitch searched the floor for his shorts as everyone converged on the bedroom. He found his clothing by the window, out of reaching distance.

Asterisk snatched the shorts up and tossed them toward him. "Looking for these?"

Stuffing them beneath the sheet, Mitch struggled to dress without exposing himself or Claire.

Ally peeked over Asterisk's shoulder. "I'm sorry, Claire. Darla and I saw you sneaking down the beach in the middle of the night. We decided to follow you."

After several tense moments, Claire said, "I thought you were my friend, Ally."

"Are you ever naïve," Darla cut in, flashing her blindingly white teeth. "Give Ally some credit, though." She nodded toward Asterisk and the cameraman. "We could've brought them last night and interrupted your little rendezvous, but she was dead set on waiting."

"Gee, thanks." Mitch glared at Ally until she looked down at the floor.

"Look . . . it's a game, OK?" Ally said. "With you out of the picture, Claire, I'm one step closer to winning."

A sideward glance at Claire showed Mitch her eye was twitching. He'd never seen her look so angry.

"Relax, everybody." Asterisk chuckled. "Chances are no one's going anywhere."

"You're wrong about that, Rupert." With his shorts finally in place, Mitch scooted from beneath the sheet and stood. "If that camera isn't off in the next two seconds," he said, zipping his zipper, "everybody who's anybody with *Eden* is going to court for invading my privacy."

Coot the cameraman looked up from his lens and over at Asterisk. Asterisk nodded and Coot switched off the camera.

"Now . . ." Mitch hooked his thumb toward the bedroom door. "Everybody out of here so Claire can get dressed."

The small crowd filed out, and Mitch closed the door. He gathered Claire's clothes off the floor and handed them to her. "I'm sorry about this. They can't fire me twice, but you'll probably get kicked off the show."

"Fine with me. I'd decided to leave anyway."

While she dressed, he slipped into his own shirt and started on the buttons. "This isn't exactly the morning-after I'd hoped for."

She smiled as she tried to tie the bikini-top string around her neck. "I know. But after being caught on camera, the rest should be a piece of cake."

Mitch crossed the room and stood behind her. Then he tied the string that secured her bra top between her shoulder blades. "My plane leaves at five this evening." He drew her back to him, his hands on her shoulders. "No matter what happens out there, I want to talk to you again before then."

Turning, she reached up and touched his face. "You want to say good-bye."

Good-bye. The word felt like a punch in the gut. Mitch swallowed. "Claire—"

"It's okay," she interrupted, averting her eyes, then easing away to scoop her cover-up off the floor. When she straightened, she tied the scarf around her hips, then took his hand. "Ready?"

Nodding, Mitch followed her into the den.

Rupert Asterisk was the only person waiting for them. Even Coot had left. "The way I see it," the show host said, "what happened this morning could be good for the show's ratings. Since you're no longer employed by Hawkeye, Talbott, Miss Mulligan didn't really break any rule by sneaking around with you. But here's the good part." He leaned toward Claire, his eyes twinkling. "When your fiancé finds out what happened, it could add an intriguing twist to the show. This isn't exactly your typical reality-TV love triangle, now, is it? I mean, you cheated with one of the *camera crew,* for crying out loud." He slapped his leg and hooted. "You'll become an instant celebrity."

"I didn't *cheat* on anyone, Mr. Asterisk," Claire said. "James Watkins is no longer my fiancé."

Mitch's heart stuttered. "Does *he* know that?"

"He will soon enough. Anyway," she added, returning her attention to Asterisk, "I don't care to be an instant celebrity or any kind of celebrity at all. I'm giving up my spot on *Eden.* Just as soon as I can pack and have a word with James, I'll be leaving the island."

Asterisk tried to reason with Claire, but Mitch didn't hear a word the man uttered, and he didn't think she did, either. They stared at each another, and in her eyes Mitch saw sadness and relief and something he couldn't name. Something bittersweet.

It took only a moment before he understood. He wouldn't be seeing her again before five; she wouldn't be there to wave him away when his plane left. When Claire walked out his door, her memory was all he'd have to look forward to.

Claire marched to the office door with Michael Hawkins's name on it and knocked. She held her breath. As far as she knew, Hawkeye's president might not even be on the island. No one she'd asked seemed willing to tell her whether he stayed permanently on-site or if he simply flew in from time to time to check up on things.

She stroked her thumb down the spine of the videocassette she held in one hand, then knocked again.

"Yeah?" a deep voice answered.

"Mr. Hawkins?"

"That's me."

"I'm Claire Mulligan. One of the contestants. Or I was up until a few minutes ago."

The door opened and the same whip-thin man who had questioned her after the hot-tub incident stood before her. "Ah, Miss Mulligan. I know who you are." He smiled. "Come in."

She stepped into a sparsely furnished office with a large picture window overlooking a stretch of pristine white beach. "I'd like to talk to you, if I could."

"Of course. Pull up a chair." He sat behind his desk.

"That's okay, I'll stand. This won't take long." She glanced at the video, at the big block letters spelling Mitch's name.

"What can I do for you, Miss Mulligan?"

Claire looked up at him. "I'm quitting the show."

"Asterisk told me. I'm sorry to hear it. You do have a knack for keeping things interesting."

234

"Funny you should say that. My ex-fiancé coerced me onto *Eden* by insinuating I'm dull."

His brows lifted. "I admit I thought so at first, too. But you surprised me. In fact, I'm wondering what might entice you to stay."

Claire lifted the cassette, her heart pounding. "The only thing you could do that would make me even *consider* staying is to watch this."

He eyed the video with interest as she handed it to him. "What is it?"

"You know Mitch Talbott? The cameraman you fired?"

He nodded.

"It's some of his work. That video, Mr. Hawkins, is the only reason Mitch took this job. He hoped to get to know you better; then he planned to ask if you'd watch it."

Looking skeptical, Hawkins tapped a finger on the plastic cover. "Miss Mulligan . . . I don't have time to—"

"I dare you." Claire lifted her chin. "Watch the video, Mr. Hawkins. See what you think. Then we'll talk about whether or not I'll stay on the show."

Thirty minutes later, Claire found James lying beneath a palm tree laughing and playing footsie with a leggy brunette named Tiffany.

Claire cleared her throat.

Sliding his sunglasses to the tip of his nose, James glanced up. "Claire?" Blinking, he scrambled to his feet. "Hi, honey. I've been worried about you."

She glanced at Tiffany. "So I see."

His cheeks turned the color of his nose. Claire shook her head. "Don't worry, James. You're off the hook."

"I'm what?"

"Off the hook. Free to carouse with whomever you choose whenever you choose without repercussions."

After a quick glance at Tiffany, James took Claire by the arm and walked her to a couple of nearby beach chairs. They sat side by side. "What are you trying to tell me?"

"We're finished, that's what. We're not going to get married or buy that house on Sunset Road we've been looking at, or have a family together or anything else we've planned over the years. As for *Eden*, I don't care if it's by ship or plane or if I have to dog-paddle; I'm out of here."

He looked confused. "You can't throw everything away just like that. If this is about last night, well, I was drunk and obnoxious. I'm sorry I got a little out of hand."

"You got more than a little out of hand, but that's not what this is all about. Not completely, anyway."

"It's this game, isn't it? I shouldn't have talked you into playing when you were so against it. I'll leave with you. We'll go back to the way things used to be."

"You don't want that." She pulled off his sunglasses and stared into his eyes. "You don't want to marry me any more than I want to marry you. We both fell into that scenario because . . ." She shook her head. "I don't know, because it seemed to be *expected* of us, I guess. Because it was easy and familiar and safe. The problem is, James, easy and familiar and safe isn't always right." Claire exhaled noisily. "Sometimes challenging and different and risky is what makes life worth living. I just didn't know it until I came on this show. So maybe I should thank you for coercing me to be a contestant."

He glanced down at his fingers before meeting her gaze again. "What about Prairie Feed and Tackle?"

"Roger Milhouse is always offering to buy us out."

James scowled. "For peanuts. He'll pay off our debt with only a few dollars to spare."

"Right now I'd take peanuts to get out from under it. You and Roger get along. He'd make a good partner. I'll sell him my half of the business for half the peanuts and pay off half the debt. How's that?"

"I couldn't stay on without you, Claire."

She made a face. "Come on, James. No more crap. If you want out, don't blame me. I'm going to have a hard enough time explaining things to my own parents; don't bring yours down on me, too. You have your own reasons for bailing. Be honest." She slipped the sunglasses back onto his swollen nose. "Might they have something to do with Hollywood?"

James's lip twitched. He grinned. "What if they do?"

She laughed. "Then I think you should go for it. I'll give old Roger a call just as soon as I get home."

After thinking that over for about half a minute, he asked, "What will you do?"

"Me?" Claire shrugged. "Who knows? Maybe I'll spend my time chasing rainbows."

Chapter Twelve

As Claire carried her suitcase into the living area of her cabana the next morning, a knock sounded at the door. The bellman, she guessed, coming for her bags. Her plane was scheduled to leave in a couple of hours. She'd been offered a flight yesterday evening at five. Mitch's flight. So she'd declined, saying she needed more time to pack.

"Come in," Claire called out. "It's unlocked."

She set her suitcase on the sofa, then glanced over her shoulder to find Michael Hawkins at her door.

"Hello, Miss Mulligan."

"Now, this is what I call personal service. *Eden's* executive producer escorting me to my plane."

Hawkins seemed taken aback by her appearance. He'd noticed the swollen, red-rimmed eyes, she supposed, choking down another wave of emotion. She'd been drowning in tears ever since the clock struck five P.M. yesterday.

He closed the door. "I'm not here as an escort."

A sense of foreboding sifted through her. Had something happened to Mitch? Or had they decided not to let her out of her contract? "What can I do for you, then?"

"I took your dare and watched Mr. Talbott's video."

Her heartbeat sped up. "And?"

Hawkins lifted a hand and for the first time she noticed what he held. "Now I'm daring you to watch this."

For a moment she didn't move. What could he possibly have that she needed to see? Footage of James with Darla? With other women? Was he hoping to make her so angry she'd opt to stay and fight, thereby boosting his silly program's ratings when it aired? "Nothing you can show me that's happened during my time here will make me change my mind about leaving the island."

Smiling, he lifted the video higher. "Watch it. I have a feeling you won't be sorry."

For a full minute after Hawkins had gone, Claire stared at the video. Finally she turned and walked to the armoire in front of the sofa. She opened the doors, exposing the television set inside and the VCR on top of it. Claire turned on the equipment, popped the cassette in, then sat down to watch.

The screen flickered to life, and Mitch's face appeared. She recognized his surroundings. He sat in the confession booth where she'd sat herself this past week and a half more times than she cared to remember.

"Um . . . hi," Mitch said with an awkward laugh. "Bear with me. It's strange being on the opposite side of the lens." He cleared his throat. "I came on *Eden* hoping I'd meet someone who would change my life. That person was Michael Hawkins. As you know, my dream for a long time has been to meet the great Hawkeye president. To have him view my work and find it worthy enough that he'd hire me for his upcoming project in Africa. I never imagined for a second that it wouldn't be Michael Hawkins who changed my life, but a sea goddess. Aphrodite herself." He smiled, flashing that dimple she loved so much.

"That's you, Claire," he said. "When you emerged from the ocean, everything changed for me."

Claire pressed a hand to her mouth.

Mitch blinked and cleared his throat again. "Claire . . . you know I'm not good with romantic stuff. What I'm trying to say is that, in a very short time, you've come to mean more than anything else to me. Thanks to you, Hawkins just offered me the chance to go after my dream." Mitch looked down at his hands, then slowly up again. "You told me recently that you always wished you had the nerve to chase rainbows. Well, here's your chance, Claire. Go with me. Hawkins is hiring people in all areas to work behind the scenes. You've run your own business. He assured me he could use someone with your management skills. The pay may not be great, but you'll learn a lot. And think of the adventure you'll have . . . the adventure we'll have together. Your heart's not in the feed and tackle business. Anyone can see that."

"Oh, my God," Claire whispered.

He leaned forward. "But I want you to know that if you aren't willing to go, that I won't go either. I'll move to Prairie and hire on at the five-and-dime taking photos of babies, if that's what it'll take to have you in my life." He sat back again. "So . . . that's all I wanted to say. Think about it, Claire. Just don't think too long. If we're going to Africa, we have to leave in two weeks. Whatever you decide, though, just turn around. I'll be there."

The video ended, leaving only a static-filled screen. Claire closed her eyes. "Oh, my God," she whispered again, ending with a squeak. She took a tissue from the pocket of her slacks and blew her nose.

"Claire—"

At the sound of Mitch's voice behind her, she twisted and jumped to her feet. He stood in the doorway, a deep, vertical groove between his eyebrows conveying his worry.

"There's one more important thing I forgot to confess."

241

She blew her nose again as he rounded the sofa to meet her. "Oh, really? What's that?"

"I'm falling in love with you, Claire." Mitch's Adam's apple bobbed. Once. Twice. Again. "What do you have to say about that?"

His arms opened wide. Claire walked into them. "I say, let's go chase a rainbow."

Hot Shot

SHERIDON SMYTHE

For Doreen Gates, my loyal, fun, crazy, wonderful friend.
I can't think of anyone who would have a better time on
a sizzling island like Mystique Island,
my friend, with your unbelievable energy and zest for life.
You would make the most of every moment.
I thought of you often while writing my story.
I love you!

HAWKEYE PRODUCTIONS MEMORANDUM

To: Dara Thompson
From: Chef Dominic
         CC: Michael Hawkins
Re: Luxury items requested for final game—please approve ASAP

1. One case of imported Tequila
2. Ten jars of caviar

Chapter One

Four months earlier . . .

"What is it, darling? Are we about to get a visit from Ed McMahon?"

Whitney Sutherland lifted her stunned gaze from the letter in her hand and focused on her mother. "I've . . . it says my application's been approved for the upcoming reality television show, *Eden*."

Barbara Sutherland—known as Babs to her friends—clapped her hands together, then brought them to her heart. "Oh, honey! That's *wonderful* news!"

"It's not wonderful news, Mom." Whitney eyed her beaming mother with outright suspicion. "I didn't fill out an application, and I certainly didn't send one to Hawkeye Productions." Her laugh came out more as a bark of disbelief. "I would be the *last* person to participate in one of those . . . those *sadistic* reality shows. You of all people should know that."

Babs's smile never faltered. "Now, darling, they're not *all* bad. I think *The Bachelor* is fascinating!"

Whitney opened her mouth to point out the obvious flaws in the show, such as the crushed women who *didn't* get picked by Mr. Wonderful, but her mother raced on before she could speak.

"And just think of the prize—a trip around the world! You've always wanted to travel, and with the prize money you could open a shop of your own, just like you've dreamed."

"I plan to do that anyway, and the trip around the world was just a dream." Whitney's eyes narrowed. "How do you know so much about the show?" When her mother didn't answer, Whitney shook the letter. "Mother, did you do this? Did you send in an application with my name on it?"

"Well . . ." Babs studied her nails. "I might have."

"Either you did or you didn't." Oh, what was the use? Whitney didn't have to hear a confirmation. Someone had obviously sent in the application, and it hadn't been her.

That left her meddling mother or her mother's best friend, Gladys. Then there were the three longtime employees of Beautiful Nails nail salon, Cathy, Regina, and Lori.

She was surrounded by meddling women hell-bent on forcing her to have some fun. Try as she might, she could not convince them that she was perfectly happy with her single life. Whitney closed her eyes, easily imagining the circle of women, very likely drunk on blue margaritas and wearing funky hats, gathered around the card table, poring over the application with *her* name at the top. Answering personal questions about *her*.

Her eyes snapped open, startling a guilty flush out of her mother. "Mom? Why? After what happened to you on *The Dating Game*, how could you possibly want me to participate in something so . . . so heinous?"

"Heinous? Whitney Charolette, I think you're exaggerating a bit, don't you?"

The use of her full name caught the attention of everyone in the salon, most of whom were regular customers. Whitney allowed her mother to pull her farther from listening ears. Lord knew she had enough people nosing around in her life!

"I see now that I shouldn't have told you about the unusual circumstances surrounding your, um, conception," Babs told her in a hushed, serious tone. "It's colored your outlook on life."

"How could it *not*? Mom! The guy you met on *The Dating Game* not only dumped you after your affair, he left you pregnant!"

"Whitney Charolette, I do not regret that affair for one *instant*! How could I? He gave me you, and you are the most precious—"

"Don't even *try* to change the subject, Mother." Whitney had her own way of emphasizing her displeasure. "The guy ruined your life, and without a second's thought!"

Babs gasped and put a hand to her heart. "Ruined my life! How can you say that? I never, ever regretted having you, or raising you alone."

"You said yourself that you had planned on going to college and becoming a journalist," Whitney pointed out.

"Dear God." Babs moaned. She rubbed her temples as if she'd suddenly developed a headache. "As I live and breathe, I will never touch another blue margarita again!"

Over Babs's shoulder, Whitney glared at the trio of women unabashedly eavesdropping. They hastily turned their attention to the tasks at hand. To her mother she said, "Are you saying that if you hadn't been drunk, you wouldn't have told me . . . ever?"

"Obviously," Babs snapped, forgetting to keep her voice down, "you weren't mature enough to handle the news!"

It was Whitney's turn to gasp.

The dozen or so people in the shop abandoned all pretense of not listening. This was simply too good to miss, since everyone knew that Babs and her daughter got on together like soap on a rope. A disagreement between them was a rarity; a shouting match unheard of.

"Mother—"

"Don't use that tone with me, Whitney Charolette!" Babs's face had flushed a rosy shade, betraying her agitation. She sniffed. "I never thought I'd say this about you, but it's true. You're a coward. You're a thirty-year-old coward, Whitney."

Her outburst stung. "A coward, Mother? You call me a coward because I'm not gung-ho to run out and make the same mistake that you did?"

"I did *not* make a mistake! *You* were not a mistake! What can I say to you to convince you of this fact?" Tears glistened in Babs's eyes. "Maybe if you weren't such a coward about life, Whitney, you could be having this discussion with your own precious, beloved daughter in thirty years."

"So you want me to do this reality-show thing and get knocked up? Would that make you happy?"

"Now you're being ridiculous. What I want you to do is take a chance once in a while, have some fun! You're thirty years old, and I can count the number of relationships you've had on one hand."

"And what's wrong with that? I just happen to be a cautious person."

"A coward," Babs murmured.

"I'm *not* a coward! Just because I won't participate in some dumb—"

"Whitney."

"—television show, like *you* did, you think that I'm—"

"Whitney!"

"—a coward. Well, it's not—"

Babs grabbed Whitney's shoulders and brought her close, this time purposely keeping her voice low. "There's another reason I want you to go on this show!"

At close range, Whitney could see the intensity of her mother's gaze. A tremor of premonition shot through her, making her mouth go dry. "What is it, Mother?" She tried to sound flippant, but her voice came out hoarse and wobbly.

For a long moment Babs didn't speak. Finally she dropped the bomb. "Whitney, darling, the host of the show is . . . your father."

Whitney didn't think the bright silver spots dancing before her eyes were a good sign. She felt faint. The host of the new, upcoming reality show was her father?

"And there's something else."

Something else? The silver spots multiplied. How could there be anything more shocking?

"I never actually *told* him about you, darling."

Whitney swayed. "You . . . you said you called him."

"Well, I did, dear. But he never returned my call, so I just let it drop." Her mother grabbed her arms to hold her steady. "Oh, darling! We just weren't suited for one another! And before you faint, you remember that gag commercial you and the girls made to shock me? The one where you're wearing a skimpy negligee, fluttering your eyelashes, and hinting that Beautiful Nails offered more than just a manicure?"

"You didn't send that in to them." Whitney shook her head vigorously. "You did not send them that horrible tape. I know you wouldn't."

Babs bit her lip. "I didn't, but the girls did."

"You can't have them." Rand McNair folded his arms and braced himself in front of the door. He tried to glower at his brother-in-law, Robin Stewart, of Stewart, McGaveny, and Sway, but didn't quite make it. He'd always liked Robin. They still played golf on occasion, and once a year he and Robin took a week's vacation to go camping and fishing.

Robin gave a helpless roll of his broad shoulders. He was clearly embarrassed by his mission. As well he should be, Rand thought with an inward growl of frustration.

"Look, Rand. Like I told you on the phone, these aren't *my* wishes—they're Bonnie's." He held out the papers in his hand. "Read it again. She clearly states that if you haven't remarried at the end of five years, then I'm to take Teddy and Dolly into my custody until you do."

"This is ridiculous!" Rand said, trying to remain calm. It wasn't easy; the thought of losing Teddy made him break out into a cold sweat. "She was obviously not in her right mind, Robin, when she made that silly clause in her will."

"I'm her brother, and I think I would know if she'd gone around the bend." His voice softened as he added, "She had cancer in her ovaries, not her brain."

Pain sliced through Rand. It had been five years since his wife's death, and he still couldn't bear to think about her without wanting to howl at the moon. She'd been his soul mate.

"Look—can I come in?" Robin asked.

When Rand reluctantly stepped aside, Robin crossed the threshold and set his briefcase on the gleaming hardwood floor. Beyond him through the open door, a plain white van idled in the driveway.

Rand shut the door to block out the sight and turned to face his brother-in-law again. "I'm not letting you take them. They belong to me. I don't care what the will says."

"*You* may not care, but the *law* cares." Robin sighed. "Rand, she knew you better than you probably know yourself. When she came to me about this change in her will, she told me that she didn't want you living the rest of your life alone."

"Taking Teddy and Dolly won't change how I live my life, Robin."

"It will if you feel as strongly about them as Bonnie believed you did."

Rand gritted his teeth, but remained silent. Bonnie had cherished them—of course he loved them. And the house would be even emptier without them.

As if he had read his thoughts, Robin said quietly, "They're a constant reminder. She knew they would be."

"I'm not going to run out and marry someone just to get them back." He snorted. "How crazy do you think I am?"

"How crazy you are isn't my business. My business is to take them into my custody. Today. With me now. Hopefully without having to bring the sheriff in on this."

With an angry growl, Rand snatched the copy of the will Robin had brought him and scanned the typewritten mumbo-jumbo. Robin had tried reading it to him over the phone, but Rand had hung up on him.

His eyes widened as he realized that the outrageous clause mentioned nothing about having to *stay* married. He swung around and eyed the elegant little antique hall table Bonnie had found in some out-of-the way antique shop.

Lying on top of its shiny surface was the day's mail, including an application to appear on the upcoming reality television show, *Eden*, and a detailed brochure about the island where the show would be filmed.

A hundred selected couples would be participating.

A hundred women looking for Mr. Right, and a hundred men looking for their dream girl.

Rand knew that Bonnie had been *his* dream girl, and he also knew there would never be another Bonnie for him. She had been his soul mate, his one and only. She had felt the same, so why was she torturing him this way?

"Rand? Are you okay?"

He gave a start, blinking as Robin's face swam into view. Was he actually thinking about filling out that application and sending it in?

A hundred women looking for Mr. Right.

Or one woman who could be bribed into marrying him, then getting a quick divorce once Robin returned to him what was rightfully his.

"Rand? I . . . I need to get started. I've got a two-thirty appointment—"

"Take them."

"I'm really sorry—"

"I said take them. They're in the bedroom." When Robin started away, Rand grabbed his arm. "You'd better take good care of them," he warned softly.

Their gazes met, each man remembering a woman they had loved, and whom they still missed. Rand softened. He knew how close Robin and Bonnie had been. This couldn't be easy for Robin, and he wasn't helping with his stubborn resistance.

He let go of Robin and turned his back. He didn't want to watch his brother-in-law leave with Teddy and Dolly. Instead he gathered up the will, the application, and the brochure and took them to the kitchen.

What he couldn't admit to his brother-in-law, he could easily admit to himself.

He wouldn't sleep a wink until he'd found a way to get Teddy and Dolly back.

Chapter Two

"As you all know, people, we're down to our last fifty contestants."

What the five-foot-tall host of *Eden*, Rupert Asterisk, lacked in stature, he made up for in voice volume, Whitney mused, glad she had taken after her mother in height *and* personality.

After the wild cheering—liberally peppered with masculine catcalls—died to a dull roar, the host tapped his microphone to get their attention. "We have two more weeks of fun ahead of us, and for the lucky five couples remaining at the end of those two weeks, we have out-of-this-world prizes." He wiggled his eyebrows dramatically, grinning. "Or should I say *around* this world? Because as you all very well know, the number one lucky couple will be awarded the grand prize—drumroll please—of a trip around the world and one million dollars.

Whitney dutifully clapped her hands as the rest of the crowd proceeded to mimic the very savages who had once occupied the island of Mystique.

"Of course, the producers of Hawkeye Productions fervently

hope the trip around the world happens to coincide with the lucky couple's *honeymoon.*"

Laughter erupted from the crowd, including the dozen or so cameramen constantly on the move around the ballroom.

Whitney didn't laugh. If *she* made it to the finish line, there would definitely be no honeymoon, so Hawkeye Productions would be fervently disappointed. They'd have to cook up another ridiculous, mind-manipulating reality television show.

With a smothered sigh, Whitney tried to relax. After four weeks of silly games played with testosterone-charged men, she was ready and willing to *swim* home. Her stint in this reality television game had reinforced her intentions of remaining single for the rest of her life, and the possibility of confronting her father grew dimmer with each passing day. When he wasn't surrounded by admiring fans—mostly screaming, giggling women—he was telling crude jokes or could be seen deep in discussion with the producers and staff.

She seldom found him alone, and when she did, she found she couldn't approach him. What would she say to him? *Hello, Mr. Asterisk. Remember the woman you used and abused from* The Dating Game? *Well, I'm her daughter—er—your daughter.*

"So good luck, people, and good night! Have a drink or two on me, will you? My wife has decided . . ."

Not even Asterisk of the booming voice could be heard over the sudden babble of a hundred people. Whitney bolted through the crowd and headed for her bungalow, praying she would get away before anyone noticed her defection.

There was always a huge party after elimination day, but Whitney didn't have the stomach for it; just hours earlier she'd witnessed more than a dozen girls leaving the island in tears, their hearts broken, their dreams shattered.

Whitney couldn't believe she had made it this far. She hadn't cared, really, and it showed. Was that the attraction for the judges? That she didn't seem to care about the stupid show?

The sandy path leading to the bungalow she shared with

Rosalyn, fellow contestant, was dimly lit. Whitney was a few yards away from her bungalow door when she heard the sound of a woman weeping.

She paused, looking carefully around her. The bushes on either side of the path revealed nothing but indistinguishable shadows. She crept closer. "Hello? Is someone there?"

The weeping grew louder.

"Rosalyn?" Whitney hazarded a guess, given the close proximity to their bungalow.

"Go away!" Rosalyn snarled, then continued weeping.

So it *was* her roommate! Whitney ignored the girl's wishes and moved blindly in the direction of the noise, sweeping lush foliage aside. "Rosalyn? It's Whitney. Is there something I can do to help?"

"Yes! You can drag that creep into the ocean and feed him to the sharks!"

Taken aback by her vicious tone, Whitney stopped a few feet away. Tropical moonlight revealed Rosalyn's tear-ravaged face and wet-lashed eyes. "Which creep would that be?" She'd been on the island long enough to have met just about every participant, and she had discovered that most of the men *were* creeps, clowns, or worse—players. There was nothing that irked Whitney more than a player.

Rosalyn's weeping slowed to an occasional sniffle. "Andrew Wilkins, that's who. He . . . he dumped me for that bimbo Darla!"

Ah, Darla. The blonde with the fake boobs, luscious figure, and insatiable appetite. Since the beginning of the show, Darla had made her rounds among the men. Stealing, seducing, bribing . . . Darla wasn't averse to outright lying to lure a man away from his girl.

Whitney had fast come to the conclusion that Darla only wanted what Darla couldn't have. When she got it, it was no longer appealing.

She stifled a sigh, not exactly sure what to say to Rosalyn. Darla was Darla, and men were . . . men.

Her roommate burst into noisy sobs again, wailing, "And that's not the worst of it! Those damned cameramen filmed him dumping me, and I heard them talking about what a good segment it would make. I'm not . . . not only a complete fool; I'm going to be a fool in front of millions of people!"

It was on the tip of Whitney's tongue to point out to Rosalyn that she had signed away her right to privacy when she decided to participate in the show, but she swallowed the words. Rosalyn didn't need a lecture.

She needed a friend. A *helpful* friend.

One who happened to have an unauthorized key to the editing room. Was it *her* fault the staff was careless with their keys?

It wouldn't be the first time she'd stolen a tape to help a friend since joining the show.

And it probably wouldn't be her last.

Rand wasn't having much luck. He couldn't believe that after four weeks, he wasn't any closer to finding a compatible, willing woman to marry and divorce. Bonnie, with her eccentric personality and outrageous sense of fun, had definitely spoiled him.

He gave his head a wry shake. If he couldn't find someone suitable among a hundred women . . .

"Don't worry, Rosalyn," a decisive, feminine voice said, jarring Rand out of his musings and bringing him to a startled halt on the sandy path.

He glanced around with a frown, realizing that he'd taken the wrong trail. They all looked the same in the dim lighting, and he'd been so distracted by his thoughts that he hadn't noticed.

"I'll make sure they never show that tape," the voice continued.

Another feminine voice—this one shrill and teary—sounded doubtful. "How . . . how will you do that, Whitney?"

Whitney. Rand's eyes narrowed. He moved deeper into the shadows and out of sight. Among the men, Whitney Sutherland was aptly nicknamed Ice Cuba. She flirted, she smiled, she laughed, but not a single guy on the show had claimed so much as a kiss. Nevertheless, her obvious intelligence and keen perception had kept her in the game.

"I have my ways. Just trust me, OK? Nobody else will witness today's humiliation. That I can promise."

She sounded so utterly convinced of this that Rand found himself believing her. Obviously the other girl agreed.

"Oh, Whitney! You are a *super* friend! Thank you."

Rand melted farther into the shadows as the woman stepped onto the path. Whitney joined her.

"Now, go dry your tears and don't give Andrew another thought. He obviously wasn't the one for you."

"Okay."

Impulsively the sniffling woman hugged Whitney before she hurried out of sight.

"The Peeping Toms should all be at the party," Whitney muttered loud enough for Rand to hear.

He held his breath as she walked past him, hips swinging, her light perfume tickling his nostrils. She wore low-riding shorts and a cropped T-shirt that emphasized her small waist and long, slim legs. After a thoughtful moment, Rand followed, his curiosity thoroughly aroused. Peeping Toms? Who was she talking about? And how was she going to stop the producers from airing that tape?

She stopped once to slip off her sandals, pausing long enough to dig her toes in the cool dirt.

Rand heard her soft sigh of pleasure, and he found the sound surprisingly arousing.

His heart began to beat faster. Maybe she was the one, he thought, his gaze now on her swinging hips. Maybe he'd finally found a woman he could spend a little time with, get to know long enough to marry and divorce. Obviously for his plan to work he needed to be a *little* attracted to the woman.

Up ahead, Whitney paused again before she turned right—away from the sound of music and the bright lights of the ball-room, heading in the direction of the cluster of bungalows housing the show's staff.

She seemed to know exactly where she was going, Rand noted, slipping from tree to tree now that she had reached open ground. What *was* the little minx up to?

She stopped in front of bungalow nineteen, and to Rand's surprise, she knocked on the door. He waited, aware that his heart was pounding as she tried the doorknob before producing a key. She glanced around before slipping inside.

Rand counted slowly to twenty before he followed.

The interior of the bungalow was dark. Whitney took out a pocket flashlight, cupping her hand around the beam as she swept it slowly around a room filled with televisions, stacks of tapes, and camera equipment.

She'd been in here before, of course, but she knew from experience that organization wasn't the camera crew's forte.

Tonight was no exception. How did they keep it all straight? Whitney wondered, moving quickly to a pile of tapes stacked precariously next to a flat TV screen with a built-in VCR.

Her foot bumped into something. Whitney grimaced as cold liquid sloshed onto her bare toes. She quickly backed away and slipped on her sandals before venturing forth again, skirting the puddle formed by the overturned cup.

Using the flashlight as a guide, she began searching the labels on the tapes one by one.

Casey and Brenda drunk at sunset.

Casey and Brenda hung over at dawn.

Darla goes topless.

Darla dances topless.

Darla plays spin the bottle with six guys while topless.

Whitney let out a soft snort. If popularity votes counted, then

Darla had already won the grand prize. It seemed that not even the staff was immune to the woman's considerable charms.

Her fingers paused on the next one. *Rosalyn getting dumped.* That was one of the things she liked about the staff, Whitney mused dryly: they called a horse a horse. At least it made *her* job easier.

She grabbed the tape, trying to decide where she could stash it. She wasn't exactly dressed for hiding things, she realized belatedly.

Warm air swirled around her ankles. She froze. The door creaked shut behind her.

Her heart leaped into her throat. She was caught. After four weeks of successfully filching tapes, she had finally been caught red-handed by . . . by . . . whom? One of the camera crew? A security guard?

"Why do I get the feeling you've done this before?"

The voice was deep and familiar, yet *not* familiar. But then, she had been subjected to a lot of deep voices since arriving on the island. Yet this one . . . this one—

"Whitney, isn't it? Whitney Sutherland." His voice deepened with a hint of amusement. "The island Ice Cuba."

Shocked into carelessness, Whitney swung around and aimed the flashlight at the man, catching him full in the face. He blinked and stumbled back, throwing up his arm. But not before she recognized him as the island's most ruthless player, Rand McNair. He'd left more than one friend of Whitney's in tears after a date, and the buzz was that he was more interested in the prize than a relationship.

"Hey," he protested. "You mind shining that somewhere—"

"Shh!" Whitney hissed, hearing muffled voices outside the bungalow. "Someone's coming!" She hastily pointed the flashlight at the floor, fumbling with the off button. Panic moved her to action. She stumbled forward and grabbed Rand's arm, jerking him against her. The shocking impact of his hard body against her soft curves momentarily dazed her.

261

The tape she'd risked everything to steal slipped from her fingers and hit the floor. She kicked it hard enough to make her bare toes throb, hoping she'd succeeded in burying it beneath a desk or a table.

He was hard *everywhere*, and warm. Very warm.

She felt an odd flutter against her bare belly, sending a strange thrilling sensation right into her nether regions.

She swallowed. Either she had trapped his hand between them, or he was—

The doorknob began to turn. Whitney flung her arms around the man's neck and whispered frantically against his ear, "I'll explain later. Just . . . just kiss me!"

"Kiss you?"

"Yes!"

"Here?"

"Yes!"

"Now?"

"Oh, for heaven's sake!" Whitney crushed her mouth to his just as the door swung open. She took his hand and moved it to her breast, letting out an aroused moan that would have done Darla proud.

Bright fluorescent light flooded the room, blinding her.

A squeaky, surprised voice exclaimed, "What the hell?"

Whitney tried to end the kiss so that she could continue the charade with an embarrassed squeal and a fumbling apology, but she found she couldn't move.

Rand had her locked in his arms, and now he deepened the kiss, lifting her up and sliding her along his body, leaving her in no doubt about his aroused state. When her feet touched the floor again, his hand returned to her breast.

The pad of his thumb scraped her nipple.

Whitney nearly jumped out of her skin. She tried to moan a protest, but found she couldn't make a sound beneath the onslaught of the most dominating, arousing, exciting kiss she'd ever experienced. No wonder the other girls cried themselves to sleep after a date with Rand! The man was a veritable expert in the art of kissing—

"Are you getting this, Will?"

"Damned right I am! It's not every day you catch a guy getting this far with Ice Cuba."

Vaguely, the conversation sank into Whitney's brain. There was that silly name again, Ice Cuba. And they had obviously been referring to her, just as Rand had been referring to her.

Well, she didn't feel like an ice cube at the moment—more like an active volcano!

And then the meaning of their conversation hit her.

Hard.

They were being taped.

Chapter Three

"Nobody authorized this interview," the second cameraman told his coworker. "You know the rules."

"The hell with the rules, Chuck," Will grumbled, lowering his camera as he gestured for Rand and Whitney to have a seat. "You want someone else to take the credit for witnessing this meltdown?"

Whitney couldn't seem to move. Now Rand would drop the hatchet on her, expose her as a thief. Point his very talented finger in her direction. They would disqualify her, possibly press charges of theft against her.

She would be banished from the island, and the opportunity to meet her father would be lost.

Not long ago, that possibility would have been a pleasant one to contemplate.

But not now. Now she had a mission just as important as introducing herself to her father. She could not, in good conscience, leave her friends at the mercy of a self-gratifying hotshot like Rand. He already had more notches on his belt than Richard

Simmons, and she could easily imagine him loving and leaving some poor woman the way her father had done to her mother.

She was Ice Cuba! She could withstand the heat of his mouth, the fire of his hands without melting into a puddle of helplessness. Okay, so she might melt a bit, but she would never lose her head.

And yes, the nickname stung a little. She supposed she was a tad conservative when it came to sex, but she never thought of herself as an ice cube. Why, she could experience passion as well as the next woman—in the arms of the right man.

She just rarely came across the right man.

Rand McNair might be arrogant and blind enough to think *he* was that man—and maybe he was—but Whitney knew the difference between lust and love. She was thirty years old, for goodness' sake!

"Have a seat, folks, and spill it." Will clapped a hand on his knee and grinned at them. "How long has this been going on, and why are you sneaking around?"

Whitney closed her eyes to pray, so she didn't see the sudden gleam in Rand's eyes until she was sitting on his lap, and she was fairly certain that wasn't a flashlight in his pocket. She quickly closed her eyes again, aware that her face had to be visibly glowing. She tightened her fingers over his shirt sleeve as the deep, low rumbling of his voice vibrated through her.

"We just can't seem to keep our hands off of each other," Rand confessed outrageously.

She squeaked a tiny protest and got a pair of hot lips against her ear for her efforts.

"Be still," he said in whisper that sounded oddly pained. To Will and Chuck he said, "But we wanted to be sure before we let everyone know."

"How about you, Ice . . . um, Whitney, isn't it? Whitney Sutherland? Do you have anything to add?"

Rand gave her hip an encouraging squeeze, prompting Whitney into a hasty, "No, I have nothing to add. We . . ." She swallowed hard, looking at the grinning cameraman. "We just wanted a little privacy."

Will's grin widened until it seemed to encompass his entire face. "Oh, I think you'll get that privacy, all right." He slanted his partner a mysterious glance.

Whitney licked her dry lips. "What . . . what are you talking about?"

"Can't say right now, but you'll know soon enough." Will exchanged another frustratingly mysterious glance with his partner. "Um, you'll excuse us, won't you? Chuck and I have some editing to do."

Whitney leaped up so fast she slipped in the puddle she'd forgotten about.

Rand caught her in his arms, laughing into her startled face. "Honey, if you wanted me to carry you, all you had to do was say so." He lowered his voice, but Whitney knew perfectly well he was aware of their avid audience. "I told you, I'm willing to try anything once."

The moment the door shut behind them, Whitney struggled out of his arms. With quick, angry strides she headed in the direction of her bungalow, aware that Rand followed, and that he was grinning from ear to ear.

He was having fun at *her* expense, the rat.

"Hey, where you going in such a hurry?"

"To my bungalow."

"Don't you think you owe me a thank-you?"

Without breaking stride, Whitney said through gritted teeth, "Thank you."

"Your sincerity brings tears to my eyes." He caught her arm, forcing her to face him. He was no longer smiling. "In case you missed it, I just saved your butt in there."

"And in case you missed it, I said thank-you."

He frowned. "Want to clue me in on why you're so mad?"

"Because you kissed me!"

Rand's eyes narrowed. "You *told* me to kiss you."

Whitney huffed. "But I didn't tell you to *keep* on kissing me! Now everyone will *see* us kissing. They were filming us!"

"And your point is . . . ?" he asked softly. When she merely angled her chin, he sighed. "Look, I'm just going to come right out and say it. I enjoyed the kiss. A lot."

"I'm sure you did," Whitney snapped. "Being the hotshot that you are, but I've got news for you, *buddy*—" She clamped her mouth shut, appalled that she'd nearly ruined her most recent plans to save the remaining female contestants from the likes of Rand McNair.

She took several deep breaths and tried to look sheepish. "I'm sorry. I guess my temper got away from me. The truth is . . . I enjoyed the kiss, too." She was dismayed to realize she spoke the truth. With an inward shrug, she thought, *Why not enjoy it?* As long as she kept her wits about her—and she would—what would it hurt to have a little fun?

Rand McNair would soon discover that he'd met his match.

Rand had been out of the dating scene for a long time, but not so long that he didn't recognize a con when he saw one.

Whitney Hot Lips was definitely conning him. Nobody switched gears that fast, not if they were truly mad.

For the first time since landing on the island, Rand felt a stirring of real curiosity for another woman. Why was Whitney Sutherland, a.k.a. Ice Cuba, a.k.a. Hot Lips, pretending she wasn't furious—when she obviously was? Was she genuinely camera-shy, or was there another reason she didn't want to be caught kissing on camera?

Rand was both surprised and pleased to discover that he wanted to uncover the truth. He wanted to find out what made Whitney tick, because unless he'd missed the mark, he'd definitely felt her ticking back at the bungalow. Big-time. Panting breath, tiny little moans, and plenty of tongue. If that wasn't ticking, then Rand had forgotten what was.

"I want to see you again," he said, watching her closely.

"Me, too."

She smiled, a soft, alluring smile that made his eyebrows shoot upward, it was so obviously feigned. Oh, not that she didn't flirt well—she did—but Rand knew instinctively that she wasn't sincere.

His ego took the punch with the barest of a flinch, while another part of him reacted as if he had no brains. What would this sexy, intriguing woman think if he blurted out that he hadn't felt this kind of instant attraction in more years than he could count?

She would probably laugh at him.

Rand stifled an ironic chuckle. After four weeks and dozens of women, he'd finally found one that at least captured his initial interest, yet *she* didn't appear interested in *him*.

Outwardly, yes.

Sincerely . . . he didn't think so. He hoped that he was wrong. All he needed was to find a woman he could get to know so that he could present his proposal. As long as she didn't get sappy . . .

"Don't worry, hotshot," Whitney said as if she could read his mind, "I'm not the type to get sappy about a guy."

"Excuse me?" Rand blinked. Her lips—lush lips, at that— were curled in a knowing little smile that made him want to soften them with another scorching kiss.

"You had that look in your eyes. That wary look that guys get when they want a good time without all the sappy, shallow, meaningless jargon that comes with it."

"I did?" Rand couldn't think of a single smart comeback to her blunt statement.

"Hm," she murmured, her gaze dropping to stare at his open mouth. She ran a teasing finger along his jaw, then gently pushed his mouth closed. "Why don't we just lay it all out in the open? You and I are interested in the same thing, I think."

"We . . . we are?"

"Yes. We both want that grand prize."

"We do?"

She let out a husky little laugh that made Rand's toes curl inside his leather sandals.

"Don't we?" she countered. "I think you and I would make a good team, don't you?"

Rand nearly said, *We would?* before he caught himself. For a startling second, a vivid image of tangled sheets and ripe lips fogged his mind.

Then her statement sank in. She thought he was after the prize, and cared nothing for finding Mrs. Right, because *she* was after the prize and cared nothing for finding *Mr.* Right.

He allowed a slow smile of pleasure to curve his mouth. Could he actually be lucky enough to have found a woman who wasn't interested in happily ever after?

Because he couldn't give a woman that. He could offer her a substantial amount of money—even beachfront property and a summer house—but not his love. His love had died with Bonnie, and he was fine with that.

"Did I surprise you?" she prompted.

Oh, she had definitely surprised him! "No, not at all." He captured her hand and brought her fingertips to his lips, kissing each one as he watched her through hooded eyes. "You have no idea how refreshing your honesty is after all the women I've met in the past few weeks." He thought her smile faltered, but decided he must have been mistaken.

"I'll bet. Then we're a team?"

He nodded, slowly lowering her hand. "You've got a deal."

And if his luck continued, it would be a deal she didn't regret making.

By the time they reached her bungalow, Whitney's cheek muscles ached from keeping a fake smile plastered on her face. She said good-night to Rand and hurried inside, slumping against the door.

"He's a player, you know."

Whitney jumped as her roommate moved away from the window. Rosalyn's eyes and nose were red from crying, but she looked considerably calmer than she had earlier. *Poor woman!* And Whitney's mother didn't understand why she avoided getting serious about a man. "I know he's a player."

"Then why were you with him?"

It was a good question, one Whitney was very happy to answer. "Because I *know* he's a player."

Rosalyn frowned as she reached for another tissue and blew her nose. "He's dated half the girls on this island. I guess you think you're immune?"

"No," Whitney said honestly. "Just informed."

After a long, searching moment, Rosalyn sighed. "Julia Benstine left the island because of Rand, and Abigail Winters threatened suicide."

"I can take care of myself."

"Yeah, that's probably what *they* thought. Half the women on the island say that after one date with Rand, the others pale by comparison."

Whitney thought about the bone-melting fingertip kissing Rand had done as if it were the most natural thing in the world for a guy to do. With moves like that, how had the man managed to remain single this long? Not that *she* was interested in marrying him. Meeting her father and damage control were her goals.

Nothing more, nothing less.

Or maybe something more between the sheets . . . if the opportunity presented itself. She wasn't a nun, no matter what her mother believed, and she was honest enough to admit that she was definitely attracted to Rand.

"If you hook him, the others will hate you," Rosalyn informed her gravely.

This time Whitney's smile was genuine. "That's not going to happen, Rosy. Even if a hotshot like Rand wanted to be hooked, he's not my type, at least not for the long haul."

271

"You can't choose who you fall in love with."

Rosalyn sounded so convinced of this, Whitney decided against arguing. "I'll be careful." She clapped her hands together, hoping to change the subject. "So! Have you thought about what I said? Are you going to forget about what's-his-name and check out the other fish in the sea?"

Blinking innocently, Rosalyn asked, "Who?"

"That-a-girl! I think I'll get a shower before bed. It's muggy tonight." Whitney retrieved her nightie from a chest of drawers beside her bed and headed for the bathroom.

"Whitney?"

She paused at the bathroom door and looked back at her roommate. "Yeah?"

"Did you take care of the problem, like you promised?"

Whitney's mind was a total blank. Then she realized what Rosalyn was talking about. How could she have forgotten? But she knew. Oh, she knew. *Rand* was the reason she had forgotten about Rosalyn's humiliating experiencing and the resulting tape.

"I think so." She had kicked it out of sight, and then she had promptly forgotten about it. With any luck the camera crew would give up when they couldn't find it.

Rosalyn visibly relaxed. "Thank you, Whitney. I'm sorry I snapped at you earlier." She flashed Whitney a wan smile. "I think you're one of the most courageous women I've ever met."

Blushing, Whitney shook her head. "Thanks, but I think you're exaggerating."

"You're taking Rand McNair on. I'd say that takes courage."

"He's just a man, Rosy."

"Yes, but *what* a man," Rosalyn said under her breath. Her face relaxed into dreamy lines. "He's every woman's dream, you know. Handsome, sexy, successful, and one of the best kissers—"

"You've kissed him?"

"No, but I've talked to more than a dozen girls who have.

They all say the same." Rosalyn cast her a sly look. "Have *you* kissed him?"

"I . . . I . . ." Whitney felt her face heat up. "Yes," she finally admitted, then added firmly, "And there was nothing extraordinary about it."

But she was lying, and she knew it.

Chapter Four

If not for the laughter and shouting of the other contestants as they surfed, swam, and played along the beautiful beach, Whitney might have dozed off under the warm tropical sun.

She sighed and turned her head, counting at least a dozen women sunbathing topless, and almost as many cameras filming them. Was she truly an ice cube just because she didn't care to bare her breasts to a million viewers? She wasn't ashamed of her body—just particular about who saw it. Did that make her a prude? Besides, they would have to censor the tape anyway. Who wanted to be seen wearing nothing but a black strip across their chest?

She cupped her chin in her hand, her gaze wandering along the crowded beach to the volleyball game in full swing. She sucked in a sharp breath as she recognized Rand among the players. Even from a distance, Whitney could appreciate the width of his bronzed shoulders, marvel at his well-muscled stomach and lean hips, and secretly drool over the sight of his powerful thighs bulging as he raced after the ball.

She closed her eyes, recalling his features from the night before. Dark chocolate eyes framed by thick black lashes, a strong, square jaw, dazzling white teeth, and a slightly crooked nose that kept him from being downright beautiful. He wore his dark hair short and tousled in a way that made him appear as if he'd just gotten out of bed.

Before Rand, Whitney had turned up her nose at that casual style.

Oh, he certainly knew how to charm the ladies, she thought, remembering the gallant way he'd kissed her fingertips. A player of the worst kind—the kind that convinced a woman she was special, when in reality she was nothing more than a challenge and a conquest.

Ha! If there was any conquering going on, Whitney was determined it would be entirely mutual.

She jumped as something warm puddled between her shoulder blades.

"You're going to burn if you're not careful," Rand said as he straddled her hips and began to rub the sun-heated lotion into her skin.

Whitney found herself hoping that she was already beginning to turn red so that it would mask her all-over body blush. He was actually *straddling* her, right in front of the cameras. His strong hands were kneading her shoulders in a way that made her knees grow weak. Lord, but the man had magic hands as well as magic lips.

She buried her face in her folded arms on the off chance one of the ever-present cameras was taping them. Maybe her mother wouldn't recognize her.

And pigs could fly.

"Of all the women sunbathing—half of them topless—why did you pick me?" she asked, her voice muffled, yet unmistakably skeptical.

"Because I *like* you. Why is that so difficult for you to believe?"

Now was not the time for honesty, Whitney decided, thinking of the many women he'd ruthlessly dated and dropped. She lifted her hot face to stare out to sea, trying to ignore the ripples of excitement she felt each time his hands squeezed and kneaded, squeezed and kneaded.

His hands dropped lower, encompassing her waist and hips. Whitney fought the urge to jump up and run for her life. As if she could, with those powerful thighs pinning her to the blanket.

She swallowed a moan, wishing he would stop, perversely dreading the moment when he did.

"There. All done."

Thank God!

Please don't stop!

"Thanks," she managed to mutter. She closed her eyes, praying he would take the hint. Her body burned and tingled all over from his touch; she didn't know how much more she could take without betraying herself. Ha! So much for Ice Cuba! They would have to think up a different name for her, something with the word *hot*, or *volcanic*.

"My pleasure."

He sounded amused, as if he knew his effect on her. Whitney scoffed at the thought. Of course he didn't know. She'd given no sign, had she? Well, that one tiny little moan . . .

She stiffened as he leaned forward, his warm breath tickling her neck.

"I'd like to see you later," he said, his voice low and husky.

After a deliberate pause, Whitney turned her head slightly so that their mouths were inches apart. The sight of that mouth reminded her of the kiss they'd exchanged the night before.

Her breath quickened, and so did her pulse.

She licked her lips, aware that he seemed to find her mouth as fascinating as she did his. "How about ten o'clock—at the waterfall?" She watched, helplessly, as he flashed her a wolfish smile.

"You don't want to be seen," he guessed shrewdly.

"Not . . . not yet. Is that OK?"

He shrugged. "I'm not exactly a voyeur, myself, but I can't guarantee that we won't be followed."

Whitney grinned. "I can. According to rumor, Darla is planning on doing a lap dance tonight in the lounge for the lucky man who can accurately guess her bra size. Sure you want to miss it?"

She sucked in a sharp breath when his gaze dropped to her exposed cleavage, lingering long enough to cause her heart to do a triple somersault. She had always considered herself average, but Rand was looking at her as if she put Darla's double D cups to shame.

When his gaze returned to hers, his dark eyes had grown visibly darker. "I'm sure."

She had a date with Rand McNair.

"Good grief," Whitney said under her breath, staring at her feet as she made her way to her bungalow to wash the sand from her body before lunch. Was she truly as strong as she had convinced Rosalyn she was when it came to skillful players like Rand?

He certainly turned her on, she mused, shivering despite the heat of the sun overhead. And that was something that hadn't happened to her in a long, long time.

So long ago she couldn't even *remember*.

The realization forced her to consider a fling with Rand. She was thirty and single. If she wanted to sleep with Rand, then she could damn well sleep with him. After all, she wasn't foolish enough to fall in love with him, no matter how talented he was in the art of lovemaking.

And she certainly wasn't foolish enough to get pregnant, as her mother had.

So what was stopping her? Nothing. Nothing at all.

Except . . . except for the fact that millions of people would know. Now, *that* bothered her, despite the fact that she had known her life would be public for as long as she remained an active contestant in the show. But so far she'd managed to keep a low profile, for the most part. And by stealing the tapes she hoped she'd kept a lot of the footage including herself out of the producers' hands.

Deep in thought, Whitney didn't see the man in front of her until she had bounced from his chest. She would have fallen backward from the momentum if he hadn't reached out and snatched a handful of her swimsuit cover-up.

When she regained her balance, she hastily apologized, looking at the man for the first time. "I'm sorry—" Her words died a quick death as she stared into Rupert Asterisk's frowning face.

Her father.

Standing before her, looking at her as if she had deliberately barreled into him. With the way the women followed him around and fawned over him, Whitney supposed it was a reasonable assumption.

She had never seen him this close. His hair was turning silver at the temples, and there were fine lines around his mouth and eyes. She saw no resemblance between them.

His frown deepened. "You look familiar. Do I know you?"

Wordlessly, she shook her head. She suspected she looked like a starstruck teenager, but couldn't seem to stop herself. She should say something—introduce herself. Perhaps her last name—the same as her mother's—would trigger his memory.

But she could get nothing past the dryness in her throat, and in the next moment the opportunity was gone. He stepped around her and hurried on down the path in the direction of the beach, leaving Whitney with a fiercely pounding heart and a sinking feeling she had just mangled her best chance at confronting her father.

"Coward," she whispered to herself. She found the nearest bench and sank onto it before her legs gave out. "This is ridiculous." She swiped a shaky hand over her face and shook her head. Why didn't she just walk right up to the man and blurt it out? What was the worst thing he could do to her?

Deny her.

But she expected that. Her mother had had a brief affair with the man, and when she found out she was pregnant, her mother had decided not to tell him. Asterisk hadn't really known her mother all that well, so he would have no reason to believe her even if she *had* told him.

So why would he believe *her* thirty years later? Did he have other children? How many times had he been married?

There were so many questions she longed to ask him.

"I just realized who you remind me of."

At the sound of her host's voice, Whitney nearly fell off the bench. She gripped the edges until the painted metal bit into her palms, staring at him in total shock.

He had returned, and this time he was smiling.

She opened her mouth to ask him who, but no sound emerged. What was wrong with her? Why did she freeze like a mindless little ninny?

"Helen Hunt," he announced with his typical flare for the dramatic. "You bear a striking resemblance to Helen Hunt. Anyone ever told you that? Well, you do." He studied her critically for a long moment. "You're actually much prettier than Helen."

His boisterous laugh made her jump.

"I'd get a kick in the butt if she heard me say *that*," he confided. Still chuckling, he headed down the path again.

He'd gotten perhaps twenty feet away when Whitney finally found her voice. It was squeaky and high, but at least her vocal chords were starting to work again. "Mr. Asterisk?"

He stopped and turned to look at her, frowning once again. "What?" His expression suddenly cleared as if she'd answered him. "Oh, sure. No problem."

Mystified, Whitney watched as the host returned, drew a glossy photo of himself from his jacket pocket, and quickly scrawled his name across the bottom. With a benign smile, he handed her the picture and gave her head a pat. "There you go, little chicken, and good luck."

Little chicken? Whitney managed to glare at his retreating back, wondering how *he* knew that she was a coward.

Next time she wouldn't be, she vowed.

The waterfall was deserted when Rand arrived a few moments before ten, confirming Whitney's theory that everyone would be in the lounge to witness Darla's latest bid for attention.

Rand had managed to elude the buxom blonde's clutches, although he'd had a couple of near misses. The last time was when he'd been relaxing in one of the island's many hot tubs, thinking about his architectural business and how he might expand it to include businesses as well as residences.

When he'd heard someone joining him, he'd thought nothing of it—after all, it was a community hot tub—until he'd opened his eyes to find Darla sitting opposite him.

Wearing nothing but a man-eating grin and an orange thong.

He'd gotten out of the tub in a hurry, luckily before any of the camera crew had time to film them together. Rand suspected the only reason Darla chased him was because he wasn't interested. There was just something about the woman that put him on red alert. She was trouble with a capital T, a man hunter.

He had met a few women since joining the show that he found mildly interesting, but that interest had been short-lived.

Taking a seat on a bench near the miniature waterfall, Rand allowed himself to think of Whitney without guilt. He knew that his attraction to her was purely physical. She was, after all, a very beautiful woman, as well as intelligent, elegant, feminine, and last but not least, sexy.

She carried herself with an almost dignified confidence Rand seldom saw, as if she knew exactly who she was and where she wanted to go in life.

Whitney was strong, as Bonnie had been strong.

But that was where the similarities stopped. Bonnie had been a wild spirit, an eccentric artist who had never ceased to surprise Rand. She had been one of a kind, at least for him. Whitney struck him as a trifle on the conservative side. Cool, filled with hidden mysteries that beckoned a man to explore.

He couldn't imagine Whitney skinny-dipping in broad daylight, as Bonnie had on more than one occasion. He couldn't imagine Whitney cooking dinner while she was still covered in paint, or stopping to gather wildflowers from the side of the road, oblivious to the traffic jam she caused.

Bonnie had been . . . Bonnie.

Rand closed his eyes, his chest aching.

When he opened them again it was to find Whitney watching him. All thoughts of Bonnie flew from his mind as he focused on the vision standing on the path leading to the waterfall.

She wore low-slung pants in a shimmering pearl color that seemed to reflect the moonlight, and a short top to match, leaving several inches of bare skin in between. The shirt accentuated her tropical tan and the feminine slope of her shoulders.

Her sandals dangled from two fingers, leaving her feet bare.

It wasn't the first time Rand had seen her carrying her shoes instead of wearing them. The reminder prompted an icebreaker. "You like to feel the sand between your toes."

Whitney confirmed his guess with a hint of a smile. "Great work, Sherlock."

Rand rose from the bench and slowly approached her, watching her eyes as they flared in slight alarm. So she wasn't as cool as she'd like him to believe. "Speaking of detectives . . . care to tell me what you were doing in the editing bungalow last night?" He knew, but he was curious to see if she would tell him the truth.

Her chin came up ever so slightly. "I was stealing a tape for my roommate. She got dumped, and she understandably didn't want a million people to witness her humiliation."

"You risked getting thrown off the show for a rival contestant?" Rand lifted his brows. "And you had me convinced you were determined to win the grand prize."

"I am." She rolled one bare, tanned shoulder. "But not at the expense of someone else's pain. Rosalyn's not just my roommate, she's my friend." Pitching her sandals aside, she climbed onto a big rock and faced the waterfall. "It's lovely, isn't it?"

"Definitely," Rand agreed, but he wasn't looking at the waterfall; he was looking at her, standing on the rock like a mythical wood nymph. He hadn't realized how lonely he'd become until he'd met Whitney, and her sensitivity over her roommate's plight increased his hope that when the time was right, she could be persuaded to help him regain custody of Teddy and Dolly. Getting them back would ease his loneliness.

She turned abruptly, and Rand instinctively grabbed her waist to hold her steady. She smiled her thanks, settling her hands on his shoulders. "So why didn't you tell on me?"

"I'm not a tattletale." He also wasn't made of steel. No doubt about it; the woman stirred a longing in him he hadn't felt in a long while. Not that he was a saint. He'd brought pleasure to several women since Bonnie's death, but the unconsummated experiences had always left him aching and empty.

Slowly Rand lifted her up and swung her away from the rock. When her feet touched the ground, he kept his arms around her, taking his time as he studied her. Her eyes were the color of storm clouds, a tug-of-war between blue and gray, and her lips . . . her lips were full and red. She wore her dark blond hair straight and shimmering, gently sweeping her bare shoulders.

He suspected that she was in her late twenties, yet there was an odd innocence about her that stirred Rand's blood. *She's never suffered a loss like I have,* he thought with sudden insight, and without jealousy. He'd never wish that type of agony and suffering on anyone.

With a tenderness that surprised him, he reached out and swept a lock of hair from her cheek. "You're beautiful."

Those lush lips of hers quirked in a slight smile. "I'll bet you say that to all the women."

He felt his own mouth quiver. "No. Just to the ones who are beautiful." Her spontaneous laughter speared heat into his groin, lighting a fire that momentarily stunned him. Bonnie had been the only woman who could stir him so quickly with a laugh or a smile, or a certain look.

"Well, you sure know how to sweep a woman off her feet," Whitney said a little breathlessly. Her tongue came out to moisten her lips, capturing his attention.

Rand couldn't resist. He swooped in and followed the path her tongue had taken with his own, taking his time exploring every curve and crevice. She stood perfectly still at first, as if she were absorbing the feel of him.

By the time Rand finished his exploration, they were both breathing hard. He blinked, amazed that the briefest of kisses had brought them to the point of panting.

"They weren't exaggerating," Whitney said, slowly opening her eyes.

"They?"

"The other women you've kissed. You *are* a good kisser."

Her bald words floored him for all of two seconds. With a rough chuckle, he pulled her against him. "You call that a kiss? I'll *show* you a kiss."

Chapter Five

She had to go and taunt the tiger, Whitney thought in the instant it took for Rand's mouth to cover hers in a searing, heated kiss that rocked her world. She had to grip his arms to hold herself upright, because she certainly didn't want to lose contact!

Rock-hard arms.

Hot kiss.

Firm body.

Lord, she was in trouble! She could feel her poor heart pounding like a jackhammer. In another moment she would be grinding her hungry pelvis in ways that would have shocked Elvis, God rest his soul.

With extreme effort she broke free of the kiss, sucking air into her lungs and hanging on to those rock-hard pecs for dear life. Shakily, she asked, "What . . . what line of work did you say you were in?"

He smiled down at her. "I'm an architect."

Whitney eyed the width of his hard, broad chest, her gaze

straying to the impressive muscles displayed beneath her tingling fingers. "You could have fooled me," she said, arching her brows in disbelief. "I took you for a construction worker at the very least. Do you work out?"

"Are you coming on to me, Whitney?"

Her jaw dropped. "Um, no. No! I was being sincere."

"Damn."

The slow, sexy grin that followed his disappointed curse stopped her heart for an alarming second. Laughter bubbled up and over as she realized that he was teasing her. "You had me going there."

"I know."

He tugged on her arm, drawing her to the bench. Whitney went willingly, grateful to be able to sit during the aftershocks following his kiss. He sat beside her.

Really, really close.

Whitney fancied she could see blue sparks zipping back and forth between the inch or so of space separating their thighs. What would he do if she jumped up and straddled him right then and there? Begged him to make love to her? To kiss her again and again and—

"So tell me, Whitney. What's a nice girl like you doing in a place like this?"

"I told you. I'm after the grand prize."

"I'm not buying that."

Whitney didn't bother hiding her surprise. "Why not?"

"Because you don't strike me as a material woman."

She had to laugh at that. "Oh, believe me, I'm a *very* material woman. At last count I owned thirty-five pairs of shoes, seven coats, and enough costume jewelry to sink the *Titanic*."

He stared pointedly at the simple gold chain around her neck. Her mother had given it to her on her sixteenth birthday, along with a pair of gold earrings she had lost in high school.

"For someone who likes jewelry, you're not wearing much of it."

"Okay, you got me there. Jewelry isn't my thing, but shoes and coats are."

"You still didn't answer my question." He put his hand on her thigh and began a slow, torturous stroking motion that made Whitney nearly bite her tongue in two.

"Hm?" She looked at him blankly, trying to recall his earlier question. What had it been? And how could she think with his hand on her thigh? Maybe she could persuade him to skip the preliminary wooing and go straight to bed. Rosalyn shouldn't object to giving them a little privacy, since Whitney had done the same for Rosalyn on more than one occasion.

A single drop of sweat made a tickling path between her breasts. She resisted the urge to rub the spot.

"Whitney?"

Were her eyes as glazed as they felt? She saw Rand through a fine haze of pure lust. What was happening to her? Why Rand, of all people?

And why not? Rand was a fun-loving guy. Just ask the other fifty women he'd loved in a fun way since arriving on the island.

That thought might have sobered her, brought her back to reality, if Rand hadn't moved his hand higher up on her thigh.

A thigh that quivered.

"This is ridiculous," Whitney said under her breath, unaware that she'd spoken out loud until he responded.

"What's ridiculous?"

"My reaction to you," she blurted out. She flushed and tried for a quick recovery. "I mean, I don't usually . . . that is, I'm not normally . . . oh, hell."

He started toying with her hair, his knuckles scraping her neck and sending delicious shivers down her spine, all the while his other hand still stroked her thigh—inching higher and higher. She was already damp. Another inch or two and he would know.

"I know exactly what you mean," Rand said on a husky note. Whitney's eyes widened. She couldn't resist darting a quick glance at his lap, verifying that he *did* know what she meant. At least the lust was mutual. She licked her lips nervously. "We . . . we could go back to my bungalow."

"What about your roommate?"

"She wouldn't mind getting lost for a while." Oh, God, Whitney thought in silent horror, she was turning into Darla!

"I don't know," he murmured. "I like the idea of driving each other insane first, don't you?"

She caught her breath as he leaned forward, his lips burning a path along her neck. Those delicious, talented fingers hovered a hairbreadth from the damp, aching spot between her legs. His voice dropped to a pulse-shattering, seductive whisper as he continued.

The man wasn't just good at seducing; he was awesome.

"Build the anticipation . . . stoke the fires."

Didn't he mean *stoke the inferno*? *He* might call it a fire—Whitney had no qualms about calling it a raging inferno. She was on the verge of exploding.

Her lips were dry, her throat even drier. Not surprising, really, considering the amount of moisture pooling elsewhere.

Maybe the cooks had put something in their food, an aphrodisiac of some kind. If that was the case, well, then it certainly wasn't her fault she was about to have an orgasm sitting on a public bench in front of a waterfall.

Fully clothed.

His hot breath filled her ear, making her shiver.

"Does that sound like a plan to you, Whitney?" he whispered thickly.

She bit her lip—hard—as he used his tongue to outline her ear. "Yes. No. I mean, sort of." What she really wanted to say was, *Hell, no!* She didn't want to tease and fan and anticipate.

She wanted him *now*.

"I think you were right, Whitney. I think we're going to make an excellent team."

She'd said that? Team? Ha! All she wanted to do was get

naked and down-and-dirty with *Eden*'s most popular player.

And the most shocking part of all was the fact that Whitney didn't care *who* was watching!

Rand dared one last flaming kiss before he pushed Whitney inside and pulled the door of her bungalow closed behind her. He hoped that she locked it instantly, because he had to muster every ounce of willpower he possessed not to barge in after her and end their torment.

Drawing in ragged breathes of warm, fragrant air, Rand turned and jogged along the path, hoping to work the tension from his body with physical exercise.

To say he was tense was a vast understatement. He had deliberately set out to soften Whitney, but in the process he had nearly embarrassed himself by climaxing like an inexperienced teenager out with the prom queen.

Fully clothed.

God, he could still hear her sexy little gasping moans she thought she'd successfully smothered, all because he'd been stroking her thigh and fiddling with her hair. What would she do when he buried his fingers inside her? Or closed his mouth over a taut, ripe nipple? Would she scream? Beg for more?

The woman was dynamite. Explosive. Irresistible.

Rand frowned as a new thought occurred to him. Maybe he *didn't* have the right woman for the job. He didn't want to become too attached to her. It wouldn't be fair to him *or* her when it came time to part.

No, it was only lust. *Only? Ha!* A powerful lust, a surprising lust.

He halted at an intersecting path and put his hands on his knees, gasping for breath. His lungs burned, but that wasn't the only thing still burning. He would have to take a long, cold shower when he reached his bungalow, and even then he was resigned to sleeping on his back.

Who would have thought he'd meet another woman who

turned him on the way Bonnie had? Not that he loved Whitney—he could never love Whitney, because he was a one woman man, and Bonnie had been that woman. He could lust, admire, even greatly *like* a rare woman like Whitney, but love? Not in the cards. Impossible. Extremely unlikely.

But if he *could* love another woman, it would be a woman like Whitney. She wasn't Bonnie—nobody was Bonnie—but she was fascinating in her own right. He'd never gotten a straight answer from her, but instinctively he knew she wasn't participating for the money. But then, he didn't think she was looking for Mr. Right, either. No, he suspected Whitney's reasons for participating on the show had nothing to do with men or money. But what could those reasons be?

He had less than two weeks to find out. Less than two weeks to discover her weaknesses and use them to his advantage.

As he began to jog again Rand felt a sharp pang of guilt at his ruthless plans, but then he thought about Teddy, and how little sleep he'd gotten since Robin took him away. And there was Dolly, possibly stuck in a cold, damp storage building, naked and vulnerable, at the mercy of leering eyes and sweaty hands.

The mere thought made Rand break out into a cold sweat. He had to get them back before anyone had time to ogle Dolly or ridicule Teddy, possibly yank out his black button eyes or rip off an arm. They were precious to him, and he couldn't live without them.

He certainly couldn't *sleep* without them. The only time he slept was when exhaustion left him no choice, and then for only a few hours. Luckily, his body didn't require much sleep, or he'd be a walking, talking, *seducing* zombie.

Up ahead, his bungalow came into sight. Rand slowed to a cooling walk, arguing with his conscience. He wasn't a total jerk. Once he hooked Whitney into his scheme and found out why she was on the show, he would do what he could to help her get what she wanted. It would be small compensation for assisting him in getting Teddy and Dolly back.

He shook his head, frowning at his feet. Just what *did* she want, if not money or love?

The more he pondered the question, the greater Rand's curiosity became.

He couldn't wait to see her again.

"You have *got* to be kidding!" Rosalyn snatched the assignment sheet from Whitney's hand and quickly scanned the list of names. "You're pairing with Rand for the scavenger hunt today. What an amazing coincidence!"

"Can the sarcasm, Rosy." Whitney knew she was blushing; she could feel the heat of it on her cheeks. She gamely stuck to her story. "I told you, I know what I'm doing."

"Yeah, right." Rosalyn stared at her so long Whitney had to glance away. "And that dreamy expression I saw on your face moments earlier was just practice, right?"

Whitney thrust out her chin. "That's right."

"You're not a good liar, Whit. It's written all over your face."

"I'm not following you."

"You're falling in love with Rand," Rosalyn said bluntly. "You claimed you wanted to save the rest of the women from that predator, yet you're falling for him yourself."

"Ha!" Whitney scoffed, sounding a little too shrill to her own ears. "Are you insane? I don't even *know* the guy!"

Rosalyn waved the assignment sheet beneath her nose. "Keep this up, and you'll know him plenty. You'll be crying into your pillow like the others."

"No way."

"Yes, way. The other girls will hate you when they see you have Rand's attention."

Whitney frowned. "They're my friends. They won't turn on me."

"Like hell they won't," Rosalyn countered with conviction.

"I'll tell them the truth."

"The truth? That you're pretending to like Rand to protect them, and that you never moaned and screamed his name last night while you were sleeping and obviously dreaming about Mr. Hotshot?"

With a gasp, Whitney said, "I did not!"

"Does, 'do it harder' ring a bell?"

The fire in Whitney's face threatened to scald her.

Rosalyn sighed as she handed Whitney the assignment sheet. "Look, Whit. I like you. I consider you my friend. I'm not going to be one of those dozens of girls who will be hating you. But I *will* be worried about you. I honestly don't think Rand can get serious about anyone."

"Why do you think that?"

Her roommate shrugged. "I don't know. Just women's intuition, I guess. Something's not right . . . almost as if he's taken."

Something cold and ugly curled into the pit of Whitney's belly. She moved to the vanity she and Rosalyn shared and sat down abruptly in the chair. "He . . . he couldn't be married, Rosy. The background check they did on all of us is too thorough. They would have known. Besides, he'd be disqualified, and if he's after the grand prize—"

"What makes you think he's after the grand prize?" Rosalyn asked. "If the rumors are true, he's got plenty of money."

"People with money always want more money. That's how they stay rich."

"You're not going to listen to reason, are you?" With a dramatic sigh, Rosalyn threw up her hands. "I give up! Go ahead and get your heart broken, but don't think I won't say, 'I told you so.' "

"That's fair enough." Whitney felt comfortable saying those words. She couldn't seem to convince Rosalyn of the fact, but she had no intention of falling for Rand.

Lusting after him—yes.

Falling for him—no.

Chapter Six

"This is crazy!" Whitney exclaimed as she pored over their list of things to find for the scavenger hunt. She felt Rand's breath on her neck, intensely aware that he was now standing behind her.

He wasn't touching her, but her nipples puckered in anticipation. Amazing.

And alarming.

Whitney hoped he wouldn't notice that her breathing had become fast and shallow. She was shameless. "Where are we going to find handcuffs? And an *orange* leather thong? Do they actually make underwear in that color? And in leather?"

"Hm. These items have to be obtainable, or they wouldn't ask for them. *Getting* them is the challenge."

"That's an understatement," Whitney said, edging forward and hoping he wouldn't notice. If he decided to press himself against her, she couldn't be accountable for her actions, and the cameras were everywhere.

"Come on, I know where at least one of those items can be found."

"Which one?"

"The cherry-flavored lip gloss." Rand's arm brushed her shoulder as he pointed to the item on the list.

Whitney swallowed a gasp of dismay. "Oh." Of course he would know, because he'd kissed half the girls on the island.

"Darla puts the stuff on all the time. Haven't you noticed?"

Wordlessly, Whitney shook her head. How did he know what flavor she used? And why didn't he just admit that he knew because he'd kissed Darla? In fact, Whitney reluctantly concluded, it would have been strange if Rand *hadn't* kissed Darla. That girl was as popular with the men as Rand was with the women.

"While we're bribing her out of the lip gloss, we should probably ask her about that orange thong."

Knowing about the lip gloss was bad enough; the thong was going too far. Whitney suspected she sounded prim and waspish, but she couldn't seem to help herself. The green-eyed monster of jealousy had reared its ugly head. "Why don't we split up? You, um, sweet-talk Darla out of her lip gloss and the orange thong, and I'll seduce the cook for the whipped cream and cherries."

To her surprise, Rand looked genuinely alarmed by her idea. He was either mocking her, or he was a damned good actor.

"Oh, no, you don't! I'm not going around that she-shark without you."

"You're afraid of Darla?"

"Damned right I am," he said with feeling.

Whitney arched a skeptical brow. "And now you're going to tell me that you don't think she's beautiful—and expect me to believe it?"

"Of course she's beautiful, and she's definitely got a body worth flaunting. She's just not my type."

"Not . . . your type?" Her voice squeaked, betraying her disbelief. Rand smiled, his gaze sweeping over her in a way that left her breathless and aching.

"I'll take a *real* woman over Darla any day."

"Are we talking about breast implants—or personalities?"

His grin widened. "Both. Come on; we'll start at the bottom of the list and work our way up. Maybe by that time I'll have you convinced I'm telling the truth about Darla."

"Fat chance," Whitney mumbled, but allowed him to take her hand. As they went in search of a can of whipped cream and a jar of maraschino cherries, Whitney considered the remote possibility that Rand told the truth about Darla. And what if he *was* lying? She had no claim on Rand. What she *did* have was his attention, and who knew how long that would last? He didn't exactly have a good track record in the attention-span department.

"Can you give me a hand? I think I'm stuck."

Whitney eyed Rand's long, elegant feet and the bottom half of his tanned, muscled calves—the only part of him sticking out from beneath the bed—and sighed. She grabbed his ankles and pulled, walking backward.

He emerged holding a life-size vinyl blowup doll with vulgar crimson lips and yellow hair. With a triumphant grin, he scrambled to his feet and held up the prize. "Got it!"

"Three items down, six to go," Whitney observed, hoping to cover her embarrassment by looking around at the bungalow Rand shared with his roommate, Clancy. "Let's hope we can get this . . . this—"

"Her name's Helga," Rand supplied with a straight face.

"Um, *Helga*, back before Clancy finds out it's missing."

"I think Clancy would understand," Rand said, tossing the doll onto Clancy's bed with the whipped cream and maraschino cherries. He began to stalk purposefully in her direction. "I think it's time for a break, don't you?"

Whitney stumbled backward, her heart kicking into overdrive at the sudden gleam in Rand's eyes. "Don't you think we should get going? We still have three items to find."

He reached her, tipping her chin upward with a finger and staring at her mouth with open hunger. "I think I need to refuel. With a kiss."

"That was corny."

Rand's lips quirked, his gaze still on her mouth. "Yeah, it was. Nevertheless, I *would* like a kiss."

"You don't have to ask." That peculiar weakness invaded her legs. Whitney fought the urge to reach out and hang on to him. She considered herself a strong woman; why did she turn into mush around Rand? And why Rand, of all men?

His breath fanned her mouth as he nibbled at the corners. "So I don't have to ask?" he murmured. "Too bad we don't have those handcuffs handy."

As his meaning sank in, Whitney tried to jerk free. He held fast. "No! I'm . . . I'm not into kinky sex, Rand." She could feel him smiling against her mouth, and her face burned. No doubt he thought she was a prude!

Maybe she really was a prude. Maybe that was why she seldom saw the fireworks other women talked about. Instead of arguing, maybe she should boldly go where those women had gone—and lived to sigh and shiver about it.

At the exact moment Whitney decided to take the plunge, Rand moved out of reach. A tiny mew of protest escaped her before she could stifle the sound. She watched, frowning, as he scooped up the jar of candied cherries and popped the lid. His languid gaze held hers as he picked up a cherry by its stem and brought it to her lips.

"Open."

She did.

"Bite."

She did.

"Chew."

Again she obeyed, the syrupy-sweet taste coating her mouth

and throat as she swallowed. Still holding the stem, Rand leaned forward and kissed her, licking her lips and running his tongue along her teeth. He made little pleasure noises in his throat as if he were eating a delicious dessert.

Her knees threatened to buckle. This time she didn't hesitate to reach out and anchor herself against him. Long, delicious moments later, he slowly ended the kiss, taking his time as he again nibbled at the corners of her lips before lifting his head. "Hm. That was good."

She stared up at him in complete agreement, dazed and aroused, vaguely aware that he looked just as dazed. Her eyelids felt heavy, and there was a hot sensation in her belly that was slowly spiraling outward, threatening to consume her entire body.

He held up the cherry stem and gave it a shake, whispering seductively, "How about a bet?"

"Okay," she whispered back. She was a disgusting ball of putty in his hands. A shameless hussy who should know better.

"I'll bet you I can tie a knot in this cherry stem with my tongue."

Whitney knew it could be done—could, in fact, do it herself. Shamelessly she said, "No way. What's the bet?"

Rand lowered his hand from her waist to her bottom. He pulled her tightly against him, making her gasp. He was obviously hot, hard, and throbbing. "If I can do it, I get to lick whipped cream from your nipples."

Her nipples obviously heard his titillating proposition. They hardened to pebbles before he finished speaking. Whitney half expected to hear tiny voices screaming up at Rand, *Do me first! Do me first!*

"And if you lose?" she asked, her voice a mere croak.

His slow, sexy smile completed her meltdown. "Then you get to lick whipped cream from *my* nipples."

Since both possibilities held equal fascination for Whitney, she nodded. She watched, barely breathing, as he put the stem in his mouth. It wasn't the stem that fascinated her, however; it was Rand and the promise in his eyes.

Seconds later, he stuck out his tongue, showing her the twisted stem tied in a perfect knot.

"You . . . have a very talented tongue," she said, then blushed when she realized how he might have taken her words.

He chuckled. "At the risk of sounding like a redneck, you ain't seen nothing yet." His fingers reached for her cropped top, his knuckles brushing her skin with each button he unfastened, lingering, teasing, exploring.

When he finished and pulled her shirt open to expose her lacy white bra, Whitney closed her eyes. She was having a wonderful, wildly exciting time, but she'd never been the kind of woman who could easily shake her inhibitions. It had always been a gradual process for her, one most men didn't stick around to witness.

"Open your eyes, Whitney."

His voice was low, husky, yet demanding. Whitney found herself obeying because she wanted to. She looked straight into his chocolate, devilish eyes in a bold move that surprised her. Rand seemed to have no problem stripping her of her inhibitions.

"I want you to watch me." He moved quickly to retrieve the whipped cream. He shook the can and, using his free hand, flipped the front clasp of her bra. He brushed both sides of the flimsy material aside, then slowly circled each thrusting nipple with a line of whipped cream.

It was cold, causing her nipples to harden more than she thought possible.

With arousing precision, he dotted each nipple, then pitched the can onto the bed again. He looked at her, his eyes a liquid, sexy brown. "You look delicious. Now let's see how you taste."

Whitney held her breath, watching his mouth inch closer and closer to her aching, cream-covered breast. When his warm lips closed over her nipple, the exquisite pleasure wrung a moan from her lips. *So this is what it feels like to have no control over your body or your brain,* she mused as little ripples of shock hummed through her body.

She clutched his head just as her knees failed to support her any longer. Rand caught her waist to hold her upright while he laved and sucked the sweet cream from first one breast, then the other. His teeth lightly raked her sensitive nipple, making her gasp.

He lifted his head and looked at her, as if seeking her approval. Impulsively Whitney moved forward and swiped a dollop of cream from the corner of his mouth with her tongue. He closed his eyes as if the mere touch of her tongue were pure ecstasy.

It was a heady feeling.

"You taste fantastic," he whispered, slowly opening his eyes. "Now I'm curious whether the rest of you tastes as good."

A delicious weakness flooded her knees at his provocative statement. It conjured all sorts of erotic images in her mind.

Erotic and time-consuming.

"Um, shouldn't we be thinking about the scavenger hunt?" It was a weak, laughable protest, and she knew it. He knew it, too, for his mouth quirked in that endearing way that was fast becoming familiar to Whitney.

"I'd rather be *tasting* you," he said in a growl, pushing her gently backward until she was forced to walk or fall.

Whitney looked behind her to the bed where Rand slept. She wanted to find out exactly what Rand meant by "tasting" her. She suspected she knew, and just the thought made her wet and quivering. If the man was half as good at *that* as he was at kissing and that wonderful sucking motion he did with his mouth on her nipples, then she was as good as gone.

So she made one last, halfhearted protest. "The door . . . your roommate . . . he could come in on us."

Without taking his eyes from Whitney, Rand strode to the door, locked it, then took a chair and pushed it beneath the knob. He lifted a dark, beautiful brow. "Better?"

She swallowed hard, then nodded, caught by the promise in his eyes and driven by her body's clamoring for more. She was hot and weak and almost delirious with need. Nothing else seemed to matter, and she wondered if this was what her mother had felt for her father. Lust at its best. Or worst.

Temporary insanity. *Oh, yeah.*

Rand came back to her, and all thoughts of her mother flew from her mind. What would he do? Could he make her see those glorious fireworks? Could *she* let him do what he obviously wanted to do?

She glanced around the room, glad the shades had been drawn when they entered. It was cool and dim, but not dark.

He looped his finger in the waistband of her shorts and pulled her to him, nuzzling her neck with lips of fire. She held her breath as his fingers began to unbutton her shorts.

One button at a time.

Very slowly.

Teasingly.

She was panting softly by the time he reached the last fastening. He locked his mouth on her breast as he pushed her shorts and panties over her hips. She grabbed for his neck, holding on for dear life.

He toppled them onto the bed, then began to kiss his way down, across her belly, stabbing her belly button with his tongue until every muscle in her stomach clenched tight in reaction. She wanted him naked with her, and in a voice she scarcely recognized, told him so.

"Take off your clothes."

He ignored her, licking a path of heat from her navel on down. Way down. He kissed the insides of her thighs until she found herself surging upward, wanting what he'd promised. She touched him everywhere she could reach, but was frustrated by the layer of clothing keeping her from his hard, naked skin.

Why didn't he get undressed? Was this part of his "game"?

In the next second Whitney forgot everything, even her name.

His mouth had found her.

He began doing exactly as he'd promised, and it was more than she could stand. She heard herself whimpering. She heard herself scream.

And there wasn't a damned thing she could do about it. Her climax seemed to go on forever, and was it any wonder? It had been forever since she'd last experienced the unmatched ecstacy of an orgasm at the hands of an expert.

Rand was indeed an expert.

Still shuddering, Whitney tugged at his hair, urging him to come back to her so that she could show him exactly how grateful she was. She wanted to make *him* moan and scream. She wanted to watch *him* lose control, as she had done.

Eagerly, her hand went to the bulge in his jeans. She could feel him pulsing beneath her fingers, through the heavy fabric, and couldn't wait to curl her hand around him. Feel his thickness, his need—

"Wait."

Whitney blinked up at him. His handsome face was tight with desire, but his eyes were still the same. Sexy and teasing. "Wait?" she repeated dumbly. She'd just had the mother of all sensual experiences, and he wanted to *wait*?

He nodded, looking pained as he removed her hand and placed it against his chest. His heart thumped madly, assuring her flagging ego that he wanted her as much as she had wanted him. *Still* wanted him.

"Don't you want to . . . ?" Whitney let the question hang. She had no doubt he knew her meaning.

"Of course I do. I just don't have any protection with me."

Dumbfounded, Whitney looked around the room. Rand's room. A room he shared with his roommate. A roommate who kept a vulgar blowup doll beneath his bed. She licked her lips. "You don't have any condoms? At all?" She just couldn't wrap her mind around the fact. All men carried condoms, didn't they?

Especially if they were going to spend six weeks on an island with a lot of half-naked women.

Six weeks.

A lot of women.

Maybe he'd used them all.

The possibility—or should she say *probability*?—put a nasty taste in her mouth.

"It's not like that, Whitney," Rand said, watching her face. Obviously she'd been very expressive in her thoughts. He sighed and lay beside her, gathering her close to him.

Now that the fire had died down, Whitney felt exposed. Embarrassed. Ridiculous. She was lying buck-naked next to a fully dressed hunk who had just given her a fantastic orgasm. He, on the other hand, didn't seem all that bothered about not finishing what he'd started.

"We need to talk about something," he said, his voice deep and sexy near her ear.

Whitney was glad her face was pressed against his chest and he couldn't see her fiery complexion. Had she appeared so needy he'd felt sorry for her? *Oh, God.* The thought was unbearable.

She tried to struggle free, fully intending to jump into her clothes and get the hell out.

He held her tight, his hand rubbing her back as she struggled. "Wait. Please?"

The *please* got her, but just barely. She lay still, breathing hard and wishing she were anywhere but on this island.

"I don't have any condoms because I didn't intend to sleep with anyone when I came here for the show. In fact, I haven't actually had . . . intercourse with anyone in a long time."

Whitney found herself on the verge of believing him. She caught herself before she made an even bigger fool of herself. "You're joking, right?" She pushed herself up so that she could see his lying face. "What normal, healthy man would come to an island full of women and not want to have sex?"

He stared solemnly back at her. The teasing light was gone. "A man who prefers to have sex with a woman he cares about?"

A tiny laugh escaped her. "You expect me to swallow that? Come on, Rand! I'm thirty years old. I know about the birds and the bees, and I know that men don't think the same as women when it comes to sex. In fact, you're safe with me, because I don't think like other women, either. I'm not in the market for a husband."

"I know."

His enigmatic look puzzled her. "You know? If you know, then why do you feel compelled to confess to me something we know is a crock of horse manure?"

"Have you always been this cynical about men?" He sighed, absently stroking her bare shoulder as if they were an ordinary couple who'd been together numerous times. "That's not what I really wanted to talk to you about."

"Mind if I get dressed first?" Whitney didn't wait for an answer. She slipped from the bed and scrambled into her clothes in record time, flushed and panting by the time she was finished. He'd watched her the entire time; she had felt his hot eyes on her as if he'd physically touched her. She was baffled. If he truly wanted her, why didn't he make love to her?

Instead of returning to the bed, Whitney moved the chair from under the door-knob and sat. She folded her arms and tried not to think of where his mouth had been only moments earlier. "Okay. Talk."

She was dying to hear what he had to say.

Chapter Seven

"I didn't join the show for the money," Rand blurted out. There. He'd said it, and there was no taking it back. The bristling woman he'd just brought to a climax was watching him as if he'd grown horns and a long, forked tail.

She began to tap her bare toe against the tile. "Let me get this straight. You didn't join the show to score with women."

"Right."

"And you didn't join the show because you were looking for Mrs. Right."

"Exactly."

"And you didn't join the show for the prize money or the trip around the world."

"You got it." Rand watched her bare toes until they stopped abruptly. He could still taste her on his tongue, a sweet, musky taste that kept him hard and ready.

"So why are you here?"

"That's what I wanted to talk to you about." Rand took a deep breath. He wished he had some inkling of how she was going to react to his proposition. It was obvious she was attracted to him, and she had made it perfectly clear on more than one occasion that she wasn't looking for a long-term relationship with anyone. Unless she was filthy rich or lying to him about not wanting to get serious, he couldn't imagine why she would turn him down.

"I'm waiting."

Rand bit back a smile as her toe began to tap to a silent beat again. He knew her ego had taken a hard knock because he hadn't finished what he'd started. But he hoped she would understand his actions once she heard his explanation. If they were to be married—even briefly—he felt she deserved to know.

He lay back on his pillows and propped his arms behind his head, watching her as he dropped the bomb. "I joined the show because I thought it would be easier to find a wife."

Yep, he thought. It was just as he expected. Her eyes grew incredibly wide. Her luscious lips parted in shock, and a tiny, strangled gasp escaped. All in all, he thought she handled the news fairly well.

She leaped to her feet. "This is not funny, Rand."

"It's not meant to be funny, Whitney," he returned calmly. "I need a wife so that I can regain custody of Teddy and Dolly. I've got a sizable savings account and a beach house. They're both yours if you'll agree to marry me. It wouldn't have to be for long, and we've already proven that we're compatible."

Her mouth opened. Closed. She clenched her fingers. "You're serious? You're actually serious?"

"I am."

"So this is all about a custody battle between you and your ex-wife?"

Rand hesitated. He wouldn't be lying if he said yes. It *was* about custody, and Bonnie was no longer his wife because she was dead. Not *exactly* . . . a lie.

He nodded, ignoring a twinge of guilt. If she asked him outright, he would tell her. Meanwhile, he would say as little as possible and hoped she wouldn't ask. If she agreed to help him, she would find out the truth soon enough.

"So what you just did . . . to me . . . was to soften me up? Some kind of twisted method of coercion?"

He winced as a rosy flush suffused her face. The way she'd put it made him sound devious and dirty. "I did what I did because I wanted to. I wanted to taste you, to bring you pleasure." He hesitated.

Her eyebrow shot up. "And?"

Rand thought her eyes looked a little shiny. Was she about to cry? He didn't think he could stand it if she did. She wasn't supposed to be so emotional about his proposition. Maybe he should have left the intimacy out of the deal.

A little late to think of that now, he thought, giving himself a mental kick in the butt. He'd gotten carried away and now he might pay for his loss of control.

Going for the honest approach, he said, "And I guess I wanted to show you that we could be good together for the short time we would be married . . . that you wouldn't . . . wouldn't be bored—"

"You conceited bastard." She said it softly. Calmly. "You know nothing about me if you think you have to coerce me with sex. I would have helped you get your children back anyway." Her gaze softened. She sank back into the chair. "You must love them very much to go to all this trouble."

Rand opened his mouth to correct her, but she threw back her head and laughed, and the words died in his throat.

"If you had any idea what I thought about you! I thought you were a player. The worst. Did you know you've been breaking hearts left and right in your search for the right woman for your plans?" When he frowned, she chuckled and shook her head. "Oh, Rand. All you had to do was tell me you needed my help. You didn't have to . . . have to—" She stopped, blushing beautifully.

"I wanted to. You have to believe that."

307

"Then why didn't *you* . . . ?"

"Just a little hang-up I've got," he muttered, feeling a big, ugly scene coming on. He was going to have to tell her the truth. He had to. He couldn't let her go on thinking what she was thinking.

"Is it the stress of this custody battle over your children?"

She sounded so concerned, which only deepened his guilt. Something had gone wrong in the telling, and now he was about to pay for it big-time.

He sat up, bracing himself. "Teddy and Dolly aren't my children." To his amazement, her eyes glazed with tears.

"You mean they're not even your biological children, yet you're desperate to have them with you again?"

She gave him a tremulous smile that twisted his gut with sickening dread. Yes, it was going to be bad.

"Teddy and Dolly are lucky to have you in their lives. I take back all the mean things I was thinking about you."

She swiped a tear from her face. Rand smothered a four-letter curse. He couldn't do it. He couldn't let her go on believing another moment that he was the guy she described.

He got up and walked to her, deliberately putting himself in the line of fire. If she kicked him senseless, he deserved it. "Teddy and Dolly aren't my children, or my stepchildren, or anyone's children. Teddy is a stuffed bear. Dolly is a statue of my late wife . . . with enormous hooters."

He was joking.

Whitney blinked up at him, searching for that ever-present teasing light that seemed to be a part of him.

He *had* to be joking.

She waited, fully expecting him to burst out laughing. To tell her it was all a joke. That Teddy and Dolly really were children.

There was no way he was *not* joking.

She refused to consider it.

"Ha, ha." She stood so that she could almost look him in the eye. Her head felt funny, as if a million tiny bees were buzzing around inside. "You're either insane, or I'm hallucinating. I thought you just said that Teddy was a stuffed bear, and Dolly was a statue with enormous hooters . . . fashioned after your *late* wife." His jaw tightened; she saw it, and was amazed and fascinated by it. He was good. He was very good.

Oh, God. He is not joking.

"I'm not insane, and you're not hallucinating. I can explain."

"Whoa," Whitney said faintly, holding up a restraining hand. The buzzing grew louder. She shook her head to clear it of the strange noise. It didn't work. "I'm sure your story would be entertaining, but I'm positive I don't want to hear another word. In fact, I don't feel very well, so I think I'll go back to my bungalow and take a nap. You'll have to finish the scavenger hunt by yourself."

"Whitney."

She did *not* care about the desperate note in his voice, or the regret she heard. " 'Bye, Rand. Thanks for a good time."

"Whitney!"

He blocked her exit at the door. She kept her gaze locked on his collarbone, determined not to look at him, not to give him the satisfaction of knowing that he'd hurt her. She was supposed to be immune.

Ha!

"What about *your* motives for being here?" he challenged. "I know you're not after the money or the trip, and you've made it plain you're not looking for a long-term relationship." He paused a beat. "Unless, of course, you lied."

Whitney wanted to leave very badly. Her voice was so cold it should have frosted his nose hairs—not that she could see any; he was too perfect for that.

Perfect, yet insane.

"I'm here to meet my father, who happens to be our host, who also happens to know nothing of my existence." She finally looked him in the eyes. He flinched. She gave him an icy smile.

"Sorry to disappoint you. My reasons have nothing to do with a stuffed animal or a big-busted statue. *Now* will you move out of my way?"

"Will you just listen to me?"

"No." To her inward relief, he finally moved aside and let her leave. She took to the path at a brisk trot, unwilling to analyze just why she was so furious with Rand.

She wasn't supposed to care.

"Won't you tell me what happened? You've been quiet for a week now, and you haven't mentioned Rand once."

Whitney shook her head, staring at the ceiling fan above her head as Rosalyn paced the room and pumped her for information.

"They're supposed to make a big announcement tonight. Some kind of mystery game the producers have planned for the final week of the show. Everyone's hyped up about it."

"Hm." Whitney had no interest in attending.

"You've got to be there," Rosalyn continued. "If you aren't, they might cut you from the show."

Like she cared.

"Aren't you curious?"

No, she wasn't. All she had been able to think about was Rand's ridiculous story. A bear and a statue. *Good grief.* If the producers got wind of it, they would use Rand to hook a few thousand more gullible viewers, and humiliate him in the process.

If she were a vengeful person . . .

Rosalyn sat before the vanity and began to roll her hair with hot rollers. Lying on the bed behind her, Whitney could feel Rosalyn looking at her in the mirror.

"I just hope this isn't another trick, like the one they pulled with the scavenger hunt. It wasn't fair, you know. Nobody knew that the couple with the least amount of items would win the most points." She stabbed at a roller with a hairpin to hold it in place. "I can't *believe* you and Rand won. Neither of you produced a single item. God knows what you two were doing while the rest of us were racing around the island."

Whitney rolled to her side so that she didn't have to look at Rosalyn's questioning face. She tried really hard not to think about the whipped cream and the candied cherry, and how Rand had easily seduced her with both.

"I told you he would break your heart."

"He didn't break my heart." She was humiliated, embarrassed, and felt like a total fool, but she wasn't heartbroken.

"Everyone thinks so, you know."

Whitney had a feeling that if she could see Rosalyn's face right then, she would be wearing a sly expression. Her roommate *knew* that would get to her. She stifled a sigh and decided to take the Fifth once again. Anything less would probably incriminate her.

"I have to say I'm surprised that you let him get to you. I mean, you of all people knew what a player he was, yet you fell anyway."

Rosalyn's shadow loomed on the wall in front of Whitney as she walked across the room. Would the woman never leave?

"I was kind of hoping you'd be the one breaking *his* heart. Lord knows he deserves it."

She agreed wholeheartedly. There was just one problem; Rand didn't *have* a heart. He was insane. Totally insane. He'd joined the show to find a wife so that he could regain custody of a bear and a statue. Amazing. Stupendous. How would the producers of *Eden* feel if they knew a lunatic lurked among the contestants?

"Whitney, if you don't go to the meeting tonight, everyone will assume they're right about Rand breaking your heart. They'll laugh at you."

"I don't care," Whitney mumbled, burying her face into her pillow. If the woman didn't leave soon, she was going to embarrass herself further by screaming.

"You *should* care, if you have any pride left at all, because Rand will probably be laughing with them. He's with a different girl every day. It's like . . . like he's got some personal goal to meet or something."

Or something, Whitney thought with an inward snort. *Like finding a woman who will agree to his crazy plan.* Out loud, she said, "I'm not going. You can fill me in when you get back."

Rosalyn sighed loudly. "Okay, but that means you'll miss out on the drawing. You have to be there to win."

Whitney rolled to her other side so that she faced Rosalyn, her curiosity getting the best of her. "You look nice. What drawing?"

Wearing a smug expression, Rosalyn said, "The one where you get to have dinner with one of the producers and our cute little host, Mr. Asterisk."

Lifting a brow, Whitney masked her sudden interest. "And I would be excited because . . . ?" She had reasons of her own to be excited at the prospect of dining with their host, but none that Rosalyn could know about.

Unless, of course, Rand had blabbed to everyone.

"Duh, Whitney! They're obviously looking for new talent. Rumor has it they're considering doing a spin-off of *Eden,* using some of the original contestants as cast members." When Whitney didn't dance for joy, Rosalyn sighed and reached for the door. "I'm out of here. If you decide to stop moping around, the meeting's in the ballroom. We're all having cocktails afterward in the lounge."

After Rosalyn had gone, it took Whitney exactly ten minutes to get ready. She threw on a short white strapless dress, twisted her hair, clamped it up with a comb, and dusted her tanned shoulders with sparkling powder. Her roommate was right, she mused as she slipped her feet into a pair of flat strapless sandals; it was time she proved everyone wrong. Besides, it would be foolish to pass up an opportunity to have dinner with her father.

She paused to view herself in the mirror, mentally comparing herself with the dozens of *Baywatch*-beautiful women on the island. Her shoulders slumped a bit. She knew that she was moderately attractive, but compared to most of the female participants, she was the girl next door. A Helen Hunt look-alike, according to her unsuspecting father.

Why had Rand chosen her? Because she looked more gullible? Because she was the least attractive woman on the island, therefore the most susceptible?

Whitney deliberately straightened her shoulders. A militant light began to gleam in her eyes. She tilted her chin, satisfied that the old Whitney had returned. Let them look and laugh and wonder. She'd soon show them that she was back in the game, and hotter than ever.

Okay, so maybe she'd never been hot to begin with. Otherwise they wouldn't have nicknamed her Ice Cuba. Whitney's eyes narrowed speculatively at her reflection. It was the final week of the show, the final countdown. Maybe it was time she had some fun.

Let her hair down.

Loosened up.

Flirted a little. Or a lot.

With anyone and everyone but Rand.

She might not make him jealous, but she'd at least show him that he hadn't touched her heart in any way.

Even if it *was* a flat-out bold-faced lie.

Chapter Eight

Rand knew the moment Whitney walked into the ballroom. And he wasn't the only one who turned to stare, he noted, fighting the urge to growl at his fellow participants as their gazes locked onto her and they began to openly drool.

She was underdressed compared to most of the women, yet the simple white dress she wore might as well have been a knockout evening gown. Her tanned, beautiful shoulders seemed to sparkle beneath the overhead chandeliers, and her legs seemed to go on forever. Rand frowned, unable to look away. What did she have that the others didn't? he wondered, not for the first time.

Judging from the expressions on several faces around him, he wasn't the only one puzzling over the same question.

Was it her frosty attitude? Her subtle challenge, a challenge that made the male population determined to conquer her? Or was it the fact that she didn't seem aware of her power? For a woman, she had enough charismatic appeal to intimidate the most self-assured male.

And Rand was far from self-assured.

Oh, he was confident enough that he knew how to please a woman in bed, but that was because Bonnie had harbored no qualms about instructing him. Bonnie had been open in every aspect of her life, including sex. Of course, he'd loved that about her. When Bonnie had wanted something, she'd gone after it with a single-mindedness that bordered on obsession.

Then there was that odd innocence about Whitney that stirred even odder emotions inside him. He didn't think she was a virgin, yet she seemed almost . . . virginal in her actions. Seductive, sexy, yet innocent.

What man could resist such a combination?

Through narrowed eyes, Rand watched as a male participant by the name of Dillon Masters approached Whitney. He continued to watch, growing increasingly tense as Whitney greeted him with an open smile and a flirty sweep of her lashes. Dillon was known for his ability to talk a woman out of her panties by the third date.

What was she up to? Ice Cuba had finally thawed, had she? In the past week she'd snubbed date after date, joining games when she was forced to, but with a careless attitude that continued to baffle the male participants and producers alike.

There were rumors that she preferred her own sex, but Rand knew better, even if the others didn't. Not that he would kiss and tell, not even to kill the rumors.

"She's something, isn't she?"

Rand turned to the guy next to him, making every effort to appear casual. "Who?"

Marty White shot Rand a knowing grin, giving him a nudge with his elbow. "Ice Cuba. You should know, huh? I heard you got lucky."

"You heard wrong." Rand's fingers tightened around the glass of Coke he was holding. He found himself wishing he'd taken that offer of Jack Daniels to go with it. "You shouldn't believe everything you hear, anyway."

"Ah, come on, McNair. Give the rest of us a break, will you? If we took a vote right now, you'd be the prom king and she'd be the prom queen. The women love her, and us guys have given up trying to top you." He said the last in a disgruntled voice that might have gotten a smile out of Rand.

If he'd been in a smiling mood.

Which he wasn't. Masters had his arm around Whitney's waist, and she wasn't doing a thing about it. In fact, she appeared to be leaning in his direction, which meant that Masters could probably see down her . . .

"McNair? You okay? You look a little green."

That would be his color, all right. Green. The color of jealousy. It was ridiculous to be jealous of something he didn't want. Not that he didn't *want* her—he did. Just not permanently.

"So what happened between you two?"

"Nothing."

"Right. That's why you're about to crush that glass in your hand, because nothing happened."

Rand made a visible effort to relax his grip and remained silent. Maybe White would get bored and go away. When the man nudged him again, he didn't bother hiding an irritated sigh.

"Sweet! Would you look at that?" White gave a low whistle beneath his breath, followed by an admiring chuckle. "Who else but Darla would have the guts to show up in a bikini and high heels?"

Because it was expected of him—and he needed the distraction—Rand followed White's gaze to where Darla stood just inside the door. She was surrounded by gawking men, oblivious to the glares of the other women. Wearing a black thong bikini, the woman had a body beyond compare, Rand had to admit. Then why did he prefer Whitney? Darla's bustline alone was enough to make a man hyperventilate.

From across the room, Darla met his gaze. She slowly ran her tongue over her bottom lip and winked at him. Conscious of

White watching him, Rand winked back, then used his Coke as an excuse to look away.

"I think you're the only guy Darla *hasn't* had," White said. "Now, why is that?"

Rand was saved from answering as their host came onto the stage and stepped up to the microphone. There was a smattering of laughter as he adjusted it to fit his short frame.

"Have a seat, everyone, and let's get this party on the road!" Asterisk instructed, his voice booming from the hidden speakers.

Not for the first time since Whitney had dropped her bombshell, Rand looked for a resemblance between their host and Whitney. Had Whitney been telling the truth? Or had her pride invented the tale on the spur of the moment? He just couldn't bring himself to believe that Rupert Asterisk was Whitney's father. They looked nothing alike.

The host lifted a black box in the air for everyone to view. Smiling, he patted it. "This is filled with names. *Your* names. After the meeting, I'm going to draw one, and if I pull out your name, you get to have dinner tomorrow night with yours truly and our esteemed producer, Michael Hawkins."

Catcalls and cheering echoed through the ballroom. Asterisk smiled and preened for his audience, obviously loving the attention.

In that way he was opposite of his daughter, Rand thought, his gaze going to where Whitney stood with Dillon Masters. She was watching Asterisk intently, with a yearning that Rand suspected nobody else could see. *He* saw it because he knew.

Asterisk gave the box to his assistant and tapped the microphone to get their attention. "Now for the big news. The producers and myself plan to end this show with a bang." Laughter swept over the crowd, then died. "We have five days left. In the next four days at an undetermined date and time, ten final couples will be chosen for a lockdown."

This time a low murmur of disappointment rose from the

contestants. Asterisk waved both hands impatiently. "Come on, people! You can't *all* win! You know that, so settle down." The host waited for a response. When his audience became quiet, he continued. "The ten remaining couples will be handcuffed to their partners and isolated in a remote location. That's why it's called a lockdown, people. You will be locked together, locked up, and everyone else will be locked out."

One of the male contestants raised a hand. "What do we do when we have to take a . . . um, go to the bathroom?"

"Good question. Although you'll get a list of the rules, I'll go ahead and answer this one. You will be allowed to remove the handcuffs five times in those twenty-four hours. Any more than that and you will be severely penalized."

"How will anyone know how many times we remove the cuffs?" another contestant asked.

"Because there will be video cameras in every room of your lockdown cabin."

"Even the bathroom?"

Asterisk sighed and shook his head. "No, moron. Not in the bathrooms."

"When will we know who our partner will be?"

Rand was glad Darla had asked the question; he was wondering the same thing. There was only one woman he wanted to be handcuffed to, but he doubted she felt the same.

"When *we* decide to let you know." Asterisk's smile was mysterious. "We want this last game to be spontaneous. Just don't be alarmed when someone comes to your bungalow, blindfolds you, and leads you out. It's all part of the game."

Before anyone else could ask another question, Asterisk hastily moved on. "Now it's time for the drawing. Julie, will you bring me the box?" When he had it in hand, he reached inside and pulled out a slip of paper. He paused, looking slowly around at his audience, playing them, teasing them, drawing out the suspense.

"Come on, Asterisk!" someone called out.

"All right, all right. The winner is . . . Tabitha Shands, ladies and gents! Tabitha, come on up here with me and get your invitation, if you please."

Rand glanced across the room at Whitney, catching her disappointed expression. *Hm.* He rubbed his chin as an idea came to him. It wouldn't make up for inadvertently humiliating her, but it might soothe her ruffled feathers . . .

"Lucky her," Dillon Masters muttered, watching Tabitha prance to the stage for her invitation.

Beside him, Whitney swallowed her disappointment and kept her smile steady, even if it did feel frozen. "Yeah, lucky her."

"I was in a movie once," Dillon told her.

Whitney glanced up to find him leering at her cleavage. She didn't think he'd once looked at her face. "Really?" And who cared? She didn't. She also didn't care that Rand didn't appear to notice her existence.

"Yeah. I played a homeless guy in an alley." He shrugged his broad shoulders, his gaze sliding away from her cleavage to the stage again. "It was a pretty important part. They never showed my face, though."

"Wow." In another time and place, Whitney would have felt obliged to point out the obvious discrepancies in his statement. But not tonight. Tonight she was determined to flirt and be nice. Live it up, as her mother would so sagely advise.

From the corner of her eye, she saw Rand making his way to the group of participants now congratulating Tabitha. Was Tabitha next on his hit list? she wondered, then immediately reminded herself that she didn't care. It was poor Tabitha's problem, not hers.

When Rand took Tabitha's elbow and led her away from the group, Whitney focused her attention on Dillon. Yes, he was a conceited braggart, but he had a fantastic body, a nice smile, and gorgeous blue eyes.

Not a bone-melting milk chocolate brown like Rand's. Not

even close, but he was easy to read and available. What more could a girl need?

This time when she smiled at Dillon, she put a little punch into it. He blinked, actually noticing her face, and an answering smile curved his mouth.

It was almost too easy.

"Want to go for a walk?" she asked, lowering her lashes along with her voice.

Dillon's smile slid into a leer without missing a beat. "Sure, babe. Let's go. I'll take you places you've never been before."

Whitney allowed him to take her arm and lead her from the ballroom, wondering if she'd be able to keep up the charade long enough to find out if Dillon was a good kisser. So far he'd touched on every emotion *except* arousal.

She cast one last glance at Rand over her shoulder, just in time to see him bring Tabitha's fingers to his lips. "Romeo," she muttered beneath her breath.

"What?" Dillon asked, bending his head lower.

She flashed him a bright smile. "I said, Let's go, Romeo."

"Hey! How did *you* know my stage name?"

Somehow she managed to contain her laughter.

Chapter Nine

"God, you feel so good," Dillon all but moaned as he soaked her neck with kisses.

Whitney didn't know a person could produce that much saliva at one time. She strained to hold herself back, but Dillon was in a world of his own, his fingers digging into her hips as he ground his pelvis into her. Nearly bent backward, she had no choice but to hold on to his neck to keep from falling.

"Um, Dillon? Could you please ease up a bit? You're breaking my back."

"Huh?" He paused a heartbeat, then resumed soaking the front of her dress with his mouth as if she hadn't spoken.

Whitney considered kneeing him in the groin—just lightly enough to get his attention—and actually lifted her knee in preparation when she caught sight of the glowing red light in the bushes.

A Peeping Tom.

They were being filmed, which meant that everyone would see them necking, including Rand. Well, *Dillon* was necking, anyway. She needed her energy and attention to concentrate on *not* doing a backbend. Who did he think he was, Rhett Butler? She wondered, giving his hair a subtle yank. When that didn't work, she whispered into his ear, "Unless you want the entire world to see you clutching your groin and screaming, you will let go of me, stand back, and keep your hands to yourself."

Her words sank in slowly. Dumbfounded, Dillon did as she instructed, his arms falling to his sides. She blew out an aggravated sigh and straightened, wondering if her back would ever be the same. It was her fault, after all, for leading him on. "I'm sorry, Dillon. It's just not working for me." She kept her voice low, praying and hoping the camera was too far away to pick up sound. With her own humiliation still fresh in her mind, she had no intention of passing the buck.

To her relief, he shrugged, sticking his hands in the pockets of his shorts. He looked mysteriously resigned. "No big deal. I should have known you were a hopeless case anyway."

Whitney forgot about the camera. Her jaw dropped. "Excuse me? I have no idea what you're talking about."

"I'm talking about Rand McNair." Dillon rolled his eyes. "He's an OK guy, but he's ruining it for the rest of us."

Her snort of disbelief would have done her mother proud. "Rand has nothing to do with the fact that you and I don't click."

"Oh, yeah?"

"Oh, yeah!"

"Then would you mind telling me what's wrong with me?"

His challenge momentarily made her speechless. She floundered. "Well, there's nothing wrong with you, Dillon; you just . . . just . . ." She gave a helpless shrug of her shoulders before plunging on. "For starters, you haven't even attempted to get to know me."

He looked surprised. "We talked back in the ballroom, didn't we?"

"For all of five seconds? And second, you haven't kissed me."

This time he looked outright flabbergasted. "I've been kissing the *hell* out of you, Whitney! How could you not notice?"

"On the *mouth*, Dillon. I'm talking about plain old-fashioned kissing on the mouth." When he made a dive for her, she quickly put her hand between them. "Whoa! Never mind now. Good night, Dillon." She stepped around him, heading down the path in the direction of her bungalow. Why hadn't she trusted her instincts and just stayed inside? She could have avoided this entire ugly episode.

"I guess what they say about you is true, then!" Dillon shouted after her. "You're a solid block of ice!"

This time Whitney had no doubt that the camera microphone had picked up his voice. Her face burned, but she continued doggedly onward. She wouldn't stoop to a cuss fight with Dillon or anyone else on this damned island.

Well, maybe with Rand, since he was the reason she was in this situation.

Damn him.

All the way to her cabin, Whitney cursed Rand, recalling every vile name she could think of remotely connected to the male species. "Him and his damned stuffed toy and big-busted statue," she muttered, jamming her key in the lock and twisting the knob.

She stepped inside. Her right foot began to slide, and she had to catch the door to stop her legs from doing the splits. First a backbend, now the splits. She'd never felt so old before, because *both* caused her pain. Stifling a moan, she pulled herself up and shut the door. She flicked on the lights, searching the floor for the culprit.

It was an envelope. Frowning, Whitney scooped it up and opened it. Her eyes went wide. It contained an invitation to dinner with Michael Hawkins and Rupert Asterisk. *The* invitation that Tabitha Shands had won? And if it was, what was it doing in *her* bungalow?

Whitney thoughtfully tapped the invitation against her palm, remembering how Rand had approached Tabitha and pulled her aside. Unless he'd blabbed to someone else, he was the only other person on the island who knew about her connection to their host.

If he had talked Tabitha—or coerced her, rather, since he was very talented in that field—into giving him the invitation, why would he give it to her? And what had he given Tabitha in exchange for the coveted prize?

The possible answer to the latter question made her stomach lurch. She put a hand over her belly to quell her nausea. What did she care if he'd promised Tabitha a night of sinful pleasure? The invitation was far more important to her than anything Rand could do or say.

Wasn't it?

Damned right it was! It was, after all, the reason she'd agreed to participate in the show.

Maybe Rand felt bad for humiliating her the way he had. Maybe getting her the invitation—by hook or crook—was his way of clearing his conscience, or assuring her silence. Assuring her silence made more sense to Whitney. What man in his right mind would want the world to know he was obsessed with a stuffed bear and a big-busted statue of his late wife?

But then, Rand wasn't exactly *in* his right mind. He couldn't be.

Whitney gnawed her bottom lip as she stuck the invitation beneath her pillow, her thoughts finally switching to the nerve-racking realization that she was going to have dinner with her father. There was no guarantee, she knew, that she would get a moment alone with him so that she could broach the delicate subject of his paternity.

What if the opportunity arose and she froze again? Whatever Rand had promised Tabitha in exchange would be in vain.

Oh, where was her brain? Rand was a man. Whatever he had promised to do he would undoubtably enjoy doing. She would not waste another breath feeling bad for him. She hadn't asked him to get the invitation.

Yet . . . he had, and she couldn't deny that the irrational side of her brain wanted to feel warm fuzzies over his actions.

Thank goodness the other side of her brain was much smarter.

"You look familiar," Rupert Asterisk said the moment Whitney reached the elegantly set table.

Whitney managed to unglue her tongue from the roof of her mouth to answer, but her voice was barely above a whisper. "We . . . we met on the path about a week ago. You . . . you said I resembled Helen Hunt."

Rupert's eyes widened. He smiled. "That's right! I remember now." He turned to Michael Hawkins. "Don't you think she resembles Helen Hunt, Mike?"

Michael Hawkins took his time inspecting Whitney. Whitney resisted the urge to fidget.

"Well, yeah. Now that you've pointed it out to me, I do see a resemblance."

Both men rose until she was seated. Whitney automatically reached for her water glass to ease the dryness in her throat. She was a bundle of nerves. When Rupert spoke again, she jerked, spilling her water onto the crisp white tablecloth.

"You're not the same woman who won the drawing," he said.

She shook her head, mopping at the water next to her salad plate. "She . . . she gave me her invitation." It wasn't exactly the truth, but she doubted either man wanted to hear her theory on how she came to have the invitation.

Rupert's brow shot upward. "She *gave* it to you? Just like that?"

Whitney had run out of water, but she kept mopping anyway just to have something to do with her hands. "Yes." Silently, she prayed he'd change the subject before she tripped over her own lie. Not exactly a promising start.

"So what shall we call you?" Rupert asked, digging into his salad. Michael did the same.

They both seemed totally at ease, while she . . . she felt on the verge of fainting. Why did the idea of speaking to her father terrify her so much? She supposed a shrink could have answered her silent question.

Too bad there wasn't one handy.

Michael graciously offered her the salad dressing caddy. Whitney took it, then said, "Call me Whitney." She shot Rupert a quick, nervous glance as she added, "My last name's Sutherland."

"Sutherland. Sutherland." Rupert frowned. "Now, why does that name ring a bell?"

Both men looked at her, waiting for an answer. Whitney had run out of things to do with her hands. She put them in her lap and out of sight. Now was her chance to refresh Rupert's memory. "You, um, met my mother, Babs—Barbara Sutherland—on . . . on *The Dating Game*. It was a l-long time ago." Good grief, she was stuttering like a fool!

Rupert's fork clanked against his salad plate. His jaw dropped. "My God! Don't tell me you're Babs's daughter!"

He'd said *Babs*, as if he truly remembered. It was more than she could have hoped for. Whitney licked her dry lips. "Yes, I am. She—"

"That must have been twenty—"

"A little over thirty years ago," Whitney inserted.

"Thirty years? How the hell is she? No wonder you looked familiar—you're the spittin' image of her!"

Whitney tried to curtail her excitement. At least he'd remembered her mother. She'd been so afraid he wouldn't recall her, and that would somehow make her own existence a little less important. Silly, but there it was.

Grinning like a child, Rupert turned to Michael. "Can you believe this? I dated this girl's mother once. Actually, we dated for a few weeks. Spent a lot of time in the sa—um, sub."

"Yes, I remember you telling me what a nice girl she was." Michael cleared his throat, obviously embarrassed by Rupert's near slip. "Tell us, Whitney, have you ever been in showbiz?"

"No." She was amazed she'd gotten that much around the tight knot of anger clogging her throat. Despite Michael's attempt to salvage the situation, Whitney suspected her father had been about to tell her more than she wanted to know about his affair with her mother. Was that truly all he remembered, that they'd spent a lot of time in the sack?

The producer continued. "And your mother? Did she get the bug after her stint on *The Dating Game*?"

"No." Whitney could feel the sting of tears welling in her eyes. She valiantly fought them back, swallowing hard. "She was too busy raising—" She clamped her mouth shut on the damning words. What if Rupert laughed at her claim that he was her father? Or worse, what if he believed her, yet wanted nothing to do with her? And did she truly want anything to do with a man who appeared to have so little respect for women?

At the moment Whitney was convinced that she didn't. Even Rand's unhealthy obsession with his late wife paled by comparison. She pushed her chair from the table and stood. "I'm sorry. I've . . . I've got a headache."

"Look, hon." Rupert got to his feet, reaching for her arm. He sounded genuinely contrite. "I didn't mean . . . I mean I shouldn't have said—"

"It's okay." It wasn't, but Whitney had had enough humiliation for one night. She forced a brittle smile. "Really." And then she blurted out, "I'm a big girl. Thirty years old, in fact." Then she slowly enunciated each word so there would be no mistaking her meaning. "Thirty . . . years . . . old."

Ha! she thought as she stalked through the restaurant with her head held high. Let *him* do the math! She was through being humiliated by heartless men. She had lived thirty years without them; she planned to keep it that way. Her mother had lived a perfectly happy, normal life without marrying anyone.

So could she.

*   *   *

From his vantage point in the hall leading to the rest rooms, Rand saw it all. He hadn't been able to hear a damned thing, which had been frustrating, but judging by Whitney's white lips and flaming cheeks as she sailed in his direction, something had gone very wrong.

What had that bastard said to make her look so stricken? Rand clenched his fists and stepped out of the hall into her path. "Whitney."

She stopped short. Her glittering eyes narrowed on his face. "You! This is all your fault, you meddling, conceited, *insane* person!"

Rand supposed he deserved every insult she flung at him. He stuck his hand in his pocket and sighed. "I take it the meeting didn't go well?"

She feigned a shocked expression. "What makes you think that? It's not every day a girl is lucky enough to find out that the one thing her father remembers most about his fling with her mother is that they spent a lot of time in the sack."

He winced visibly. *Ouch. Double ouch.* "I'm sorry it didn't turn out the way you planned. If I had known—"

"Sorry? *You're* sorry? Believe me, you're not as sorry as I am for coming to this island, for meeting you, and for thinking my father might be someone I'd like to get to know. Now get out of my way!"

Wisely, Rand moved aside before she mowed him down. He ground his teeth, glaring at the table where Rupert and Michael sat with their heads together. If he knew it wouldn't make things worse for Whitney, he'd march over there and give their host a blistering he'd never forget.

Instead he turned to follow Whitney's progress through the door, wishing he could turn back the clock, and in the same instant wondering what he would do differently if he could.

Bonnie had been his one and only true love. When she died, she'd taken their love with her. He could never love like that again.

But if he could . . .

330

Chapter Ten

"Why are you wearing your clothes?"

"Why are *you* naked?" Whitney countered, keeping her gaze averted from her new roommate.

Darla rose from her bed that had once been Rosalyn's and stretched slowly, purring like a cat, completely uninhibited in her naked state.

Not truly surprising, Whitney mused, given Darla's apparent aversion to clothes. She blew out a sigh, wondering how on earth things could get any worse. Mentally, she went over her list of woes.

She was forced to share a bungalow with the oversexed *Baywatch* wanna-be Darla, since Rosalyn had been eliminated yesterday—just two days after Whitney's disastrous dinner date with Dad of the Year. As if that weren't bad enough, Darla talked of nothing but Rand, Rand, Rand.

Rand was wonderful.

Rand was sexy.

Rand was a hottie, a hunk, a god among men.

Whitney suspected Darla's obsession stemmed from the fact that Rand still refused to be caught in her carnivorous clutches, but knowing didn't help much. It was just damned hard not to think about him when Darla was constantly mentioning his name.

Then there were the drums. Constant and annoying, they played on her frayed nerves as if they were truly the ominous warning of a savage tribe intent on attacking. She knew the sound was coming from well-placed speakers, a manufactured symphony designed to lend authenticity to the producers' silly plans to capture and take captive the ten remaining couples.

But knowing didn't help much in that department either. If they didn't show up soon, she was going to run screaming into the ocean.

"I'm going to be handcuffed to Rand," Darla announced for the hundredth time. "I just know it. They all know I want him, and they love me. They'll give me Rand."

Give her Rand? As if he were some kind of barbaric love offering? Whitney smothered a snort. She couldn't think of a more fitting end to the show.

Rand and Darla, handcuffed together. And with Darla naked. Well, why not? They were the most popular players, yet they had never been together. Whitney didn't blame the producers for looking at the big picture.

"Shh," Darla said in a hushed whisper. "I hear something."

Whitney rolled her eyes; she hadn't made a sound in over an hour, and the only thing she heard was those damned drums. If the people who came to get them were dressed in loincloths and wielding handmade spears, she was going to laugh so hysterically they would be too afraid to touch her.

"I think they're coming!"

Good, Whitney thought, although every muscle in her body went taut. Anything had to be better than being cooped up with Darla and the ghost of Rand McNair.

The drums stopped. Whitney braced herself, half expecting the bungalow door to come crashing down.

She jumped as someone knocked lightly on the door.

With a squeal of excitement, Darla rushed to answer it. Whitney noticed that she'd had the decency to throw on one of her infamous leather thong panties and a bathing suit cover up. As for herself, she was glad she wore comfortable shorts, sandals, and a T-shirt.

Slowly Whitney rose and faced her jailers, Dannon and Gage. After six weeks on the island surrounded by the *Eden* staff, she had no problem recognizing them. Silently she stood still as Dannon tied a blindfold around her eyes.

"Just follow me, please," he instructed, placing her hand on his arm.

"Ooh! This is so exciting!" Darla squealed.

Whitney was glad when Darla's voice began to fade, indicating Gage was taking her new roommate in the opposite direction. "Thank God," she murmured with heartfelt sincerity.

Dannon chuckled. "She's something, isn't she?"

Yeah, Whitney thought. Darla was something. But what?

They walked for about ten minutes before Dannon halted. "Step up. We're getting into a cart."

Feeling foolish and more than a little disoriented, she obeyed, sinking onto the cool leather seat. She felt around until she found something to hang on to. The vehicle took off, plastering her against the seat. Wind rushed at her face, carrying the heavy scent of lush tropical flowers and a hint of sea salt.

"I don't understand why we have to be blindfolded," she said, not entirely certain Dannon was the one behind the wheel. She thought she'd felt the brush of his arm against hers, but it could have been the wings of a bat or the brush of foliage along the path, for all she knew.

"I don't make the rules," Dannon said, proving he was indeed with her. "I just follow them. I suspect, though, they're doing it more for effect than for the need to hide your destination from you."

Whitney stiffened. "We're being filmed right now?"

"Randomly, yes."

After that she clamped her lips shut. What purpose would it serve to let them know how very weary she was of the entire show? She'd tried to leave after her regrettable dinner with Daddy, but she'd been informed that the island had been sealed to keep out the reporters.

During the final days, no one was allowed to come or go until the show was over.

The road became bumpy. Whitney clung to the bar in front of her, trying to keep her body from slamming into Dannon's. Where were they taking her? She sensed they were climbing.

Some twenty minutes later the car came to an abrupt stop. Whitney let out a sigh of relief. She flexed her aching fingers. She'd never known how disorienting and frightening it was to be blind.

"Step down, please. Watch your step—the path is rocky."

"If I break an ankle, I'm suing," Whitney muttered. She held her free arm out to ward off unsuspecting trees that Dannon might forget to warn her about.

"The cabin's just up ahead," Dannon said.

Belatedly, Whitney wondered who would be her partner for the lockdown. Since yesterday morning everyone had been instructed to remain in their bungalows, so other than Rosalyn, she didn't have a clue who had been eliminated, and who remained for the final showdown.

Maybe Rand wasn't even *on* the island, she mused. The possibility left her feeling empty and aching. What a fool she'd been for thinking he wouldn't get to her.

"Here we are. We're going through a doorway, so watch your elbow."

Prudently, Whitney pulled her elbow close to her side. She

felt carpet beneath her feet as she followed Dannon another few yards before he finally stopped.

"I"m going to put on the handcuff now."

"Oh, what joy," she murmured, her earlier tension returning. Something hard and cold circled her right wrist. She heard the sound of the cuffs locking; then Dannon was fumbling with the knot of her blindfold.

He whisked it away and abruptly left the bungalow.

Whitney blinked rapidly, her eyes slowly adjusting to the light. Without much enthusiasm, she turned to see whom Dannon had shackled her to for the next twenty-four hours.

She quickly closed her eyes, certain she was hallucinating. *Praying* that she was.

"Hello, Whitney."

She wasn't. It was Rand, all right. His voice. That smile. Those damned bone-melting eyes.

God help her.

She wasn't happy to see him.

Well, what had he expected? Hoping to lighten the tension, Rand tried joking with her. "Hey, it's not for life. Just twenty-four hours."

He didn't expect what happened next.

Whitney bolted toward the door, yanking him with her. Rand tripped over his own feet and went sprawling, yanking her back like a yo-yo. Whitney landed on top of him, her eyes wide, her breathing erratic.

Rand didn't kid himself; he knew it had nothing to do with passion. His ego took a beating as he stared into her panicked eyes.

"You . . . you were supposed to be handcuffed with Darla," she said, panting, pushing at his chest with her hands. She didn't get far, since they shared the handcuffs.

Rand wasn't joking when he said, "Then *I'd* be the one kicking and screaming to be let out."

She blew a strand of hair from her eyes and glared at him. "I'm not kicking and screaming."

"No," Rand said slowly, seriously, "but judging by the panic in your eyes, you're not far from it." He sat up, rolling her from him until they both sat on the floor side by side. As if they had a choice. "Are you actually afraid of me, Whitney?" He knew she was attracted to him—or had been before he'd botched it—and he knew that she now disliked him, but he'd never considered that she would actually *fear* him.

He didn't like the possibility. Not one bit.

She yanked at their shackled wrists to push the hair from her eyes, nearly jerking his arm out of its socket. She flashed him a derisive look. "In your dreams, buddy, in your dreams."

"You *look* afraid," Rand pointed out. He crossed his legs Indian fashion and she did the same. Their shackled wrists lay between them on the carpeted floor.

Whitney blew out an explosive sigh. "I'm *not* scared of you. Cautious, maybe, but I think that's a normal reaction, considering the fact that you're insane."

Rand frowned. "Oh, yeah. You mentioned that before. Why do you think I'm insane?"

She deliberately widened her eyes in mocking disbelief. "Surely you know? Maybe you don't. Maybe that's part of your sickness."

Sickness? Rand's gaze narrowed. He didn't like the sound of that. It hit too close to home. "Explain yourself."

"Don't order me around." She shook their shackled wrists. "This doesn't give you that right."

"Okay. Will you please explain what you mean?"

"You're obsessed with a stuffed bear and a stone statue in the image of your late wife." Her expression softened slightly, as if she realized she was being rather harsh, considering she believed he was mentally ill. "I'd say that qualified you for a bed in a mental ward, or at least a good year's worth of therapy."

Her diagnosis stung, although Rand wasn't ready to admit

why. Maybe he was a little obsessed, but wacky? "Tell me something." He scooted closer, lacing his fingers with hers. Just that simple contact made his heartbeat kick into overdrive. Her skin was hot and damp and smooth. She tried to pull her fingers free, but gave up without much of a fight.

A small victory on his part, but a victory nonetheless.

"Why are you *really* mad at me?" he asked. "If you're really mad at me because you believe I'm insane, then that would be rather heartless, wouldn't it?"

Her gaze slid from his face to their linked hands. Rand watched as her breathing became fast and shallow. He was secretly pleased to know that she wasn't unmoved by the contact. Gently, he nudged her. "Whitney?"

After a long moment she spoke. "I guess I'm angry because I thought you were . . . you were interested in *me*. Physically, of course," she added hastily. "Then you revealed the true reason for your interest, and I suppose it sort of . . . kind of made me feel used."

Rand flinched inwardly. He had suspected as much, and was still kicking himself for being so insensitive. "I'm sorry, and you're right. I *was* using you. I guess I was hoping we could make an even exchange—"

"You thought I was *that* desperate for sex?"

He stared at the rosy flush on her cheeks and managed not to smile. "For money and property. That's the kind of exchange I was talking about. The other—pleasuring you . . ." He swallowed hard. Just saying it out loud aroused him all over again. "Pleasuring you was a spontaneous thing. I wanted you." His voice deepened, grew husky. "I *still* want you."

Her snort was like a slap in the face. "You mean you want to please me, yet remain true to your wife's memory. I think I saw that movie."

He didn't know how to reply. How could he explain to Whitney the terrible shame and guilt he experienced at the thought of intercourse with another woman? She was probably right and he *did* need to see a shrink, because it didn't make sense. He had no qualms about pleasing a woman as long as he didn't please himself in the process. In some twisted way, holding himself back kept him true to Bonnie.

With Whitney, Rand had sensed a disturbing change, because he'd enjoyed bringing her to a sexual peak more than he'd believed possible. To be perfectly honest, he'd nearly climaxed himself, not once but twice in Whitney's company, and without the guilt and the shame.

"I'm thirsty," Whitney announced, scrambling to her feet and forcing him along with her. "And it doesn't look like I have any choice in taking you with me."

Although Rand had broached the subject, he was relieved to let it go for now.

He didn't have any answers.

Chapter Eleven

Whitney stared at the fifth of tequila in the cabinet in disbelief. "You've got to be kidding! Nothing to drink but tequila? Isn't that breaking some kind of law or something, leaving us with nothing but alcohol? What if one of us is allergic?"

"They'd know that by now," Rand said. "Besides, we both signed a release form, freeing Hawkeye Productions from any liability."

"Well, sure, but does that mean they can poison us and get away with it?" When Rand nodded without smiling, Whitney belatedly realized he was mocking her. "Drop dead," she said in a growl.

"If I drop dead, you drop with me," he countered, staring pointedly at their shackled hands.

She hated the fact that he was right. She also hated the fact that she was beginning to forgive him. He seemed genuinely sorry for humiliating her. So he had a few hang-ups about his late wife. Was that truly a crime? Whitney swallowed a wistful sigh, daring to admit that she was more than a little envious of a ghost. It had to be envy she was feeling, because it couldn't be jealousy. Experiencing jealousy over a hopeless case like Rand would imply that she lacked common sense, and she wasn't ready to go there.

"Come on. We'd better inspect the rest of the cabin and find out what we've got to work with." She started to tuck her hands in her pockets, but remembered in the nick of time that she would also be putting Rand's hand in her pocket. Although the idea made her nipples pucker, she steadfastly ignored her reaction.

The cabin had a simple layout. There was the living room/kitchen combination, a bedroom with a full-size bed, and a small bathroom. Everything was spick-and-span—and disturbingly bare.

One bed, one cover, and a camera in every room save the bathroom.

Whitney decided not to tax her brain over the implications of the one bed and one cover, or the box of condoms in the nightstand next to the bed. She pulled Rand back to the kitchen and opened the refrigerator door.

"We've got limes, fruit, and a snack tray. Looks like cheese and ham. Oh, and there's a jar of caviar." She yanked him back to their starting point, opening cabinet after cabinet. "Crackers . . . peanut butter and no glasses." She pulled open a drawer, cracking his knuckles in the process and becoming increasingly exasperated. "No silverware. Good grief! They're forcing us to live like barbarians."

"They're probably hoping we'll act like them, too," Rand suggested in a voice far too innocent to be believed.

Their gazes locked. Whitney pressed her free hand to her stomach as heat flared low in her belly. Why did his eyes have to be so damned sexy? She told herself that she hated her reaction to him, but her body cried otherwise. She did her best to remind it that Rand was taken. "You're enjoying this, aren't you?"

His smile was wolfish and totally endearing. "I cannot tell a lie. The simple truth is, I'm glad we're getting this opportunity to get to know each other."

Before she could respond to his confession, he glanced beyond her shoulder and nodded.

"I think I've just found our instructions."

Relieved at the distraction, Whitney whirled around, taking Rand with her. She snatched the list from the wall and held it between them so they could read it together.

His warm breath tickled her ear, making it hard for Whitney to concentrate. She felt the heat they generated as he pressed his arm against hers. How was she going to manage the next twenty-four hours shackled to a man she had the hots for?

Desperately, she focused on the list. Her gaze zeroed in on one particular item. "Truth or Dare," she mumbled out loud. "I haven't played that game since I was in junior high."

"Hm. I don't think I've ever played it."

Whitney couldn't keep the sarcasm from her voice. "Then you're in for a treat. And look." She pointed with her right hand, which ended up being *two* hands. "Oops, sorry." Prudently, she switched hands. "It says we must choose six activities from the list." She thumped the piece of paper. "You know, we don't have to follow their silly rules if we don't want to. I don't care about winning."

"Neither do I, but since we're this close . . . what do you say we give it a shot? Who couldn't use a million dollars and a trip around the world?"

"Have you forgotten my association with our host? I think that automatically disqualifies me from winning." Whitney tried really hard to keep the hurt from her voice; she didn't want Rand's pity.

His expression softened, telling her that she had failed. For an insensitive jerk, the man was certainly perceptive sometimes, she mused. She had always believed the two attributes were mutually exclusive.

But then, she had discovered there was nothing ordinary or normal about Rand McNair, even if he was an unfeeling, obsessive brute.

"Not if he doesn't acknowledge you."

"I don't think I have to worry about that," she said. "Because I don't think he *will* acknowledge me."

"I'm sorry, Whitney."

His sincerity made her eyes tear up. She blinked rapidly. Rupert Asterisk wasn't worth crying over. In fact, she hadn't yet met a man who was.

Until Rand.

Belatedly, Whitney's alarmed gaze went to the camera installed near the ceiling in one corner of the kitchen. "Damn," she whispered. "I forgot we were being taped."

Rand moved so close she nearly jumped out of her skin. He put his free arm around her neck and drew her in so that his mouth was next to her ear. His warm breath sent shivers down her spine and made her yearn for things she couldn't have.

Things he'd made it clear he couldn't give her.

"You didn't specify what your association was," he whispered. "You could have been talking about an affair."

Whitney's face grew hot. She turned her head until she could whisper against *his* ear, hoping she disturbed him as much as he had disturbed her. "You're right, but *I* would know, and you would know." She licked her lips, inadvertently catching the lobe of his ear with the tip of her tongue. He jerked and drew in a sharp breath, much to her extreme satisfaction. "Besides, I dropped enough clues about my age for Daddy Dearest to have figured it out by now, unless he's as short on brainpower as he is on legs."

His husky chuckle nearly buckled her knees. His wife had been a lucky woman, she thought. Rand's sex appeal was downright lethal.

"I won't tell if you won't tell," he said.

"That would be cheating." They continued to whisper. Whitney suspected they appeared as lovers to anyone watching.

"Then why have you stayed in the game this long if you knew you couldn't win?"

"Because until the dinner, I hadn't given up hope of confronting Asterisk about being my father. After that I couldn't leave because they sealed off the island. Nobody can come in and nobody can leave."

"What about the the contestants who were recently eliminated?"

"I think they took them to the other side of the island."

"Hm." Warm lips nuzzled her neck. "What do you say we give them a show they will never forget?"

Whitney caught her breath and held it. What, exactly, was he implying? If he thought for one minute she was going to do anything risqué in front of a camera, then he didn't know her at all.

She licked her lips. "Why . . . why would we do that?"

"Because we're here, we're together, and unless I've missed something, we don't have anything better to do."

A naughty thought flashed through Whitney's mind like a hot zing of electricity. *She* could think of something better to do, all right, but it wasn't anything she was brave enough to mention. Oh, why did she have to get stuck with Rand? He was the only man on the island she couldn't resist.

Damn him.

"Come on, Whitney. Take a chance. Let's do something spontaneous."

"I think," Whitney murmured dryly, "we did the spontaneous thing in your cabin."

His voice dropped abruptly, his tone suddenly low and intimate. "So you *do* remember."

"Of course I remember." She sobered quickly. "How could I forget? That's where you first told me about Teddy and Dolly."

He groaned. "You're not going to let me forget that, are you?"

343

"Nope. I'm surprised you want me to, since they are obviously important to you."

"Not as important as they once were," Rand admitted. "When I saw how much I had hurt you—"

"You didn't hurt me. You embarrassed me." It was imperative to Whitney that she make him believe this. "To hurt would imply that I care about you."

The handcuffs clanged as Rand slid his arm around her waist and brought his mouth close to hers. "And you don't?"

"No."

"Are you absolutely certain?" He nibbled the corners of her mouth, reminding her that he was a fantastic kisser. The best.

"Y-yes." She tried pushing him away. He didn't budge. "What about you? Have your reasons for being here changed?" He hesitated a moment too long. She swallowed an aching ball of disappointment and pushed him again. Harder. "Don't start something you don't intend to finish, McNair. It's no fun playing alone." She was lying: it *had* been fun; she couldn't deny that. But afterward she'd had nobody to share the moment with, because Rand had remained on the sidelines.

She hadn't realized until that moment that she wasn't quite as liberal about sex as she had convinced herself she was. She *did* want to bask in that fabled afterglow, that shared intimacy where she curled up against his chest and listened to the pounding of his heartbeat slow. She wanted to feel that deep satisfaction every woman experiences when she knows she's pleased her man.

Her man. *Oh, Lord.* She hadn't meant it. Really.

His fingers tightened at her waist. "If you knew just how badly I wanted you—*still* want you—"

"If you wanted me that badly," she whispered back, "then nothing would stop you."

"Is that an invitation?"

"No." She blew out a loud, exasperated breath. He was not only twisting her words around, but he was mangling her feelings as well. Of *course* she wanted him, but not if he had to force himself, and not if it meant she would end up humiliated again.

She leaned back and grabbed the jug of tequila. Uncapping the bottle, she turned it up and took a long drink. When she lowered it, she found Rand watching her in amazement. She wiped her mouth with the back of her hand—out of necessity— and grinned. "Don't look so shocked. I have a high tolerance for alcohol. I think I got it from my mother's side of the family."

He realized he was gaping at her and closed his mouth. He shot her a lopsided grin that made her heart do a triple somersault. "I guess getting you drunk and taking advantage of you is out of the question, then?"

Whitney gave the bottle a thoughtful look. "Probably." His teasing question prompted an idea. It was outrageous and not very nice of her, but the devil in her couldn't resist. "How about you?" she asked, deliberately making it sound like a challenge. "Can you hold your liquor? Or do you want to save yourself some embarrassment and admit here and now that I can drink you under the table?"

"That sounds like a challenge, Miss Sutherland," Rand said softly.

Her smile was quick and impish. "It was."

"You wouldn't be thinking about getting *me* drunk and taking advantage of me, would you?"

He was too damned astute for his own good, Whitney thought. She took another long pull and slowly held out the bottle. "Why don't you find out for yourself?"

Chapter Twelve

Ten minutes later they were both a little glassy-eyed as they went over the list again.

"Let's play Truth or Dare," Whitney suggested. She hiccuped, casting him a sheepish smile. "Sorry."

"Don't mention it." He traded the jug for the list and looked it over while he took a drink. "I'll make you a deal. I'll play Truth or Dare with you if you'll play strip poker with me."

She giggled and hiccuped again. She wasn't drunk by any means, but she had a pleasant buzz going on. "Strip poker isn't on the list, silly."

Rand opened a drawer, withdrew a pen, and scribbled on the piece of paper. "It is now. See? Right there at the bottom."

"You can't do that."

"Says who?"

Whitney floundered. Finally she used the jug to point at the camera, then said in a stage whisper, "Says *them*. They won't like it if you stray from the list."

"Maybe you're wrong. Maybe they *want* us to be spontaneous

and do whatever comes naturally. Remember the scavenger hunt?"

How could she forget? She had to squeeze her legs together every time she thought about it. She nodded and reached for the bottle, squinting as she held it up to the light. "Okay, you've got a deal, but there has to be a stipulation."

"What's that?"

"We cover up the camera while we're playing strip poker."

"Bashful?"

"No." She feigned surprise. "I was thinking about you, and how embarrassing it might be for you to have to strip naked in front of millions of viewers."

"Ah," Rand said. "You're assuming you'll win."

She shrugged and tried to look modest as she said, "I've never lost, but I guess there's always a first time."

"Your modesty astounds me. First Truth or Dare question. Name something you're *not* good at."

Whitney set the jug down and hopped onto the counter, secretly pleased when Rand moved between her knees and settled his hand on her leg. She rested their shackled hands lightly on her other thigh. She was once again struck with the natural way they did the couple things . . . as if they *were* a couple. "That's a tough one," she drawled teasingly. "Let me see. Something I'm not good at." Suddenly she snapped her fingers. "I've got it. I'm not good at judging men. Most of the nice ones turn out to be jerks."

Rand visibly winced. "Ouch. That hurt."

Solemnly she said, "It wasn't personal. My turn. How many lovers have you had?" She was surprised when he didn't immediately answer. In her experience, men loved to boast about their lovers. Maybe Rand had had so many he couldn't remember, she mused. The thought left a sour taste in her mouth.

She took a drink of tequila to wash it away.

"I'll take the dare."

In the nick of time, Whitney turned her head so that the

mouthful of tequila she spewed went over his shoulder. She coughed and wiped her mouth with her hand. "Are you for real? Most men can't wait to boast about something like that."

"I'm not most men, Whitney."

He sounded too serious to be teasing. Whitney swallowed the rest of her surprise. She had to come up with a good dare, something that would force him to think twice about taking the dare again in the future.

Finally she held out the bottle of booze. "I dare you to drink until I tell you to stop."

"You're determined to get me drunk," he muttered, taking the bottle. He turned it up and began to chug.

Whitney stared at his throat, finding his bobbing Adam's apple sexy as hell. She wanted to lean forward and suck on his neck like a hormonally charged teenager. When her mouth began to water, she hastily stopped him. "Okay, that's enough. Save some for me."

He set the bottle on the counter beside her, swaying slightly, his eyes a few shades darker. "My turn, you little devil. What is your favorite position when you're making love?"

"So typical," Whitney said. Inside she was quivering. The man was a tease, she decided. A flat-out tease. "With the right man, I like *any* position." She tossed her head and tried to look him in the eye as if she answered intimate questions all the time, but found her gaze sliding away and a flush suffusing her face. Before she could stop herself, she blurted out, "What is *your* favorite position?"

It was the tequila talking, she mused, biting her tongue. She glared; he grinned.

His hands closed over her thighs, then slid slowly upward. He moved in closer, closer still, until she could feel him pulsing against her. "I favor this position," he told her in a husky whisper. His hands moved around to cup her bottom, twisting her shackled arm behind her back. The position forced her back to arch, pushing her breasts against his chest.

Her nipples sprang to attention; her breath quickened. His beautiful mouth hovered an inch from her own parted lips. She cradled his erection, feeling her own inner muscles contract in reaction. What if they didn't have the barrier of their clothes between them? Would he sink himself into her, make love to her as he so clearly wanted to do? There was no question about what *she* wanted. . . .

"Damn it, Whitney," Rand muttered raggedly against her mouth. He kissed her roughly, almost angrily. Whitney felt as if her bones were melting beneath his onslaught. She kissed him back, tasting tequila.

Tasting heaven.

"I've never been with anyone since Bonnie, never dreamed I'd *want* to be with anyone but Bonnie. Yet the moment I start kissing you, I forget my vows."

So lost was she that it took a moment for his words to sink in. No need to wonder who Bonnie was, or what vows he spoke of. Inwardly cursing her rotten luck, she pulled her mouth free and turned her head aside. He was breathing as harshly as she was, but what did it matter? She wouldn't make love to a man who couldn't stop thinking about his wife.

His *deceased* wife.

Gently she said, "Rand, I've never been married, but I believe the marriage vows say 'till death do us part.' Most of them do, anyway." She gave a start of surprise when he buried his face in her breasts. She could feel him trembling.

From desire? Or was it regret? Regret that she wasn't his precious Bonnie?

"Rand?" She tried to pull his head up, but he resisted, turning in her arms so that his back was to her chest. She couldn't see his expression, and she suspected he preferred it that way.

"Maybe I *am* crazy," he said harshly.

Whitney propped her chin on his shoulder. Obviously *he* needed to talk about his late wife. With a sincerity that surprised her, she said, "Tell me about her." He hesitated. She could feel the tenseness in the set of his shoulders, and it caused a curious ache in her heart. Just when she thought he wouldn't speak, he did.

"We were high school sweethearts," he said slowly, painfully. "We were married fourteen years. Five years ago she died of ovarian cancer."

Whitney blinked back tears and swallowed hard. Jealousy and sympathy warred with each other. "Fourteen years is a long time. Sounds like a match made in heaven." And what chance did that leave her? None.

Rand chuckled, but his voice cracked as he said, "She knew I would have trouble letting go. That's why she made that silly stipulation in her will regarding Teddy and Dolly. She left instructions with her brother—he's a lawyer—to take them if I hadn't remarried after five years."

"Don't take this the wrong way, but what's so special about a stuffed bear and a statue? I know the statue looks like your late wife, but I don't get the bear."

"She slept with the bear." He laughed, but the sound of it made Whitney want to weep. "I used to hate that bear for coming between us. She got the bear from Elvis Presley at one of his concerts when she was twelve, and claimed she couldn't sleep without it. I used to make fun of her. Then she died, and I tried to pack that damned bear away, but found that I couldn't. I ended up sleeping with it."

She easily pictured him lying in bed with a teddy bear tucked beneath his arm, a sexy five-o'clock shadow on his jaw, his dark hair tousled from sleep. Even the strange image couldn't lessen his appeal in her eyes. In fact, it made her want him even more. She gave her head a slight shake. "What about the statue?"

"It was a joke, a gag gift from me to her on our tenth wedding anniversary. At least once a year Bonnie threatened to get a boob job. She hated her small breasts, although I constantly assured her that I loved her just the way she was. She kept the statue in our bedroom to remind her of how ridiculous she would look with big boobs."

What a lucky woman, Whitney thought.

"Now do you understand why I wanted to get them back?"

Whitney told herself that it would be dangerous to put any emphasis on the fact that he'd spoken in the past tense. Honestly, she said, "Yes, I do understand." Sadly, she did. "I'm not a shrink, but I think I also understand why Bonnie did what she did. As long as you have those precious reminders of her, you can't move forward."

"Until you . . ." Rand turned around, cupping her jaw with his free hand. His slightly moist eyes blazed into hers. "Until you I never *wanted* to move forward. Just the thought of sleeping with another woman twisted my insides into knots." He looked bewildered as he continued. "Meeting you, realizing that I really wanted to make love to you, well, it scared the hell out of me."

Whitney held her breath, afraid to speak, afraid to break the spell that seemed to be weaving around them. She couldn't be sure if it was the tequila talking, or Rand. But she could hope.

"I want you, Whitney. I want to make love to you. I want you like I haven't wanted a woman since Bonnie."

She curled her arm around his neck, her body quivering with anticipation. "I want you, too."

He picked her up, locking her legs around his waist as he staggered to the bedroom. Still holding her, he moved to the far wall and leaned against it, the position placing them beneath the camera and out of range. Slowly he set her on her feet, his hot gaze holding hers as he unbuttoned her shorts and pushed them over her hips. Whitney stepped out of them. Rand reached down and scooped them up, then rose on tiptoe to cover the camera lens with the discarded garment.

"That should muffle the microphone, too," he said.

Smiling, he picked her up again and carried her to the bed. Whitney was on fire, wanting him with a fierceness that stole her breath away. She could see the determination in his eyes, and easily read the stubborn angle of his chin.

Maybe if she hadn't seen these signs, she might have kept quiet and enjoyed something they both wanted badly, repercussions be damned.

But she couldn't in good conscience ignore the signs. She cared too much.

With a muffled curse directed at herself and her blasted conscience, she grabbed Rand's hand as he reached for her. "No. Let's wait until the booze wears off."

He grew very still, staring at her intently. "You think I'm going to do something I'll later regret?"

Reluctantly, she nodded. He'd never know how hard it had been to stop him. She ached to the point of screaming, but she had to be honest with herself. It wasn't just lust that she felt for Rand, and because of that she had to be sure that *he* was sure.

"You're an amazing woman," he said softly, kissing her forehead so tenderly tears sprang to her eyes.

She bit her lip, feeling anything but amazing. Stupid, maybe. "Let's see if you still think so when the booze wears off, OK?"

"No."

Her startled gaze flew to his face. "Wh-what?"

"I said no, it's not OK. For the first time in five years, I want to make love with a woman. Not just *to* her, but *with* her. Do you have any idea what this means?"

Whitney was tempted to let herself believe that he meant what he said. In the end she was too afraid. "Don't read more into it than there is, Rand. For both our sakes."

He smiled and shook his head. "There is more, Whitney. I'm going to prove it to you, too."

The promise in his eyes fanned the fire already burning inside of her. "Rand?"

"Close your eyes, baby, and hang on."

Chapter Thirteen

Whitney had been having so much fun at the thought of drinking him under the table, Rand didn't have the heart to tell her that back in his college days, he'd held his own when it came to liquor.

Which was why he knew that his feelings had nothing to do with the tequila, and everything to do with the amazing, sexy, beautiful, big-hearted woman lying beside him on the bed. She was staring up at him with her heart in her eyes, her need of him a powerful aphrodisiac.

He kissed her slowly, passionately, tasting the tequila on her tongue, thinking he could kiss her forever if she'd let him. When he felt her fingers at his waist, he groaned and lifted his hips, accommodating her.

She panted against his ear as she quickly opened his belt, then his shorts. She reached into his shorts and pulled him free.

He moaned when her fingers closed around his thick erection.

"Hm," she murmured with laughter in her voice, "Rand's a *big* boy."

With her inquisitive little fingers stroking him and her provocative statement in his ear, he nearly came right there on the spot.

Hastily—and prudently—he moved her hand to his hip, smiling at her protest. "I don't think I'm going to last very long, honey, so let me love you first."

"Mm." She cupped his jaw and stared into his eyes, her own sultry and hot. "You mean like you did the last time? No. I want you inside of me. Deep." She hesitated, then dropped her gaze.

Rand marveled at the blush that bloomed on her cheeks.

"I want you hard and fast the first time," she added. "We've got all night to do it slow."

All night to make love to Whitney over and over again. Rand took a deep breath. He couldn't believe his luck. Nibbling her lips, he said, "You've got a valid point, babe. Let's get out of these clothes."

They undressed in record time. Her breasts were perky and firm. Just right. Her nipples . . . Rand leaned forward and sucked one into his mouth. She cried out, clinging to his head, her nails digging into his scalp, arousing a primitive side of Rand he didn't know existed. He'd always been a slow and thorough lover.

Right now he wanted to take her fast and hard, just the way she'd said.

It was the catalyst that pitched them over the edge of determined restraint into a frenzied rush to touch, taste, and feel each other. Whitney became an aggressive she-devil that spun Rand out of control.

When she took him in her hot little mouth, he cried out and grabbed her arms, pulling her away just seconds before he exploded. She laughed and wound her arms around his neck, kissing him, sucking on his tongue, driving him crazy with desire. He didn't want the moment to be over.

Not yet.

Breathing hard, Rand quickly sheathed his erection with a complimentary condom, then pulled her wrists above her head and held them in place with his shackled one. Soft and sexy and wild, she smiled up at him. She began to move her hips against him, trying to capture his throbbing erection. Trying to pull him inside her, where he would be lost.

With a rueful smile, Rand shook his head. "No, baby. Not yet."

Her luscious lips formed a pout. "But I want you inside me. I want you badly."

"And I want you," he said. "*Too* much, which is why we've got to cool down."

"To hell with cooling down!"

She reached up and caught his bottom lip, sucking it between her teeth. He fancied he could feel the heat between her legs, tempting him, teasing him. She whimpered. "Please, Rand? I'm burning up!"

He knew that. So was he. His arms were trembling with the effort to hold back. He sucked and nibbled on her breasts until she was squirming and bucking beneath him.

And then it happened. One moment he was holding on by the skin of his teeth; the next he was engulfed in flames.

The minx had managed to capture his surging erection, surrounding him with her tight, hot feminine muscles that squeezed and stroked him. She locked her legs around his waist and surged again, driving him deep.

Pushing him to a place where he knew he would be lost. With a low growl of surrender, Rand closed his eyes and threw his head back. He clutched her hips and began to move, his strokes fast and hard.

"Hang on, baby," he managed to strangle out. "I can't slow down. . . ."

"I don't want you to slow down," she said breathlessly in his ear. "I want it just like this. Wild and primitive."

And then she was matching him stroke for stroke, her frantic lips on his neck, his chest, sucking at his flat nipples. She moved back to his mouth and kissed him, thrusting her tongue into his mouth in perfect harmony with the thrusting of their bodies.

Rand struggled one last time to regain his lost control. He didn't want to leave her behind, didn't want to shoot to the moon without her. It was too glorious a trip to make alone.

Then he felt her squeezing him, her muscles contracting around the impossibly hard length of him. She whimpered against his mouth, her arms tightening around his neck. "Rand?"

She sounded bewildered, awed, and Rand realized they were going to shatter together. He wondered, briefly, if they would survive.

"Oh, God, Whitney!" Rand locked a scream in his throat, gritting his teeth as he let himself go. His climax seemed to last forever, prolonged by the sheer beauty of their timing.

They stayed locked together for long, long moments after the shudders subsided. Finally, reluctantly, Rand moved to lie beside her. He gathered her close and held her tight, bombarded with a myriad of emotions.

One of them was guilt, but it was a guilt prompted by the realization that Rand had never, ever, experienced a climax quite like the one he'd just experienced with Whitney.

What did it mean? Was it a powerful, all-consuming lust? Or was it . . . love?

Whitney thought her heart would simply quit, rather than continue beating at such a murderous pace. What they'd enjoyed was beyond fantastic. She felt as if she had just given Rand everything. Her heart. Her soul. Her mind. Her body.

Everything.

Placing her free hand against his chest, she listened to his thundering heart. She smiled. "Are you OK?"

He chuckled. His voice sounded gruff and sexy as he said, "I don't know. Ask me again in ten minutes."

Ten minutes later, Whitney asked again. "Are you OK? I mean, with everything?"

"You mean am I feeling any guilt?" When she nodded, he continued. "At first I did." She stiffened, and his arms tightened soothingly around her. "No, it's not what you think. I felt guilty because . . . because I've never experienced anything so wonderful in my life."

Whitney's heart stuttered to a stop. "Ever?" she said in a squeak. *Even with Bonnie?* Her heart began to race again as she waited for him to answer.

"Ever," he confirmed quietly. "Whitney, I think I love you."

"You . . . but you don't know me!"

"How can you say that?" He came to his elbow, his expression serious. "After what just happened between us?"

"But—"

"But nothing." He took her chin in his hand, his voice rough as he said, "I'm not asking you to make a commitment right now. Just think about it, OK?"

She bit her lip and nodded, afraid to open her mouth and say something *he* would later regret. Snuggling into him, she closed her eyes, thinking she would just rest a moment. Then she would gently remind him that anything said in the heat of the moment usually didn't mean diddly-squat the next day.

Or an hour later, when lust had cooled.

Despite his reputation as a player on the show, Rand had been out of the dating loop so long he'd just forgotten. What kind of friend would she be if she didn't remind him?

Unfortunately, she wanted to be more than Rand's friend.

"I'm going to take a shower," Whitney announced, sliding from the bed. She turned with her hands on her hips, surveying her prisoner lying spread-eagled on the bed. One wrist was hand-cuffed to the bedpost. For the other hand she had used a pillowcase taken from one of the pillows. She'd used his belt for his left ankle, and his boxers for the right ankle.

She'd never had so much fun in her life. Rand was not only a great kisser; he was an inventive lover. Playful. Talented.

At the moment he was paying the price for his inventiveness. Sweat beaded his forehead and upper lip. His voice was husky to the point of a whisper as he said in disbelief, "You're *not* leaving me like this . . . are you?"

Whitney pretended to look thoughtful. "You mean, like *you* left *me* when it was your turn? As I recall, you had me to the point of begging. Instead of taking pity on me, you took a nap."

"I wasn't really sleeping."

"And I'm not really taking a shower," Whitney countered, lying smoothly. Her gaze traveled the length of him, pausing on his rigid erection. Liquid heat streamed and pooled between her legs. They'd made love so many times she'd lost count, depleting the complimentary box of condoms at an alarming rate. How could she still feel this barbaric urge to mount him and ride like the wind?

Technically, she didn't think they should be able to walk. "Listen, Tonto—"

"I thought I was the Lone Ranger."

"You mean the *Long* Ranger," Whitney corrected, deliberately widening her eyes. He ground his teeth and surged upward.

"Whitney, I swear when you let me go I'm going to make you sorry for this."

"Promises, promises," she *tsk-tsk*ed. Reaching out, she ran a finger along the length of him, smiling as he groaned and struggled against the bonds. She knew he could easily work the bonds loose, just as he knew it. Catching her thumbs in the waistband of her panties, she slowly drew them over her hips and down her legs. She flipped them into the air with her foot. They came to land on his head. He growled and snagged them with his teeth, making her giggle.

She watched him watching her as she slowly, teasingly lifted her T-shirt over her head. Her nipples were hard and aching, her breasts full and heavy. She draped the T-shirt over his erection. "You really should save your strength, you know," she purred sweetly. "You're going to need it when I get out of the shower." Deliberately wiggling her behind, she turned and headed for the door.

"Whitney! Get back here!"

"Take a nap, Rand." She laughed her way to the bathroom and shut the door. Her legs were weak and wobbly as she turned on the water and adjusted the temperature. Maybe, she thought as she stood beneath the invigorating spray, the producers of *Eden* had forgotten about them, because surely they'd been disqualified the moment they covered the camera with her shorts?

Had that really happened *yesterday*?

She chuckled as she lathered her hair, thinking she might try eating caviar from Rand's navel, or grapes from his ears. Possibly she could smear his pleasure rod, as she had so aptly named it, with peanut butter, and proceed to lick it clean.

Still plotting their next erotic adventure, Whitney stepped out of the shower and wrapped a towel around her damp body. She tucked it securely beneath her arm before she opened the door.

And came face-to-face with Rupert Asterisk.

She screamed.

He jerked back, holding up his hands in a defensive gesture.

Whitney clamped a hand to her mouth, feeling her eyes bulge. "Wh-what are you doing here?" She wasn't surprised when her voice came out squeaky and shrill; she had given up being articulate in his presence.

He slowly dropped his hands, sounding as nervous as she felt. "I wanted to talk to you before everyone gets here."

She put a hand to her throat, swallowing hard. "Everyone? Everyone is coming *here*?" Belatedly, she remembered the position she'd left Rand in. She glanced to the open doorway, then back to her father. Her heart sank, and heat crept up her neck and into her face. She knew that it was unlikely he'd missed seeing Rand.

Impatiently he waved a hand. "Camera crew, makeup, wardrobe—you name it, and they're coming." He looked grim as he added, "The voters picked you and Rand."

"Voters?"

He nodded. "The lockdown was live to the staff and producers." He waved in the direction of the bedroom. "We let them be our judges for this grand finale. They picked you and McNair."

Grand finale. Whitney's face grew so hot she fancied she saw steam rising from her cheeks. She and Rand had had a grand finale, all right. More than once. "We . . . we covered the camera," she stammered. "They couldn't have seen us . . . us . . ." No way could she say the words *making love* in front of her father, not even a father she knew nothing about.

"No, we couldn't see . . . but we could hear most everything. Those microphones are state-of-the-art, designed to pick up a whisper at thirty paces."

A *whisper?* The fierce heat in Whitney's face spread to the rest of her body. She'd never heard of anyone dying of embarrassment, but that didn't mean she wouldn't be the first. "Why . . . how could you let them . . . them—"

"I stopped them at 'Hi-ho, Silver.' It was the most I could do."

"Oh, God."

"Yes, well. Why don't you get dressed and meet me in the living room? We can talk in there, and don't worry about the cameras. They're dead."

Oh, sure, Whitney thought, clutching the towel as she hurried to the bedroom for her clothes, now *they're dead.*

Rand had obviously wriggled out of his flimsy bonds and was up and getting dressed, looking unperturbed by their host's presence. Maybe he'd forgotten that their host was also her father.

"When we leave the island, let's fly to Vegas and get married," he said, pitching her shorts to her.

Whitney didn't know if her heart could stand another shock.

She whirled around, glaring at him. "Didn't you hear what Asterisk just said? A lot of people have been listening to everything we've said and done. *Everything.*"

His lips twitched. Whitney felt a surprising urge to smack him.

"It doesn't matter. I love you and I want to marry you."

"Rand," she said slowly, "this isn't the Middle Ages. My reputation hasn't been compromised. You don't have to marry me."

"I want to." He hesitated, looking uncertain. "Do you love me, Whitney? Because if you do, I don't see what the problem is."

She clenched her hands. Obviously he hadn't been listening. "The problem, Rand, is that the entire staff—not to mention the producers of the show—heard me shouting 'Go deep,' among other things, and I'm pretty sure they knew we weren't watching football."

He winced visibly. *Finally,* she thought, watching him approach. He took her hand and brought her fingers to his lips. Leisurely, he kissed each fingertip. She caught her breath and tried to snatch her hand free. Didn't he know this wasn't the time or place? Her father was waiting in the living room, no doubt practicing his I-don't-need-this-in-my-life speech.

"Whitney," Rand said softly, pulling her against him. "We're consenting adults." When she tried to pull back, he held her tight. "Don't. Don't shut me out. We're in this together."

Together. Whitney had to admit she liked the sound of that.

"You've got the Asterisk ears," Rupert stated the moment Whitney was seated on the sofa.

Rand sat beside her, holding her hand and offering his silent support.

She licked her dry lips, wishing she had a drink of water, or better yet, a bracing shot of tequila. "You believe that I'm your daughter?" She hadn't meant to sound so surprised . . . or so hopeful.

Rupert paced in front of them, shoving his hand through his thinning hair. He blew out a sigh and stopped to face her. "When you dropped that bombshell at the dinner table, I admit that all I wanted to do was pretend we hadn't met."

Rand's hand tightened on hers. The action gave her courage. She thrust out her chin. "What changed your mind?" To her surprise, Rupert flushed a dull red. He shot Rand a fatherly glare and pointed.

"*He* did. When I heard who you'd been partnered with for the lockdown, I felt a strange urge to come storming in to save you." His eyebrows met in the middle as he continued to glower at Rand. "I've heard about you, McNair, and how you've left a string of broken hearts all over this island."

"Mr. Asterisk—" she began.

"Call me Rupert." He paused, then added, "Or you can call me Pop."

"Rupert, Rand isn't what you think he is. He was . . . well, he was still getting over losing his wife—"

"You actually fell for that cock-and-bull story?" Rupert roared suddenly.

Whitney blinked, hiding her shock at his reaction. Inwardly, a warm glow was spreading inside her heart. "His story was true . . . Pop."

That stopped the host of *Eden* cold. "You called me Pop."

"Yes." Whitney felt tears sting her eyes. "I called you Pop. Does . . . does anyone else call you that?"

Rupert shook his head, his eyes shining with unshed tears. "No. You're the only one. I had a bout with prostate cancer by the time I was forty, and the treatments wiped out my chances of fathering a child. My wife—the love of my life—can't wait to meet you."

"You told her?" A tear trickled down her cheek. Rand tenderly wiped it away.

"Yes." He cleared his throat. "After you mentioned on camera that you and I had a connection, I had to tell her something.

She would have thought . . . well, it doesn't matter what she would have thought. It's done. What I need to know is if you're okay with going public on this. It would mean you'd have to forfeit the grand prize."

Smiling through her tears, Whitney shook her head. "I don't care. Just out of curiosity, who'll get the grand prize when I forfeit?"

Rupert rolled his eyes. "Darla Brimbeau and Dillon Masters. Ninety percent of Darla's votes came from men. Oddly, seventy percent of *your* votes came from women. You beat Darla by twenty votes."

Beside her, Rand convulsed with laughter. She chuckled, squeezing his hand. Her heart felt as if it might burst with happiness.

"We need to smuggle you two out of here before the horde descends," Rupert said. "Dannon's waiting outside. He can take you to my private plane."

"We're going to Vegas," Rand told him, daring Whitney to argue. "We're going to get married. Aren't we, darling?"

Whitney got lost in his eyes. "Yes," she whispered, bringing his hand to her lips.

Slowly, she kissed each fingertip.

Ronda Thompson
Scandalous

Christine is shocked that she's agreed to marry. Her intended, Gavin Norfork, is a notorious lover, gambler, and duelist. It is rumored he can seduce a woman at twenty paces. The dissolute aristocrat is clearly an unsuitable match for a virtuous orphan who has devoted her life to charity work. But Christine's first attempt to scare him off ends only with mud on her face. And, suddenly finding herself wed to a man she hasn't even met, Christine finds herself questioning her goals. Perhaps it is time to make her entrée into London society, to meet Gavin on his own ground—and challenge him with his own tricks. The unrepentant rake thinks she's gotten dirty before, but he hasn't seen anything yet. Not only her husband can be scandalous—and not only Christine can fall in love.

___4805-1 $5.50 US/$6.50 CAN

LISA CACH

DR. YES

Dr. Alan Archer doesn't seem evil. But Rachel Calais knows the insidious truth: The doc is down in Nepal searching for the lost city of Yonam—and a plant that, when properly refined, will have every female in the world on her knees . . . or her back.

Rachel's mission: Stop Archer at any cost. B.L.I.S.S.—an international organization fighting such dastardly villains—has given her a kit to help, as well as a dangerously sexy man who knows how to watch a woman's back. With a stun gun, infrared goggles, and other less conventional forms of protection, Rachel is a regular Jane Bond. She doesn't know that playing spy will make her pay the ultimate price: her heart.

ROBIN WELLS
OOH, LA LA!

Kate Matthews is the pre-eminent expert on New Orleans's red-light district. It makes sense that she'd be the historical consultant for the new picture being shot on location there. So why is its director being so difficult? His last flick flopped, and he is counting on this one to resurrect his career. Maybe it is because he is so handsome. He's probably used to getting women to do as he wishes. And now he wants her to loosen up. But Kate knows that accuracy is crucial to the story Zack Jackson is filming—and finding love in the Big Easy is anything but. No, there will be no lights, no cameras and certainly no action until he proves her wrong. Then it'll be a blockbuster of a show.

CALDER'S ROSE
KATE ANGELL

Dare Calder is the kind of rough-riding, fast-shooting hero who will never let himself be saddled with just one woman. Unfortunately, Shane McNamara has agreed to co-write the next book in his *Texas West* series, and his collaborator is a curvaceous temptress who makes it mighty hard for a man to stick to his guns.

Devin isn't sure which is more dangerous, the Old West or the come-and-get-it look in Shane's eyes. As they corral their characters into courtin', Devin swears she'll leave Shane free to roam the range. But with their face-off more likely to come at midnight than high noon, she realizes no one can prevent a happy ending for their story.

EUGENIA RILEY
The Great Baby Caper

Courtney Kelly knows her boss is crazy. But never does she dream that the dotty chairman will send her on a wacky scavenger hunt and expect her to marry Mark Billingham, or lose her coveted promotion. But one night of reckless passion in Mark's arms leaves Courtney with the daunting discovery that the real prize will be delivered in about nine months!

A charming and sexy British entrepreneur, Mark is determined to convince his independent-minded new wife that he didn't marry her just to placate his outrageous grandfather. Amid the chaos of clashing careers and pending parenthood, Mark and Courtney will have to conduct their courtship after the fact and hunt down the most elusive quarry of all—love.

THE LAST MALE VIRGIN
Katherine Deauxville

Leslie expects a great deal of publicity for Dr. Peter Havistock—heck, the hunk has survived a plane crash, spent nearly fourteen years living with a Stone Age tribe in the wilds of Papua New Guinea, and returned to write a best-selling book about it. But his tour of colleges is too wild. Frankly, Leslie has never seen a doctor of anthropology act the way Havistock does. And while his ceremonial g-string is . . . authentic . . . she doesn't see the need for him to go flaunting his perfect body across the nation. And then he announces on *Harry King Live* that he is a virgin! And that he is looking for a wife! And that he'd like to marry her! Well, she decides, there is a first time for everything. . . .

Those Baby Blues

SHERIDON SMYTHE

Hadleigh Charmaine feels as though she has been cast in a made-for-TV movie. The infant she took home from the hospital is not her biological child, and the man who has been raising her real daughter is Treet Miller, a film star. But when his sizzling baby blues settle on her, the single mother refuses to be hoodwinked—even if he makes her shiver with desire.

Treet knows he's found the role of a lifetime: father to two beautiful daughters and husband to one gorgeous wife. Now he just has to convince Hadleigh that in each other's arms they have the best shot at happiness. He plans to woo her with old-fashioned charm and a lot of pillow talk, until she understands that their story can have a Hollywood ending.

AN ORIGINAL SIN

NINA BANGS

Fortune MacDonald listens to women's fantasies on a daily basis as she takes their orders for customized men. In a time when the male species is extinct, she is a valued man-maker. So when she awakes to find herself sharing a bed with the most lifelike, virile man she has ever laid eyes or hands on, she lets her gaze inventory his assets. From his long dark hair, to his knife-edged cheekbones, to his broad shoulders, to his jutting—well, all in the name of research, right?—it doesn't take an expert any time at all to realize that he is the genuine article, a bona fide man. And when Leith Campbell takes her in his arms, she knows real passion for the first time . . . but has she found true love?

___52324-8 $5.99 US/$6.99 CAN

NINA BANGS
FROM BOARDWALK WITH LOVE

The world's richest man, Owen Sitall, is a flop at a certain game, but now he's built an enormous board so he can win on his own. His island is a playground for the rich. But he doesn't know that L.O.V.E.R.—the League of Violent Economic Revolutionaries—has come to play in his hotels . . . and the plans to bankrupt him have already passed Go.

Camryn, novice agent #36-DD of B.L.I.S.S.—the international organization that fights crime anywhere from St. Croix to St. James Place—finds her assignment clear: Protect the fanatical Sitall from financial ruin. But being a spy doesn't just mean free parking. Before this is over, she'll be rolling the dice with her heart.

Bait & Switch

DARLENE GARDNER

To catch a criminal and save his sibling's skin, Mitch agrees to switch places with his identical twin. But nothing could prepare him for the gorgeous knockout on his doorstep. The blond bombshell is spitting mad, and Mitch's course of action is clear: He will have to win back his brother's girlfriend. Wooing the funny, smart, and caring Peyton is no hardship. It's keeping his hands to himself and ignoring all the steamy fantasies she evokes that is pure torture. And it doesn't take a crack detective to realize Mitch has set a baited trap, but it's *his* heart that has been ensnared. Which leaves only one question: Has Peyton fallen for him or his mirror image?
